BERRIGAN'S RIDE

JAN ELPEL

Silver Sage Studio & Press, LLC

Berrigan's Ride

© 2016 Silver Sage Studio & Press, LLC
Cover Art and Illustrations by Jan Elpel
Cover Design by GRAFFITI

Publisher's Cataloging-in-Publication Data
Elpel, Jan 1937–

Berrigan's Ride / By (Author), Jan Elpel

ISBN: 978-1-892784-37-7 $16.00 Pbk. (alk. paper)
1. Historical Fiction. 2. Montana Territory. 3. Gold
Rush. 4. Post-War Trauma.
I. Elpel, Jan. II. Title.

Silver Sage Studio & Press, LLC

Published by
HOPS Press, LLC
12 Quartz Street
Pony, MT 59747-0697
www.hopspress.com

Author's Notes

All characters in *Berrigan's Ride* are imaginary and their relationships based on a sliver of well-documented time. Legendary figures are cited in historic context because their stories are better than fiction. These include Henry A. Ward, superintendent of Midas Mining Company in Sterling, who traveled back and forth across the country in a superhuman effort to conduct company business. A 10,267-foot peak is named in his honor in the Tobacco Root Mountains above Sterling. Ruins of the Midas mill remain to this day. (See *The Mechanics of Optimism* by Dr. Jeffrey Safford for a fuller appreciation of Ward's achievements and that of the Creighton brothers).

John and Edward Creighton expanded the telegraph system west of the Mississippi for Western Union, and extended a line from Salt Lake City to Virginia City, Montana Territory, in 1866, linking the States and Territory in an unprecedented way.

Judge Hezekiah Hosmer, Chief Justice of Montana Territorial Supreme Court, owned claims on Norwegian and Rattlesnake creeks.

Actual mining operations include Midas Mining Company, Denton stamp mill on Norwegian Creek, Boaz mine in Lower Hot Spring District, Revenue mine on Gold Field and the Galena Lode on upper Hot Spring Creek. The Crocker and Venture mining companies are fictitious, as well as the Comet stamp mill at Summit in Alder Gulch. Barnstone Telegraph Company of Santa Fe is fictitious although it was inspired by Tillotson, a company that extended telegraph lines to remote areas. All cities, towns and streets are actual places with the exception of Woodland Hills, Georgia, the birthplace of Kent Berrigan.

The gold camp of Sterling was west of present day Norris in southwest Montana. In 1863, Alexander Norris, an Irish immigrant, purchased land that became Hot Spring District with Sterling as its center. Sterling remains on many maps of Madison County.

The Tobacco Root Mountains, considered part of the Jefferson Range, became known as the Ramshorn Mountains and years later were renamed the Tobacco Roots, likely after mullein or arnica roots used for tobacco. Distinctive Hollowtop Peak in the Tobacco Roots was formed by glacial rather than volcanic action.

The early name, Fifteen Mile Canyon, is used instead of the present term, Bear Trap Canyon. Gold Field has since been renamed Revenue Flats.

Pony, Montana, a gold camp established years after the town of Sterling, occurred after the scope of this story and is not to be confused with Pony Gulch north of Sterling.

Boulder Hot Springs and the Boulder–Helena road were relatively undeveloped at the time of events in this novel.

Bruce Flesch (deceased) of Pony, Montana, related a story of Mrs. Mendenhall driving a buggy bearing hidden gold from Alder Gulch to Helena for her husband. The story is unverified although the Mendenhalls invested in mines in Alder Gulch.

The story of the Long Walk was told by a descendent of the little Navajo girl to a group of horse riders at a hogan in Monument Valley, May 2007, and is retold as best as I can recall.

Attitudes and relations between North and South in Montana Territory are based on historical documentation and reflected in previous sectional conflicts in California and the Southwest. The expansion of transportation and communication across the United States is related in historical sequence. However, this book is a work of fiction and any and all errors of facts or interpretation of history or ethnicity are mine alone. Readers' comments and corrections are invited.

U.S. expansion in the Northwest led to the near decimation of the Native population and their way of life. This novel refers to earlier campaigns by the U.S. military. My sequel, *Healers of Big Butte*, describes more conflicts leading up to Indian Wars of 1877- 1878.

—Jan Elpel

Historical Perspectives

1864 Gold was discovered on Hot Spring Creek, Madison County, Montana Territory, with Sterling at its center. Montana Territory was separated from Idaho Territory with Bannack as first Territorial capital and Sidney Edgerton Territorial governor. Mullen Road was built from Fort Benton to Corrine, Utah, with roads to Virginia City and Bannack.
The Long Walk was a forced march of the Navajo Nation from Arizona to New Mexico led by the U.S. Army.

1865 The Confederate States of America surrendered April 9 at Appomattox, Virginia, and Abraham Lincoln was assassinated five days later.
The Virginia City area gained a population estimated at 10,000, with cultural amenities including the telegraph.

1866 Montana militias were sent to defend the Bozeman Trail from attack by the Sioux.
The Boaz Lode discovery occurred in Lower Hot Spring District, known as Red Bluff.

1867 The United States surveyed federal lands in Montana Territory. Sterling's area population was estimated at 500.
Shoshonis camped on the Madison River and visited Virginia City and Sterling.

1868 The Midas Mining Company of Sterling shut down operations.
The Treaty of Bosque Redondo freed Navajos June 1 at Fort Sumner, New Mexico

1869 The transcontinental railroad was completed at Promontory Point, Utah.

1875 Helena became Territorial capital and Virginia City became seat of Madison County.

1889 Montana gained statehood on November 9, twenty-six years after early Montana gold discoveries.

1

Montana Territory, 1866

Kent Berrigan shuffled his priorities. The assay office could wait. The stagecoach to Virginia City came in late in the day from the four to five day trip from Salt Lake City. The surprisingly fresh face of a woman peered from the dusty windows of the coach.

Kent turned to follow the passengers into the Varina Inn, a fine edifice despite the remoteness of the boomtown. Crystal chandeliers lit wall adorned with elegant tapestries of gold and red thread accented by blue stitchery. As colorful and delightful to his eye were women in silk gowns; even the gingham ones looked good to Kent. Most of the travelers were still covered by long dust coats. A young woman with coppery hair straying from her bonnet briefly checked in at the desk. She soon turned and met his gaze as she went out the door. He was sure she was the one he had glimpsed in the stagecoach.

He wheeled to ask, "May I – uh—"

The words were lost in her inquiries of a gentleman who appeared to be as drawn to her as Kent. Checking his impulses, Kent scanned the new arrivals for one who might be her escort—father, husband, uncle who would no doubt accompany such a remarkably wholesome young lady to the frontier, did not appear. Later he saw her alone at the Overland Stage office, a slight figure in a tan ankle-length dust coat. She continued to quiz townsmen and miners about their success or lack of it in the Territory.

Kent dropped off an ore sample at the assay office. He had a feeling it was high grade. The claim could conceivably build the house he had in mind. Buoyed by the prospect, he rushed to the Clerk and Recorders office to check on claims an investor had raked in next to his. A thin young man in a baggy old-style brown suit looked up without uttering a greeting. Packing crates held stacks of papers next to a sputtering wood stove and two shabby desks.

"Good afternoon," Kent said. "I'm—."

"Whatever it is, it isn't ready." The clerk indicated the workload around him with a sweep of his arm.

"I see you need a great deal more help. Surely there must be—"

"Surely there must be intelligent life in the camp," the clerk interrupted. "but they make more money on the claims. I must be guarded about my health so I refrain from heavy labor."

"I hope you keep the fire blazing in this drafty office," Kent said, hoping the clerk would not catch pneumonia. I could whip through this logjam myself, he mused, not the first time he'd have had to fall back on his accounting experience.

If processing was held up, Crocker Mining Company's claims could fare no better. Kent's were safe for the time being. He climbed uphill to Idaho Street and found a cheap hotel among many boarding houses not far from the noisy Leviathon, a large structure built for an arena that served for fist fights, traveling shows, occasional weddings or cultural events. The center generally blazed with lights and drunken activity until well past midnight, enough to drive Kent to Stonewall Hall with its upstairs reading room. New and old *Montana Post* newspapers were scattered about. A few classics clung to a shelf. Obviously, some emigrants brought books with them and encouraged rudimentary refinements of life. A billboard advertisement caught his eye:

POETRY READING
PURELY FOR ENTERTAINMENT OF CITIZENS
ON SUNDAY AFTERNOON IN THE GREAT HALL OF THE LEVIATHON

"Now poetry reading would be a real asset for citizens of Norwegian Creek." He laughed at images of Jake and Benson listening to verses of Wordsworth, Thoreau, and Tennyson.

The next morning the young woman he'd seen at the Varina Inn boarded the 5:30 a.m. stage for Sterling along with Kent and several German speaking miners who nursed *kolsch* ale from Gilbert's Brewery.

"Excuse me, ma'am. I am Kent Berrigan of Sterling. May I inquire if you are traveling alone?"

"Marion Patton," she said extending her gloved hand, a slight smile lighting her small oval face. "I usually say that I am with my father but I am not. I am actually a representative of his mining company in Coloma, California."

In the confines of the stagecoach she made no pretense of feminine wiles. She asked about the quality and variety of minerals in the ore that Kent was finding, the number of mills and their capacity as well as the number of stamps.

"And how are the Indian troubles in this part of the Territory?"

"Certainly no problems with Shoshonis camped around Sterling or Virginia City, ma'am. Bannack travel down the Madison River to hunt buffalo near the headwaters of the Missouri. They have been friendly and seldom appear in the camps. We have more troubles among ourselves. An aggressive mining company would like to edge prospectors off Norwegian Creek north of Sterling."

"I am sorry to hear the usual mining conflicts arise in Montana Territory, Mr. Berrigan. I was a child when my family moved to Coloma, California, with the '49ers. We have experienced the competition and frequent corruptness of the camps."

This is no debutante, Kent mused, astounded at her forthrightness compared to the parlor talk of women he had known, but he dared not disclose his hopes for his latest claims. He managed to stammer increasingly vague responses to her questions. He felt thrown off center by her audacity to travel alone, not to mention the apparent depth of knowledge her job entailed. He marveled at how the camps had molded her character, a striking contrast to women who conformed to finishing school protocols.

The torrent of words gradually became blurred as proximity to her strong shoulders bumping against his in the stagecoach further rattled his composure. He had a chance to study her face when she turned toward the window. Her skin glowed like sunshine, fresh, and scented with the clean smell of a utilitarian soap, not the lavender or chamomile used by his mother or Miss Olivia. Up close he detected a few freckles on her nose, cheeks, and glimpses of the backs of her arms between the long gloves and her coat sleeves. Pert. She was pert and defied definition, unlike any woman he had ever met.

He felt the German miners' blunt stares searching for any sign of him succumbing to her presence. Yards of tan cotton canvas-like material separated his thigh from hers but he felt her heat—and his. Occasionally the men peered out of the window on a landscape that swept away in often terrifying drops below the stage road which was carved high around winding hillsides. Kent took these opportunities to breathe deeply and coolly discuss the relative merits of mining in Virginia City, Bannack, and Hot Spring District. As much as he knew, not that he was the expert.

"I have been too preoccupied with my own affairs to entertain these other prospects," he said. "Certainly I have missed a great deal by sequestering myself on my claim." The compliment, or hint if she cared to take it so, was lost on his female traveling companion. The German miners conversed among themselves, making what might have been suggestive remarks, given their knowing smiles.

If one of them winks at me or at her I'll open the door and shove him out, Kent vowed to himself. The thought gave him some satisfaction that he was not getting from his efforts with Miss Patton.

In Sterling, Marion alighted from the stagecoach to be met by a bouncing, long-haired dog before Kent stepped from the coach to be effusively licked. Startled, Marion connected the two then turned to go.

"May I escort you to an exceptionally fine dinner at the boarding house just down the street?" Kent hurriedly attempted to interrupt her pursuit of business.

Marion's hazel eyes widened as she pushed back her straw bonnet to gaze steadily at this quiet, serious gentleman who looked extremely uncomfortable at the moment.

"Why certainly. I shall be pleased with your recommendation. Travel fare whets one's appetite for reasonably well prepared meals. And what will become of this dog that seems overly fond of you while we dine?"

Kent laughed in relief that Shag disrupted the formality. "Shag was a stray. She lived at Callahan's boarding house until I took her. The Callahan's two youngsters, Angel and Donovan, take in every animal that comes along. Sterling has been good for me—it is my home now." Left unsaid was anything about his place of origin.

Small tables by the front windows of the boarding house were occupied. Kent and Marion squeezed onto the bench at a table down the center of the room. Heads turned and conversation attained a sustained octave above normal. His neighbor, Jake, stared. The likes of Miss Patton were not everyday visitors in Sterling. Before the family style plates and platters of food made the rounds, a scuffle broke out at the other end of the table.

"Traitors, the lot of ye." Benson punched futilely at a handsomely dressed newcomer across the table. The man's partners rose to face off with the stocky miner in suspenders. Miners nearby put down their forks and moved aside. "Ye ain't to be braggin' about profitin' from sellin' guns that killed my pa," Benson thundered, fists failing the air.

Kent rose and flanked Benson on one side. Jake leapt over a bench to collar the Rebel. Dishes clattered and miners' chairs scraped the rough wood floors. They whisked Benson out the door and angled him down the street towards the Dixie Saloon to leave him among friends.

"I don't much like my cookin', but I like the company in town less," Jake waved at Kent. "I'll see you back at the Gulch."

Behind them Mrs. Callahan's voice rose in a shrill command.

"Ain't ye got no manners nor upbringin' to be around decent folks?" With her wide hips bunching under a loose dress, she flourished a broom to chase the braggarts out of the boarding house. The gentlemen sought refuge in the crowd and dust in the street. Mrs. Culbertson wiped her hands on her apron and caught the approving glance of most of the diners. Rebels far out-numbered Federals in Sterling.

Kent regained his seat next to Miss Patton, his temples throbbing. "Excuse the ruckus, Miss Patton. I hope this scene does not deter you from remaining in Sterling for a time." Without divulging past loyalties, he scooped potatoes and gravy onto his plate. The gravy tasted flat. A healthy dose of cayenne like we do in the South might clear my mind, he mused.

"I am not naïve about violence in the mining camps, Mr. Berrigan. My father has long been a speculator in various associated enterprises in California and beyond. Tensions invariably exist where stakes remain high."

"Unfortunately, that reflects the present situation in Sterling and on Norwegian Creek where I live. However, the land is open and beautiful. Might I interest you in a riding tour of Gold Field since you seem to be knowledgeable about the mining industry? Horses are readily available for hire at the livery stable. I believe you would be impressed with the distinctive character of the land and the view of four mountain ranges."

Marion glanced at her ankle-length split skirt and boots, riding habit that functioned as daily wear in her active life. "I have only a short stay here. I had hoped to visit several of the larger stamp mills. We hear they are copied after those in California."

"You will find the Crocker, Venture, and Midas mills here in Sterling. We can ride to the Galena Lode. I will arrange for mounts while you visit here." Her eager eyes and ready smile were all the encouragement he needed. At the stable, Kent met some old friends, a full complement of captured wild horses from the Madison Valley herd that ranged on this side of the Tobacco Root Mountains.

"That tall one, he's got a good disposition and he ain't skitterish, We had him in here for a couple months. I caught him from the herd off the mountain. He's strong. You got to git a good handle on him."

The stable owner volunteered more than Kent wanted to hear. The stakes were high, Miss Marion's safety as well as his. He hadn't ridden for over a year, and never in a western saddle. He feared the bay might want to run away on the land where he had roamed free with the herd. Will this be a showcase or a dog and pony show? Kent grinned at his own audacity, his thoughtless plunge as he led a four year-old Percheron-thoroughbred cross and a spirited black and white pinto down the street to meet Miss Patton.

"We will have to round the foothills since the creek up this gulch is excavated. Uphill will be good for these energetic horses. I'll take this tall one." His voice came evenly, certainly not reflecting how he felt inside.

Marion swung herself onto the pinto and quickly curtailed its excited circling. Kent clambered aboard the seventeen-hand bay; the withers registered at about his eye level, thanks to his heeled boots. The bay listened for commands, enormous brown eyes alert to every movement, his powerful legs rooted on the earth overcoming natural instincts of fight or flight.

"You'll do fine, buddy," Kent told him, raking his fingers through tangles of long uncombed mane.

Marion was a natural horsewoman who apparently feared nothing. Her bonnet fell back on her slim shoulders, letting the wind twist her frizzy hair. The clatter of hooves on scattered limestone and granite shale limited conversation of any depth. Shag raced after Miss Marion and rested only when her horse paused for breath. The shepherd's quizzical brown eyes under one raised eyebrow after the other sent adoring messages to the woman. Kent envied their immediate connection. A swoosh of adrenalin reminded him he hadn't enjoyed a woman's company for a long time. And he had never felt like this.

"I love the lavender lupine on these long slopes. And is that wild geranium? The smell of sage bites my nose! That must be the Galena Lode on the promontory."

Marion's delight more than rewarded Kent for the ride. He reluctantly shifted his attention to their destination. A frame structure rose on a stone and concrete base to house the Galena stamp mill. Ore dumps over the sidehill attested to the tons of rock already processed. Considerable activity around the mill convinced Kent they'd better ride on up to timberline. Looking back they fell silent at the sweeping 180 degree view, the long pale violet ridges of the Bridger and Gallatin ranges in heavily saturated atmosphere contrasted with sharp outlines of the nearby snow-crested Madison Range. A glint of silver in bottom lands traced creeks that fed into the Madison River. Clumps of cottonwoods lining stream beds displayed dense shades of earthy greens.

At last Marion turned to Kent. "I shall remember Montana Territory. I am most grateful for this opportunity to view it with you." Her gaze lingered with his, sunlight turning her eyes to what Kent beheld as smooth bourbon. A hint of a smile softened her features and tugged at his formality. He wondered what she was thinking, indeed would have given his last dollar to know.

"A pleasure, my pleasure," he assured her, his voice low, uncertain, as the strange tension this woman so effortlessly created threatened his composure. She seemed so unaffected, natural; no, primal like the hidden places of the land he had found on his lonely wanderings. Places he suspected no one had ever seen. She was unspoiled, truly a natural beauty with an alluring hint of purity.

He conjectured that this woman wasn't likely to bury herself in a book, a far cry from Miss Olivia Spencer he'd known who taught literature in a women's academy. The itinerant nature of Miss Patton's life and her freedom were quite a jolt to Kent's Southern sensibilities. Intriguing, stimulating—more than that, the two of them sheltered in spindly fir, lone figures seated on their horses in the patterned edges of the timberline.

A slight breeze whisked clouds from the 10,000 foot peaks of the Tobacco Roots, dipped to encircle the couple, and robbed time of its linear march. It stirred the sweet warm scent of summer from the hill grass inviting one to stay, to breathe the intoxicating air, laugh and leap or tumble in the soft bed of pine needles, leave cares and secrets in the shadows, follow one's senses, chase one's desires. There was now and forever—in Kent's mind—without an empty tomorrow. Unaware or unheeding of the daring excursions the moment held for him, Marion kicked her horse for a rapid return to catch the next stagecoach out of Sterling.

Sideswiped from indulging in fantasies, he could think of nothing to deter her. He felt lightheaded; his usual resourcefulness escaped when he most needed it. As they galloped over Gold Field the pinto kept a tension on the reins, straining to have his head. Miss Patton maintained a firm seat while her mount deftly skirted sagebrush and jumped small dry washes. The bay's black mane flowed in heavy streamers into Kent's face and his hooves tattooed the hollow-sounding ground, flinging limestone shale like shrapnel which Shag quickly learned to avoid.

"I could get to like this horse, Big Ben," he called to Miss Patton for lack of a personal connection with her. Ben's huge strides moved with the ease of his wild forbears over rugged landscape, a familiarity with the terrain so natural that he could keep one ear and eye attuned to his rider.

Soon back in Sterling, Kent felt a biting sense of loss when he held Miss Patton's hand in a brief formal separation before he returned the horses to the stable.

"I would like to further our acquaintance," he ventured. Pressured at this fatal moment, he had to say more, to invite her to stay longer, but he spoke more to the back of her head as she moved away, already discussing business with teamsters on the street while the stagecoach was being loaded.

"I want to see you again," he breathed, but she was out of earshot. He knew—he became convinced that he needed to spend time with her, show her more of Montana Territory, talk at length of their lives, to at least make his intentions known. The fresh scent and image of rusty-colored frizzy hair and recognition of his own needs stayed with Kent long after her abrupt departure.

By the time Kent walked the seven miles of the north-south running Norwegian Creek road to his shack he had argued himself out of reasons why he stayed in Montana Territory or why he prospected on Norwegian Creek. It was a thousand miles from California and the home of Marion Patton. That felt like an insurmountable distance. In any case, she would likely link him to Benson and leave the memory of their ride in the past. And Georgia was a thousand miles in the other direction where he left Miss Olivia Spencer when he fled to the West. She had no doubt also scoured her memory of him. Kent now questioned his fate. He felt like a misfit in Montana Territory, about as useless as his former thoroughbreds, Donegal and Bonnie, would have been in the West. Like himself, their destinations were unknown.

Norwegian Creek sliced thorough the Tobacco Root foothills and became an enclave of Southerners despite its name, one of the richest placer discovery sites in Hot Spring District. All the land on Gold Field had been staked when he arrived. Miners had already shifted over to digs on Norwegian Creek, saturating its upper reaches.

At the abandoned squatters' shack Kent had appropriated on the flats above the Gulch he heated the wood stove and stirred up a pan of beans for supper.

"Benson won't let it go." Kent rehashed the flare-ups that often aroused his own trauma. The war was over but not the effects. Benson's gripe was legitimate. The arms companies that sold to both sides in the war enriched themselves and the gun runners. The unimaginable profits of the war upturned the order of wealth and society in a few short years. A familiar darkness settled over his spirits, a mood he'd been hard-pressed to shake since he fled the South a year ago. Shrugging, he filled a bucket of water from the hand pump out front and fell onto his bunk hoping for a rare good night's sleep.

Later that night he awoke to a distant rumble like thunder. He grabbed a shirt and ran outside, recognizing the sound of wild horses running down from the ridge. Loosened stones hurtled over granite boulders, a pulse of the mountains he couldn't fathom yet couldn't leave alone. The pounding had its own cadence. A rhythmic drumming echoed off sheer cliffs until it was above his shack, then became a discordant stampede as if the herd would split north or south of his place. Hard to know which way they'd head, or if they might loop down past Jake's place to spirit off his old mule. Or rip into settlers' haystacks, the last winter feed for domestic stock, provoking enough outrage that they'd be rounded up or shot.

Kent felt his own pulse again stimulated to breaking in this land of intemperance, temper, maybe indifference with an edge on its own terms. He hadn't readily adapted to being a placer miner, settler, or any other hardy individual attracted to these parts. The unconventional notion of leaving home had never occurred to him, not until he and his mother were forced out by the war. But he'd heard the call. He'd come west and squatted in an abandoned shack on ground now shaken by horses running in shadowless dark. Horses bound in a rush of thick swirling dirt, their exhausted milling announced by snorts. Horseflesh that smelled of hot breath, rancid sweat, and torn sagebrush.

Kent stood in the doorway, feet in wool socks, and inhaled now familiar odors, his veins bursting with wanting to ride with them, wanting something he couldn't put a finger on—until he had ridden with Miss Marion Patton. The heartbeat beneath his jaw felt irritating, kept him restless as he recognized himself in the turmoil of the herd that disappeared down the slope of Norwegian Creek. Like the horses, another life formed a past he ran away from—or a future he could be running toward, he wasn't certain. But it made it harder to think of ever leaving Montana Territory.

The shadow of a great horned owl swept low over pastoral foothills that in daylight showed ravages of mining. The raspy screech of a night hawk was answered by either an echo or a distant hawk. He fumbled in the dark for a pipe and tobacco—ironic, a tobacco farmer here in the Tobacco Roots. The pipe lay unlit, tobacco pouch empty.

"Oh hell. I have to go back to town for tobacco."

A draft fluttered the thin canvas covering of the windows, swept around corners of the shack and into the seams of his trousers. Kent sucked in the cold air, his gaze drawn above. A blue-black sky looked back at him like a mirror whose paint had worn off leaving fantastic shapes telling fortunes that were hopeless to decipher. The squatter's place and claims? Sell to Crocker and go to Nevada or Colorado? Or chase the rusty-haired woman back to California?

A turquoise rim over renowned Hollowtop Peak spoke of other worlds in distant stars that capered over his former, much grander home in the war depressed state of Georgia. A home now owned and occupied by his brother, Randolph Berrigan.

Still awake hours later, Kent Berrigan watched as dawn crept over the Madison Range. His quiet grey eyes searched the semi-darkness for early spring birds, their songs lonely sounds drifting in chirps from one gulch to another. He sighted along a series of quartz outcroppings than ran up a slope nearest his shack and reappeared on a lower slope towards the north. None of it was on his claim, however, Kent speculated that the vein he had staked his mining claim on ran across this property. The assay report from Virginia City would tell him if his hunch was right. He had quickly secured title to the land with the shack on it just in case. Today he let out a long breath, still unable to believe where he ended up the past six months.

After coffee he closed the damper on the makeshift woodstove in his shack and left to pick up tobacco in Sterling, a two-hour walk as the crow flies. He pulled a dark tweed cap with a bill snuggly over his hair and let out the flaps over his ears. A bulky black coat and wool trousers tucked into boot tops braced him for the early chill.

Sterling originated four years earlier following the gold rush to Alder Gulch, an unlikely settlement in a narrow rugged canyon framed by massive oblong boulders on the ridge above. Smoke from cabin fires rose in white columns above the muddy complex of shelters and false-fronted businesses that served a growing population. Two huge stone buildings under construction awaited shipments of mills from iron and steel industries located on the East and West coasts. The camp was well on its way to becoming one of the largest towns in the Territory. Saloons captured most of the business downtown.

To Kent the place had the look of havoc wreaked upon once undisturbed foothills and a tree-shaded stream. Hammering, chopping and digging accosted one's ear on all sides. Kent's recollection of his family's stately brick mansion and white fenced stables in Georgia faded to the present reality of ugly, exploited turf. Here Southerners were derisively dubbed "the left wing of Price's Army" after Confederate Major General Sterling Price, the likely origin of the gold camp's name. But it offered amenities like tobacco and liquor and the ever present lure of riches from Hot Spring Creek that spouted a geothermal outburst three miles to the east.

He bought tobacco and headed for Callahan's boarding house, a structure of plain, rough-hewn boards that was architecturally not much different from the livery stable, but it carved out a facsimile of civilization along Sterling's east-west Main Street. The boarding house and its exuberant Boston family represented the warmth and hospitality he sorely missed from home. Kent chose his favorite seat near the kitchen so he could enjoy the banter of other people.

"Mr. Berrigan, my lad and lassie ask about the pretty lady you brought here. I 'spect they fear losing your attention," Mrs. Callahan teased him. A platter of boiled spuds spun out from one elbow to land on the table in front of him, and a checkered, dish towel-lined basket of hot buttermilk biscuits descended from the embrace of her other arm.

"I enjoy them. It's a whole passel of fun to see them growin' right out of their britches." Kent strung out his southern drawl, entertaining himself by indulging in down home vernacular. Mrs. Callahan put out a good meal three times a day for the men and still managed to take care of two children and do the wash. Angel and Donovan were too young to go to school yet old enough to create a constant ruckus of their own. Today they were entertained by armloads of kittens from a litter of eight, all wriggly, tiny fur balls with the roundest blue eyes Kent had ever seen.

"Do ye want to hold one?" Angel held out her arms so Kent could take his pick. "They're really nice. Ye could have a kitten to take home. Father said we cannot keep all of them. Only I want this one and that one belongs to Donovan," indicating with a nod of her head which was which. Long, cloud-like hair fell over her shoulders and down the back of the cotton print dress that she wore under a dirt-stained pinafore. Four year-old Donavon in knickers and knee socks edged behind his sister, a role Kent suspected might last a lifetime.

"Shag might run off and be a stray again if I brought a kitten home," a fact of life the children understood.

The dining room had cleared out except for four men at a corner table. Several wore rounded bowler hats and dressed in dark, mid-length coats over vests and high white collars common for businessmen. Three of the four officials puffed Meerschaun pipes signaling a luxury fantasized by men in camp. The larger man in a top hat, expansive lapels, and a pleated shirt stepped over to Kent.

"I represent Crocker Mining Company of New York," he announced. "I'm here with these gentlemen who have an interest in expanding our holdings on Norwegian Creek, where I understand you are prospecting."

This portly individual with thick, peppery beard and mustache did not stand on ceremony about his intentions, taking Kent aback by the suddenness and forthrightness of what appeared to be a proposition. Kent held the calculating gaze and his thoughts as well. The men at the corner table halted their conversation to listen.

Without any preamble or explanation, the speaker came to the point. "We're looking at four places up the creek—yours, Benson's, Jake Hanson's, and the Colter brothers.' We'll make it worth your while to sell out along with the others."

The room swirled as Kent managed to prop his elbows on the table and give a non-committal response. He didn't know what the others had committed to, but the potential of new claims on the squatter place made him hold back. This offer felt like a threat to him and his present uncertain situation.

"Time will tell whether it's worth buying or selling." He muffled the words to hide welling emotion, a surprising feeling of attachment to the 160 acre dry land homestead and placer claims paced off 100 feet by 200 feet and marked by stakes at the corners.

The Crocker representative moved away from Kent's table and soon the gentlemen made their way out past the children and kittens. One of the men said over his shoulder, "It might be a good idee' to go along. The mills aren't going to process your ore if you don't."

"Who were they?" Kent asked as Harland Callahan cleared tables and swept the floor.

"The higher-ups, the one's taking yer money in fees. A justice of the peace in Virginia City, a recorder, and a commissioner, the one who warned about the mills. I didn't recognize the fella in the top hat, but he took over a bunch of claims around Bannack." Harland's long narrow face betrayed nothing as though he recited last week's menus, but quick glances checked passersby outside the window. Kent recognized the proprietor's self-interest. They were all customers or potential customers in Sterling.

"Ye'r not the only one being badgered to sell. These big outfits need a steady supply of ore to keep their stamp mills running. So many companies are pouring in with buckets of money, they'll likely crowd each other out."

"Thanks for keeping your eyes open, Mr. Callahan," Kent said. He felt a hollow spot in his stomach despite Mrs. Callahan's platter of meat, potatoes and gravy, and apple pie. This morning it hadn't mattered whether he stayed or left. Now he sensed that there was more to his sojourn here than he knew, that he was reacting to the possibility he could be forced off his property.

"No," he said half-aloud. "I have nowhere to go." He heard echoes of his former servant Ephram when he told him he was free to go or stay on the Berrigan estate. "I 'spect we be here till everbody comes home. We done got no other home."

Outside, Kent went the opposite way of the businessmen, his spine tingling with a yet unperceived concept of how this threat would play out. The terse, unvarnished intentions of the group shocked him out of any new-found complacency he harbored about his tenancy in this rough country.

While he prospected on Norwegian Creek, another gold rush had occurred at Red Bluff near what was called Fifteen Mile Canyon of the Madison River. A typical miners' camp had risen near the Boaz stamp mill located two miles south of the Bozeman Trail which cut over the foothills to the farm towns of Gallatin City and Bozeman. Crocker Mining Company of New York had astutely muscled their way into the Lower Hot Spring area to acquire promising claims around the Boaz. This unnerving development reminded Kent that he, Jake, Benson, and the Colter brothers were not immune to takeover on Norwegian Creek.

Spring of 1866 was generously warm and bountiful well into June as it painted whole hillsides in astounding yellow arrowleaf balsamroots on south-facing slopes. Elusive pink bitterroot blossoms appeared in windswept patches of native sod. Tiny buttercups, their cadmium hue concentrated in soft round petals, peeked from isolated spots. Benches below the foothills formed relatively flat, open land slashed by ravines and small washes. Shadows of dense aspen groves encouraged spritely glacier lilies in traces of receding snowbanks, and masses of silvery-leafed lupine spread lavender blooms on lower slopes. Dark junipers scattered over the draws, descending from heavily timbered mountains where tumbling streams of snowmelt continued the age-old process of erosion, washing sand, soil and gravel, a process the prospectors duplicated.

Weeks went by and Kent had not heard more about the Crocker proposition. He let it lie until rumors surfaced about fierce competition between the mills for ore to process. Now he needed to sound out Jake's opinion of the offer.

"Halloo. Berrigan here," Kent called from outside Jake's log cabin. "I see Hoot's still here." The name triggered a smile since Jake always asked, "Did you ever see a mule that gave a hoot?"

Jake finally appeared in the doorway in his long underwear. "Come in for coffee. You already got me up. Yeah, I keep the darn fool picketed or he'd run off with the mustangs." Jake grumbled around a drag on a lumpy hand-rolled smoke and put on a pot of coffee. Heating the old cookstove enough to boil coffee took time. Kent lounged on a hand hewn chair and waited. Jake dressed and talked.

"That was bad business about Benson needling the Yankees. A man could get hisself shot for less. Or us." Jake's voice was low, throaty. If Benson had another name it was unknown in the camp. "I oughtta move on. The bastards come here and wave their money around to offend folks, then bring in more stamp mills. Neither are what I came west for."

Jake had come last summer and worked Hot Spring Creek up and down till, the easy placer gold was gone. Recent findings were not as rich or else the gold was mixed with other troublesome metals in the ore. Everybody was getting testy.

"I came for a good strike, not to keep the war goin'. I figured my luck was as good as anybody's, but I guess it ain't. I'm stranded in the Territory." Jake rounded up his gum boots and jammed then on his feet. "I left Tennessee early to work in tobacco fields of South Carolina. My folks weren't makin' it on tenant land with seven young'uns, me the oldest. But folks in the back hills were looking to marry off their daughters. I had to run like hell!"

His lopsided grin dimpled up a cheek and made Kent laugh. "So you got out of there. I've had similar experiences among debutantes. Believe me, I skedaddled!"

"I got caught up in a drag for conscripts in New Jersey. Me a Yankee? Not on yer life! But I couldn't go home. Either way I'd be shot. So I come out here." Jake had experienced a lot of hard knocks from an early age that left Herculean muscles on his medium tall frame and brightened the twinkle in his blue eyes. He was everybody's kid brother, except perhaps for his own siblings that he hadn't seen for awhile.

Kent also felt he didn't have to reveal all of his story, only his misgivings about the way he left Georgia, the way his own family had been split by the war, Rand fighting for the Union, his own choice to serve the South.

"If the gold don't pan out, I'll hightail it somewhere else. It's a two day ride to Bannack. Maybe git Benson to leave town with me," Jake went on. The boomtown and erstwhile Territorial capital had sprung up on Grasshopper Creek in the Pioneer Mountains a few years earlier. Jake leaned his chair on its back legs and propped his feet up on a chunk of firewood.

"Or leave when the fish don't bite," Kent chided. Jake could pull out for any excuse. "I received title to the squatter's place I live on. You might find me turned into a settler yet."

"The value of plain land right now couldn't be something to write home about, not when it's given away for free under that Preemption Act."

"Looks like a man could take his chances on something above ground same as what's below it," Kent countered.

"If you're wantin' to settle those 160 acres, you might consider that there's more rifts occurrin' among the men. If they aren't able to make a strike they start blaming everybody else for their ancestors, upbringing,' or loyalties. There's a lot of drifters, not the right kind for around here."

Kent's face went blank, his inclination to settle having fallen on deaf ears. "Yes, of course, I know of the tensions. Didn't we all leave home for these very reasons? Why duplicate them out here? God, it's over." Silence held the room close, tense. Light slanted through the doorway cutting a swath in the dark interior. The air smelled of wood smoke, coffee grounds sludge, old leather mule collars. Shag questioned the impasse with a keen stare before she slipped out to investigate dogs barking down the creek.

Kent heaved himself to his feet, the joy gone from his face. "If we don't hang on to what we have title to, Crocker Mining Company will buy up everything around us and pressure us to sell cheap."

Jake's chair came down with a thud. "Say, man, this may be an opportunity for all of us to git out. Let's see how we can generate this into a real attractive prospectin' deal!"

A glimpse of what it meant to be transient struck Kent with a new reality. Why should he stay if Jake and the others go? Suddenly Jake's one-room log cabin felt crowded. It was superior to the shack Kent occupied yet the presence of two men at the hand-hewn table filled the space. The scent of crushed sage around the doorstep mixed with rancid cooking odors as the men calculated current values of a myriad unknowns peculiar to prospecting. All were calculations unfamiliar to the business of accounting that Kent had engaged in earlier. Their claims were well sited with access on the Sterling-Norwegian Creek road and had suitable water for sluicing. The veins might continue to run in a generally north-south direction if they connected the dots from the Rattlesnake diggings north of here to south to the Meadow Creek Lodes.

Yet Kent found their figures and speculation tiresome and unnecessary. He recalled the lucrative business of skimming fees by the county recorders. Unrestrained by laws, they charged and pocketed all the traffic would bear until recently. Miners were rising up in protest, beginning in Hot Spring District. A rising sense of indignation compelled Kent to stand and firmly address Jake about his own inclination.

"I'm going to stay. I have no other plans or destination. In addition, the fee for filing nearly drained my finances. Fees that line the pockets of the Crocker bunch, I daresay. You might consider staying and partnering with me to withstand what will surely be pressure to sell our holdings. I have a suspicion the prospects are still good."

Jake paused. Then in a turnabout just as unexpected, he said, "The Justice of the Peace was innerested in speculating. And Judge Hezekiah Hosmer holds a lot of claims right here on Norwegian Creek. It might be better than we know. You've got hold 'a the tail of something larger than yourself, Berrigan. You've been the voice of reason after some petty disputes. Benson and the Northerners, Patrick and Jackson, gotta hear about this even if you and me sell or don't sell."

"I won't forget it, Jake." Kent shook the younger man's calloused hand.

"I guess it don't matter much whether I go or stay." Jake's blue eyes twinkled, an easy going look that made him a favorite with the girls in the camp.

That night Kent's mind was at ease for the first time in a long while, since he left the only home he had ever known. The ridges of the Tobacco Roots silhouetted against the deep royal blue sky above the shack appeared less formidable. The cry of the nighthawk spoke of familiarity, less aloneness. Kent stretched his arms and inhaled, expanding his chest with a sense of strength that struck him as a gift of the West, this crucible that remolded him from the inside out.

2

Western Union's new telegraph system extending to the West Coast had spread news of the Hot Spring District discovery. A line found its way to the mountainous niche of Virginia City, Montana Territory, in 1865, a legendary feat thanks to the Creighton brothers who set posts and hung wire on trees, fences and cliffs. Along with the telegraph, the Montana Post and Montana Democrat newspapers disseminated reports to the East that exaggerated the ease with which gold could be found at this new discovery site. Still, the flush of the 1864 discovery had only slightly abated since more men were working for the mining companies than for themselves. Kent stayed alert to these sharp rolls of boom and bust fortunes, but the constant unrest was disturbing. He sensed an urgency to apply himself to his claims after receiving a promising assay report. He decided to settle. Build a house. Buy a horse. This last objective sent him to Sterling. The sense of riding over the benchland with Miss Patton was a constant reminder of how that felt.

The horse he was looking for in the livery stable had been leased out. Unable to make an offer on Big Ben, Kent noticed a heavily muscled, trail worn Morgan that had just come in. His glance fell to the rider's knee-high riding boots and the blood drained from his face. The unmistakable black leather with sienna stitching and faint imprint of the *fleur-de-lis* labeled them made by Dubrinski, the Georgia cobbler his family patronized, the same style of boots he was wearing.

His mind went numb, refused to accept that he had been found, before a long simmering resentment bubbled to the surface—Rand ruined my life once. I won't let him do it again. An impulse to slip out unseen clashed with his need to absorb all of Rand, all of the weary but dignified figure in front of him, the older brother who had endured the war and lived to come after him.

Rand's tired eyes searched the crowd passing the doorway of the livery stable, sweeping over Kent without recognizing him in a beard and miners clothes. The sadness in the depths of his eyes struck Kent in the few merciful moments he had to collect himself, to gather pieces of their tangled lives. He turned to go—I have nothing to say to him—nothing that can't wait. The impetus to run leapt from his stomach to his chest; he sensed the beat of wild horses, a mindless adrenalin rush not unlike herds stampeding in the night on Norwegian Creek.

Wait until I'm ready—not now, but he turned back to face his brother. Surprised brown eyes met his own grey gaze. Kent, by nature, dearly wished to embrace him, yet his feet wanted to take flight. A long silent reunion occurred across the span of dirt-stained horses and mules. Rand remained aloof as if he'd come far enough. His lips tightened, a message that asking one more step was too dear a price.

Kent tried to hold back, maintain his resolve, until he broke in spite of himself and met Rand's bear hug as they had as young lads. The heights and hollows of the gold camp of Sterling in Hot Spring District, Montana Territory, witnessed more than one strained relationship in its four years as a boom town, post-war divided loyalties typical of an all too common experience.

"We need to talk." Rand led the way to a shady spot along the creek behind the stable. The sweet permeating scent of cottonwood sap claimed the air that Kent stole into his heaving lungs. Thick chokecherry bushes drooping with heavy clusters of small purple berries spread among red willowy dogwoods and aspens.

"You look good, Kent. Strong. What are you doing here?"

"I came to the livery to buy a horse."

"No, I mean here in Sterling."

Kent felt his throat close, close as decidedly as a front door. Only the men's unreadable stares breached the distance of the last two and a half years. Rand had the firm Berrigan features although his face not as long as Kent's, nor as sensitive. He wasn't as tall but his broad shoulders gave him a look of authority. Dust-caked trail clothes hung loosely over a once fashionable high- collared shirt that Kent recognized from long ago. Even the fitted riding pants, vest and short coat had a distinguished cut. He wore a black neck scarf formally like most men wear a tie. Ever the gentleman farmer, Kent noted. Even Rand's deep cultured voice seemed out of place here.

Mute, Kent continued to assess this phenomenon in front of him, Rand from Woodland Hills, Georgia, who showed up in Sterling. He looked older, wiser, a bit stooped; the war had taken its toll on him, too.

"Last year I looked for you in Illinois among father's relatives, but you'd left for St. Louis. Your last letter to Mother came from Montana Territory, so I followed the trails and asked in the camps. She would have been devastated if I hadn't found you."

Rand's words came slowly, strangled from being compressed in his mind and heart for months of the overland journey. His eyes, like Kent's, were moist, his hands visibly shaking. He shuffled in discomfort, declining to sit on the jumble of boulders beneath shady aspen boughs. Filtered shadows now felt ominous. Towering granite boulders on the hills overhead dwarfed the two men below. Even the rippling of Hot Spring Creek emerged from beneath alders and elderberry bushes with a chilling effect. A fine mist of dust clogged their nostrils from dozens of wagon teams hauling freight and ore in and out of Sterling.

Straining under the timorous silence, Rand half spoke, stopped, and reached out as if to grasp Kent for fear of losing him again. "I know I'm unexpected, and maybe unwelcome, but I didn't come this far to fail. It's been a hardship, the trail and heat and storms, only to chance creating a greater divide in the family than existed before. We feared you might have died, Kent."

Kent's mouth worked, felt dry, his eyes narrowed to encompass the other side of the coin, his brother's side. He stared in amazement. Rand take the high ground? "You betrayed us, Mother and me. You left us like Father did—."

Rand's chin jutted but he did not deny the charges. "Take me to your place," he said, gently shifting from a confrontation.

The plea slammed into Kent's remaining reserves. "You are not welcome in my home."

Rand laughed, throwing his head back. A big brotherly I-know-you laugh that always came before Kent gave in. Kent riffled through the stand-offs over the years, a long tunnel of memories that led to similar encounters, different circumstances. Rand's laugh. His own sense of defeat. His own loss of self-respect.

"I came here to be alone for a reason. That has not changed." Kent knew Rand would not allow him to stay in such squalor. The shack and mining claim would have Rand's imprint, his all-knowing advice stamped all over it, and surely his disapproval. He would demand that Kent go back to Georgia with him. He recalled his pain as a lad when Rand's wishes had overridden his own. He felt cornered then and now. The inclination to turn his back on Rand seized him; he turned but caught himself. His stoutly muscled frame whirled back, bringing him square with Rand.

"I want to leave things as they are, with you, with Mother." Kent's voice was even, given his innate good manners and deep fealty to this brother.

"I traveled over two thousand miles because Mother is sick and mourning her life away for you. Listen to me—I cannot go home without you." Rand raised himself almost to Kent's height, exercising his authority and power to the fullest, a stance that had long worked during past brotherly altercations. His dark eyes flashed with impatience, a growing fury.

"I will go see her soon, but not now," Kent countered, his drawl low, halting. He knew either going or refusing to go would be a mistake. He preferred to drop the whole thing, to escape Rand once again. "Give me some time. You don't understand."

Pain bled inside as he inwardly raged. *I can't go back. The war haunts me, don't you see? I lost you and Mother and myself when all I wanted was for us to go on as before. My very existence depends upon staying sane.* None of this he revealed to Rand.

"Time! It's been, what? A year and a half. Mother feared you might have been attacked by hostiles since your last letter from the Territory. Doesn't that mean anything to you? I cannot fail Mother. She dotes on you. She's always doted on you." Rand's temper flared, flushing his wind-dried cheeks, knotting his fists. "What don't I understand?"

Cowed by the strident tone, Kent heard only their father's voice when they were young. He felt himself slipping into his five or six year-old shoes, his hair cut in childish bangs, his knickers expensive but his feelings dashed. Wavering under the barrage, he heard his voice come out high, thin.

"I—I must hang on to something I've found here." His jaw slacked, his will crushed. The knotty relationships with Rand, Mother, even his long absent Father, swept over him inciting a dilemma—he envisioned himself fleeing Richmond, Virginia, with townspeople who must surrender their beautiful Confederate capital to the enemy or set it on fire in a final demonstration of rage and rebellion. He had sprinted across the last bridge over the James River, and hitched a ride on the final Richmond-Danville train only to dodge the Home Guard of Unionists in the Carolinas.

With the flashback a sense of reeling out of control left Kent's eyes red and a chunk lodged in his throat as if flames sucked at his lungs, tortured his soul. Kent's grey eyes grew round, boyish, and watered as his brother became a grim reminder of the suffering he had endured, still endured. Never before in his life had Kent experienced such a bitter taste of rebellion. Not with his parents, not with the war, or with Rand.

Rand misunderstood the tearful look for weakness until Kent's fist struck him.

Days after the confrontation Kent wandered the foothills and benches, avoiding his now inhospitable shack, his former refuge, the shack he had refused to show Rand. The late afternoon sun coaxed sprouts of barley from settlers' newly tilled fields and buds to form on wild roses along streams stemming from the Tobacco Root Mountains. Nature's bounty responded to the short growing season in the northern climate, but for Kent it was unseen. The fifteen-foot sluice box he had worked so hard to seal dried out and the boards separated. He struck out early each morning to prowl up and down Norwegian, Canadian, and Rattlesnake creeks, walking long and hard among stands of juniper and clambering over piles of tailings that hosted last year's tall, dry mullein stalks. He drifted through camps to be with people and away to be alone. Daily living felt like a chore. He became gaunt, stooped, a ghost haunting the hills and in turn, haunted by ghosts within.

Kent stood on a promontory in renowned Gold Field above a branch of Hot Spring Creek, a vertical distance from benchland below, and south of the tree-lined spot where he had struck Rand. Bent forward, eyes down, his hands trembled in the pockets of his wool coat, his spirit shaken by cascades of regrets. Each breath was still a sharp intake with a long, controlled exhale. He felt like the tumbleweeds that scurried ahead of prevailing west winds, teasing sagebrush on their way to pitch over the rim of massive boulders that stood on end like staunch guardians above Sterling. Steep slopes of the foothills, dense with shrubs and fir and blackish in the depths of the shadows, dropped along the east side of the Field. Eerie plumes of steam spouting from the hot spring three miles distant reinforced the supernatural landscape features that might have frightened native tribes, especially the way the creek disappeared from view and abruptly popped up downstream as if guided by a coyote trickster. Gold Field had kept its secret of untold riches in this rugged, remote land of startling beauty until recent discoveries drew men to its folds. Yet today Kent's eyes were vacant. Blow flies buzzed unnoticed beneath his sweaty hat brim, emboldened by this lone, alive but unaware creature in their territory

Rand had gone, riding out on the next stagecoach without attempting further pursuit. Kent confirmed this information with Harland Callahan, owner of a boarding house in Sterling, who reported seeing the Morgan for sale at the livery stable. But the long shadow of Rand's presence remained. Kent cursed himself.

"I should have stood up to him instead of leaving home before he returned from the North—but I couldn't face him." At last the words were spoken aloud, left to drift aimlessly over open benches of Madison County, to wander with the spirits of the wind over the mountains. Weary of their family schism he acknowledged, I couldn't follow or support Rand's treason to us in the South. If Rand was true to family blood that meant that I was in essence a deserter.

"Still, it was unforgiveable to strike him."

He shook his head as a painful awareness broke through earlier denial. He had left Mother mourning as surely as if he had died; Catherine Berrigan, the stately presence with the low gentle voice. The image gave way to a blurred recollection of his father, Brogan Berrigan, the once privileged stockman from

Dublin. Strange that he would think of him since he left when Kent was seven, a vague memory from a photograph when his father was in his mid-twenties. About his age now, Kent realized. Brogan had the same tall lean build, thick unruly hair and angular features with the penetrating Irish eyes of his sons. An uncomfortable intensity radiated from him that Kent recognized in himself and Rand.

Was I striking out at Father, not Rand?

A small rock cut loose from beneath his Dubrinski boots, prompting another image of Rand. Startled, he found he'd braced himself over a looming precipice. A ker-chink told him the stone hit another rock, a thud relayed its progress into another as it marked a gravelly course among the clumps of dried grass, gathering larger rocks and momentum until a crash resounded against distant boulders at the bottom.

"I felt Father's temper as my own when I struck Rand—I hated how both of them left me." With a renewed surge of anger, Kent dislodged a dozen other boulders to follow the first, scrapes drawing blood on his knuckles.

"I guess I ended it with my brother. I'll likely not go back."

He wondered if he had thrown his life away coming here. Certainly he had lost any claim to the family estate. And Miss Olivia Spencer? He likely forfeited any prospects of marrying her, the woman he had known from their respective boarding school days. That seemed even more remote since he'd met Miss Marion Patton.

Echoes of the avalanche below stilled his burst of anger and despair. He stepped back from the precipice and turned toward home.

"We have all been uprooted and resown like so many seeds in a field of sparrows. We will make of it what we will." He absently brushed the flies from his brow. A hint of the acceptance he would eventually embrace surfaced, but blessed relief eluded him.

Tinted layers of evening light bent over the Tobacco Root Mountains scattering pinks and purples in the few glass windows of the saloons along Sterling's main street.

"Say, this looks pretty good." Jake Hanson admired his reflection that showed his fresh shave left only a full goatee. He pushed back dirty blond hair that flopped over his brow and matched golden fuzz visible above the few buttons left on his shirt. He knocked mud from his gum boots, sniffed his armpits and swore.

"I'm wed to the Almighty diggin's, sweatin' out more crik water than I take in." He followed a blast of Louisiana-style music into the Dixie saloon, a false-fronted building, dark as a cave, with a long bar flanked by a string of rickety stools. Kent rubbed his own scruffy chin and edged in behind Jake. An accordionist summoned lively tunes from an eight-chord squeezebox, catchy old folk songs complemented by a fiddle, and a washboard that anyone drunk enough could play.

Several of the miners they knew on Norwegian Creek were at the bar with drinks in hand. Those who made the original discoveries usually christened the land and its features—Canadian Creek, Preacher Creek, Norwegian Creek. Soon, because of the opportunistic nature of miners to cluster around good prospects, the Confederacy was well represented on the windswept mountainside, many of them from Missouri. Lately, Jake took comfort in the gathering of Southerners. He and Kent and spent more of their long evenings in Sterling, alert to rumors of riff-raff and incidents.

Kent wouldn't have traded his shack on Norwegian Creek for all the saloons in Sterling, but he was uneasy about Jake frequenting the hot-spots in town. Rebels were tinder to the sparks of Federals' taunts of treason. Things could go bad if miners drank too much or failed to pan out enough gold or tempers flared for no reason at all. Down the rough wooden bar a conversation ceased abruptly between two sun-blistered, grimy faced miners when he and Jake slid onto the stools nearest the door and fished for cigarette papers and tobacco from small muslin pouches.

"Evenin' gentlemen." Jake nodded In their direction then pointed to a jog of corn whiskey whichh the bartender poured, splashing it over the edge of the glass.

"No news is good news. As long as the shipment of big stamp mills is delayed, we kin continue prospectin' without a lot of problems."

"Sure and what are you goin' do with yer ore? Beat it to death yerself and melt it down on the cookstove?" The taunt came from the far end of the bar. The men guffawed. Jake shuddered at the tone of the drawl. It was not the usual banter he enjoyed at the saloons.

"Business will be good for whoever gits one here first," Jake admitted, "though they'll try to run us out."

"I sez run them out, the big money. They made fortunes sellin' guns to Abe Lincoln. Are we gonna let 'em take over agin? I don' like it." Benson harped his grudges too often, too loud, a constant reminder of tensions in the Territory.

"Yeah, he's right," someone chipped in. "The North still has the country in its grip. They don't answer to us."

"The discovery of gold on Silver Bow Creek is drawing customers from my business," volunteered the bartender, changing the subject to dissuade the miners from taking dangerously polarized positions. The roomful of hard-nosed customers laughed and relaxed.

"Let's head on back to the Gulch," Ken urged, more impatient than he wanted to let on, but

Jake parlayed the visit into a chance to glean any gossip that might pertain to the security of his claim and that of his neighbors. Miners outside bypassed the Dixie Saloon for the even rougher Golddigger. These were not likely to be Southerners, but you never knew. Folks each had their reasons for affiliation and all hid their stories, their past, as if their lives depended on it, and often they did. All Southerners were suspect for being deserters, or they'd fought on the wrong side or didn't fight at all. Seceshes they were called. As if being displaced or losing everything were not enough, each prospector had his own grim story, regardless of region of origin. Most did not find the anonymity they sought in the West.

In the noise and stink and dust of the joint, Jake became pensive. The scratchy, offbeat music sounded jarring and dissonant. "It's been a long time since I sent a packet of money home. My brothers must be old enough to help out, hard to believe they might be grown up. Wish I knew them better. I thought I'd get back to Tennessee some day, then again, I'd have a lot of explainin' to do. Jake downed his drink and slid off the stool and headed for the Golddigger with its garish green and yellow sign lit by an oversized kerosene lantern.

Kent made the rounds with him, amused at what Miss Olivia Spencer would think if she could see him now. His pale Southern complexion had given way to burnished leather around his straight nose and firm jaw. The grey eyes might have been the same but the look was different, sharp, even piercing to reflect the clarity of the thin atmosphere. His former slim horseman's hands represented the most drastic change; prominent knuckles bore workman's scars, ingrained dirt and calluses.

"Here I am, Kent Berrigan, late of Woodland Hills, Georgia, at the Golddigger Saloon in Montana Territory—already this far deviated from you—and my past. Miss Olivia, I do believe yo' all would find me quite changed, aye! A sappy smile played around his lips, the speech below his breath. At times the contrast between where he came from and where he ended up was almost laughable. His present one room miner's shack was little different in construction than the saloon, a frame building of board and batten, roofed in the same, which was neither warm nor particularly waterproof. He sensed that Miss Marion Patten woould not be quite so shocked. She seemed to accept him as another miner, or did she? Their short time together revealed little of his life, but she seemed at ease with him.

Sterling was located on a major road tying Bannack to Virginia City and Bozeman, so most travelers visited the Golddigger just to say they had. The saloon was dark and crowded with customers. A blast of hot, steamy air reeking of whisky and sweat emerged, even with the front and back doors open. The rank smell of spilled cheap beer and garlic sausage was steeped into its very walls. Kent nearly backed out the door.

"I'd rather enjoy a whiff of homegrown tobacco and Old Jake Beam," he choked.

Charlotta Ann Marie was first to get her hands on Jake. Laughing, she tucked her slim white forearm into the unresisting crook of Jake's arm and led him to the bar. Her small white teeth and fresh cream complexion gave her the look of a schoolgirl, Jake had a hard time looking into her eyes rather than at prominent mounds of bare flesh where the dressmaker had apparently run out of material.

"You're like one 'a them pretty finches I see flitting all over the place." Jake slipped an arm around her. A tight red-orange satin bodice flared into an overlay of her gathered skirt with scallops caught in tiny bows around larger floor-length ruffles. Charlotta turned just in time to find Harriet Eloise snatch Jake in her usual expansive embrace and pinch his cheek.

"When you goin' to grow up, honey?" she teased in a gravelly voice, "How long do I have to wait for youse?"

Jake flushed scarlet as miners hooted at this old ploy. He managed to wriggle loose and cut into a poker game at the corner table. Kent tuned into the discussion of news about Crocker Mining Company's escalating buy-up of land and claims. A smattering of comments did little to enlighten either the speakers or the listeners. By the time the saloon girls made their move on him, Kent nodded to Jake that he was leaving.

Kent prospected with renewed vigor over the next few weeks. Returns from the newest digs were gratifying, confirming his earlier hunches. Shag explored wide circles around him, chasing cottontails, and stirring shrill killdeer from among the bunch grass and rabbitbrush.

"You are quite a sight, Shag," he laughed, picking sticky weed out of her long hair.

As usual on these rambles, Kent packed his gold pan and leather pouch to collect findings. He scooped sand and gravel into the pan and squatted at the creek with a bit of the usual anticipation. He dipped the pan carefully underwater to float off loose dirt and leaves, then rotated the contents back and forth in a washing action to separate the remaining dirt, clay and large rocks that he gently tipped over the edge of the pan.

"Panning" generally had a mesmerizing effect to which Kent readily succumbed, the prospector's eternal dream that the next pan or the one after would yield riches—the swirling motion formed concentric circles from eons of eroded matter that was readable to the practiced eye. A sheath of white granules toward the outside surrounded fine black sand centered with radiant ruby-like garnets in the bottom of the pan. A flash of fool's gold against the black sand aroused Kent from his reveries, but the lightweight particles were iron pyrite. Weighty gold flakes or nuggets that he looked for failed to show this time in the pan. Kent emptied the remains back into the creek and stretched his cramped legs.

His mind drifted back to lazy afternoons he had spent with Miss Olivia Spencer. A sense of her thick, amber hair fluttered within the edges of his consciousness, recalling a hint of her gardenia cologne. The enveloping sense of her waist-length tresses lingered with him today, a contrast to the rust-colored, frizzy hair of Miss Marion Patton. Miss Patton—her image came at odd moments, reminding him how he felt galloping on a wild horse over Gold Field with her. Tempting as it was to try to catch up with her, he recognized he'd made a choice to first seek healing his soul in the expanse that was Montana Territory. With a reluctant shift from his fantasies, he picked up his gold pan and Shag leapt to his side for their next adventure. Only then did he notice tiny wild strawberry plants blooming along the creek banks, their round, saw-toothed leaves shining with moisture.

Sometime after midnight a few weeks later, Kent was awakened by shouts from down the creek. Coyotes yipped and prowled along the foothills, their voices echoed by packs of dogs. Wild horses whinnied and stampeded. Kent grabbed his lantern and ran toward the swinging lights he saw ahead. He arrived at Jake's place along with a dozen other alarmed citizens of Norwegian Creek. Jake had been shot.

Foot and mounted posses circled, issued orders, revised plans, and disagreed on strategies. Tempers ran hot; fear brought chills. Side arms and rifles hung on every man's person. Hovering black clouds rumbled with thunder. Rain bit bare heads and arms unprepared for the night's crisis. Men were finally dispatched in all directions in search of the murderer. A high-caliber bullet had pierced Jake's skull behind the left ear while he filled his water bucket outside. Blood and dirt matted his beard and long blond hair beyond recognition.

Kerosene had long ago run out and candles burned down in lanterns of those still milling about. Hours later Kent stumbled home alone in the dark through the sagebrush, staring unseeingly at the indistinct trail. He again felt the weight of Jake's solid body as they'd moved it inside Jake's cabin.

"Damn," Kent murmured, "Jesus, what of his family?" He spit into the brush to get rid of the sick, sweet scent of blood. Death, so indiscriminate. Or was it? It could've been any of us— we're still Rebels to some folks. Oh, hell, I ought to leave, get out of here while I can. Why Jake? Did Benson stir up old grudges charged like gunpowder used to blast solid quartz?

The interior of his shack took on a new and ominous presence. He started to poke up the fire for coffee, but slammed the stove door and stepped outside. Jake had wanted to sell out, but Kent had prevailed upon him to stay. Had Jake sensed a threat to his life? Kent's boot sent a stick of wood flying into the brush. He'd had a sense of rejection when Jake wanted to sell out to Crocker. He hadn't told Jake about the series of outcroppings, but he had opened his confidence more than usual. Anyhow, Jake had come around in support of holding on against those with money and power. A good man.

The cloud cover shifted, revealing chiseled blue-grey sky that showcased a bright star over the ridge of the Tobacco Roots as if nothing had changed since the world began. Kent dropped his chin toward his chest, struck by the beauty and its contrast with this wretched night.

"It's not worth it," he told himself. "How can I notify his folks? Jake and Hoot—they were my family here on Norwegian Creek."

His limbs hung weighted with exhaustion when he fell into bed only to wake when his fist splintered the flimsy pine wall, shaking dirt from between the cracks in the ceiling over his head. He flung back the rough Army blankets and sat upright— a drama still churning unfinished in his mind. His shoulder length black hair released dirt from the ceiling into his lap. Fires raged as he and an unknown private fled broken streets and eerie landscapes of Richmond. Tall formless figures with armloads of elongated weapons emerged from the flames, silhouetted against live oaks erupting in cinders. He dove for cover in a swamp only to find his brother Rand standing over him—implacable amid thundering rounds of cannon mortars.

Kent staggered outside, his chest shirtless to invite the pain of cold to assure him which world he was in. Head in hands, he tried to dispel images of broken men in the war, silent, as voiceless as he felt right now in the wake of the murder of Jake

Hanson. The biting air usually chased away haunting memories, but it was too early, dreams too disturbed.

"These damn flashbacks ought to be gone by now," he groaned, but the night's shooting had brought them back.

Long hours passed until it was light enough to catch a stagecoach in Sterling that was bound for Virginia City where he would find a coroner.

Virginia City, Territorial capital of Montana, had amassed a diverse population, a thriving town center, and a reputation driven by vigilantes, although citizens struggled to give it a sense of dignity. The Creighton block of low stone stores and offices anchored the east end of Wallace, the main street. The Creighton brothers' Western Union telegraph line ran west of the Mississippi and extended it to Virginia City, upending any romantic notions of the camp being isolated from civilization. Blocks of decent wood frame houses flanked downtown businesses, but the concentration of livestock traffic created fetid street conditions. Garbage, dogs and pigs added to the disagreeable odors and mayhem, defying pretenses of sophistication, though a few stone Victorian homes were grand dames among a preponderance of log cabins and shacks. Union-style, conical Sibley tents, brush wickiups, and a number of converted covered wagons served as questionable human habitats on the hillsides.

Searching for a coroner, Kent walked past blacksmiths who hollered and hammered in forges in a half dozen shops while miners, freighters and farriers demanded services day and night. He dodged drivers who angled a crush of teams, some hauling three or four wagons lashed together, in front of saloons and mercantiles to load or unload. The Diamond R Freighting Company's drivers shouted and swore at teams of six to sixteen horses, mules or oxen, offering no niceties in the city's melee. Interesting, Kent thought, that some drivers wore soldiers' long

Union blue overcoats. General Ulysses S. Grant had charitably allowed defeated Rebel officers permission to keep their horses, uniforms, and guns after the surrender if they'd go home. Apparently the general had done as much for his own men.

An arrastra made of heavy stone discs for crushing ore was turned by a plodding mule on a rare level spot on the edge of Cover Street north of Wallace. The coroner, who also served as pharmacist and physician, worked out of a log cabin on Cover Street. Space for offices was found in any available structure that could be built, leased, or borrowed. The hell-bent-for-gold public opposed funding any civic or Territorial projects.

"Did he have any relatives that you know of?" The coroner's thick white mustache framed the deep voice, and settled into his bushy beard.

"He talked of a number of siblings," Kent remembered. Jake had found his estrangement from them as baffling as Kent found his split was with Rand.

"Do you know where he came from?"

Kent regretted the one code of ethics the men observed in the camps, avoid personal inquiries, however, he agreed to handle any of Jake's affairs back on his claim. The coroner would dispatch word of Jake's death to surviving family members when they could be located. The older man shuffled off to deal with other problems, all urgent and probably few pleasant.

Kent circulated, too, asking about connections Jake might have had in Virginia City. A clerk at Wells Fargo Express, where mail was sorted for transport to the camps, rummaged in bags in search of letters addressed to Jake. Quite a few had accumulated, either unclaimed or undelivered, Kent wasn't sure, but they did have return addresses. He was pleased to give this information to the coroner and agreed to follow up on the correspondence as he tucked the letters in his inside coat pocket.

3

The stream of prospectors to the Hot Spring area continued into the fall of 1866. Several new stamp mills were already established on strategic sites ranging from Norwegian Creek to Lower Hot Spring, but many were soon in trouble. The quality of ore processed from both the mill owners' holdings and those of individual miners was often disappointing. The yield rarely paid for the high cost of processing and, in many cases, the ore was practically worthless. The enterprising Midas Mining Company became the center of a debate about the potential for gold to be found in any worthwhile amounts in the Hot Spring area. Superintendent Henry A. Ward believed that gold would increase in quantity at a greater depth, similar to hardrock mines in Nevada and California. He optimistically extended his operation up Hot Spring Creek above Sterling, where he built Midasburg, a new company town. Managers of other operations, particularly in Lower Hot Spring District around the Boaz mill, boasted that resources were infinite, or seemed so based on earlier rich discoveries.

Kent Berrigan gleaned information about Crocker Mining Company in an effort to protect his self-interests. It appeared the Company was here to stay. Believing that gold discoveries were yet to be made, Crocker accelerated its acquisition of small claims while many miners and investors held out, speculating on higher prices to come. However, the out-migration of laborers was in full force by the time a mid-September blizzard whipped across the foothills of the Tobacco Roots, harbinger of a merciless winter ahead.

The turn of events magnified Kent's inertia. He began to dread his promise to Rand that he'd soon return to Georgia. Anxiety and a raft of emotions raised by Jakes' death and his own war trauma plagued him day and night. He settled Jake's affairs on Norwegian Creek, where underlying fear stalked the lives of those still in the camps. An inquest into the murder by the fledgling office of the Territorial magistrate further antagonized Southerners who felt threatened by any questioning. Angered that Northerners occupied the appointed seats of power throughout the Territories, they were not forthcoming. The inquest listed robbery as a motive, as well as possible claim jumping, gambling debts, intemperate remarks, or jealousy over a woman at the Golddigger. The investigation was inconclusive and faded into the background. Lacking any evidence, suspicions that the Civil War continued in isolated pockets of the country were not entirely unfounded. Old grudges, class warfare, and unabated feuds from myriad conflicts remained among the displaced and disadvantaged who had little to look forward to and nothing to go back to. Kent's eavesdropping and intuitive hunches led him to believe that one of the miners had shot Jake, mistaking him for Benson, who lived in the next cabin down the creek.

"The greater loss is mine. A pity the country isn't big enough for all of us," Kent lamented. "I tried to outrun my own demons but feel confronted by them at every turn."

The shorter days of fall, known by locals as Indian summer, and its longer nights at this high latitude added to unease in the camps. Picking up Jake's habit, Kent dropped in to saloons in Sterling to keep abreast of affairs in Hot Spring District.

A young man preening his first moustache made his way up the street past the Dixie Saloon, then turned back to enter. The din of conversation quieted, the hush typical of a stranger's arrival, an appraisal of the mixed blood *mestizo* longer this time. Thick dark hair crowded under the man's black flat-brimmed hat, accenting a tailored black cotton shirt and trim pants, an outfit rarely seen in the Northwest. Kent moved his drink over on the bar, leaving room for the newcomer who apparently welcomed the gesture as he strode quickly to the space. The racket behind them resumed and Kent introduced himself.

"Ray here," the lad said, though the name did not fit the Spanish and Indian look or accent. "I come with wagon train from Utah, few days ago. I be camp tender. Pay my way."

Kent's eyebrow rose at the name.

"It's better, Ray. I be *Americano*. Git along with *el hombres!*"

"I understand," Kent smiled. "We both have to figure out how to be Americano and keep out of fights!"

They laughed. Up close, Kent noticed Ray had a serious, mature look older than his years, probably close to twenty. His large dark eyes were fringed with long black lashes. This young man obviously had a tough, gritty character, but Kent sensed a vulnerability. Kent suddenly felt paternal, a sense of connection with someone similar to Jake.

"Cigarillo?"

Kent accepted the readymade. "Thanks. Having been a tobacco grower, I've maintained a high standard for my smokes. The miners' roll-your-own Durham doesn't suit me."

They talked for awhile, mostly about the odds for success in prospecting around Sterling. "Some miners come in and do well for six months or more, but most are gone in two or three," Kent said. "News of richer strikes comes along and off they go, recently to Last Chance Gulch ninety miles north of here."

Ray revealed little except that he came from California gold country. Long silences hung between their comments. Kent realized he was unaccustomed to talking with anyone these days. In this case, he was grateful for the easy distance between them. He was happy to listen if the lad wanted to talk. Ray had the kind of presence that made a person pay attention. Sadness hung in his eyes where shades of give-in or give-up acceptance stripped some of his vigor. That's not to say he doesn't have guts, Kent knew, given his willingness to venture to Montana Territory.

Ray briefly surveyed the occupants of the saloon and moved to leave, though not before catching the eye of one of the girls. She had him dancing a two-step to an impromptu Latin beat the accordionist provided with a wide toothless grin. Ray grinned, too, when he left.

Kent saw him again in Sterling a week later and they had dinner at Mrs. Callahan's. This time Ray was more talkative.

"This new country for me. *Muy grande!*"

"How long were you on the trail from California and what was it like?"

Ray related little, his stories sketchy. He drifted from one idea to another without divulging much, a little like Jake had been, restless but good company. Kent tried to shake his own heavy mood, but he couldn't match the energy of this young amigo who soon left as if he had pressing business.

For Kent, the following week became one of especially painful recollections that slammed into current reality. Jake was gone. The loss felt like a ragged hole. Kent had come to Sterling late in the fall a year ago and now faced another winter alone except for Shag. He'd stacked the woodpile higher than the roof of the shack, but any passion he'd had for using a pick axe on frozen ground dissipated last winter. He exercised every effort to avoid his promise to Rand, yet the fierce early storm felt damn cold to a Georgia man. In disgust he tossed his meager belongings into a pile on the bunk, gathering wool socks, a wool scarf, a felt hat he'd made, and sheepskin leggings he was particularly fond of. In the shuffle, the packet of letters to Jake fell from an inside pocket.

Neglect of the correspondence had been on purpose at first. These letters seemed so personal and private that Kent felt it would be invasive to open them. The coroner had the addresses and entrusted disposal of the lot to Kent. He sliced open the seals with a kitchen knife and glanced through the contents.

"Half a dozen bills, ha! Maybe that's why Jake didn't pick up his mail," Kent laughed, relieved. He owed for the mule he "borrowed" to get to gold country. That was Jake!

There were a couple letters in women's handwriting from home that Kent felt too uncomfortable to read—they brought up the emptiness of his own alienation. And last, a nicely embossed birthday card. Jake was twenty-three years old.

———————

Seeking company to counter the isolation, Kent left Norwegian Creek with Shag for a walk to Sterling, tramping through another early snowstorm. Snow-covered domes of haystacks marked settlers' farms where squares of plowed land caught drifts in furrowed rows and wind rattled dry leaves of broken corn stalks. Stark corner posts of claims like Kent's cast long shadows, changing the character of once uninhabited land. Piercing, sideways gales of snow again reminded Kent he was from the deep, warm South.

In Sterling, kerosene and candle lanterns glowed like tiny fireflies along the streets, sheltered somewhat in the mouth of the canyon. Smoke curled and lay low over cabin chimneys up and down Hot Spring Creek. The smell of wood smoke was warm and inviting, the crunch of his boots the only sound. The Golddigger had a fire roaring in a pot-bellied wood stove, attracting a few miners, who stamped their feet free of snow and hovered around the stove before retiring to what were probably less habitable structures. Kent recognized the German miners he had met on the stagecoach. Now the gentlemen spoke in camp-style English mixed with German.

Kent asked questions similar to inquiries Miss Marion Patton made last summer, an exceedingly dull enterprise without her. After hashing over the weather, few subjects arose other than the quality of assays, the constant breakdowns of the stamp mills, and the sorry business of transport from the States to the Territories. The fact the transcontinental railroad was being hammered into place at an astounding pace was barely known or comprehended here or elsewhere in the mining districts. Clever mechanics improvised from iron and scrap steel to repair the mills, but steel milling manufacturers were in the East, three months away for spring orders, almost a year away for orders in late summer. As winter bore down, everyone complained.

"Our jobs depend on cranky capitalists in New York or Missouri who expect quick returns and threaten to yank operations if we don't meet expectations," one miner said.

"Mining wasn't born yistiddy. They oughtta know somethin' about keepin' mills runnin' and gittin' orders in early."

"The women say their outfits are outdated by the time they get here. Hats with them flowers are out of style. They want the ostrich feathers or sich."

"The mines are gonna hafta pay a lot more'n they do now if we hafta buy ostrich feathers."

Kent's face scarcely disguised his boredom. He wondered why he ended up here with day laborers who growled about being idled, isolated, and far removed from amenities in the country, then realized he was guilty of the same.

"I hear new discoveries elsewhere top Hot Spring District—Confederate Gulch, Silver Bow, Idaho, Oregon," he said, without stirring much attention.

Inevitably, rumbles of Indian conflicts reached far flung enclaves. "I hear they're callin' up volunteers for fightin' the other side of the Yellowstone into Wyoming. Ain't good, the situation there, attacks on the forts 'n all. I 'pect they be callin' on us right when the weather and minin' gits good."

The German miners said they worked on North Meadow Creek near the rich Washington Bar. The Galina operated with minimal shifts, but they didn't have much to do except wait out the winter.

Kent had heard enough griping. He bundled up and strode to the boarding house to stay where Shag could sleep inside on a crocheted rag rug. By the time he returned to his shack the next day, he'd made up his mind to go to Georgia. A longing to visit home was wearing on him. He wanted to see fine horses and green pastures among stately sycamore trees. Miss Olivia Spencer, a longtime friend from a wealthy family, teased his thoughts. Dwelling on reuniting with Rand and his mother raised less comforting prospects.

"I didn't plan my life this way, my friend," he muttered to Shag. At age twenty he had considered no other life than management of the family estate. Marriage, a constant buzz in his social circle, he'd handled with an arm's-length relationship with Miss Spencer. Now seven years later he sensed her sultry cologne, and her long hair blowing free against his shoulder—Olivia, bright, ambitious, intellectually formidable, and available as far as he knew.

Miss Marion Patton's recent visit stirred his imagination even more, but she had come into his life and left without a backward glance after their short, fast ride. She'd said she would remember Montana Territory—she on the flashy black and white pinto, he on a striking oversized bay that reminded him how much he loved to ride, but that was blessed little to sustain one's hopes through a cold winter.

"I best be going, as they say out here," he told Shag. If he went during the spring or summer it would take away from his mining time and from precious summertime in the mountains of Montana. "You'll be all right, my friend. Just hang on and we'll see if Callahans will board you."

Nostalgia brought back the fun he and Rand used to have in a tree fort they'd built and furnished with crates from their cook's pantry. In humid summers they'd dash to a small lake on the estate and dive in from a fat overhanging branch. Later, as adolescents, their lives revolved around horses they raced recklessly beyond the surveillance of Mother or the stable hands. The recent realization he had acted out his father's abandonment of the family lay heavily on his conscience. Did Catherine Berrigan have an invisible hold the men in the family were forced to break? Kent shook his long, black hair to dispel unbearable reflections. Surely his leaving after the war had to do with Rand; however, he'd learned that speculation about why he did what he did was not a gold miner's way. It seemed they lived faster, worked longer, drank harder, and let bygones bury bygones.

Shag's floppy ears waggled back and forth as if honoring his confessions. She stared uncertainly as Kent packed a few things in his old Army duffle bag, gathered his guns, which he couldn't leave behind, and pulled down a clean coat and pair of trousers from a peg on the wall. At last he threw himself on the narrow bunk for a short night's sleep before an early departure on the stagecoach. He intended to make connections to St. Louis by taking passage on a swift mackinaw down the Yellowstone to the Missouri. Trusting in a revival of the Indian summer, he figured he'd get started and adapt to travel situations as he went along. By the time he again walked to Sterling in a blast of headwind, a watery sun had been up a few hours.

"Hallo, man, where yer going at such a pace?" The voice was unmistakably Ray's. He was leading his horse, its head down in the wind. Kent was so glad to see a familiar face he threw his free arm over Ray's shoulders, the gesture eliciting a grin beneath the well-trimmed moustache. Same *vaquero* hat and long black hair, but now he had a trace of a goatee and a fancy scarf knotted inside his collar.

"Good to see you! Where are you going with those saddle bags and bedroll on your horse?"

"Out with wagon train to Californy. This time I be outrider." Ray was clearly pleased he'd be a step above camp tender. His mousy tan and grey mustang danced impatiently, primed to buck or rear, anything except stand still in the cold wind.

"You don't say! You strike it rich already?"

Ray grinned. "I might be goin' back to see a girl. You ought to go with me. I ain't seen you on a horse yet."

"Hmm, let me think about that. It sounds a whole lot better to me than going East." Kent pulled down his cap and thrust his head into the wind, mulling the possibility. "This might be a lucky coincidence, a chance to get out of here and put off going home. California, why not? I might have gone anyway if I hadn't claimed title to the land."

Ray nodded as if he understood. They went to get a cup of coffee, along with three more cups and a half dozen of Mrs. Callahan's doughnuts, a specialty of the house.

"You know, Ray, I think you have a good ideer there." He drawled for fun, for being saved from what felt like his own folly. Not only saved, but given the fateful opportunity to pursue Miss Patton on her own turf—if he could find her. Coloma, did she say? "Maybe I will go with you. Say man, let's see if there's a horse for sale at the livery stable."

The change of plans would cost him half a day, but the wagon train was a notoriously complicated business to set in motion so it would undoubtedly be going out later. Kent found Big Ben, the handsome bay he had ridden with Miss Patton, and negotiated a trade for him and a saddle with a silver-handled pistol he had saved for such an emergency.

"This is my lucky day, young fella," he said, tightening his cinch.

At once he felt a sense of freedom, "a heady experience a man could get to like," he smiled to himself, recapturing the elation he'd felt at peak moments here in Montana Territory. Meeting Miss Patton ranked highest among those. He had no problem reliving the intrigue he'd felt when he met the woman from California with the sunburst frizzy hair, nor his attraction to that same glowing, vivacious woman when they rode to the sheltered timberline of the Tobacco Roots not so long ago.

Big Ben's large solemn eyes surveyed Kent up and down, followed by snorts from his great muzzle. Kent smoothed the tussle of black mane to calm him with long easy strokes over his chest, withers and barrel. Later, when he had experience with the giant horse, Kent would have bet the poor soul at the livery stable had eagerly traded Ben because he couldn't afford his feed! Ben waited impatiently, the nature of a thoroughbred sire that had mated with a Percheron mare back in the mountains. Ben had the heavy black mane, tail and size of the mare, probably someone's prized draft horse that got away. The farrier charged extra to shoe him, but Ben was friendly as a pup, nudging Kent with a tweak that would have sent a lesser man flying backwards. Kent was over six feet tall and he could barely see over his mount, but fortunately his long legs enabled him to mount the gelding easily. In short order the two worked out who was doing the nudging.

Shag was safely boarded at the Callahans' under the watchful eyes of Angel and Finn. The freighters unloaded foodstuffs—sardines, oysters, molasses, salt pork, and gloves, suspenders and overalls, pick axes and shovels at the Mercantile, a rambling false-fronted building on Main Street. Crates of whiskey hastily moved from hand to hand into safekeeping in backrooms of saloons. Just as quickly, the narrow wagon beds of outgoing rigs filled with road-building and repair tools, extra harnesses for the teams, ore samples for more sophisticated mineral analysis, and an occasional trophy moose rack stashed on top.

Paying passengers vied for seats above the load. A pair of Belgians led an eight-horse team pulling two boxcar-like Shuttler wagons full of freight in gunny sacks. Cargo in other wagons consisted of local goods to be sold or traded elsewhere—deer and elk hides, and wolf, coyote and beaver furs. Bags of Montana grain to be cached along the way for returning mule teams completed the freight.

The cumbersome train moved out under the whip of John Kepling, a trail worn wagonmaster who had made this trip dozens of times. Along with curses, the teamsters chewed and spit on pace with the braying of the mules and barking of the dogs.

"This would be a good market for Georgia tobacco," Kent chuckled to Ray. "I ought to tell my brother, Rand!"

With a break in the weather, the wagon train of six teams, each pulling two or three wagons, was destined for its first overnight southwest of Virginia City where the animals could graze on patches of dry grass. Everywhere he looked, Kent noticed Ray on the spirited mustang enjoying the excitement of his new position as outrider, helping line out the freighters and riding ahead with other outriders to clear the road. Kent felt he had his hands full becoming acquainted with Ben, easing him into the grinding, shouting parade without spooking him. Tiny red veins exploded in the whites of Ben's eyes, eyes seeking to break free, weeping tear drops on flared nostrils. Young and jittery without much experience, the wild horse had a lot to learn, but Kent felt reassured when Ben's large soft ears flicked front to back, monitoring the activity, listening to his rider.

"We'll get along just fine," Kent said, bending forward to rub the powerful neck that was already moist and warm, the touch alone speaking to the quivering beast. One ear tipped back in answer before the Percheron's attention was captured by Ray trotting alongside with a mile-wide grin. No wonder women fall for him with that charm, Kent thought.

"Wanna trade?" Ray offered.

"Not on your life. I couldn't stay on that bronc you have. We rode English style on well-trained horses in Georgia, but I suppose these two will settle down on the trail."

The plodding routine of the wagon train soon quieted their mounts. Kent took the opportunity to recheck his belongings. His deer rifle rested in a hand-stitched leather scabbard he'd made which was well supported by Ben's generous withers. With the necessity to obtain his meat year-round, Kent had developed a keen eye shooting whitetail deer, pronghorn antelope, and elk that grazed slopes above his shack and on grassy benches below. His Army duffle bag loaded with bedroll, winter clothing, extra wool socks and soap pretty well accounted for his travel gear. He regretted not packing the sheepskin leggings for this trip. He'd sorely need them crossing the Sierras into California, but he'd packed expecting to go east and south to a warmer climate. He also left without a book, pen, paper or any other trappings of civilization.

"I've become something of a mountain man, I guess." He fingered his long beard and patted his tobacco pouch.

Ray laughed, a short rolling chuckle Kent found engaging.

The wagon train traveled the tricky dirt road of the Bozeman Trail that led to Virginia City from Sterling. Small drifts of early snow clung to hollows where the road was wedged into sidehills, though the trail did its best to skirt steeper and higher hills. Heavily laden wagons rolled and tilted at heart-stopping angles before they leveled out again, thanks to much cussing and hollering by the drivers. Working and straining most of the way, they made a last big push to gain altitude crossing the notorious Virginia City hill, where freighters often wrecked within sight of their destination, ironically after traveling hundreds of miles through hostile Indian country. This time Kepling's small train successfully descended the hill, continuing west downstream along Alder Creek to a sheltered camping place.

The next day they passed through a rich valley bordering the small but exquisitely pristine Stinking Water River. Grass belly deep on the horses revealed summer's largesse. Moose, deer and antelope gazed fearlessly at the ungainly outfits that split the solitude with their rumbling passage. The fairy tale-like Snowcrest Mountains formed a dramatic backdrop. Wagons hauled hard on this stretch of dirt, two-track shortcut through high Sweetwater country, following a course that bypassed Bannack to reach Idaho Territory. Several times the riders tied lassos to wagons to pull them up steeper ascents or through slushy snowbanks on the north sides of the hills.

"Ben, show me how to do this," Kent urged, feeling as uneasy as the horse when the rope tightened and began to sing with the tension between his saddle horn and the tie-down hitch on the front of a wagon. The Percheron shifted into the pull comfortably enough until he hit the end of the rope, then his hindquarters plunged down and sideways, hind legs staggering for a foothold, head rearing with wild eyes, trying to free himself from what felt like a fearsome trap.

"Give 'em his head and keep clear 'a the damn rope," Kepling yelled, simultaneously lashing his mules to create a little give in the lasso. Ben felt the give and steadied, then repeated his alarmed response several times until he understood his job and settled in to throw his shoulders against the taut line. Kepling nearly catapulted off the driver's seat.

"Whoa, man, hold 'em in!" The wagoneer swore and grabbed for a handhold on the rig.

"This Percheron heard his calling," Kent jubilantly yelled back. Kent's first cowboy experience sent his adrenalin rushing. "If this is any indication, this trip could be a real education for Ben and me." He savored the moment, thinking of the contrast with his previous life in Georgia where he'd had a relatively pampered ride after Ephram tacked up his horse. With the rush still coursing his veins he kicked Ben into a lope. The outriders headed for Monida Pass on the Montana Trail, which connected with the Corrine Road in Idaho Territory, a major corridor of transportation running four hundred miles between Bannack and Salt Lake City.

Ray and Kent reined in their mounts to view the dazzling white-crested Centennials that rose out of the grassland and swamps of upper Beaverhead valley. Quaking aspens, bright with golden autumn leaves, formed a necklace below the range.

Ice flirted along the edges of Red Rocks Lakes which mirrored the mountains in spectacular shades of azure and emerald. Snowy peaks set off the blue vertical range like a diamond tiara, its reflection clear in the shallow water. Silence fell over the travelers as if they had come upon the Swiss Alps—only Kent felt the comparison would be inadequate. The Centennials were vast, limitless, seeming to occupy the western portion of the continent, the edge of a boundless universe. Pale blue mountains slipped away in every direction, melding into sky in a seamless bowl of electric air so sharp it stole his breath.

Kepling halted his team and raised his hand to stop the procession for a breather at the top of the rise. As wagons creaked to a standstill, a palpable reverence swept over those assembled in the presence of so much majesty.

"Lewis and Clark couldn't have seen it any purtier than this," Kepling said. "They explored the Beaverhead on their way to the Columbia River." His arm motioned the direction of their trail over the pass into Idaho Territory. "It was known as the Louisiana Purchase in them days."

With a lack of inhabitants or their effects as far as the eye could see, it struck Kent that he was now deep in the Far West, owned by flocks of Canada geese blackening the sky over his head. Squawky calls of spindly-legged, long-necked sandhill cranes punctuated the honking of geese and Mallard ducks.

"This is a migration path. The cranes oughtta be heading down south by now, 'specially after that storm blew through. Must be a nice Indian summer comin' to keep them here." Kepling used his binoculars to scan the acres of fowl.

Kent observed that the wagonmaster's weathered face softened in this land he wore like a cloak. His voice that withered mules in their harnesses struck a tone of tenderness, simplicity.

"Ye oughtta see the trumpeter swans," he said. "Damnedest beautifulist sight ye ever seen." His gesture drew a huge, graceful fowl in the air. "A wingspread of six feet or more." He waggled his head as if no words could describe what he had seen. "They could be there, but I don't see 'em right now."

Kent felt a tinge of sadness to ride over the pass toward unknowns, away from the enchantment of the Centennials and Montana Territory. Unknowns that tempered his newfound sense of liberation. The thrill was part of the journey, the fears another. He found the men who accompanied this wagon train a rough bunch. Norwegian Creek seemed like a cradle of domesticity in comparison. There the predominance of Southern laborers was at least within his life experience. Here he felt caught in a tide of foul-mouthed mule skinners of questionable origins, of desperados masked as outriders. Even most of the passengers and ne'er do well camp followers who had lost everything gambling were crude and untrustworthy. To hear the stories told by these "gentlemen" one would think they were good citizens. They claimed that the real threats existed along the nine hundred mile trail from Montana gold camps to camps along the American River. Marauders, road agents, and outright murderers preyed on innocent travelers, they said. Their Springfield single-shot muzzle-loading rifles, likely purloined from the Army, attested to the men's sense of unease.

Ray rechecked his stash of weapons, the two early Smith and Wesson pistols on his person, an ivory-handled piece he'd won off somebody, and an older model musket-type rifle that kicked the daylights out of him. Kent's new Henry, a rare model rifle he'd bought from a destitute settler passing through Sterling, garnered a few comments. The bulky coats of others betrayed hidden weapons in addition to the inevitable rifles slung from pommels of their saddles. Several of Kepling's men on guard duty prominently displayed Sharps carbines that had replaced older Union rifles in the war.

Kepling boasted that the only purpose of his sawed-off Confederate cavalry shotgun "loaded with a mix of slugs and shot" was to ward off grizzly bears. In any event, no one messed with the wagonmaster. Reports were that Indian troubles were not as bad in Idaho as they might be going east unless they were attacked by the Nez Perce, the Nimií pu on Idaho's Clearwater River. This was unlikely if they honored a treaty to stay on their reservation, an agreement the government made with two representatives of the tribe, Chief Yellowtail and old Chief Joseph, father of the peaceful young Chief Joseph.

"Strange how violence or threats of violence follows humans wherever we go." Kent asked Ray if ongoing conflicts were the same in California.

"*Mi familia* in Mexican province on Colorado River long time. Be peaceful with Navajo, Hopi if they stay on own land, but it's same wars if tribes attack. We let 'em alone. They leave us alone. I think California more like this bunch." He nodded disapprovingly toward the wagon train.

It was a long speech for Ray. Kent wondered if he was homesick.

"Will you be going home this trip?"

"No!" Ray's answer was too hasty. Kent waited.

Ray looked up rather sheepishly. "It be about a girl in Colorado, grownup woman now, probly married." He obviously regretted whatever had or hadn't occurred between them when he was younger.

"So you left home on account of a woman? Well, I may be doing the opposite—going to California to see one. At least to find one I have in mind."

"I followed one to Montana. *Ella vino y se escapo' volando como un pájaro*, she came and flew away like a bird."

The conversation was getting too close to Kent's rising anticipation of seeing Miss Marion Patton, who had likewise vanished, an urgency that triggered an uneasy flush in his body. He kicked the gelding into a lope and left the straggling wagon train for a breather. Ahead on a bend he pulled to a halt and rubbed the horse's stout neck and ruffled his mane. Ben, who seldom seemed to tire, pranced and pleaded to be let out on the rein.

"You're a hoot," Kent laughed, recalling Jake's mule, then caught himself. God, there was violence and murder enough on Norwegian Creek—what could possibly be worse out here? Mother would be saying Hail Marys if she knew.

"I have to take a chance on carving out my own life," Kent said aloud, his voice thick, tenuous, strange to his ears. Only the word 'chance' stuck in his mind. He stroked Big Ben with confidence, knowing the gelding was carrying him to his big chance.

4

The road agents struck on the banks of the Snake River in Idaho Territory, only they were not immediately recognized as such. They did not fit the description of those known to ambush stagecoaches at Robbers' Rock on the Bannack to Helena road. Kent had heard the story of masked men with rifles easily relieving passengers of their gold and valuables—a long slope up to an outcropping of massive boulders favored the holdup agents. Later these same agents removed their masks and returned to lives of ordinary citizens, one of them rumored to be Sheriff Henry Plummer.

Kent was pleased to find Idaho was surprisingly warmer than Montana with little evidence of snow. At noon on a bright sunny day, the wagon train pulled into a dry, dusty open spot on the road near the Snake River. A few sheds and several hovels that apparently served as homes sat by the landing. A stash of battered rafts and rowboats were heaped at the edge by a worn ferry. A wiry, grey-haired fellow in tattered shirt and trousers rose from a chair on the porch and beckoned the wagonmaster over.

Kepling yelled back asking him what he wanted. The man spat and demanded the wagon train pay a toll to cross and an extra fee to have freight ferried. Kent had no idea if this was an expected confrontation, but he could see they had trouble. Not one to take orders from anybody, Kepling took his time handing his team to another driver. He slowly climbed down from the seat and stretched his short legs, his canvas pants revealing powerful muscles that came from crunching down with all his might on the brakes of the heavy wagons. Three outriders dismounted and flanked the boss.

"Ye tell me where we can git down to the river and we'll be gone outta here and be no trouble to ye folks," Kepling said.

"Ye ain't passin' here big as ye please, scarin' away all our fish and tearin' up the river banks for nothin' I tell ye." The old man puffed out his chest, a sorry defense but evidently the only one he possessed.

"Wal, there's crossins' and there's crossins.' I don't 'spect I haffta cross at this one."

"They all charge, ever one of 'em. Ain't no reason ye need go outta yer way—"

"I ain't goin' outta my way," Kepling barked. "This is the way I come back and forth year after year. Ye hear me?"

"We ain't got nothin', no work, no money, an' we won't hurt anybody if ye do right by us'ns." The tollman's mouth, empty of most of his teeth, sagged with spit and tobacco juice. A woman, evidently his wife, stood with youngsters in the doorway of a rustic building that appeared to be home, café and stage stop all in one. The hapless family that owned my homestead might have been like this, Kent thought—like many he'd seen in the South. They had the blank, staring eyes of lost souls, victims of boom or bust times stranded on this godforsaken canyon of lava rock that in places plunged a mile to the river bottom.

Eighty mules shifted restlessly in their harnesses under the stifling sun and sounded their foghorn-like voices at this inconvenience. Kepling looked at his men and took about one second to make up his mind. Take him, he indicated with a nod of his head. In one sweep, the men whipped the bullying extortionist around with his arms behind his back and forcefully marched him into the building, pushing his family ahead of him.

Then shots rang out up and down the rim of the river. Diverted by the ambush, drivers lashed the startled mules to retreat back up the road amid screams and hollering of both crew and passengers. Outriders hammered their horses to get beyond and behind the attackers, but the shooting ceased as scared young lads climbed over the rim and vamoosed toward the buildings with a couple low caliber rifles dragging at their sides.

"Let 'em go," Kepling said, "and get those damn mules straightened out and back on the trail. We'll cross about a quarter mile down below that pile of boats." He stomped around giving commands and finally mounted a horse to inspect the crossing he had been advised to take by previous teamsters.

Ray cheered. "That was big song and dance!"

"Did anyone get hurt?" Kent breathed, after experiencing his first holdup. But Kepling interrupted.

"Ray, Kent, throw that top crate off my wagon by the house and lets git outta here."

The old wooden box labeled EXPLOSIVES looked daunting, but Kent understood the goodwill gesture and knew that boxes were often reused. He cracked open a slat to display gallon cans of tomatoes, peaches and beans, the crew's own food supply.

The Snake was well-named for its twisting incision in the earth's surface, looping over a thousand miles from the Grand Teton Mountains through Idaho Territory. Gathering tributaries, it emerges in the northwest on its way to the Columbia. Kepling told stories about the land of the Shoshoni and Nez Perce, tribes that flourished since pre-history on the plentiful salmon that migrated up from the Pacific Ocean. Knowing little about the West, Kent was attentive to the man's knowledge. The Snake's endless vertical canyons were shaped over eons by what appeared to be a tiny river far below, but the depth of the canyons and size of the river were deceptive. The Snake was actually wide and powerful in many places, though not always deep this late in the year.

No incidents occurred in the crossing, and fortunately the shots had gone wild, maybe by chance, maybe intentionally, except for one. It damaged the bung on a keg of apple cider vinegar strapped to the side of a wagon, cider that served multiple purposes from preservation of food to disinfectant, and treatment for stomach ache and venereal disease. Enough vinegar dripped on the wagon wheels that the train could've been tracked by the smell all the way to Elko, Nevada.

The following days were less eventful but still challenging. Kent mentally added hoodlums and beggars to the list of road hazards and desperados. In the meantime, his body didn't take kindly to long hours in the saddle after months of squatting on streambanks panning for gold. He was relieved to lay over a few days in Salt Lake City where they changed to another wagon train. This was the end of the line for Kepling who ran the Salt Lake to Virginia City freight.

Salt Lake City was a crossroad for emigrant trails to the northwest and south. The new train left on the California Trail, and pressed on through parched, alkaline stretches that reached from Utah far into Nevada, taxing men and mules to the utmost. Remnants of previous outfits littered the wayside. Old bedsprings, broken wooden wagon wheels, ox yokes, and bones whitened in the relentless sun. A bleached mahogany chiffonnier with intricate carvings of leaves and flowers lay intact in the dry climate. Each artifact left by gold rushers represented a sad tale no one wanted to know lest they abandon their own journey.

Kent shook away unwelcome fragments of thought. His past seemed barely real now that he'd left his early life behind as others on the trail had done. He had cut loose from what were, in retrospect, tight reins—Mother had lost two men—she valiantly attempted to hold on to the last one. These thoughts, like random shots, accompanied him wherever he went. How far must I travel to escape, he wondered.

"Race?" Ray rousted Kent and caught him up in the mood. They walked their mounts quietly some distance out of sight of the wagon train, then urged them on. Ray's mustang was swift and sure-footed as they pounded over brush, sandbars, gopher holes and stones, flushing rabbits and a napping fox from their hiding places. Ben's large hooves tossed clods of alkaline soil, his long strides keeping pace with the mustang until he was hot and heaving. The men laughed and cantered back, innocent as school boys. Kent felt like a lad again with Ray who was a stand-in for the younger brother Kent never had.

Nights became colder as they approached the Sierra Nevada mountains. The new wagonmaster, Jones, urged the party to keep moving, heading out earlier in the mornings, continuing later into the short evenings. Kent had more than enough time in the saddle to anticipate finding the woman who would make this discomfort worthwhile. Nights filled with dreams of folding her in his arms and sinking into soft secluded grass away from prying eyes—before cook banged on a pan and bellowed that hotcakes and coffee were ready. Jones provided quickly prepared suppers of biscuits and beans that facilitated camp setup. Dutch oven apple pie and chocolate pudding had long vanished from the menu. Eventually, after trudging through the flats of Nevada, they passed small farming and mining towns where goods and foodstuffs could be supplemented. Every effort was made to prepare for the trail over the Sierras where notoriously early winter storms could catch them en route.

For the next hundred miles, the jolting of steel-rimmed wagon wheels over granite boulders proved the storied tales of the Sierras to be true. Passengers chose to walk. Drivers of the ten, twelve, and fourteen-hitch mule teams were not so lucky. They had to ride out the bone-jarring bucking of the wagons. Whips flicked over straining backs, while Kent, Ray and other outriders gave an assist or scouted the best track through heavy stands of timber, snowpack and muddy stream crossings on both sides of the passes.

The Sierras, granite ridges protruding from a vast four hundred fifty mile-long batholith of magma, left nothing to the imagination. Snow-capped peaks speared a tense blue sky by day; by night a tinseled blanket woven of the Milky Way lay overhead. Lofty elevations purified the air and invigorated the heart and lungs. Resolute ponderosas mocked the Georgia pines of Kent's homeland. Forbidding boulders amassed on passes, along ridges, and in streambeds where amber water bubbled beneath crystallized ice. He took it all in, one astounding view after another, marking his journey toward chance with a thousand and one small epiphanies. He rejoiced feeling the wild horse beneath his saddle, and saw himself running with a different herd—this migration to California that represented yearnings out of reach for many.

The trail, or braided trails long established by Forty Niners, left sculpted corridors even in lingering snowdrifts. Kent breathed in his first experience west of the Sierras, one inviting titillating possibilities—Miss Marion Patton remained foremost in his mind. She was a woman suited to these mountains, as well as those in Montana; a spirit with rusty-red hair and plum-shaped face who enticed him over the Sierras. For Kent, this pursuit had already become laced with remarkably graphic images of her. His goal was clear, but attaining the object of his desire was clouded in uncertainties. He knew very little. She lived in Coloma. She worked for her father. She failed to succumb to his overtures on their first encounter. These overheated inclinations provided Kent with diversions from the hardships of the Sierras; beyond that he couldn't count on the gamble he'd taken to find her.

However, once they scaled the Sierras and traversed foothills into California, Kent felt like a new man in a new landscape; in fact, in a new state. California was admitted to the Union in 1850 on the heels of the Gold Rush of '49. He wondered how these seasoned gold camps would look now compared to those in the young, upstart territories of Montana and Idaho, but soon concluded that gold camps were gold camps, regardless of larger geographical or political realities.

Days warmed the further they descended from the passes. Behind him were Jones' unsettling stories of the Donner party and others who dared to travel over the dark, timbered mountains in winter. Nights now carried the thick, organic scent of humid valleys. Prospects ahead were heartening. He had to admit the image of Miss Marion Patton sparked his feelings with a constant glow that, exasperatingly, kept eluding his grasp.

Not all his musings dealt with such fantasies. His prospector's eye had been carefully honed by observing and learning from California miners who had migrated to Montana's Hot Spring District. Now he studied the lay of the land in terms of streams and the way they angled into rivers that formed wide fertile valleys. The American River, his destination, formed in rivulets from hidden places high in the Sierras. Garnering force, it created its own snake-like canyon as it pummeled its way down the foothills, pummeling that washed gold from its lodes and laid it bare along the shores. Quartz mines, some operating, some abandoned, clung to the western foothills of the Sierras.

From his experience in Hot Spring District, Kent understood how the camps must have sprung to life nearly overnight in 1849. Eighteen years later, roads following a spidery network of original explorer trails were still rugged. The wagon train lurched into Nevada City and Grass Valley—towns with an air of maturity—established churches, schools, apple orchards and an occasional vineyard. Ray engaged in lively conversations in Spanish with people he knew, and he did not show up when the wagon train resumed its route to Sacramento. Kent switched to a small contingent of other freighters headed for Coloma in the Calaveras region north of Placerville.

Without his riding partner to enliven the days, Kent concentrated on how to pay for his stay in California and eventually get back to Montana. He had to feed Ben, no small consideration. His reserves were substantial, but limited to what he could safely stow on his person. His first claim on Norwegian Creek was not considered a great strike, but as his intuition indicated, the quartz outcroppings to the north offered yield from what he surmised was the same vein. He had claimed these outcroppings on the hundred and sixty acres that he owned, since mineral rights were granted separate from surface rights. At any rate, besides being driven by a distinctly romantic nature at present, he felt pressured to prove himself employable. Kent's travel-weary face crinkled in a grateful smile at the prospects ahead.

The town of Coloma sat in a gentle valley fifty miles east of Sacramento, on the South Fork of the American River where Sutter's Mill discovery set off the California gold rush. The wagon train eased into town to unload freight. Scattered white frame homes amid overgrown ore dumps attested to the staying power of the legendary site. Riches continued to be mined where portions of the river were rerouted, feeding active mills similar to those in Sterling. It was evident, as one miner said, that hydraulic mining ripped out more earth than was excavated from the Panama Canal. Twisted piles of boards from old chutes and flumes were scattered like bleached bones in the desert. Placer miners used rockers with hoppers for gravel, and long cleat-lined boxes to catch the gold. Sun-bronzed miners in light cotton shirts, and pants soaked to the knees in the streams, gave little notice to passing freighters.

A sense of impending fate, for better or worse, bedeviled Kent's already heightened anticipation of finding the woman he had dreamed of for the past thousand miles, a woman who tended to be short on social encounters and unusually focused on business. His impulsive notion to go to California had not yet merited any intelligent follow up. Pursuit of a dream, he smiled to himself, had overridden his ability to plan ahead.

"Where might I find Miss Marion Patton?" he asked immediately after his contingent straggled into town.

"She was in the store. You'll probably find her at the telegraph office." A local resident indicated the direction.

Everyone knows everyone, apparently. I find her this easily and I look like a scruffy miner, he moaned to himself, but he made arrangements for Ben and let his buoyant heart and step carry him uptown. He soon located her at the well-used office where an aged clerk bent over the only desk. Kent looked twice to recognize Miss Patton. Her petite body, encased by a wide sash over a no-frills, ankle-length skirt, had a girlish look rather than that of a hard-nosed mining representative. No dust coat, no bonnet, no flurry of activity. Catching himself, revising his memories, separating fantasies, he quickly determined that she might come up to his shoulder since she was wearing the same high-heeled riding boots. Her face appeared smaller than he remembered but still piquant, pert, a bit freckled and sunburned. Large round hazel eyes turned toward him.

Marion looked puzzled for a moment, her gaze as direct as he remembered. Then he caught a little gasp. "Montana Territory," she said. "How could you leave your beautiful mountains to come here?"

"Easy," Kent drawled, wanting to say "because you are here," but said instead, "I had an opportunity to ride along with a reputable wagonmaster. It is my good fortune to see you again, Miss Patton."

Extending his hand, he said, "Kent Berrigan from Hot Spring District."

Marion offered her gloved fingertips. "We discussed the operations of Crocker Mining Company," she recalled.

"In its ascendancy then, probably descending now," Kent said. But he didn't want to pursue that line of conversation. "I recall your excellent horsemanship." The words sounded affected and distant, like those of Kent Berrigan of Woodland Hills, Georgia, not the rush of words he wanted to express—I remember how you made me feel, how the air on the mountain was lighter with you and my world became alive. Instead, he ventured a bit awkwardly, "I mainly recall your hair and riding boots!"

"And I remember your dog with the funny looking eyes!" she countered. They both laughed. She invited him to sit in one of the captain's chairs in the telegraph office next to her. She crossed one booted leg over the other, fully at ease, presenting a side of her character Kent hadn't seen during their brief dinner and horse ride in Montana. Welcoming the casualness that replaced her former brusqueness, he leaned back in the chair, wishing he could sit here with Miss Marion forever, feeling the warmth of her puffed sleeves against his upper arm. Breathing in this reward for the damn long journey to California, he began to wonder what her life might be like here. Unsaid 'what ifs' circulated underneath as they talked.

What if she was already taken? Or she was going off on another business trip? Or she did not care to spend time with him? If Marion was still working for her father, she didn't say. She listened quietly to his tales of the overland trip, then asked, "Where is Big Ben now?"

"He's getting a good feed and new shoes at the other end of town. I want you to see him again. He's the one I rode when we visited the Revenue mine. I've been more than impressed with him on this trip. But first, a piece of apple pie!"

As they stepped out on the boardwalk, Kent was conscious of his worn and dirty trail clothes. Even the Dubrinski boots were caked in dirt. "In this condition my horse is more likely to impress you than I will," Kent admitted. Marion disregarded his remarks, and led him up the street a few doors to a coffeehouse, a slightly upgraded version of Callahans' boarding house in Montana Territory. But the pies seemed like the sun and moon and stars all at once to Kent.

"Imagine that!" Kent stalled to make a choice among the lemon meringue, local blueberry, chocolate cream and apple pies arrayed in a tall, green pie saver decorated with floral vents in the doors. Finally he selected the apple pie he had mentally savored for the last two hundred miles.

They barely had a chance to talk when other men drifted over to their table and sat down, irritating Kent by their intrusion. He forgot he'd planned to stay this side of the Sierras for the winter months with ample time to get acquainted with her, but the room felt crowded when he wanted Miss Marion to himself—alone. His usual genteel nature disguised the resentment, and his reactions were further obscured behind a thick black beard that brushed underwear exposed above his shirt front. A deep line separated his sunburned face and naked white brow, previously covered by a hat he'd hung on a deer antler rack by the door. Facilities at the livery stable for cleaning off trail grime were limited to a hand pump and a horse trough. He looked like the teamsters whose uncouth appearances he'd questioned when he first saw them.

Marion introduced him as a miner from Montana Territory. He soon had his own crowd of admirers and interested bystanders, not the ideal reunion with Miss Marion he'd imagined. He was drawn into a round table discussion about operations in Montana and the Sierra foothills. He found he had a surprisingly good grasp of general processes from his short time mining in Sterling. Questions flew his way. What do you think the future is for gold discoveries there? What is this Last Chance we hear about? Is it really the last of it? How many stamp mills are operating in your area and what is the quality of the yield?

Kent did his best to be forthright in sharing his knowledge, allowing of course that mining is highly speculative, and that he'd be a rich man if he knew for sure.

"You folks are the experts. Crocker and Midas mining companies pay handsomely for advisors from California since y'all have years of experience under your belts." He was glad he had visited with miners in Sterling and wished he'd visited the Boaz mill near Fifteen Mile Canyon, given that local gossip has more veracity than reams of gold rush hype in the newspapers. He made an effort to be gracious and deferent, while Marion remained attentive to the news, but the conversation was tiresome and the room felt oppressive.

"My guess is the next big strike in Montana will be in silver, maybe copper. You're aware, I'm sure, of the rich silver lodes in Nevada."

He steered inquiries away from personal disclosures or commitments except when one gentleman insisted Kent meet Mr. Bowman of the Coloma Mining Company the next day. The men's talk soon became a distant buzz as fatigue overcame his faculties, and he relaxed with a deep sense of relief at having arrived safely. Beholding Miss Marion across the table is worth more than gold, he assured himself. She toyed with a curl of hair as if she, too, was distracted—her mind elsewhere—and where was her heart? He wanted to kiss her slim hand, her sunburned forearm, unbutton the sleeve and run his hand along her arm to her elbow, kiss her soft lips, all fantasies from wretched cold nights on the trail that flooded back—all worth the occasional hardship to be here now.

After the others left, Kent found Miss Marion appraising him with real interest for the first time. She had propped her elbow on the table to listen to the men's exchange, her pie tasted and pushed aside.

"Are they taking you away from me just when I have discovered your talents?" For the first time the hazel eyes held a bit of coquetry. "Seriously, you might think twice about visiting Bowman and his company. I feel they are less than upright competitors to my father's company."

"You haven't said much about his business." Kent reluctantly pulled himself back from the fantasies.

"Father tends to have rather grandiose ideas, and what started as a small Coloma mining and shipping outfit is now known as International Consolidated Mining and Shipping Company, with the main office in San Francisco." She paused to see how the somewhat ostentatious name went over with Kent whose unwavering gaze held hers.

Lack of transparency was not an issue for Marion, reaffirming Kent's impression from their first encounter. She wanted to know if he was impressed. So was she interested? Still, he guessed, it was unknown what remained inside this inveterate business woman's head and heart after business was accounted for. Looking down at her hands now capped over each other on the table, Marion apparently assessed the same thing about him. Clearly the discussion could have taken place anywhere, anytime in the camps, but her interest intrigued Kent. Was it because he'd been center of attention or because he represented something more exciting to her? She was quiet, wistful, as if sorting out a jumble of thoughts. Did he meet her expectations? And what did she expect?

Kent found this bit of uncertainty very appealing. He covered both her hands with his large palm. At once she became shy, demur, revealing a womanly charm that surprised Kent, until she pulled her hands into her lap and laughed, showing even rows of teeth behind full red lips. This headstrong woman wouldn't be easily tamed, Kent thought, and joined her laughter.

"Come see my thoroughbred," he urged, eager to prolong their time together. They walked half a dozen blocks to the livery stable where the oversize bay filled a box stall in the rear. At Kent's call a whinny responded and a great muzzle appeared over the gate, seeking a familiar face.

"Big Ben! He is larger, more a draft horse. You have been teasing me about a thoroughbred." Marion removed her gloves to rub the long chin whiskers. Ben reached far over the stall for her touch, nickering softly at the attention.

"I owned thoroughbreds on the family farm in Georgia. This was the best I could do in Montana. Not that there is a better horse than Ben. He pretty well earned his keep on the trip down here." His voice wavered with emotion that surprised him. He knew he loved the horse, but how much of it was about Miss Marion?

After the horse talk ran out, he didn't know what to say, yet they did not immediately leave the stable. Marion mentioned going to San Francisco; he didn't hear clearly. He leaned against the stall, entertaining a crazy image of a Chinese fortune cookie that held clues to his future with Miss Patton. Evening shadows enveloped the figures in the stable. The quiet spaces filled with the soft rustling of hay tossed around by the horses and their steady munching. Marion turned to go, then faced Kent. Her arms fell to her sides and her eyes were intent, serious.

"Hold me," she said simply, suddenly yielding to her own emotions and the privacy offered by the dimly lit interior.

For Kent, a thousand miles of travel weariness and pain fell away in an instant. All the harrowing incidents, the heat and cold and fears of his trek disappeared. His tall, slim frame surged with a forgotten sense of his own masculinity, his own need. Deep sunburned lines in his face softened. Words flooded his mind that his lips did not—could not—utter, the pulse on the side of his throat too loud in his ears. Thank you, Lord, he managed to breathe. He gathered Miss Marion in his arms, dirt, travel perfume and all, for a long embrace. Her petite supple body folded as softly into his as he had dreamed time after time after time. His lips gently brushed her hair, cautious so as not to frighten her away. The moment was sweeter than he had ever imagined.

5

Three days after she had pie with Kent, Marion left for San Francisco to personally deliver contracts to the head office of her father's business. She had not run into Kent again, and they'd made no arrangements to meet. Still, she felt his arms firm around her shoulders, his breath warm against her cheek. She looked for him several times at the coffeehouse, smiling again at his appetite for apple pie. However, few men stayed long in the mining camps, a constant tide of humanity searching for something, a better life, instant riches, their very souls. She wasn't sure what drove Kent; many men had a gambler's nature, staking everything on a perilous cross-country trip to the gold fields, a gamble that cost many their lives.

Marion's father, Henry Patton, was little different than these men only he had come to the camps in the early heady, chaotic days of the first gold discoveries in California. He built a lucrative business, the Midland Merchandise Company, by serving multiple needs of the growing population in the foothills. With later extensive connections abroad it became the international company that Marion had mentioned to Kent.

Marion frequently traveled to the main office located on Montgomery Street in San Francisco. The trip involved going overland by horse or wagon then down the Sacramento River on a passing barge or freighter and taking a ferry across the Bay.

Occasionally, she rode her horse all the way to San Francisco Bay, especially in late February or March when the world came alive with cherry blossoms and flowering plums. On these trips, her mare sensed the burst of life and fairly flew over the grassy, open countryside and down the valleys from one stage stop to the next.

This time Marion boarded a wagon that served as postal carrier, passenger coach, and freighter to meet the boat above Sacramento at Roseville. The westward route meant rumbling over dirt roads for hours, the monotony a familiar aspect of the miners' lives and hers.

"Morning, Mr. Cobb. It's me again." Darkness had yet to concede to light for the early departure and wouldn't for awhile this late in the year.

"A pleasure, Miss Patton. How's your father?" Benjamin Cobb was best known as a lively link in the region's grapevine.

"He is quite well, Mr. Cobb, and sends his best wishes," she said, without revealing that her father was in Brazil. Marion took care to spread few crumbs about the owner of the major business that contracted with Cobb on this freight line. He'd known the Patton family since Henry and Elizabeth moved with their young daughter to Coloma.

Henry, successor to a family of distinguished San Francisco traders, had served in border skirmishes prior to the Mexican-American war. He married Elizabeth, an attractive woman from San Francisco when he returned home. He determined he'd make his fortune by astute investments rather than by pick and shovel. Shipping inland to remote camps proved to be an overwhelmingly successful venture within a few years. At first Elizabeth Patton had an adventurous streak that led her to the handsome go-getter, Henry Patton. She gamely cooked, washed, and sewed, but soon wished for the old days when they had a house in San Francisco. The stress of hype and hopes, as well as the tedium of the foothills, was too much for Elizabeth. When she found she was with child, she took Marion and moved back to San Francisco where Dora was born and she established a permanent home. Elizabeth later gave up raising a tom-boyish girl in the city and let Marion stay with her father and the family's long-time cook.

In Coloma, Marion had a dog, a pony and a wagon, all of which gave her endless childish amusement while her father sought financial investments near and far. Marion grew up content in the familiar surroundings of the foothills, but today the old freight wagon creaked and groaned at a maddeningly slow pace as it maneuvered winding roads through dense brush, madrone and manzanita saplings. A collage of chopped hillsides, broken implements and forgotten flumes were evidence of prospecting years before hard rock mining defined the current industry. She shifted position on the less than comfortable seat of woven padding that was nevertheless about as hard as a human body could stand. Finally she scooted up front with the driver. Mr. Cobb heard most of the region's gossip first, and he was only too willing to share it, true or false, with anyone willing to listen.

"The last passenger told me they're headin' to Last Chance Gulch in Montana Territory," he said. "Lots of folks are pullin' out for the North where gold is layin' right there on the ground. And if ye know what to look for and ain't in too big a hurry to pick em' up, they's rubies and sapphires big as yer thumb right before yer eyes. Agates, too, with those ferny things inside. Kind of a mystery how they got there. From what I hear Montana is God's country." He hiked the reins to prod the four-horse team that could have found its way in the dark on this route.

"Tell me more about what you hear—will it last, do you think?"

"No, no, fickle stuff, this gold. It's superstitious to believe yer'll be that lucky. I say work an honest day and be grateful to God fer yer pay."

"It's the fever, Mr. Cobb, it's the fever!" Marion laughed. She had heard these stories and admonitions since she was a child.

Laboring was fine for those who didn't have gambling in their blood. The thought that her dreams might be gambling always sobered her—where do we go from here—when does it stop, if ever? A hint of what her mother might have felt crept into her consciousness and as quickly she snuffed it out. After all, her father was very successful in business at home and abroad.

"I went to Montana Territory earlier this year," she confided, knowing this news would have a long shelf life with the driver. He glanced at her in surprise, his brushy, grey eyebrows raised at this juicy information.

"Ye, lass, youse gone off where them Indians and robbers attack the freighters? Ye won't git me out there for all the gold and gemstones. What'd ye do that fer?"

"For Father. I'm helping him with the business now. He can't be everywhere at once." She allowed Mr. Cobb to digest this second bit of information while his large, red-rimmed eyes appraised her. With a little smile, Marion continued. "They are hiring advisors and mechanics from California for mill operations in Montana. It seems their mills are always breaking down and they often have to improvise parts."

"Advisin' is it?"

"Good paying jobs, yes, and not half the work." Marion knew that Mr. Cobb would relay this message to passengers coming and going for awhile. "Oh well, that's what I saw and overheard," she shrugged and gave up conversation to the drone of hoof beats of the old team.

At age twenty, Marion was expected to be married or at least trained in some womanly endeavor. With her unconventional upbringing, she sometimes wondered what her future held. The touch and grace of the man from Montana Territory remained with her, but he had apparently moved on. She bit her lip and forced her attention back on the tiresome trip to her father's office in San Francisco.

The first vessel out of Roseville was a shallow-draft, steam-driven riverboat that primarily hauled freight. Marion usually traveled on the leading California Steam Navigation Company's line, but in haste she took the freighter and paid for guest quarters which were hardly better than those provided for the crew. She read posted shipping labels: molasses, brandy, pickles, flour, all in barrels lashed to the deck. Below were crates of dry goods, tools, books, and farm products including fruit, rice and beans.

"I could live well for a long time on board," she remarked to a steward, and grudgingly endured the slow passage hampered by winds and turbulence.

The riverboat muscled steadily down river, navigating through sloughs and the shipping congestion around Sacramento. Steamboats jockeyed for position to disgorge passengers and freight in the capital. Mexicans, Chinese, and Kanakas from the Pacific Islands, worked the docks on crowded levees among freighters and hangers-on. Wagons bearing lumber and potatoes edged into Sacramento's J and K streets' stream of commerce. Weary teams of horses rattled their harnesses, mules brayed, and oxen stoically inhaled black woodsmoke from the steamboats, their eyes smarting and watering. Marion glimpsed the inland city of Sacramento where a surprising pretentiousness marked recent growth. Stately frame and brick homes occupied quiet sections where tall trees and lush growth had been preserved away from the waterfront.

She went to her cabin and slept until an orchestra of foghorns sent gulls squawking as the boat eased into the port of San Francisco, where it waited far out on Long Wharf, pilings that ran a half mile into choppy waters of the Bay. Ahead was a line of ocean going steamers as well as traffic off the Sacramento River. Paved with planks, the wharf rumbled under handcarts, wood or iron-wheeled wagons, carriages of the wealthy, and throngs of porters, sightseers and pickpockets. Sailboats of all sizes mingled with tugboats, barges, and steamers. Sailing ships flying international flags hogged the best and biggest docks. Chaos reigned on the water and didn't appear to be any less so on land.

"We'll get you there fine and dandy," the steward assured her, taking a double look at her slim figure and plain but distinctive riding outfit.

Few women rode the freighters and none alone. Marion increasingly understood why when she came into the fiercely competitive port where mine owners, longshoremen, naval staff, and merchants hustled up business, a significant part of it predatory; the city was known for its ruthless market cornering and gambling by monopolies. Guttural male voices jammed the air with shouts and insults. Burley men, young and old, sweated as they wrested cargo from vessels to wagons. A prevailing fishy scent of the Bay's murky shore saturated the air, though she knew that daily catch came in fresh for merchants and restaurants.

San Francisco had already reinvented itself after six disastrous fires in previous years and become established as a gateway port. Stone, brick, and frame buildings marched over hilly terrain from the Bay to Nob Hill with the abandonment of a free woman. Gracious new hotels replaced false-fronted boarding houses. A dozen or so daily newspapers chronicled life bursting on land and sea. Chinatown threw up fire-resistant edifices for multiple "Companys," designating provinces of China, that immigrated to the "land of gold." The port, born of fur traders and foreign explorers, now yearned for maturity. Fed on news, gossip, and excesses of raw resources, the banking and commerce industry anchored the City's importance among international ports of the Pacific Rim. Its adolescent exuberance echoed among clanging bells of trams, foghorns, and uproar of the Long Wharf as if it couldn't get enough of its importance. Palatial gambling houses on Portsmouth Square exuded the daring and audacity of the '49ers.

Quickly disembarking, Marion hired a hack to take her to the Montgomery Street office. Handmade brick buildings in the financial district took on an air of permanence compared to much of the city. The International Consolidated Mining and Shipping Company occupied the entire second floor of a stucco, four-story office building showcasing ornate iron doors and shutters. Marion was always delighted to tread the off-white marble staircase imported from Italy by an extravagant architect.

"Miss Marion, you are as pert and pretty as ever," Mr. Holcomb greeted her. "Only you stay away too long." The manager, who preferred to think of himself as Chief of Operations, straightened his tall thin frame and checked to see if the creases in his pinstripe trousers fell properly to his polished shoes.

"Yes, Mr. Holcomb. I brought two contracts for you, small ones to be sure, but I think you will be interested. At least my father's board assures me that you will take valuable time to examine them."

Mr. Holcomb lost no time slitting open the heavy mailers with an ivory-handled letter opener from his orderly desk top. He pulled spectacles from his silk vest as his eyes raced over the neatly hand-copied pages.

"South America, eh? What is he doing in South America?"

"He went to a Portuguese city on the coast of Brazil. I'm sure you've heard of their considerable resources, even supporting the war, but I couldn't tell you right now whether they supported the North or South. Father believes a thorough investigation into their reportedly infinite minerals may lead to prosperous exchanges."

"Another gamble, eh? I must admit he finds interesting prospects. Too often they are just that, prospects. It's in the blood, I guess."

Again Marion laughed at the "fever." Anyone with half a heart and a little ambition could be accused of "chasing the elephant," whether it was prospecting or speculating—not a harmful activity she supposed, as long as one invested one's own money. She guessed that Father had avoided briefing Mr. Holcomb about his travel plans before he left for fear of being discouraged from going. Speculation was the linchpin on which investors turned. The board had backed a great many enterprises that proved to be worthless, relying primarily on Henry Patton's original shipping business to pull the Company through good times and bad. Marion chose to tolerate Mr. Holcomb's grudging remarks for the eventual support she might want her father to provide. She played her cards carefully, holding her new found interest in gold, silver, and copper in Montana Territory to herself. Mr. Holcomb still treated her like a child. He would never believe the opportunities Marion foresaw opening in the unexploited Rocky Mountains.

"I'm off to visit Mother and Dora," she said shortly after her unexpected arrival at Company headquarters. "Good day, Mr. Holcomb." Marion left, thoughtfully questioning her budding business sense, and yet also aware of the excitement she felt speaking frankly to the manager. She wandered boardwalks and cobblestones of Mission and Market streets in the opposite direction of her mother's home, while her mind toyed with the gist of the conversation—Mr. Holcomb's conservative obstruction to new enterprises and her own intuitive sense about their potential. Horses jostled each other as wagons passed in congested streets, and men in top hats and silk-trimmed waistcoats crossed with an air of entitlement through traffic. Women in fur muffs and collars paraded past store windows featuring elegant capes and gowns from Paris and Milan, hats with rows of Irish lace, and undergarments that made Marion cringe with discomfort.

The approaching holiday season added zest to the scene with trimmings of holly and pine boughs. Marion drifted downhill toward Embarcadero Street and the piers, walking rapidly in long strides downhill, her skirts picking up grime of the city. Dense acrid smells of fish, freshly-sawed lumber and stale produce drifted up from the Bay marketplace. The produce came in at four a.m. and rapidly sold to city restaurants, grocers and traders. Piles of damaged leftovers remained to be carted away for hog and chicken feed by those in the scavenger business, usually the Chinese or Negroes.

City life was heady, fun and always fascinating to Marion. Small shops and hawkers vied for her attention. She bought hot clam chowder with tomato, West Coast style, accompanied by a huge sourdough roll, and found a bench where she could sit and eat. A red-orange sun set across the Bay, casting spangled ripples in its wake. The spiky tips of sails caught the last bits of color like bobbing rainbows. Hours passed and Marion realized it would be very late by the time she reached her mother's place on Ocean Street. She hailed a passing hack and the driver flicked his horse into a smart trot across town, up and down the city's rolling hills.

Elizabeth registered neither surprise nor dismay at her daughter's arrival. She was accustomed to Marion's unorthodox life, but she openly vowed that Dora would be brought up a lady. Elizabeth's long auburn hair was intricately curled on strips of rags for bedtime, the latest styling technique. Any grey she might have had was tinted to match the thick locks that Henry adored.

Father should see her, Marion thought. She really is an attractive woman in her pink housecoat, embroidered in an Oriental pattern, and lovely slippers to match. The port of San Francisco had much to offer and her mother took full advantage. The yellow frame row house fitted its narrow three stories tightly against similar houses running down the slopes toward the beach. It seemed more like an apartment to Marion, but it was spacious enough and manageable for Mother and Dora. Sweet, brown-haired, sixteen-year-old Dora, whom Marion would see in the morning.

Marion removed a few combs used to tame her unruly hair, a concession to expectations in the City, and fell into bed without washing. She wondered how she had felt so invigorated earlier wandering the streets of San Francisco past admiring dockworkers and fishermen compared to disappearing in this low key, predictable world of her mother and sister. In one respect, it was a quiet interlude in an often calamitous world, she mused, but it is no wonder Father is in South America.

Late December delivered deluges of rain interspersed with astoundingly clean blue skies over San Francisco. Imported eucalyptus trees scented the dampness with their strong menthol fragrance. Dora claimed sisterly rights to the wayward Marion, who pinned on fashionable hair *pièce de résistance*, but had yet to try on a gown with a bustle.

Two weeks after New Year's Day 1867, Henry Patton returned from South America, and reunited with Marion and his family in San Francisco. After celebrating late holiday festivities, he and Marion journeyed on to Coloma.

The quiet town wrapped in wintery storms set a pace at odds with Marion's mood and outlook. She still felt the throb of industrious, smelly, foggy, enchanting San Francisco calling her back to the vitality of the streets, markets, even the staid company office. After all the dallying with Dora, a notion of engaging in something much larger than herself kept her on edge and restless. So far it was unclear what that would be, and she declined to discuss her ambitions with her father. Certainly the early days of the '49ers had given her a rush she was unlikely to forget or duplicate, but that made it hard to gain an objective perspective on anything less compelling.

Days dragged on. Drifters flooded into California for jobs and better weather than where they came from. In turn, California transients left for Montana, Oregon, or Colorado where they'd heard that untold riches abounded for the lucky. Her discreet inquiries about whether her father's competitor, Mr. Bowman, had hired a Mr. Berrigan failed to turn up her former visitor's whereabouts. Kent of the gentle touch and winning smile had disappeared without a trace. The suspicion that he had ridden nearly a thousand miles to see her was entirely unprecedented and unsettling, but not unwelcome.

I liked him, she admitted to herself. He was handsome and diverting—the man could carry on an intelligent conversation. His soft drawl and deep warm laugh came to her at odd times, along with fantasies of his muscular arms enfolding her. In those fleeting moments in the stable he had felt strong, manly yet refined, leaving an indelible impression. But a physical attraction was harder to acknowledge; she concluded he must have returned to Montana Territory, and she therefore put him out of her mind. There was nothing to do but bide her time until she could exercise her own interests.

In the days after Kent met Miss Marion Patton on her own turf he appraised his prospects as a potential suitor and found them wanting. He had forgotten he was not Southern landed gentry, but a displaced tobacco farmer on a hard scrabble homestead in Montana Territory. His frantic efforts to locate her in Coloma only deepened his disappointment. Stunned how easily she could, and did, walk into and out of his life, he resolved to make his intentions known—if she stayed put long enough. Holding her those brief moments revived his belief he needed to corral the wayward Miss Patton. His blood ran hot at the thought of her, cold at the possibility of losing her. He realized she represented a spirit that would give him new life. A reason for life. But any optimism he'd had about Marion's affections dimmed after she left for San Francisco for an indefinite stay.

He waited for her return, alternately castigating himself for his reckless pursuit of an independent woman, then pining for the womanly love that now besieged his dreams day and night. He did not interview with Bowman's Coloma Mining Company, and he did not have the audacity to apply at the International Consolidated Mining and Shipping Company for the subversive but entirely obvious reason of pursuing the boss's daughter.

Kent finally left town unannounced in search of Ray. He met Mr. Cobb who informed him that he'd heard a young *mestizo* had been in a scrap and was jailed in Placerville, a common occurrence, and if that was the one he was looking for, he'd be only too glad to help. Cobb could be a saint, Kent admitted, only he talked too much. Since Ray had not continued on to Coloma as he had planned, Kent was concerned. He knew reconnecting with his young friend would cost him a week or more and possibly his relationship with Marion, but he took Big Ben for a fast trip down the trail to an El Dorado gold camp jail.

A deputy nodded towards a long corridor without getting up from his desk by a window. "I dunno anybody by that name, but you kin have a look."

The thick stone walls of the cells kept the interior damp and musty. Most of the inmates appeared dark skinned—whether from race, weather, or grime Kent could not be sure. He recognized Ray's scarf before he caught sight of his face.

"Have you been in a fight over a woman?" Kent asked, recalling that Ray had fled once before over a woman.

Ray slumped on a bench, his head propped on his elbows. "Yer needn't come here botherin' about me." The old camaraderie was gone. After a long, uncomfortable silence, Ray corrected the assumption. "No woman." He conceded he had been beat up in a fight and robbed of everything—his mustang, guns, money and bedroll. He was missing a canine tooth.

"There be three of them, one of me. Sheriff not know me— he know others."

"Why didn't he arrest them?"

"He not catch 'em. Only me. I be knocked out." Ray's voice was flat, muffled.

Whether the story was true or not, the scenario didn't look good to Kent. His previous opinion of law enforcement in Montana seemed consistent with what was happening here, and for that reason he didn't want to go off and leave the lad.

"Even if I git out, what I do? This town not good for me."

"Come on. What could you do? I've seen you handle a difficult job."

"Probly git in more fight."

Clearly Ray had hit bottom and was very depressed. His face was still bruised, lacerated and swollen days after the fight. Kent went out and bought cigarettes, hoping that a solution would arise. They sat and smoked for a few hours. Prisoners yelled and cursed and pounded on the jail walls, pockmarked from abuse but stout enough to last a hundred years. The deputy walked by the cell with other inmates a few times but let them alone.

"Is there anywhere you want to go?"

No answer.

"Say, man, we went through a lot on the trail and I want to do some more riding with you." Kent finally resorted to a firm approach. "I don't know exactly what your situation is, but I want to see you out of here with a good start on a job." Kent began pacing outside the cell like an inmate.

Ray lifted his dark eyes to meet Kent's gaze, then looked away. Kent guessed the shame was pretty hard for him to take, and he wasn't sure he could do anything to help. It was sad to see Ray's handsome face marred by the missing tooth.

"Tell you what--I'm going to settle the fine, and you can decide what you want to do." Kent extended his hand but Ray refused to look at it.

"Ramos, huh? He's known around here as Ramos." The deputy stored the fine in a safe behind the desk. Kent took the opportunity to scan inmate belongings hung on wall pegs and dumped on a wide shelf in hopes of spotting something that belonged to Ray—er, Ramos. He had the feeling the scruffy officer might sell or trade goods on the side.

He and Ray parted on the rickety front steps of the jail. Kent's intuition told him the mess could get worse. He boarded Ben at the livery and hung around town for a few days. Miners bought him a lot of coffee and drinks, querying time and again about mining in Montana. Kent saw Ray only once when Ray was loading freight onto wagons. The lad waved to Kent in what appeared to a friendly acknowledgment.

By the time Kent returned to Coloma, Marion was still in San Francisco, and he had his own bout of depression. Last year, not long after he arrived in Montana Territory, he'd attended Mrs. Callahan's community Christmas party. Northerners ate wild turkey, danced, and drank with Southerners without batting an eye. Here, as the holidays turned over in California, he found his funds were running low, and he faced a bleak winter without the woman he so earnestly sought. This prompted him to accept a position with an accounting firm in Auburn whose services were indispensible in the high rolling days of gold and trade in the foothills of the Sierras. Kent was handsomely rewarded in the firm's employ, a short, satisfying stint, though at one point he barely restrained himself from spending a week's pay to buy back Ray's mouse-colored mustang from an auction sale ring.

I'm getting into this too deep, he acknowledged, and tried to drop the self-imposed sense of responsibility. He started inquiring when wagon trains might cross the Sierras for his eventual return to Montana. He had no desire to make that trip in the cold again. But he was drawn to first see Miss Marion, recalling his vow to make his intentions known.

Auburn did have its advantages, one being its location in a relatively temperate zone between the Sierras and the sprawling Sacramento valley. Gold rush wealth contributed to construction of lovely colonnaded mansions that occupied prominent sites with expansive views. Auburn's air of comfort and charm reminded Kent of his hometown in Georgia, a welcome change from the frenzied and generally dirty life he had been leading.

"Clip the beard close, no, shave it clean except for the jaw. Leave a little more on the chin," he told the barber, "And take off about four inches of this damn hair."

The heavy-set barber laughed and took off five inches, then combed the straight ends down in a nice line around Kent' neck. He took extra time trimming Kent's moustache and whisked away the ends with a thick, soft brush.

"The gentlemen, they wear hair like this. We're far from San Francisco, but I keep up on styles for the gentlemen. You get a city cut right here in Auburn!"

Kent peered into a huge old mirror on the wall, his image mostly obscured by silver and black snowflake veins that covered most of its surface. "Some mirror you have here. It makes a man look better than he ought!"

"Exactly. It belonged to my grandfather and to my father, now me. It came on the boat with the hair clippers and all. You found the right place for a shave and cut." He polished a long razor blade on a rag as he talked and rubbed hair off the scissors on his apron. Kent paid him and walked out feeling like a new person, or at least a semblance of the gentleman he used to be.

Early spring flushed the Sacramento valley and foothills with pinks and whites of flowering cherry and crab apple trees. Kent concluded his assigned tasks at the accounting firm and gave notice he would be leaving. Privately, he had become very anxious to see Miss Marion, his heart often ruling his head by turns of 'yes' this is a good idea, and 'no' I shouldn't assume she'd be attracted to me. The contradictions blessedly wiped away resident wartime flashbacks and he slept better. By day he pursued his dream of becoming acquainted with Miss Patton.

6

The winter of 1869 had not passed without Marion devising a plan of her own. Long after her return from San Francisco she watched for Kent Berrigan, wondering why he'd come so far to see her and left so abruptly. With the nagging concern that something may have happened to him, combined with her increasing restlessness, she soon found Father's presence wearing. He was constantly preoccupied with mining interests, particularly that of solidifying his foreign contracts.

"I want to go to New York," she announced one day at breakfast, their only regular time together, though Father usually buried his nose in a battery of newspapers. He looked up askance, this coming unexpectedly from his young daughter.

"You want to go to New York? Now what have you been dreaming, Miss Marion?"

"Father, you know I've traveled since I was sixteen to San Francisco, and last year you allowed me go to Montana Territory. You cannot be surprised that I want to explore other parts of the country. I'm sure you understand."

"New York would be a fine city to visit. I hear it has lost some of its seediness since the war. In fact, money flows like water through New York from investments in various industries and enterprises. We should go after our company agreements are signed in Brazil." Henry warmed to the idea of new prospects.

"I'm not sure you do understand," Marion interrupted. "I want to leave on the next wagon train going east. I feel closed in,

Father. You are needed to oversee operations here. Early spring is a good time for me to travel." Her jaw was set, her voice low and firm, not unlike her father's at times. The attitude framing her small face with those earnest hazel eyes could be very persuasive. Father had seldom, if ever, denied her wishes, and she felt he had no reason to do so now.

This time he hesitated, then looked at her anew. Marion shifted uneasily under the appraisal. She sensed he saw the woman she had become, though a male appraisal was far from new for her. A small, uncertain smile played over her lips, belying the power of the personality inside—fooling anyone besides her father, that is.

"You will do what you want to do, my strong-willed Marion." He paused and cleared his throat. Moments dragged on. Finally he said, "The daughter I know is strong, steady and lacking the impulsiveness I often fault in myself, yet I wonder about this woman across the table from me."

Marion had not grown as tall as either her father or mother, but she made up for it in a lively spirit under her tussle of coppery hair. She wore her starched collar turned up, while her sleeves were wadded above the elbows for convenience. A particular slim, tan riding habit she constantly wore irritated him. His lectures that she dress properly, according to the status of the family, went unheard. She didn't own a silk gown or any clothing trimmed in fashionable Irish lace.

Marion remained silent, suspecting her father had a great deal more to say. In a sense, she had taken the place of a wife, overseeing domestic affairs and handling purse strings related to their home. Her presence at the breakfast table, taken for granted, was probably the role he enjoyed most.

"Had you not known I would one day fly of my own accord?"

"No, I certainly had not." He stammered in wide-eyed wonder, "I mean--I thought--I hoped this worked well for both of us until—." He became flustered and Marion was not sure why she was seeing this unusual behavior.

"Of course it couldn't have to do with a gentleman, or could it?" he blurted.

Marion laughed with relief. "I have no plans, Father," she said. "I assure you I have no plans." She added quickly, "With the telegraph, I could let you know how I am faring in New York." The matter was dropped as both pursued their own thoughts.

The next day Henry Patton fidgeted with his china coffee cup, tapping it annoyingly with a silver sugar spoon until Marion asked, "What is it, Father? Are you thinking about my desire to travel to New York?" Provoked, she questioned whether he thought of her at all given his unfailing interest in one business affair or another.

Henry again cleared his throat, nodded assent, then murmured, "Marion, I'm struck by the grown woman you have become—I was not aware—." His authoritative voice trailed off.

"You are afraid for me to travel alone now, are you, Father?"

His knitted brow betrayed concern as his eyes, hazel like hers only darker, met hers, warmly at first stemming from their close relationship, but soon changing to a dogged stubbornness.

"Are you sure you want to do this, Marion? To go against my wishes—as your mother did long years ago?" His feet heavily hit the floor as he rose. Marion sensed that she had won, but the conquest came without joy.

Two days later, Marion prepared to leave with the freighters, other wagons and outriders. Kent showed up in Coloma on a stagecoach in time to catch her before she left. *This woman is elusive as hell. I could have missed her*, he heard himself saying repeatedly, with stunned reaction to that possibility. *I wouldn't have gone without some answers, not again.* He bounded across the clearing to the assembled travelers, confronting the mirage—or reality—of finding Miss Marion.

"My god, Miss Patton, I--I didn't expect to find—"

"And who didn't expect to find me?"

Words formed and dissembled in Kent's mind; thoughts chased one another away. She didn't know him? Or remember him? Or remember being in his arms? Oh hell. Hell. At last his formal etiquette surfaced in an unconscious extension of his gloved hand to hers. He tipped his new bowler hat and bowed slightly, his eyes never leaving hers.

"Of course you have not seen me dressed as a businessman. What was I thinking?" He laughed a bit off key. "I am the grubby, trail worn miner from Montana Territory that you had pie with, remember?"

It was Marion's turn for lack of words. She appraised him in disconcerting directness. He wore a handsome tailored black suit over a light grey wool vest. She mimicked the way he said "trail worn miner from Montana Territory," dragging out the words, painting them in subtle charm, her lips playfully teasing. When she dipped a curtsy in response to his bow that was too much. Kent grasped her arm and led her away from prying eyes.

Still shaken, he said, "I was afraid I wouldn't see you again before I left."

"Apparently we are traveling in the same direction. Are you going first class?"

Kent looked down at his business wear and joined in her merriment. "If your wagon train is delayed, I'll have time to change clothes and collect Ben and my gear from the stable. Otherwise I will ride hard to catch up. I have to tell you that I would be terribly disappointed if I lost you again."

"Lost me again?"

"Yes. I went to find my travel companion in Placerville and missed you when you left for San Francisco. So you see, I must apologize for my forwardness, but this chance encounter makes up for months of waiting in Auburn where I found employment. I--I had hoped we might become further acquainted, Miss Patton."

Dodging the implications, Marion said, "Your travel companion? Is he—or she—"

"Ray or Ramos as he is known here." Kent expressed his uncertainty about Ray to Marion.

"He came to Coloma," she said, as if these altercations were commonplace and of no significance. She had certainly witnessed years of upheaval among the masses that preyed upon each other in one way or another. She offered no other information. The matter was dropped when they discovered they had independently planned to take the route to Salt Lake City. Kent would travel north to Montana from there, and Marion east to St. Louis. Circumstances favored them traveling together, a fortuitous happenstance that seemed equally agreeable.

Kent could barely contain his joy in this arrangement, however, the intimate moment in the stable months ago seemed to have been forgotten. Marion was now fully engrossed in realizing her dream to visit New York, leaving little desire to repeat it as far as Kent could see. She was animated but distant, a barrier she apparently set on purpose. Grudgingly, he accepted the limits and enjoyed their occasional companionship on the trip.

Their wagon train going east faced an endless migration west. Covered wagons with pitchforks and hay hooks hanging on the sides passed coaches with fashionably dressed women. Children led pet goats while older lads brought along flocks of sheep. The continent was on the move, shortly to be augmented by the Union Pacific Railroad. A spirit of determination, conquest and discovery carried individuals from the smallest child to the eldest adult into the path of unimaginable hardships, not all of them surviving the ordeal. Hundreds of oxen would die on the trail across Nevada and Utah, and human life was even more vulnerable to thirst, starvation, the desert furnace, and winter temperatures dipping well below freezing. A special urgency to cross the lower Sierras through unpredictable weather kept them moving.

If the rigors of overland travel were not conducive to bringing Kent and Marion closer, neither did it separate them. Tempered by her experience growing up almost exclusively among men, she exhibited a casual, disinterested approach to most. Kent, though, felt he held a favored spot with her. When he rode beside her wagon her brusqueness faded to a natural charm, appealing to a soft side of Kent of which he'd been unaware. At these times he tended to share bits of his personal story and feelings that he wouldn't previously have thought to express. He felt like a lone cottonwood tree bending into the wind, changed bit by bit by external circumstances altering his solitary way of life.

"I feel cared for with you on this trip. I wish Father knew. He would appreciate having someone look after me!" she confided in turn. In small matters she leaned on him enough to hint at a femininity that engaged his courtesies. When the bumpy wagon ride became unbearable she scooted from the hard wooden seat to walk or ride.

"Ride Ben," he urged. "He wouldn't even notice you. He'd think it was a flea!" Marion gratefully rode while Kent walked alongside, her split skirt allowing her to ride astride. His preoccupation with Marion and the surprisingly benign March weather meant their crossing the southern portion of the Sierras was without undue hardship despite snow-covered passes. The traveling party soon relaxed into the lesser demands of the Nevada desert though dust rose in clouds from grinding wagon wheels and iron horseshoes. Kent and Marion laughed at each other's dust-caked faces. Marion is like the sister I never had, Kent thought, but he wanted more—eventually. There was not much either could do under the watchful eyes of busybodies.

But he didn't stop thinking about her—Marion, the wood sprite, a charmer with the simplicity and straight-forwardness of the Callahans' five-year-old daughter, Angel. Kent sensed that Marion was not burdened by the deep guilt and regrets he painfully harbored beneath the surface. It must be nice to be free of self-reproach, he sighed. Marion was seven years younger than he and seemed to find her way in the world rather effortlessly. Her confidence in herself and in achieving favorable outcomes to her ventures, including this trip to New York, distracted her from otherwise opening to intimacy that Kent hoped for.

"I will call my next good yielding claim *The Marion*," he teased, without yet declaring his intentions. This was as close as he could get at the moment. His own difficulties too often intruded upon these idyllic times.

"I ought to be tending my affairs on Norwegian Creek. The claims need to be worked to keep them valid. Shag must think I've left for good, but I promised my brother I would visit my mother in Georgia. That was in the spring of last year."

Silence stung the air until Kent admitted, "Well, I intended to go until I had the opportunity to go to California."

"My visit to my mother in San Francisco unleashed many conflicting emotions. Dora, my sister, was wildly excited to see me. We had a blissful time sharing our lives. Dora vicariously lived my adventures, and I redeemed myself with Mother by doing whatever Dora wanted. That involved fixing each other's hair, trying on dresses in expensive shops and splashing our feet in the ocean. Dora could have gone on with our being together forever, but it soon became tiresome for me. I assume there are differences in your family as well."

Marion correctly guessed there was much more to Kent's confession, too. She waited.

"My family split over the war. I did nothing to distinguish myself, let us say. I don't know if I want to go back. Something seems to prevent me from making a rational decision about it, even though I heard from my brother, Rand, that my mother is ailing."

"Then you must go to her."

Blinders fell from Kent's eyes as the answer lay so clearly before him. He looked with awe at this remarkable woman who could so deeply alter the contours of his life. She said no more and he stumbled on, catching his breath at the way she drilled her way so straightforwardly into the core of his being. I need you, he told himself, his eyes moist, but the need was too great to express. Her words had been factual, blunt and insightful. No, obvious. His thoughts of Mother had been buried in the tangle of family relations and finally lost in his pursuit of Marion, his promise delayed to fulfill his own yearnings.

"I could go east from Salt Lake City rather than north to Montana Territory," he said, reorienting himself to a change of plans in keeping with his promise to Rand. "I could purchase another horse in Salt Lake for the remainder of the trip to St. Louis, and continue to Georgia by rail from there. Ideally, I could meet up with my old wagonmaster, John Kepling, in Salt Lake, and persuade him to take personal charge of Ben's transfer back to Sterling."

"I'd certainly appreciate our traveling together on the wretchedly long Overland Trail," Marion admitted.

Pleased with the altered plans and Marion's rare overtures, Kent enjoyed an infusion of hope that he'd further his relationship with her as well as fulfill a deep desire to see his mother. The remainder of the tedious yet uneventful extended journey to St. Louis afforded plenty of time to also hope for a positive outcome reuniting with his brother. Of these prospects, the most heartwarming was his undeclared courtship of Miss Marion Patton while they traveled over the Rockies, past pioneer landmarks of Scotts Bluff and Chimney Rock, and through the awakening of spring across the Great Plains of the continental United States.

The city of St. Louis commands the west bank of the Mississippi River below its junction with the Missouri. This natural location has all the advantages of being midway between the continent's decisive north-south ranges, the Rocky Mountains and Appalachians. Early in the westward movement, St. Louis became a thriving trade center, rivaling the largest fur and hide markets in the world, largely in export of buffalo hides for robes and beaver pelts for much-demanded beaver hats. The city now sustained not only the main port for Mississippi steamboats, but was second only to Chicago in rail service. Kent had passed through the city in the fall of 1865 and now again in the spring of 1867. On both visits, he found that river and rail transportation discharged immigrants, their belongings, and freight west of the city on primitive oxcarts and horse-drawn vehicles, but he knew these antiquated means of cross-country travel would change in a few years with railroads linking East and West coasts.

"The noise and hustle of the St. Louis waterfront reminds me of the port of San Francisco," Marion said, "except for the absence of ocean vessels. I miss the elegant, tossing fans of sailing ships." Here workhorses of the river—tugs, barges, and freighters—supplied transport sorely lacking in the West. Bearded longshoremen muscled tons of cargo off incoming steamships, replacing it with hundreds of tons of outgoing freight and cords of firewood on lower decks.

"This energetic city is indeed a center of a recovering country," Kent agreed with some regrets, again feeling the overwhelming effects of industry on his southern sensibilities.

""If this is St. Louis, imagine how vigorous New York City will be."

"Miss Marion, my dearest, I cannot imagine anything without you in it. Not the next hour or day or month or however long it will be before I see you again." Kent's clear grey eyes searched her face, his wide firm lips quivered, uncertain. He tried to memorize the lilt of her voice, the tiny sun-baked creases around her mouth and the essence so unique to this woman.

Marion paused to absorb his declaration. His cheeks flushed in immediate confusion. Young porters vied for her small travel trunk, annoying Kent to no end. Marion sent them off with her usual aplomb, smiling with amusement that Ken's battered Army duffle bag attracted no takers at all.

From the Mississippi ferry, their transfer to rail routes, hers northeast and his south, was so hectic that parting was hasty.

"Wait for me, please," Kent pleaded. "Be here in six weeks, no five weeks, to meet me. Come back to Montana with me." Never had he simply asked, longingly, for anything in his life of privilege. He felt stunned by his own words, but knew in an instant that they came from the deepest place in his heart. He was no more able to suppress the plea than to leap the Mississippi River. "We'll take a riverboat like that one over there to Fort Benton!" he promised, pointing to a triple-decked sidewheeler gaily flying flags over its gingerbread façade.

"You amaze me!" Marion responded to the need and urgency in his low voice by stalling for time, obviously assessing her own desires, perhaps sorting out this proposal that was less than marriage, yet more than friendship. He grasped her hands and pulled her close to his chest. Serious now, her earnest hazel eyes in her upturned face reminded Kent of Shag's quizzical look. He assumed she must have been asking herself "Why am I doing this?" In the long hesitation, a shaky moment that stretched beyond the horizon for Kent, she made her decision.

"Yes, I will be here," she whispered, swaying into the curvature of his arms.

Kent stooped to gather this slip of a woman next to his heart, this time kissing her hair, her lips, her fingertips, holding so tightly she could barely utter, "I must catch my train." The pulsing of his breast matched a rising response in hers, both a familiar drumming to Kent like the flight of wild horses in the night. She shoved him away, breathless, to stare at this man as if she'd never seen him before. In that quiet span of mutual contemplation whole worlds vanished and were refashioned in a different light, softening the edges and valleys of their separateness.

7

Dense green foliage of the southern countryside struck Kent with its myriad hues after his trip across the Plains. He traveled east by rail with a smile on his face, picturing the youthful woman he had come to love—Miss Marion with her high-heeled boots, uncontrollable windswept hair, and puffed sleeves rolled up to bare her arms. She's a match for anyone, Kent thought, unknowingly echoing the very sentiment of her father. How she'd come from being the inquisitive mining company representative to his soon-to-be riverboat partner was hard for Kent to fathom. But why question a welcome change of fortunes? A sense of chasing his big chance still lurked in the edges of his consciousness.

Kent admitted that his trip back to Georgia contrasted with his mindless flight when he'd left the state two years earlier. However, his mood became increasingly anxious as the train progressed over rickety rails through Missouri, Tennessee, and finally into Georgia. As a former Army dispatcher, he understood that the South's railroads presented a proverbial Gordian knot. Owned by private companies, the rails were built to different specifications, therefore size and width varied. Transport through to destinations was impossible, a major liability during the war when rapid, reliable railroads were critical for moving troops and supplies. In contrast, the Union had seventy percent of the country's standardized railroads, thanks to early federalization of the rail system. Therefore, they had the advantage of consistently compatible trains and rails, affording maximum mobility. In addition, most of the steel mills and heavy industries were in the North. The strategic advantage was obvious, Kent lamented.

The Confederacy was forced to use Richmond's Tredegar Iron Works and the South's limited number of manufacturers for shipbuilding materials, guns, and ammunition rather than allocate scarce metals for railroads. Not being an industrialized region of the country, procuring more steel was often futile. Reliving the horrors, Kent recalled "Sherman's neckties," rails bent by Union troops on dangerous curves to purposely derail Rebel trains. More often than not mules packed the South's supplies and ammunition to the front lines, and the Rebels laid down a trick or two of their own. They retaliated by loosening spikes on the outside rails of Sherman's supply lines. As a result, engines crumpled like tin cans over steep hillsides, their rusting hulks visible from Kent's train window.

Similar mishaps appeared imminent for lack of maintenance during and after the war. My life and good fortune could be lost on this wretched track, he fumed. Rotting logbeds barely upheld rails over swamps and streams. Bridges spanning chasms, restored with matchstick wooden trellises, shuddered and howled as the train passed over.

Shacks of wood butchers' still lined the railways, homes to those who clear-cut Georgia pines and hardwoods hundreds of years old to fuel the trains' steam engines. Other forests were burned to rob the Union army of resources. Poor, small farms now occupied these clearings along bramble-filled dirt roads. An unnatural quiet prevailed over a once thriving countryside; a pall had settled over the broken land. Only the grinding of rail car wheels on wavering tracks and wail of screeching brakes offered a concert to turn the heads of passers-by.

In contrast, Kent's mind flitted to the endless unspoiled landscape of Montana with its generally peaceful stillness, thrilling him with the sudden, improbable prospect of taking Marion to the Territory with him. But the realization he would soon face Rand began to hit home. Each would bring their long-avoided paths to bear when they met. The fact that he had struck Rand in fear and rage rode heavily on his mind. Shame or personal defense? He could not be sure. *Will we come to blows again?* Kent envisioned this worst case scenario, rather, the worst case would be if Mother had died and he had not been notified.

Kent transferred from the train to a stagecoach going north toward the Piedmont Plateau, "upcountry" rising above the coastal plain. The train continued on to Atlanta. He noticed transportation seemed to be thriving. The Chattahoochee River was busy with small boats and barges. Great swaths of burned land showed new life in thick grass and shrubs, and vines and palmettos had begun to reestablish distinctive characteristics of the devastated countryside. Maples, beeches and hickory trees would take decades to grow back.

He was startled to see the red soil that had blessed his homecoming from Richmond two years ago, when he'd begged to get on one of the last *Richmond and Danville* railcars heading south. In the Carolinas, he'd plunged for days and nights through underbrush eluding the Unionist Home Guard until he collapsed by a stream. He vividly remembered sinking numbly to the earth, his fingers kneading the soil on both sides of his mud-caked uniform. He'd uttered "out of sick ward and I'm losing myself again." Disoriented by fear and fatigue, the shadows became assailants, imagined footsteps pursuers. His eyes and ears, then his mind, began to shut out images and sounds. The entirety of his life came down to that moment, his face reflected in a small pool. Survive. The earth felt cool, receptive to his overtures. Ripping away a deep layer of leaves with both hands, he sought the damp, naked earth underneath, earth familiar to a tobacco farmer. The world had gone mad—no, he had gone mad, but the earth healed his torment and he slept.

Fully immersed in events of two years ago, he now struggled to free himself from the anguish and pain that supplanted thoughts of Miss Marion Patton, but a fleeting recollection of a letter from his mother anchored him in the past. She had sent it to him in Richmond at the Army Supply and Dispatch complex where he'd been stationed.

My Dearest Kent,

This will be brief. I heard from Rand. He is a captain and doing well with the Federals. And how are you, Kent? Suffering, I am sure, from the terrible conditions of this conflict, but Rand is confident they will soon win and he can come home. I could meet up with you at your uncle's place in Jacksonville until we sort things out.

Always your devoted mother

Today Kent realized the letter stating "Rand is confident they will soon win and he can come home" had prompted his running, his stampeding with a wild herd of his own choosing, or rather fate had chosen for him. Kent's old friend, Ephram, had saddled Kent's horse, Donegal, and packed his mare, Bonnie, with blankets, food staples, and guns.

"Tis Master Rand you're leavin', isn't it sir?"

"Yes, no. Mostly myself, I think, Ephram."

"If you don' mind my sayin' so, 'tis hard to run away from yerself."

Kent had galloped out of the driveway into a stream of displaced families, his flight aimed north toward his father's relatives in Springfield, Illinois. The visit opened more wounds than it healed. Who were these unknown uncles and cousins with the Berrigan name? They speculated that Brogan, Kent's father, might have returned to New York or Dublin, or more likely, migrated to Australia, portraying him as a rootless or irresponsible individual. The insinuations angered Kent, yet forced him to examine his own running.

"I'm not the adventurous type. I prefer returning to the South, but that is an unbearable option at this time," he said, which in turn antagonized his northern relatives.

He had accepted a mid-level position in a wholesale company and endured assimilation of sorts into the now dominant culture of post-war industry, a contrast to the ease of pre-war South. By fall 1865, his identity ripped to shreds, he headed for St. Louis, where he departed on a wagon train for the Territories.

Kent now realized he was gripping the seat in the stagecoach until his knuckles hurt—he recalled selling at auction the prized thoroughbreds he'd raised from foals, their intelligent eyes wide and questioning. Bonnie's knowing gaze had tracked his emotions, plumbed his heart, and eventually acceded to the separation. That day at the sales ring Kent had crunched his hands, tempted to buy them back. They were purchased by a Southerner, which meant something might be familiar in their new lives. Kent had turned away swallowing rivers of piercing memories, moments accumulated over the years they shared—they had carried him in a headlong dash across Georgia's uplands that fateful day in April when he'd left his home.

Dazed, he now traveled past resurrected cotton and tobacco fields and gardens, his inner world torn between the former complacency of the antebellum period and the present signs of upheaval. He remembered that women had rioted in desperation to obtain food for their families when soldiers made off with their cows. "But we had superior cavalry and took better care of our horses than the North." The words murmured aloud spelled the least bit of pride from the vanquished.

The coach passed deserted ruins of plantations, signature handiwork of the Union's advances south. The driver explained these incursions were presently followed by carpetbaggers flooding the South under Abraham Lincoln's banner reconciliation and reform, a plan in disarray after his death. The lofty aims of Reconstruction to provide education and assistance to freed slaves were often lost to corruption, greed, revenge, and unlawful takeovers by those sweeping up spoils of war. With yet another internal threat, thousands of Southern families were relocating to Brazil.

"I travel the continent back and forth, but the passions remain and could be rekindled like fire to tinder." Kent, a war torn man, aired his fears and regrets to an impassive stranger; his once quiet nature alternately seethed and trembled as he journeyed home. He winced at unhealed stories of atrocities on both sides; the brutal onslaught of Grant's army, the South's Andersonville Prison leaving only a few skeletons of Union soldiers alive to see the end of the war. He turned his eyes from the sight of burned squatters' huts and slashed stands of hardwood forest that felt like personal assaults—wreckage buried deep in the depression of his soul.

"I should have done more—damn, I'm still divided over the larger divisions in the country. I think the war was about class. My family was a part of that, whether we want to admit it or not. Those with names and wealth tried to maintain oppression of the working class—a class I can only view kindly given my nanny and stable hand."

The driver nodded, seeming to accept rather than argue unresolved societal and political issues. They passed fields of cotton, soybeans, and modest homes, finally arriving in Woodland Hills. Kent inhaled the warm, moist Georgia air bearing the fragrance of damp forests sheltering wild roses and violets.

"The air at least is the same. I fear precious else will be."

The small town showed her mature countenance; one of resignation to a world altered in so many ways. Kent braced himself for this latest assault on his senses. The proximity to the family estate aroused even greater apprehension as he hired a surrey pulled by a stunning bay pacer to transport him the final lap home.

The square Georgian brick mansion with its long, curving carriage drive loomed in sight. A glance over the pacer's arched neck as he paid the driver revealed that the family home and property were intact but badly deteriorated. His heart raced as he made a quick inventory of his appearance in his travel clothes. Without the aid of a mirror, he didn't know what he looked like anymore, mirrors not being a necessity in the gold camps, wagon trains or rail cars. Resolutely, he walked up the steps to the front door. Enormous drooping camellias flanking both sides of the colonnaded entry seemed as strange as knocking at one's own door. He would have preferred a respite to visit the stable, where movement indicated that life went on as usual, where he might not feel so out of place. As he formally presented himself at his childhood home, he wondered if he would be welcome.

"Why, is zat youse, Master Kent?" Gracie stared hard at the stranger before recognizing Kent. Her spare, medium-height frame had wilted beyond her aged years. She had stifled cries, her fist in her mouth, when he left the last time he'd seen her.

Kent laughed and held out his hand. "Gracie, I am happy to see you. You are looking lovely." Seeing her there, he wanted to crush this nanny, this housekeeper, this woman like a great aunt, into his arms. He had spent a great deal of time on her lap when he was a child. In turn, she devoted hours to untangling fishing line for "her" two lads, Rand and Kent.

She flushed and backed up, ushering him into the foyer. Same Gracie, Kent was relieved to find, only her hair, which was thinner and whiter, looked like a halo above her black skin. Gracie, of all people, made him feel like the lad he had been in this very house. He hung his long coat on the pedestal coat rack, his nerves relaxing a bit while she fussed.

Gracie's angular features softened as a huge smile played over her lips. Her large dark eyes couldn't believe it was really

Kent, that he had come home at last. Her words tumbled over each other.

"Master Kent, youse is a handsome soul as ever was yerself," she said, urging him to follow her into the parlor until Kent managed to interrupt.

"If you don't mind, Gracie, I'd like to visit the stable first. When I get my bearings I will change from travel wear and spend time with everyone."

He strode through the long hallway, a bundle of feelings lodged in his throat—home. Home, though the hollow sounds of his footsteps echoed words Mother had said to Rand when Rand declared he had joined the Union, and to him when he signed with the Rebels, "Just go if you must."

Today he paused at the staircase where he'd lurched up the steps on his last trip home, the effort draining the last of his reserves. He had tried to pass Rand's room with averted eyes and closed mind, but he'd been drawn to open the door. It swung, rasping on unused hinges, to clunk against a cluttered dresser. An accumulation of stale odors from Rand's clothing escaped from the room. Though Rand had been gone three years it was as if he'd never left. Kent recalled how his own body had sagged heavily against the door frame, his chest heaving. Rand's neatly made bed exuded confidence, an authority that stripped Kent of self respect. A blurred vision of Rand emerged from the bedposts as if it demanded, "What the hell were you doing brother?"

Kent had fought the voices, the visions, and sought relief in his own room. How long he'd lingered there he did not know. Eventually the smell of chicory, a substitute for scarce coffee, and the sound of pans rattling in the kitchen brought him back to his immediate task, to leave before Rand arrived. Gaunt and starving from the struggle to get home, he had roused enough energy to gather his belongings.

Now that he was home again, he hurried past the stairs to get outdoors and shake the chill of memories. Surveying the outbuildings and stable, he found that time and neglect had taken hold, yet the old white oak and maple trees were as magnificent as ever, casting a comforting shade over the courtyard and carriage house. When he left, he feared the estate would be overrun in the aftermath of war by refugees, looters, soldiers, uprising slaves or Indians. Kent felt a huge sense of relief seeing the old trees and the tree house where he'd tucked a wicker fishing bag that as youngsters he and Rand had hauled to the creek a hundred times— something meaningful for Rand to find when he returned from the war.

Kent notified a stable hand that he would go for a walk and be back to meet with Mr. Rand before supper. He outwardly viewed the property that felt so familiar to his feet, the rolling lush green so much a part of him, but inside his thoughts scrambled to focus not on his last homecoming, but this one, and his projected meeting with Rand.

Kent spruced up in a high starched collar Gracie provided, and changed into a morning coat and pressed trousers, thanks to valet services in St. Louis. His boots with the faint *fleur de lis* imprint of Dubrinski gleamed after a brisk polishing along the way. He looped a string tie in a loose knot around the white collar, a stark contrast with his sun-browned hands.

Gracie ushered him into the library. Rand sat reading in a chair by the fireplace. Kent's immediate impression was that the furnishings and Rand's mid-thigh burgundy dress coat were outdated. He wore a thin clerical collar above a starched shirt with small pleats. The two gentlemen quietly assessed each other. Rand did not attempt to rise but indicated with a casual gesture that Kent sit opposite in a matching chair. The gesture felt hospitable to Kent, and he gratefully seated himself, crossed his long legs and leaned back. If Rand recalled being struck by Kent on their last encounter, he gave no hint of it.

"Ephram took care of my horse and surrey at the stable and informed me of your arrival," Rand said. "I drove to town to serve on a board implementing reforms. I am invariably considered part of the occupation and my services often resented, but that is more than you want to know."

Though Rand was only twenty-nine, his face appeared to have deeper lines and his sideburns showed some grey since his trip to Sterling, evidence of strained family relations and his difficult reentry into Woodland Hills, Kent guessed.

After a long pause, Rand resumed. "Well, you did come. And you are welcome. I am glad to see you, Kent. You look good." He cleared his throat. "You probably heard from Gracie that Mother no longer lives here. She moved permanently to Savannah to be with Aunt Margaret. She is quite dependent, you know, though she is barely fifty years of age."

"Indeed, Gracie informed me. How is she?" Kent had digested the news of her move before meeting Rand, and in his anxiety, he had pushed Mother to the back of his mind—it was less stressful to deal with only one family member at a time.

"Her condition has stabilized under the care of her doctor there. He prescribes laudanum, I believe. She has great confidence in this physician. Appropriate medical care was entirely lacking in Woodland Hills, so the move was a satisfactory one for her. In addition, there were too many memories for her here." Rand chose his words carefully as if to maintain the calm, even mood of their conversation. Clearly he desired to avoid a confrontation, an effort Kent noted with gratitude. This initial meeting unfolded not only civilly but cordially compared to Kent's expectations, yet their talk lacked the substance he'd hoped for.

Rand continued in the absence of his brother's response. "The staff manages to carry on with hardly any direction from me. My wife, Elena, is quite competent about domestic affairs, but most of her time is spent with the children."

At this news Kent sat bolt upright.

"I am happy to hear you have married, Rand, and have children, too! Surely that makes me an uncle!" At last the brothers chuckled easily and a long-awaited thaw seemed imminent.

"Oh, I was young and brash when I married a woman behind the lines. When we were at last reunited here after the war, we had one child, a girl, then a boy came along in due course. How long since there was a girl in this house, Kent? I wonder if she will take over the tree house and post it for girls only!"

The mood had truly lifted by the time Gracie called them for supper. Elena joined them in the dining room. The children had already eaten in the nursery. Rand haltingly walked in, stooping slightly as if he were in pain.

Rand's wife is a beautiful woman, Kent breathed. No wonder he married her at once and let the future work its inexorable course. She was tall and slender, giving her a stately appearance enhanced by fine, pale features and a crown of thick auburn hair looped in a French braid. She graciously offered her hand, at last meeting Rand's errant brother. Kent worried what she did or didn't know about him and his disappearance.

Polite questions about the Territories and prospects in the gold fields sustained the conversation and gave Kent a chance to find familiar footing by sharing his experiences. His description of Big Ben, the half-thoroughbred, brought a hearty laugh from Rand, who'd once shared Kent's penchant for hot-blooded horses.

"Ben hauled a good many wagons out of the mud and snow. That brute is a pulling fool—and I only have to feed him twice what a normal-sized horse would eat." He gestured the height and girth of the huge horse, which drew laughter all around.

Kent did not have to feign an appetite for the stuffed quail, baked sweet potatoes, and steamed collards served on a family heirloom tray. "Who is the bird hunter?" he asked.

"None of us, unfortunately. There are few wild quail since the land was stripped. We raise our own now." Rand spoke easily on this subject, one pertaining to his interests and comfort level. He described his efforts to make the property self-sustaining.

"Raising quail and pheasants has become a practical as well as an enjoyable pastime. You may be surprised that we—I—have taken other initiatives in growing and curing tobacco. Thankfully, most of the field hands stayed with us. There are too many unknowns for the families to leave. So, you see, we continue on—with considerable success under the circumstances."

Gracie refilled Kent's plate from the tray and a tureen he remembered from his childhood. While he wondered how family treasures had been saved, he dared not turn the conversation to the war. Neither did he disclose a word about Miss Marion, the woman who seemed distant to his present world. It is safer not to arouse speculation so early, he thought, but a twinge of excitement shot through his body at the possibility that she might become a part of his life.

After dessert, Elena left to care for the children and Kent caught up with Gracie in the hall. "Bless you, Gracie, you have the memory of an elephant and a heart as big. I haven't had pecan pie since the last one you made for me."

She curtsied, her long black dress sweeping the immaculate floor, and gave him such a smile he couldn't help feeling that he was, and always had been, her favorite.

Rand and Kent retired to the library to smoke, an indulgence Kent had largely forfeited on his Spartan journeys. The dark mahogany paneling reflected an orange evening light. The men lit cigars, their private thoughts circling like the smoke while the grandfather clock in the hall struck as always, and outside crickets sang their evening song. Rand removed himself from intimate discourse by describing the intricacies of cultivating new strains of tobacco, and his expansion of the estate's gardens and orchards.

Kent's mind wandered, willing to address the heart of his visit, yet anxious regarding the outcome. He braced himself and said at the first opportunity, "I'm sorry I wasn't man enough to join you when you enlisted or even remain here to talk after the war. You well know my subsequent course of action. We have all suffered because of it."

Rand squarely faced Kent, his eyes betraying hints of both affection and anger towards his earnest younger brother. Kent's face portrayed an infinite sadness; his hand holding the cigar shook. His voice came thick, uneven.

"I was weak, Rand, I couldn't face you when you returned from—from—serving the North and—and ultimately breaking us in the South. My abrupt departure was a poor decision, one I can never make up to you and Mother." The words trailed. "You said in Montana she was devastated. I have lived with that fact every day since I left here—especially since she suffered similar abandonment by Father." Kent reached into a breast pocket for a handkerchief. Rand rose to pace unsteadily back and forth in front of the unlit fireplace, sensitive to his brother's emotion.

"I suppose I was closer to Father than you since I'm the eldest," Rand replied in a tightly controlled defense. "He was an idealist, an immigrant deeply indebted to the North. I was convinced of the cause or I wanted to please him, I'm not sure. I can understand your being closer to Mother and her roots here." His jaw twitched in a manner that annoyed Kent.

"I couldn't get my mind around the Northern cause, the politics of equality and loss of state's rights." A familiar fog clouded Kent's mind. "My heart was with my homeland." He did not divulge that Mother had forbidden him to leave the estate until they were forced out near the end of the war. She had always held the reins, even before her husband, Brogan Berrigan, had abdicated, but beneath the power she yielded, Kent sensed she was dependent upon him, especially after Rand chose to follow family ties to the North.

"I am aware that I also abandoned Mother," Rand confessed. "The consequences were starkly apparent when I returned. She became as ostracized as I am now because her son was, and continues to be, often considered a traitor."

Kent had heard the word "traitor" invoked by Jake, Benson, Yanks and Rebels alike, all summing up complexities of a nation turned upside down, dispersing its dissidents to the West, to Brazil, to ongoing strife in the South. An image of the swirling contents of his gold pan prompted him to question, "Where or when will it all settle out?"

Floor to ceiling shelves of leather-bound books staged the occasion, the vision of Mother being abandoned thrice—by her husband, her eldest who fought for the Union, and her youngest who fled. A strong, elegant woman at one time with beautiful dark hair, she bore the firm broad features represented on the faces of her two sons, at this moment both deeply stricken with the realization of how it must have been for her.

Kent could only guess her appearance since Rand said she required close medical supervision though she was far from old age. But his attention turned to Rand. "If I may, I wonder if you have suffered greatly yourself. I see you have some difficulty moving about."

Rand straightened. "Yes, I incurred some wounds in the course of action—minor, I daresay, compared to most. I carry on as before."

This last statement was hardly believable, but Kent did not dispute the assertion. Only too vividly did he recall his brother riding into Sterling having traveled nearly two thousand miles in search of him. The furious reception and blow he had given Rand then seemed unwarranted now. Rand had offered no resistance—as though the starch had gone out of him since the war. Rand now attempted to dismiss the subject of the war, to let it fade into the past.

A tenuous new connection formed between the brothers— one Kent had never dreamed possible but perhaps had risen once he'd bared his soul. God, he groaned, I would apologize one thousand times over if it would dissolve all the pain our family has suffered.

8

Days passed quickly on the eighty-acre Berrigan estate, where freed men and women worked fields of tobacco cultivated for its distinctive aroma and light ochre leaves. The estate occupied a surprisingly fertile location midway between the tail of the Appalachian mountains and the distant coastal plain. Orchards and pastures ranged into wooded foothills above. The heavy scent of magnolia blossoms saturated evening breezes while honeysuckle's sweet fragrance claimed sun-filled days. Moss-draped trees hid in the shade along small golden streams, and grapevines draped arbors bordering the kitchen garden behind the mansion. The garden burst with well-tended plants: watermelons and honeydews, cantaloupe and berries. Pimento peppers, unknown in Montana Territory, found favorable conditions to flourish here. Kent half expected Mother to arise from gathering spicy basil, rosemary and lavender in her apron. The smell of damp soil and pungent plants crushed beneath his boot triggered a memory of meeting Gracie in the garden two years ago.

'I must leave now, Gracie. The war has split us, Rand and me." Tremors had shaken his tall, skeletal frame. Her lips had quivered, words failed to come. Misty eyes held his own. He'd faltered in the face of her love, the gentle kindness. Her glance fell to the unkempt Confederate uniform sagging from Kent's stooped shoulders and to his Army boots caked with mud.

"You've been a godsend, Gracie. From the beginning you fed and rocked Rand and me and kept us out of trouble. Thank you." Thank you seemed so inadequate, then or now.

Kent exhaled resident tension tinged with unacknowledged bitterness, and forced his thoughts back to the present. He had summoned courage to confront Rand with "breaking us in the South." The bold, bald truth held few, if any, repercussions as far as Kent could see. If his brother had recoiled at the accusation, he'd held it inside.

Kent occupied a guest room, happy that his nephew and niece used his bedroom for a nursery. He felt honored to be treated with every kindness, especially that of being called Uncle. Early attempts by Rand and Elena to set him up with women he had known came to naught, however. He declined social engagements and dances in the vicinity. Thoughts he'd indulged in the West of the beautiful Miss Olivia Spencer were given short shrift now they were both far removed from their respective boarding schools. At that time their mutual interests in literature and history had engaged them in lengthy academic conversations.

"We'll leave law and politics to intellectuals to riddle with their high-minded debates," she had stated. "I'll contribute to higher education in the humanities. What will you do to establish yourself, Kent?" Olivia was unusually outspoken and self directed for a woman, Kent reflected. He had entertained notions of courtship, not that he pursued it after the war began. Now he wondered why she wasn't married since she must be nearly his age. But her pointed question struck him again—he hadn't yet established himself.

However, he took advantage of the respite at his old home to fall back into a familiar routine, up early to exercise the saddle horses on the red dirt roads in the rolling hills of the Piedmont. Dense forests of beech, maple, pine and white oak shaded the forest floors, limiting undergrowth except remarkably aggressive rhododendrons. He found lily of the valley trees that would later bloom with hanging clusters of white bell-shaped flowers, source of the area's distinctive sourwood honey. The energetic strides of Kent's horse flushed out an occasional raccoon that scurried out of the path. Long accustomed to hunting with Rand, he knew where to look for families of opossums tucked into branches overhead.

On a crest he savored a view of the Blue Ridge Mountains capped in pine and hemlock, the ranges spilling over to the north, becoming lost in the mist-saturated atmosphere. He recalled having seen the sun rise over the Atlantic, spiking Mount Mitchell, the highest peak east of the Mississippi, with golden rays. Kent saw the distinctly eastern character of the land with a new perspective since being away. Lavender, soft violet and purple edges traced cobalt mountains that wandered northeast, skirting the Smokies. Warmth inched down into valleys, awakening remote small farms hidden in dense groves of elm and rhododendron. He shook off the damp chill from the overnight rain, glad of the reminder that mornings could be invigorating, though stifling humidity was sure to follow.

After these early contemplative rides, Kent had breakfast with Rand before Rand began his full day's schedule. Rand had little interest in the horses. Instead, he cultivated large orchards and botanical gardens that attracted the attention of horticulturists around the state and beyond. The thriving tobacco fields continued to provide a limited income as they had in the past. As usual, this was supplemented by Mother's considerable resources. Typical of the South's small farms, the Berrigans had owned only five or six slaves, most of whom chose to remain with the family after the war. Only a tenth of the planters in the South owned slaves at the onset of the war, while a few owned as many as five hundred, making post-war changes in the labor force radical for some, but not for all.

The Berrigan family was getting by and not unhappy that reduced circumstances necessitated a modest existence consistent with the times and the lives of others. In fact, they felt extremely fortunate compared to many. Elena was especially careful to ease their way back into a community that was not always receptive. She also cautioned Rand not to overdo his exertions about the place. A nurse when they met, she was attentive to his welfare.

"As you surely must see, the South has been in frighteningly poor shape these last few years," Rand said. "There are severe shortages of most basic necessities, and the economic shambles appear hopelessly irreparable, especially when one is preyed upon by the strong and revengeful as well as the usual riff raff. You may be uncomfortable with the comparison, Kent, but I understand the North is rebounding quite robustly."

"The contrast is well represented in the gold camps. Those with money and connections who have invested heavily in procuring the best claims and means of processing ore are centered in New York and Des Moines. With the exception of Missouri, I can't think of a single major company from the South, yet the bulk of the laborers, particularly in my area, are Southerners. The criminal element you refer to is represented, but most are fine, upstanding settlers who provide staples for the camps with their industrious farming and ranching." Kent felt he was speaking from the heart about Sterling and Norwegian Creek, places that had taken on an outsize meaning in his life.

These discussions with Rand were satisfying in the sense they could converse civilly and exchange bits of their lives that helped clarify many of Kent's own thoughts and actions. Talk of past hunting and fishing felt comfortable, but the day he'd struck Rand behind the livery stable in Sterling? Rand let it pass. The two years it had taken for Kent to come home? Forgiven. I wonder what I expected from this long and vigorously avoided encounter, Kent asked himself. Still, he felt he had gained little traction in addressing a deeper wound, his conviction that he had failed or deserted the family. If the visit was to be healing as he truly desired—as he desperately needed—it appeared unlikely to happen in any interchange with members of his family.

He was soon drawn away from home to make the promised visit with Mother in Savannah, one that aroused a host of mixed emotions. He needed to see how she was, and find out how he might be received.

Before he left, Elena met him briefly in the garden. She wore a simple, ankle-length dress in pale pinks that reminded Kent of dogwood blossoms.

"Rand has suffered from a terrible condition since the war. He has violent dreams and wakes crying out. These invariably lead to a bout of melancholy—or worse. The neighbors have shunned us. We're quite alone—having aided the enemy." Her eyes misted, pleading for him to understand, possibly to help if he could. "I think he is much better since you are here," she added.

"The visit has certainly helped me clear regrets of the past. I hope that it is equally comforting to Rand. I know how the wretched flashbacks persist despite our efforts to leave the war behind." Kent's voice came low and full. "I am sorry this trauma intervenes in your life with Rand. If there is anything I can do—"

The offer felt too little, too late; if he could do anything in the world to make things better he would—not that he had that power over his own life. Elena nodded, her features sad, tender. She extended a hand which Kent grasped in both of his.

Elena's disclosure wrung Kent's heart, but also brought some measure of solace. Kent had placed blame solely on himself for upsets in the family. The fact they equally shared regrettable experiences served to renew their relationship. For that he was most grateful.

The visit to his mother was somewhat heartening as well. She greeted Kent with open arms—the prodigal son—he remembered the story from his elementary school catechism.

Tears filled his eyes when they embraced, his face resting in her soft greying hair. Aunt Margaret fluttered over the two until Kent freed himself to give her a hug. At about his height, she was a force to be reckoned with.

"Y'all come in and have tea," she insisted, speeding off to call the maid.

Again Catherine held him, this time at arm's length, her hands white and unsteady. Her grey eyes, like Kent's, seemed to search the past, seeing him as a boy, as a young man, and now as a tanned and weathered gentleman she hardly knew.

"I'm sorry, Mother, for everything," he blurted. "For everything that has happened to you. For every bit of sorrow I have caused you." Kent did not wipe his eyes. "I wasn't cut out to fight epic battles." He choked over the words thinking 'except when my own flesh and blood pushes me too far.' "I didn't mean to desert you, but I needed to gain some perspective."

"That's all right, Babe. You came home and that is all that matters." Catherine patted him on the back. Her rosewater cologne matched the dusky rose of her long, flowing gown, cinched at her waist and trimmed with wide ochre lace at the bodice and throat. She stood well past his shoulder, an imposing woman with the eternally smooth skin of women in the dewy southern clime. They gravitated to wicker chairs on a shady side of the veranda. Kent strained to regain his composure from the unexpectedly tumultuous emotion that had unleashed his impromptu apologies. Again, inadequate apologies by any measure, but he wondered how they had been received, how his mother felt deep down. And when, if ever, she might discuss those past days and events.

Her questions about his welfare tumbled over one another. Her attention, though, quickly wandered before he could relate his story. Her eyes drifted to darker times and sadness crept across her face, a familiar bit of which he'd grown up with as a youth. Now the setting sun revealed lines of stress and pain that settled over her in a palpable way.

"And you, Mother, how are you these days?" Kent asked, gently linking his elbow with hers on the arm chair. His long repressed concern surfaced, stifling his words. He wondered why he'd failed to come sooner.

Catherine straightened herself, a resolute set to her mouth. She paused as if not knowing where to begin. "I am quite fine, Kent, darling. Thank you. Margaret has been most solicitous of my every need, and I find it highly satisfactory to be living with her in the city. As Rand may have told you, my physician here has been especially helpful treating my rheumatism and headaches. I could not do without him."

They sat in silence for a long while, hands fiddling with frosty glasses of peach tea. Her words were not quite convincing, but Kent couldn't see that she overtly suffered any debilitating condition. The malaise was common among gentlewomen; in Mother's case, more likely a deep melancholy which in retrospect seemed endemic to his family. Most apparent was her lack of energy, the absence of a once proud and defiant spirit. Mother had literally raised her two sons under her wings. Now, though she solemnly searched his face, she held back, maintaining a distance, as if protecting herself.

I am to blame for that, Kent admitted privately. My penance for leaving. He swallowed and looked down, momentarily succumbing to the South's prevailing mood of weariness, as if it struggled for an affirmation of life after its defeat. A defeat he'd taken with him.

Catherine had been a diligent homemaker and patron of community affairs, and she had wielded a firm hand behind the management of slaves and their families who worked the tobacco fields. Kent knew there would be no planting or harvesting without them, nor stable hands nor house servants. They are fundamental to us in the South. My parents, Mother mostly, made it possible for us, as well as the Negroes, to live in a tolerable fashion. With a start, Kent realized he had readily fallen back into a southern way of thinking, at least that of those who retained considerable family wealth. The absence of such unequal relationships in the West had not erased his inherent views in the two years he had been away.

A cobwebby feeling blurred his thoughts—he saw his reflection everywhere in the South and found it disturbing, as if he needed to make an internal adjustment to external realities. The charm and dignity of Savannah had survived, yet it harbored pain that had recently criss-crossed the land. Conventions entrenched a few years ago now seemed archaic, even questionable with the abject shortages of basics such as coffee, salt and sugar. Hanging on to old roles and customs suddenly appeared pointless and inconsistent with brighter moods in the West and North. Or with that of Aunt Margaret.

He looked up in time to see her sail out to the veranda with a tray of small cakes and shortbreads delicately iced with frosting and dusted with powdered sugar. Kent's eye for fashion couldn't help but recognize that her light cotton sun dress looked like the icing with its bits of pink, rose, and pale green embroidery on white, an exceedingly feminine dress for a woman of such vitality and self assurance.

"Catherine, Kent, here you are dwelling on the past, I'm afraid. Can you not see that we have our lives and a future awaiting us? And a homecoming to celebrate? I do think we should have a party for Kent and invite just the right people, some dear friends who would love to see you, Kent."

She turned her bright, flashing smile in his direction thoroughly expecting him to comply with her every whim. Kent laughed at her energy and sparkle as the conversation ran on largely independent of Mother and himself. Clearly, the inherited melancholy, if that was the case, had skipped over Aunt Margaret.

"There are the Adamsons next door. The Harveys have moved here from upstate, and your uncle in Florida should be notified. Surely we know young women among our acquaintances. I do believe the Daniels have a lovely girl named Lou Anne."

"Aunt Margaret, I am no longer young! And I have barely stepped in the door to have a nice visit with you and Mother. Truly, that is all I desire, and here you are arranging a marriage. I am nearly thirty years old, twenty-seven to be exact, an old man, and not by any means a suitor for these young candidates you so eloquently describe!"

Catherine smiled absently while Margaret conceded they could make reservations for a popular concert the next evening, stating that folks they knew would attend. "We're so proud to have you visit, Kent. We must show you off. You really are quite handsome, and the dark tan becomes you."

Kent flushed, the frock coat and snug cravat suddenly felt as stifling as Aunt Margaret's heavy, floral drapery that darkened and closed her house.

"I do see a great deal of resemblance to your father when he was your age, just before he left. You can be proud," she added. "He was a fine man. It just wasn't his nature to settle down as a country squire." Margaret glanced at the now quiet faces, apparently assessing the fallout from her transgression. Bringing up the name of Brogan Berrigan in the presence of his abandoned wife and son had been tacitly forbidden.

"After all these years it's 'water under the bridge,' I know," her voice trailed, "but truly, Kent, you're his spitting image. Your mother cherishes you, my nephew." Unable to resist filling the stunned ensuing silence, Margaret continued, "Brogan was quite caught up in politics and aspired to be an ambassador to France or somewhere. He was forever chasing rainbows and finally he didn't come home at all."

Kent nodded. Losing his father at age seven was burned into his memory, but he was too young to understand his father had such high aspirations. The notion intrigued Kent; he felt it gave him an insight into the parent he barely knew. Had farming the estate not been enough for him after experiencing New York as an immigrant? Brogan had not brought wealth to the marriage. The Berrigan's depended upon Mother's inheritance then and, to a degree, now. Ruminating, Kent realized he'd done the opposite, emigrated from a relatively affluent, cultured society to untamed Montana Territory. He noticed his mother shifting uneasily in her chair. Her hand dismissed the remarks as readily as she had moved on after Kent's burst of regrets. At the apparently familiar signal, Margaret caught herself and changed the subject.

The abruptness alerted Kent. Margaret knew something he didn't. A scandal that had been kept from Brogan's sons? Kent was aware his father had not abdicated with Catherine's money. Had he run away with another woman? Had Margaret not blundered but revealed the truth indirectly, the only way she could in his mother's presence? Kent's eyes squinted, puzzled about the mystery surrounding his father's absence. He sensed Aunt Margaret needled futilely in an attempt to clear a lingering unknown for him, without intruding on her sister's secrets. Bless her. She wouldn't overtly spill the beans, but her suspicions now confirmed his.

Kent lifted a brow and responded evenly, "I'll take your kind words as a compliment, Aunt Margaret. I know Mother married a fine man." That was as far as Kent could go. A tinge of disappointment crossed his face as the conversation was redirected.

"I'll have Bessie stir up our favorite pimento cheesecake and cornbread for a light supper," Margaret said, forgetting that Rand and Kent always graciously demurred at the offering. Fortified with jalapeno cheese and filled with chili pepper-infused honey and pimento cheeses, the "favorite" required better men than they, the nephews had agreed.

Kent would have welcomed disclosures to fill gaps in their family history. He'd held back questions about his father's disappearance when he was a child. As adults, why not open their hearts to embrace their common loss? However, the opportunity for that outcome passed, despite the fact these two women were the few living persons who held answers to his unspoken pleas.

Over the length of Kent's visit his mother and Aunt Margaret did not return to any substantial revelations about his father's past or their shared history. Heart-to-heart talks were simply avoided. Nor did Kent reveal his deepest feelings, particularly those concerning Miss Marion Patton. As a result, the next two weeks of constant flurry and tutelage by Aunt Margaret about the joys of civilization in a fine Southern city were more than enough for Kent. He paced the wide veranda that sheltered two sides of the three-story frame house, a home set well inland from the constant shuffle along Savannah's river channel. Heavy limbs of familiar Southern live oaks hung graciously over a cool side yard. Terraced paths circled dainty beds of pansies, primroses and forget-me-nots inset with ornamental stone bunnies. Moist, limp jasmine blooms lent a seductive scent along with other florals—azaleas, sweet bay, white honeysuckle and dogwood that Kent enjoyed until restlessness drove him inside.

By now the slightly tarnished, etched silver platters arranged in the dining room appeared dreary, as well as the mahogany sideboard displaying an heirloom gravy bowl and a soup tureen belonging to the fine china stored inside. Glass doors of a corner cupboard revealed a set of Syracuse red-patterned daily service he had chipped as a child. Pale ivory wallpaper with its raised velvet garland design rose above varnished wainscoting, a mockery of the plain pine walls of Kent's Montana residence.

Kent chuckled at Aunt Margaret's breakfasts, feasts fit for kings—at least royalty favoring the excesses of Southern home cooking, a contrast with his own slather of bacon grease on hardtack and a cup of coffee. Steaming pans of fried cinnamon apple slices swam in syrup, and plump white biscuits topped with maple syrup and pecans drowned in thick red-eye gravy.

Not to mention creamy yellow cheese grits with a mushy consistency. He patted his expanding waistline, worrying that Marion wouldn't recognize him in St. Louis.

Sitting back after one of these feasts, he begged off scheduling further parties and excursions arranged for his benefit. "I want to spend a few days in Woodland Hills. My niece and nephew will soon forget they have an uncle if I don't show up. What a joy they are! And I've barely reacquainted myself with Rand. I'd like for us to resolve our affairs, you know, before I depart for Montana."

This announcement set off a stir in the henhouse.

"Whatever could compel you to return to the arid West, my nephew? It is too remote and primitive even to contemplate. Surely you did not tell us of a gold strike, nor any other business that binds you. Dear me, there must be a woman—what else?" Aunt Margaret fanned herself and exercised all her feminine airs to entice him to reconsider.

Mother was kind but less effusive. "I need you, dear Kent. You understand that better than anyone, though I always want the best for you. Go if you must. You have my blessing."

It was the familiar push-pull that she and Rand used so effectively to bind him. This time, he chose to listen to the latter part of the message, to his own heart. Images of Mother's hands opening to release him caught Kent off guard. He feigned a smile at this unexpected, genuine gesture—so profoundly opposite his previous desperate leave-taking.

"Mother," he stammered. He knelt at her side to wrap his strong brown arms around her pale, thin frame. The pulse pounding in his ears muffled any reply she might have made.

The Randolph and Elena Berrigan family in Woodland Hills quietly cared for their children, planted gardens, and contributed to Reconstruction efforts to the extent an often resentful community permitted. Kent's brief return seemed to enliven their usual routines. When pressed for details regarding his need to return to the Territories, Kent admitted he owned one hundred sixty acres he acquired under the Homestead Act, specifically the Preemption Act since surveys had not yet established property boundaries.

"The homestead is not a notable acquisition since the land is granted freely for filing with a small processing charge," he hastened to add. "I took the opportunity since I only have to invest my time to maintain it," he finished, uncertain how this news was accepted. Becoming landed gentry in Montana Territory might have sounded absurd to Rand, or perhaps Rand thought that his younger brother flaunted his large property. Kent couldn't guess from their blank faces, but their shock revealed how far he had removed himself from the South.

"It is about enough to feed a few jackrabbits and antelope." Kent downplayed any advantage over the eighty acres owned by Rand and Elena.

The children were old enough to understand "rabbits." They climbed upon Kent's knee, their little faces eager and voices piping, "Bunnies, bunnies!" They reminded him of Angel and Finn with their successive menageries, and he had to laugh. The tension was broken and his plans left unchallenged.

At the last moment, Kent met with Miss Olivia Spencer, admittedly his first flame, though the courtship was intermittent long before he left. The prospect of seeing her again had been much more compelling when he was alone in a long, isolating Montana winter.

Olivia styled her waist-length hair in a French bun for the classroom when she taught at the Women's Academy, but with Kent, she tossed it freely and seductively; her gardenia cologne also moderately interfered with his concentration. He found her as interesting as he remembered, and fun now that she was a self-described fully emancipated, self-supporting "old maid."

She shared verses she liked from Elizabeth Barrett Browning, whose liberated thinking was in keeping with her own. "Certain issues might be challenging for you, Kent," she cautioned. "You recall Miss Browning was one of England's earliest abolitionists. Social and political issues became subjects she addressed passionately and forthrightly."

Kent remained non-committal. If she was goading him for his views on current events, he chose to avoid entering the discussion.

"And her love poems are most explicit for a woman," Olivia added with a sidelong glance, checking his reaction.

Her flush betrayed her purposeful taunt; Olivia wanted to know how he felt about her, not necessarily how he felt about the poetry. He had never engaged in intimate conversation with her—the word "love" carried a charge he was quite unprepared to discuss with her. If he blushed in turn, he hoped she didn't see it.

Olivia continued, "She openly defies domination by men—even while endlessly declaring her love for Robert Browning."

The literary discourse tended to remain one-sided. Kent guessed she might have desired less independence if she had a suitor—and that she might be hinting for his favor.

"Perhaps you'd find Lord Tennyson's endlessly intellectual works more appealing, particularly the relation of man to nature." Olivia resorted to another tactic.

"Are you assuming, Miss Olivia, that I have gone back to nature in the West? Certainly the Midwest, Great Plains, and Rocky Mountains invite one's immersion in almost overwhelming nature." He paused, tempted to confide that he usually felt spiritual in the immensity of the land and the endless reaches of sky in Montana Territory, that it was easy to drift into deep contemplation in the sanctity of solitude—to vow to live simply, to find forgiveness in his heart, and at times, rest in His grace. But he was aware he wasn't the type to exchange confidences, and

Olivia had not sensed this serious side of him, or encouraged him to express his deeper feelings.

"I assumed Tennyson's poems inspired by classical works would be in keeping with your early studies. Really, Kent, I don't know who you are anymore without the bookishness. I wonder that you recognize yourself when you look in the mirror."

"I don't have a mirror! Nor a shelf for books that rats and mice can't reach," he replied wickedly. "You would be most surprised to see my accommodations. However, since I doubt you're ever coming West, I shall not worry about impressing you!" They bantered back and forth as Kent reflected how far he had fallen from the accepted world of learning, not to mention the basic niceties of normal life.

Every discussion that touched on his home in Montana Territory spurred him to return to St. Louis and, hopefully, to an even more wildly independent woman. Conversations with Rand seemed increasingly superficial. Despite Kent's efforts to renew the sharing they had in their youth, or even so recent as their talk in the library, exchanges lacked depth. Perhaps it was the price for his extended absence, for the intervening years and events, he concluded, or perhaps it was a matter of maturing and going their separate ways.

Rand seemed agreeable, settled, and distant. This tendency to generally ignore Kent those last days of his visit conveyed a message—if he'd become a fixture like the hat rack in the hall, it meant Rand had gone on with his life and Kent needed to do the same.

Kent's train rumbled west toward St. Louis, concluding his promised visit home. He felt his spirits lifted by the family reunion, as if he'd released burdens of guilt and regrets. Yet in leaving he had to wrench himself from the lassitude, a low key southern pace that sharply contrasted with the postwar bustle of the North and West. He wanted most to pull himself away from the heaviness that beset his Mother and now had its grip on Rand. Mother's lethargy might be explained by the sedating effects of the opiate-based laudanum, but despite a façade of tranquility, Rand had been robbed of his unquestioned confidence. Remaining though, and reinforced, was Rand's loyalty to family and an idealism that had led him to serve the Union. Kent saw Rand now trying to resurrect the South, while internally he was given to flashbacks, as Elena had said.

Not unlike myself, Kent admitted, knowing he had not been alone in leaving after the war—and carrying the war with him. After the surrender at Appomattox, conflicts between the states continued to rage south and west across the Mississippi, spurred on by General Jeff Davis' refusal to surrender. Kent witnessed stricken, exhausted families with wagon teams going both north and south, hauling their worldly goods in silent processions. He had urged his own horses on faster as if he could outrun the meleé—and his own conscience.

"Lives are inextricably intertwined across the continent," he moaned, "but bah, that's old plowed ground." He grasped for the reality of a new threshold opening for him far from his previous way of life.

His musings were shortly curtailed by plans to meet Miss Marion Patton at the Gateway Hotel near the waterfront. Kent had sent a letter ahead instructing the hotel to reserve rooms under his name, and make reservations on the next northbound riverboat. That done, he paced the rail cars, obsessively worrying whether Marion would forget their plans, or worse, reject their last minute promises. Daily news bulletins littering the cars tried his patience along with the deplorable travel conditions. Capricious winds blew wood smoke inside, leaving a blackened residue, or as readily sent clouds of steam sideways, dampening even the most earnestly starched white collar. In addition, the always prevalent picnic baskets toted over passengers' elbows left trails of crumbs, sticky jam, and crushed soda crackers. Irritated to no end, Kent wiped the seat with a handkerchief prior to sitting down. Amid numerous transfers and delays, he managed to have his suit and shirts cleaned, pressed, and carefully bundled.

At last he arrived in St. Louis, pleased to have reached their destination before Marion to ensure she was not waiting for him—or that she would not come and leave without him. He felt anxious yet obliged to talk with her about embarking on this impulsive riverboat trip, and was more than a little aware she might have changed her mind. Interrupting his thoughts, a noisy group shouldered its way from the ferry landing toward the hotel with Marion in its midst. Several young men took their cue to desist and depart when Kent approached. Overly eager baggage handlers conspicuously turned over responsibility for her trunk when she handed out coins for their service. Kent recalled his first image of the young woman who had arrived in Virginia City—brusque, assertive, self-contained—an image that momentarily set him back. Would he be talking to the back of her bonnet while she pursued business interests? How had they left things between them? That resolved look she had given him? He feared New York could have shot things to hell, until she turned fully toward him.

A fresh glow lit her vibrant features, and he sensed a deeper affection traced her small youthful face. He squeezed her hand, steered her among the crowd, and breathed a prayer of relief.

At the hotel in the hubbub of arrivals and departures the couple shared only public greetings before trailing others to the dining room for a light supper. Long spaces in their conversation invited trivialities. Neither Kent nor Marion flooded the lapses in this uncertain time of readjustment. Kent tried to prepare his heart to accept what she might and might not be willing to give, but his mind took flight with possibilities.

"I'm wondering, Miss Patton, if you feel comfortable traveling with a Montana miner without benefit of nuptials. I might be taking liberties with my assumptions—"

Marion started and squelched a smile, murmuring, "I trusted you in the shadows of high timber the first time I rode with you."

Kent threw his head back with a long burst of laughter. She trusted him in the stable in Coloma, too. She seems to trust her impulses, he decided, and they retired to separate rooms in the hotel.

The next day they prepared to board the Inland Flyer, a Missouri riverboat as Kent had promised, with destination north to Fort Benton, Montana Territory. Kent bought their tickets while Marion supervised loading her now worn trunk. It was assumed they were man and wife, and he said nothing to deny this.

"You are returning from a solo trip to New York City and will no doubt be running the boat before we get to Fort Benton!" His amusement brought her back to his side. He took her arm and walked "Mrs. Berrigan" with her long white gloves and graceful white straw hat on board. Marion's eyes boldly met his twinkling grey gaze. She carried herself like a princess, twirling before him in a full-skirted, green silk gown, exposing slender hightop button shoes that Kent had not seen before.

"You are staring, Kent. A girl must shop in New York, you know. How often will I get such an opportunity to outdo my sister in San Francisco? I had a perfectly delightful time having a few smart dresses fitted by an excellent seamstress while I was there. Are you impressed, or do you prefer the dust coat?"

The foghorn blasted repeatedly as the riverboat shoved off, a ceremonial gesture since there was no fog on such a beautiful, blue-sky day. The swish of waves raised by the sidewheeler's paddles assured a concert they would enjoy for hundreds of miles except for occasional sections of turbulence. The Missouri was characteristically muddy with spring runoff, a disappointment to Marion who had seen the pure, drinkable water of small streams across the Territories and, more recently, enjoyed the sweet water of the Alleghenies that served New York.

Heads turned when they promenaded the upper deck. As a young man in Georgia, Kent had escorted debutantes on scripted coming-out parties, their elegant silk or satin gowns in every hue of the rainbow. Heavily powdered dowagers who felt entitled gave him petite pecks on his cheeks, and spunky young girls flirted with him when chaperones were otherwise engaged. Yet none of this prepared him for escorting Miss Marion Patton. The astounding life and beauty of this New York-styled belle sent his temperature soaring and apparently that of every other male on board.

A bride. She looks like a bride, he thought. On his arm she turned the enormous barrel-shaped skirt of the silk gown, giving a curtsy to acknowledge "Good day," and a tip of her broad-brimmed hat toward women who stared. Men's mouths dropped discreetly out of sight of their wives. The couple turned after the length of the deck and whispered their way back in waltz-like steps, enjoying their own parade.

"You are so beautiful. You will set the boat on fire by creating such envy." Kent tried to suppress a smile that accompanied a constant, crazy feeling of disbelief. Excitement widened her round hazel eyes, sent roses into her cheeks, and a bright coral-red flush into full pouting lips.

"Kent, are you teasing? You have until today only seen me in my riding clothes. Isn't a woman to be admired? Surely you have not been so insulated in your life. These women are beaming at you like bees to honey. You look positively handsome with your beard trimmed so."

He laughed, shaking off nerves he hadn't realized he had. He tugged at his collar; his neck felt hot, tight with tension, with worry whether all would go well. He feared this fleeting dream might be dashed on the first stiff winds catching the riverboat midstream. What then? But Marion appeared enchanted with the slow cranking forward of the shallow draft boat, the faint chords from a string ensemble in the salon, and the awakening of her soul to her own blossoming. Kent's fantasies ran rampantly until he led her in a proprietary manner to the staterooms on the upper deck. He hardly dared think his dreams over the Sierras were about to come true. Marion took one look at the neat, compact room for double occupancy and understood what he had done. She turned, and without wanting to see either amusement or conquest on his face, she ducked into his arms, the "trust" evident in her response. Both gave in to overwhelming longing.

"This cabin is more spacious and comfortable than my shack," Kent warned as elbows and heels knocked on the thin partitions, and their laughter sang with gentle laps of the river, distant shorebirds, and the novelty of personal intimacies.

9

That evening in the dining room Marion's silk dress caught the flickering light of gas lamps and reflected watery green waves around her body. She had tamed her sunburst of gold-rust hair with two inlaid abalone combs Kent had given her.

"Kent, they are beautiful! How the shell catches the light in pink, green and silver! Do I look well-dressed now, dear?" She flirted with a coquettishness he had not seen, tilting her head and smiling as she extended a stylishly shod foot in a kid and cloth button shoe.

Kent's eyes softened. He wanted to sweep her up again but for passengers filing into the room, all bracing against quiet swells of the wide river.

Supper was served from a long, ornate sideboard bearing great urns, tureens, and platters of hot, delicious-smelling dishes. Baskets of warm baked breads shared space between trays of cheeses, fruit and small desserts. Tethered samovars dispensed hot water and apple cider. The smorgasbord offered fare of both East and West. Kent bypassed oysters to select trout and fried potatoes along with steamed collards, not forsaking his Southern roots. Marion chose chicken pot pie over a heavier venison stew or baked ham. Supper became less about the menu than rediscovering each other. The world had turned and neither was in their habitual place or role. Sentences dropped midway, thoughts became disconnected, experiences re-examined—the time they met in a stagecoach with two non-English speaking Germans, the day they embraced in the back of the livery stable, the promise extracted when they went separate ways in St. Louis. Silly plans were suggested and discarded, all becoming part of their shared history. The next days, weeks, and months would hold new stories.

Beneath the shared reflections, Kent sensed Marion's subtle reserve. He felt she tended to quietly appraise him, apparently in wonder at his fascination with her—or she assessed her response to him. He'd like to know more, what she felt and thought. But he was endlessly pleased she kept one hand on his arm as if ensuring that this gentleman of the South belonged to her.

After supper rowdy troubadours bounded into the salon with their banjos and side shows of burnt cork-face Virginia minstrels. The traveling song, "Follow the Drinking Gourd," became louder and increasingly repetitious as the crowd relaxed under the influence of Captain's rum. Kent and Marion slipped out of the noise, heat and humidity to find a small table with two chairs on deck. The evening breeze was not to be missed, nor a moment of their time on the river, yet Marion's attention often remained on her recent journey to New York.

"I felt so alive there, Kent. I walked for miles and miles up Park Avenue and back on Fifth Avenue. Not in these shoes, mind you. Distinguished men in handsome coats and tails paraded with their walking sticks. Women wore enormous feathered hats and great bustles. Despite their adherence to cumbersome fashions, many women are forward-looking and support women's rights. Their movement creates quite a stir among politicians seeking rights for freedmen equal to those of white men. Political leaders fear women's demands for the same rights as freedmen born in the United States would jeopardize the chance of passing the 14th Amendment." The complexity of issues momentarily distracted her. She scanned his face for a reaction.

Seeing none, she continued, "The shopping! My sister, Dora, would have loved it! Massive windows everywhere displayed costly jewelry. Pocket watches with gaudy gold nuggets from California, silver pendants from Mexico, and the loveliest imported ivory cameo brooches. I bought one for Dora, the darling. The shop mailed it to her.

"The hotels, too, were extraordinary. The beautifully restored Colonial with its quaint balconies and stairways was the loveliest. The New Englander with a sea decor served huge platters of fresh lobster! Even San Francisco is rough and pale in comparison. Hacks and carriages made an awful racket up and down cobbled streets. The air fairly buzzed with activity."

Clearly, Marion had fully experienced the dazzle of New York City. Kent sensed he had missed a significant event in her impressionable young life.

"I toured Lower Manhattan's financial district, of course. From what I learned by discreet visits to various offices, these were infinitely wealthy firms of investors exercising great confidence in the future of the United States."

Marion had shifted from a girlish delight to that of a mature observer beyond her now twenty-one years of age. "Union Pacific Railroad and Overland Stage Shipping Company have headquarters there. Sterling's Crocker and Venture mining companies, along with New York First Company and dozens of others were well-represented, clustered on Pine and Nassau Streets near the piers.

"I never tired of exploring New York City with its soap and candle shops, and brokerage firms with shiny brass plaques on the doors. New York seems like a very old city compared to San Francisco. Both are crowded with immigrants speaking dozens of languages. I understand the Irish fare badly in New York. The off streets are like farm lanes with ruts, animals and trash. Considering the wealth I've mentioned, living conditions are shameful for many. I was warned by more than one hotel manager to avoid certain streets and sections of the city. But I wanted to see more of the East so I took a train to Rochester for a brief stay. I found it an enterprising city that would vie with any in California. The main office of Western Union is there, as well as the headquarters of Montana's Midas Mining Company of New York.

"You would be amazed, Kent, at the power and energy driving this country. It is reassuring to find the continent is connected East to West by increasingly modern means of travel and communication." In her enthusiasm, she failed to notice his increasing discomfort while she related her story.

Kent felt a familiar blur of confusion. The reality of the newly unified Union, the unstoppable force that obliterated his former life, seemed to be marching on with or without him now. That he did not yet know his place accounted for the sinking feeling, yet she seemed to sense hers. He watched her face glow with animation, reflecting the beat of New York and perhaps the winds of emancipation for women.

"I telegraphed my father at every opportunity though it is shockingly expensive, and I wrote letters to both Father and Mother. They know I am well and that I am now in good hands." She squeezed his arm, at last roused from the long dream-like travelogue.

Kent quietly held her hand, absorbing the effervescence of Miss Marion Patton who now gazed steadily back at him. I want to propose marriage, he thought, but a wall of caution subdued the impulse. Her interest may be fleeting judging from her experience in New York—would life in the Territory suffice for this woman enamored of New York City? And besides, what could I offer? A shack?

In any event, he had planned for this contingency in case they traveled unmarried. Since she couldn't always wear the customary gloves in public, he slipped a small gold band upon her finger.

"Quite right, Kent. I am safely in your hands." This from the Marion he loved, the Marion who simply stated her feelings but whose deeper feelings were still unknown to him.

They listened to shore birds in the darkening trees. Heavy odors of river mud and slime clung to the boat. Georgia pines faded into a hazy memory as Kent questioned what lay ahead. Uncertainty chased certainty in his thoughts. He wondered about hers. After a time, he stirred to bring his face near hers. His breath, warm on her cheek, captured her full attention. His grey eyes hinted of some concern.

"And what is it you want for yourself, my dear, after all your travels and experiences?" he asked with an undercurrent of apprehension.

"I want you, Kent."

"Honored, Mrs. Berrigan!"

He bowed over her hand and they rose to go inside, his arm encircling her waist. Kent wiped his brow and stifled a sigh, knowing he'd not reopen the subject for fear she might change her mind.

———

The Inland Flyer claimed a romantic interlude before the test of northern waters. The season favored river traffic, encouraging more than the usual number of boats to navigate turgid spring runoff in channels of the upper Missouri to Fort Benton. However, long gone were sumptuous smorgasbords and troubadours. Fare often consisted of venison or buffalo hunted on shore by rough woodsmen who cut fuel for the boat's steam engines. The lucrative business of carrying up to 650 tons of cargo on the 250-foot-long boat took precedence over comfort of the passengers. Midway a few passengers chose to travel by wagon train on an overland route towards the Yellowstone River. Kent determined that he and Marion would brave the currents to the furthermost inland port in the United States. Luck afforded them rare good weather and river conditions for their May arrival.

Cheers sounded from Signal Point when their riverboat rounded a bend between steep, dark slopes. They docked at the levee among other veteran riverboats, keelboats and smaller steamboats. If the Missouri had its jaw-dropping turbulence at times, Fort Benton's Front Street was little different with swarms of freighters and teams. The adobe Fort opened wide for business, an already legendary trading partner with Indians, trappers and hunters, and a perpetual stream of newcomers. Trading stores, saloons, and shipping company offices crowded along the street. Mounds of cargo dwarfed men who toiled to supply northern outposts for winter, while relieving them of furs, buffalo hides, grain, and gold destined for the East. Seldom were so many oxen teams seen in one place as those lined up to load or unload a succession of wagons on the levee at Fort Benton. Tipis silhouetted against the western skyline spoke of inhabitants of the land, their colorful tribesmen longtime traders at forts on the Missouri.

Kent and Marion quickly boarded one of a string of stagecoaches for the three hundred mile trip to Sterling on the well established Mullen Road that passed through Helena. The coach sped west day and night, stopping every ten to fifteen miles for a change of horses at 28 Mile Springs, Birdtail Divide, Sun River, Sieben, Little Prickly Pear, Silver City and others on the way to Helena. With increased anticipation Kent and Marion departed Helena for the final leg to Sterling. News spread that the ramshackle gold camp had become one of the largest towns of the Territory. Kent wasn't sure what to expect since he'd left the previous fall—a disappointing rougher version of the camp where Jake had been shot, or a relatively livable center offering basic amenities.

He soon found that Hot Spring District had gained a population of five hundred or so and Sterling had attracted a slew of saloons, two boarding houses, two hotels and a half-dozen blacksmith shops, in addition to livery stables, general stores, and a billiard hall. Relieved to find Callahans' boarding house, Kent and Marion stopped there first to greet friends and collect Shag and Ben.

"I went away one and returned as two," Kent beamed, introducing Marion. Harland grasped Kent's shoulder and gave him a hearty clap on the back. "You might recall her brief visit here last year. It was a turn-around stage stop, but we ate dinner here."

"I remember her." Angel uncharacteristically sucked her thumb, betraying her sense of ownership of the children's favorite customer.

"Shush. Children should be seen, not heard," Mrs. Callahan warned. Angel and Finn ducked behind their mother's flowing apron, staring in wonderment at this woman's takeover of their own Mr. Berrigan. Mrs. Callahan curtsied, a brief formal dip of her ample waist, and managed to keep her always busy hands to herself.

"I am a bit surprised to find myself back here," Marion interrupted, "but I do recall a tasty shepherd's pie. Your children are lovely." Angel's shy smile revealed she'd lost two front teeth. Finn had nearly outgrown his short knickers.

Behind the Callahans, dishes clattered to the floor. Miners' dropped their forks and shoved back the long bench beside the dining table. Chairs scraped rough wooden floorboards as other customers scurried aside to avoid the conflict.

Harland spun around. "Give me a hand," he gestured to Kent, "Benson is starting a fight."

"Dirty treasonists, the lot of ye." Benson punched futilely at a big newcomer across the long table. The newcomer and his partners dressed in business clothes rose to face the blistering miner wearing suspenders over a red flannel shirt. "Ye ain't to be braggin' about selling guns that killed my pa," Benson thundered.

Kent and Harland whisked the Rebel out the door, but not before he denounced the Northerners for profiting from the war.

"They're backed by Hadley and Sons Arms Company," he growled. "What are they doin' here? We oughtn't put up with them who committed treason against us."

Mrs. Callahan eyed the newcomers. "Ye get out, too. Ain't ye got no manners nor upbringing to be around decent folks?" Swinging a broom, her shapeless loose dress bunching over wide hips, she chased the unsuspecting offenders into the dirt road in front of the boarding house. With a last sweeping flourish, she wiped her hands on her apron. The culprits sought refuge in the crowd and dust.

"Ye folks sit down and have dinner," she gestured towards Kent and Marion, and went to tend the fire blazing in a double-oven cookstove.

"There's always trouble brewing, and ye's got trouble about the claims," Harland was quick to say after the upset and uneasy formalities. "'Tis Crocker Mining Company. They're moving more equipment and men into Hot Spring District this week."

"Possibly that is good news if the rate of return on the mines has picked up that much," Kent said. "This could mean a substantial boost in all of our prospects."

"No, no good news for ye, sir," Harland insisted. "To be sure ye been away a long time, and they found out you left the country. I 'spect they think yer didn't prove up on yer claims. They grab claims that's been abandoned."

Kent quickly determined that Harland's warning came none to soon since he'd extended his trip to travel south, but he turned to Marion to assure her, as well as the faithful Callahans, that he would take care of it. "Right after more important business of having Mrs. Callahan's famous dinner and looking after Shag and Ben."

The children bolted outside to release the dog. Shag streaked into Kent's waiting arms as he knelt to greet her, a wriggling bundle of shaggy hair whose wet tongue licked Kent's hands and face in a flurry of kisses. Her eyes searched his, inquiring uncertainly if he would stay, a cinnamon brow quirking in anxiety. Kent gave her an extra hug, ruffling the white collar around her neck, his eyes moist in gratitude for her loyalty.

"I hope Ben doesn't get this excited," Kent said, trying to regain his balance. They laughed and went to see the "thoroughbred" he joked about. Ben cantered in from the hill pasture at Kent's whistle. A huge sense of relief welled up in Kent's throat. Home. This time he sensed home was here in Sterling with his gelding nuzzling his shoulder in the old familiar way, and his dog nudging his legs for attention.

Marion quietly watched the emotional reunion, sobered by the depth she witnessed in Kent. "You seem like part of the country here, the land and horses and people. I feel as though I'm seeing you for the first time in a different light."

Kent beamed, clearly revealing he felt he had it all—or least all that mattered.

They leased a sorrel horse, Rusty, from the livery stable for Marion. If she liked him she could discuss a long term arrangement or purchase the horse.

After Mrs. Callahan's hearty pot roast and potato dinner, they packed an accumulation of mail and old *Montana Post* newspapers and left for the shack. The Sterling-Norwegian Creek road was well traveled by increased traffic due to new mines and mills in the District. Soon the stark outline of Kent's weathered shack came into view over the hilltop. The privy sat well back from the building, and a hand pump stood outside the front door. Shag had reconnoitered the entire place and made her second or third lap when the riders reached the corral and turned in their horses.

Kent shouldered open the heavy wooden door of the shack, its oversize hinges squeaking mightily from disuse. He stepped in ahead of Marion, unsure if mice, rats or snakes would scurry past his feet to make their escape. The late afternoon sun flooded the interior through a south-facing window. Marion followed, her heels tapping a hollow sound on the wide, bare boards that served as flooring. In took her about a minute to inventory the entire contents of the one room home she would now occupy, but for Kent it took a bit longer.

"My sheepskin leggings and work boots are missing," he noted right away. "And it looks like someone made coffee, judging from the dirty cups by the wash pan. It could be worse considering I've been away over the winter and spring months. Indeed, it would have been worse if Harland was right about the scam—"

Words fell unattended on Marion's aimless rounds of her new home. Grasping her sense of shock at this first impression, Kent stopped in mid-sentence, seeing the shack as she might view it. Overcome by her hesitation and her presence in what had been his sole domain, he took her into his arms. Choking, he held her against his throbbing chest.

"Marion—." He tried again, "Marion, my deepest wish is that you might be happy—with me—here with all its shortcomings. That we can be happy together and—." Promises rushed like a waterfall through his mind only to be cast aside unsaid, promises he feared he couldn't keep; assurances he'd like to express were discarded as being exceedingly foolish in the stark circumstances.

"Are you up for this, my Marion? A prospector's life—?"

Her flyaway hair lay soft on his cheek. The refusal he'd half-expected did not occur. Her energy vibrated against the length of his body, the warmth reassuring to him, flushing his ardor. Silent prayers he hadn't said in years tumbled about. She's so young, so precious, so wise, thank you, Lord. His eyes wet, he smiled into her upturned face.

"So lovely, so much a woman," he said aloud. She laughed, a throaty chuckle as grounded in her person as her sense of adventure. She held him at arms' length, at once taking charge of his uncertainties and her own future in the Territory.

"I'm not sure my father would exactly say that. He still sees me as a child."

"Tis' my good fortune to be your husband, not your father. And as your husband, I need to do something about extending this single bunk until we establish a suitable home."

Marion moved around the limited confines of the room, checking out the Dutch oven on the back of the half-barrel stove and the large cast iron skillet hung from a hook above.

"I hope they have a lot of canned goods at the mercantile. Father always retained a cook. Most of what I know I learned from camp cooks on the wagon trains—beans, salt pork and biscuits."

"We'll live! I can cook an elk steak you can't beat anywhere. We'll have plenty of meat starting this fall when the weather turns cold." This time Kent felt he could be fairly confident in his assurance.

———

Several days later two men in a buggy drove up the Norwegian Creek road and stopped at Kent's shack. Kent recognized the man wearing a top hat as the Crocker Mining Company representative he met at the boarding house a year ago. The gentlemen came over to greet Kent.

"Good day. I am Chester Johnson from Springfield, Illinois. You may be acquainted with Mr. James Morgan from Virginia City." Johnson held a sizeable leather portfolio and did not offer a handshake. "I – we – did not expect anyone to be here. I believe you are Mr. Berrigan if I recall correctly from a chance encounter in the boarding house." Kent had not acknowledged either man, in fact, the very mention of Springfield, Illinois, set his teeth ajar.

Silence was all Mr. Johnson needed to assert "Norwegian Creek is in our hands now." He patted the portfolio. "Crocker Mining Company whom we represent has acquired abandoned claims up and down the creek. Even settlers who are disinterested in mining have sold claims on their properties for substantial remuneration. However, our records indicate you are the owner of claims that have not been worked or maintained for a year. As you know, that represents a breach of ownership. Therefore, the claims have come into our possession."

Mr. Morgan cleared his throat and stepped forward. "Titles to all your claims have been deeded to Crocker Mining Company by the Clerk and Recorder's office. You retain title to the property because mineral rights are deeded separately. I'm sorry you and the – uh – missus seem to find this a surprise."

Kent moved toward the men, his boots crunching the dirt walkway. He was hatless with sleeves rolled up, his voice even and firm. "I worked all of the claims steadily with the assistance of two young miners less than a year ago. I understand Patrick and Jackson Colter are still in the area. They will attest to that." He stared pointedly at James Morgan whom he knew to be County Justice of the Peace. "Moreover, your visit here was uninvited and it is unwelcome."

Chester Johnson waved his arm towards a series of corner posts on Kent's claims, his rage knocking his hat askew and flapping his coattails. "I sent two wagons and four men to your farthest claim to load ore stacked there. I am sure you do not want to make this difficult, Mr. Berrigan. The rights are ours now, and legally you cannot deny us access to the claims."

Marion shuffled her feet in the doorway and held a tight grip on Shag. Kent glanced around to find her looking alarmed.

"Let me see those papers." Kent extended his hand while Mr. Johnson righted his hat and dug in the file for the requested documents. Mr. Morgan snatched the papers and pushed them near Kent's face.

Kent could see at once the dates had been altered from the time of filing to lengthen the time he'd been away. The claims were false. Another form stated abandonment based on failure to maintain the claims within the past year.

"I'm sorry gentlemen. As you can see for yourselves, I am very much present, which obviously comes as a surprise to you.

I intend to maintain ownership. Assay reports will verify that I was here last fall, and that the claims were worked, except for winter months, well within time constraints. You have no legitimate basis for this presumptive action. Good day. And call off your damn ore wagons."

Shag rumbled with a low growl, and Kent stomped back to the shack. After a bit of wrangling among themselves, the officials boarded the buggy and lashed the team to hurry down the road. Threats of immediate removal of the ore appeared untrue. No other outfits came up the road or across the property. This wait and watch was not the homecoming Kent wanted for Marion, but it was, in essence, one all too familiar to her from gold camps in California.

"I understand," she said softly. "It is not unknown for those invested in mining affairs to engage in theft. Indeed, it's all too tempting and easy for men with money and power."

They sat in the shade on the step, Kent holding her free hand while her other restrained Shag. "I'm sorry, Marion. After Benson instigated a fight, I didn't need another hassle. I could use a stiff drink. Rand kept a bottle of Old Jake Beam on a sideboard." He sighed, at loss for a drink and a peaceful homecoming. "Confrontation is not in my character, but they won't get my claims." His voice sounded more steely than he felt.

"Not with all of us!" Marion playfully nudged him, "And how about the neighbors? I wonder if they went through the same thing while you were gone."

Within the next few weeks they visited the Williams, Colter brothers, and others to establish solidarity. However, they found that the people who had taken over Jake's place had moved away, and others were forced off Norwegian Creek. A few had sold out. Only a little gold deposited in pockets by spring runoff showed in the creek, discouraging prospectors. The trend toward hardrock mining accelerated, leading to aggressive measures such as those practiced by Crocker to supply ore for their mills. The upshot was a community disturbed by pressure from Crocker and other large mining companies.

"I'm damn lucky to have returned home in time." Kent drew Marion's to him and silently thanked a benevolent God or guiding star that blessed his path in more ways than he could count.

The strikingly clear, sharp air of Montana Territory constantly amazed Marion. "It has a heady bite of pure exhilaration," she told Kent, "so unlike anywhere else."

Buoyed by the novelty of being married, she spent her days relishing her own becoming—becoming a woman, becoming one with Kent. The expanded cot had its challenges, but it comfortably nested two. Her restless touch smoothed his brow, his beard, the firm ridge of his nose and strong cords of his neck. "I'd like to find ways to let you know how much I care—," words lost in his smothering kisses.

"I'll take this," he murmured.

They shared cooking and washing clothes, and she eagerly pitched in to help work the claims and property. Early June prompted farm work. They plowed a few acres with borrowed implements, turning resisting native sod into pliable soil for planting. Marion led Ben, thoroughbred-Percheron converted to plowhorse, up and down the rows. Kent bent over the plow's hardwood handles, guiding the recalcitrant machine in straight furrows. At the end of each row, Ben looked back with soft brown eyes as if to chalk up progress the three of them were making. Kent debated the merits of different crops they might plant, but not having sufficient experience at this altitude he failed to reach a decision.

"Next spring will be soon enough to plant. I need to ask the settlers for advice. I hadn't expected to suddenly identify with Rand's agronomist tendencies."

Their reward after a hard day was a leisurely walk up Norwegian Creek. Kent had long ago widened the creek for a lazy channel to accumulate a proper depth for bathing behind large boulders. There, a chilly current sought the deep pool sheltered by crusty junipers, the water so clear a collage of rocks on the bottom shone with brilliant rusts, yellow-browns, purples and copper greens. Kent and Marion stripped and slipped in with little yips prompted by the cold. Their bare skin lay on slick rocks, chests heaved in air cooled by snowmelt.

Her lips lightly traced the outlines of his wide mouth under a dark uneven moustache, her breath strummed soft and shallow as his hand fondled her hair. His beard wet, heavy, brushed her cheek while toes fluttered in depths of the mountain pool. Low chokecherry boughs caressed her white shoulders. A thorny twig of wild rose swirled with the current, enticing pale blue juniper berries to be fellow travelers downstream.

For Marion, the world becomes enchanted and enveloped in mystical hues, the present moment sharpened by a planetary cold. A dream—she feels as though she awakens in a watery dream of wild horse and man. She envisions Kent's hand in Big Ben's tangled black mane. His long slim fingers draw small circles on the damp hide, the touch alone speaking to Ben from his heart. Ben yields to the touch, his great head arching toward Kent, equine lips forming words of joining.

What kind of man knows the soul of a wild horse? In the quiet splendor of man and woman in nature, she breathes in his ear, "I know not with whom I share this forbidden swim, nor do I truly know myself." Unknowns cluster behind her half closed lids. A sense of timelessness coalesces images of man and horse, man and woman, yearning, trusting. Marion senses the boy in him, he who would have forgotten supper when foals were born, he who gathered wounded birds in warm towels in a basket.

"You must have been terribly hurt to feel so deeply," she whispers. His eyes open, wondering. He nods yes and no as if the notion were purely inconsequential. His tanned face reflected in the placid surface is serene, his skin white above the line of his hatband. A bronze arm captures her tiny waist drawing her chilled porcelain body into his embrace, leaving small ripples to entertain themselves. Elderberry leaves drift into quiet eddies, bunch like a congregation of ballerinas, then swoop over the boulders on a surge of waves.

Marion feels a sense of weightlessness buoyed by his arm lifting her haunches in the pool, unburdened by cares. Toes seek the silty bottom among mossy stones. He draws her slight form into the cocoon of his lean bare body. She nuzzles like the gelding into his beard believing the wild horse wouldn't love Kent so if he were but empty promises.

"This feeling, this feeling, I do not know why I am drawn to you, so much a stranger to myself," Marion muses. But his hands tell her she is cherished in more ways than she can name. The stream, scented with juniper, sage and wild roses cools his neck, inviting a taste. She kisses his fleshy lower lip, hot and split by the mountain sun.

High on this creek in 1867 nature is as its best, the way it was before Lewis and Clark, before trappers and hunters and Natives, even millennias before time was recorded. Forces heated and compressed strata containing gold-bearing veins deep inside the earth, and relentlessly urged granite to the surface. Weathering exposed oxidized ore, where the bumbling efforts of man discovered "free gold" that easily separated from other minerals.

"So silly in the vast sequence of things," Kent and Marion agree while claiming their secluded spot beneath fragrant junipers, swim, talk, and make love. They knew mankind could not improve on this pristine landscape running from Preacher Creek on the ridge of the Tobacco Roots to the Madison River below. As they walk down the hill, a cursory glance follows the line of intrusive corner posts on Kent's claims marring the landscape.

10

Marion frequently took Ben with their newly acquired wagon for a drive to the mercantile in Sterling, more as a social outing than a shopping trip. One day she came bouncing into the shack with a large box from California delivered by stagecoach.

"Something from Dora! I can hardly wait to see." She slit yards of string with a fillet knife then carefully removed layer after layer of brown wrapping paper, since paper found a second or third afterlife in the Territories. On top of the gift was a note from Dora saying she was excited about Marion being on the "frontier," and discreetly did not press for details—a concession from Dora who would never drag her gowns through dirty camps, who believed they were inhabited by common criminals. Marion lifted out an extra large, hand-stitched patchwork quilt, Dora's artful style in every choice of blues, lavenders, and purples worked into an abstract design representing mountains.

"Bless her, dear Dora! She could not be more thoughtful and kind. All those beautiful stitches and so much ticking—it is really heavy. See, it is for both of us." Marion spread the splendidly colorful quilt over the entire bunk, its well padded edges hanging below the sides. She sat down upon it and turned the corner to feel the thick, baby-soft flannel on the underside. She looked up at Kent with misty eyes, for once speechless and caught in an inexpressible tide of emotion.

Kent planned their trip to Virginia City as a holiday among the bourgeoisie in the "City," after they righted the Crocker infringement on Kent's claims, but the distasteful nature of the business threatened to steal the joy. He sided with angry miners of Hot Spring District who raised the problem of claim jumping, a practice Crocker had blatantly attempted in an effort to steal his claims. The Justice of the Peace, Mr. James Morgan, who had accompanied Crocker's representative to Kent's place, was implicated in the scheme. In addition, other insiders gained undue advantages, a hot campaign issue. Seats for Territorial representatives, local sheriff, coroner, and justice of the peace were up in the next election.

"This election can't come too soon to suit me," Kent told Marion. Norwegian Creek offered its most vociferous candidates. Sheer numbers of Southern Democrats there seemed likely to tip the vote.

Given her lively interest in business, Kent briefed Marion on the historical background of the area. Shortly after the 1864 gold strike by William Fairweather in Alder Gulch, the entire gulch was staked around small camps for fifteen miles to the summit. The largest camp on Daylight Creek was soon incorporated and its first officials elected.

With a population of prospectors, opportunists and ne'er-do-wells, Madison County was established by an Act of the First Territorial Legislature with Virginia City as county seat. The county, as chaotic and lawless as it appeared, was governed by civic-minded men who were instrumental in swiping the designation of Territorial capital from Bannack. Part of the coming of age of the city was acquisition of the telegraph that ran between Virginia City and Salt Lake City, linking the remote outpost to the States.

In Virginia City, Kent left Marion at Rank's Drug Store to enjoy society lacking on Norwegian Creek. He proceeded to the Clerk and Recorder's office, a frame building on west Idaho Street. Kent hoped the impertinent young man he'd met before would not be present. The gunny sacks of claims papers and applications had been replaced by substantial files. Several older clerks wrestled thick, bound record books. Kent presented documents verifying his presence on Norwegian Creek the previous fall, and that he'd worked the claims in a timely manner.

"Protecting the rights of citizens is a duty of this office." Kent flashed a card with his name and employment as an accountant in Auburn, California.

The clerk closely examined the papers, ducking his face behind the high oak counter so that his thin hair, greased straight back on the top of his head, was all Kent could see.

"These have—umm—irregularities not associated with our office. I assure you, our books are in good order. If any monkey business occurs, it is outside of this office." He produced the original filing record with the correct dates corresponding to Kent's receipts. "This is not the first case of claim jumping called to our attention, nor will it be the last. You could help by reporting names of transgressors, and I suggest you serve in county government yourself."

Kent left fuming with contempt at how cheating, robbery and murder often eluded the hands of justice in Montana Territory—a notion in keeping with Harland Callahan's views. Claim jumping was considered a long and honorable practice in the eyes of many. The code of the West went only so far. Kent briefly considered serving in some capacity on behalf of small miners like himself. He was well aware miners demanded adherence to historic mining regulations, and that they had created rules for local conditions. From the first discovery in Alder Gulch it was essential to establish legitimacy of mining operations. Regulations designated length and width of claims which had to be acquired by filing, purchase or preemption. Other than in winter months, at least three days' work had to be done each week to maintain ownership.

Kent also knew that Hot Spring District's rules varied from these due to different conditions, but the principle was the same—claims must be worked except in winter.

"I stretched the time considerably by traveling east," he admitted; nevertheless, the Crocker scheme hadn't been processed legitimately.

Seeking recourse in miners' court seldom proved to be an unbiased experience. Jurors often included those present or twelve selected men. In either case, most were drunk, partisan, or both, and decisions were arrived at accordingly. Kent headed up Boot Hill to work off seething anger before he met with Marion at the drugstore. Coming upon still raw, upturned dirt of road agents' graves, he found them a sobering reminder of so-called justice. The Vigilantes had been disbanded due to their own notoriety the previous year (1866). Kent hastened on, shaking the gloom associated with the hangings. He resolved to relish the sunshine and a few days break from mining to enjoy the woman he loved. He checked his breast pocket to be sure a surprise gift for Marion was safely tucked inside.

From Boot Hill he gazed across town, noting it was remarkably well developed since his visit a year ago. The narrow gulch above Daylight Creek held Virginia City's packed commercial strip within its steep confines. Kent circled east of town then back down Cover Street where a few Victorian houses with window glass replaced shabby cabins with oiled paper panes. H.S. Gilbert Brewery occupied the corner of Boot Hill Street and Cover, its false front wafting heady fumes of *Kolsch* ale, a specialty of its German proprietors.

The chatter and garble of many languages dominated the west end of town. A brace of shacks represented Chinatown, its pervasive scent of burning sandalwood distinct amid the scent of pine and sage in the mountain air. Clotheslines strung with suggestive women's clothing signaled residences of women of the night, Chinese and whites.

"We transplant ourselves with the same human conditions," Kent muttered, and spun around past the "elephant corral," a so-named horse corral along the creek. There a sprawling lumber yard occupied the back alleys of several blocks below Wallace Street. Workmen everywhere bent, lifted, and hauled mining tools and supplies—tons of buckets, stoves, pickaxes, wagon wheels, and food. Kent glimpsed men in articles of blue or grey uniforms that served as a change of duds from the miners' rough hickory shirts and pants, though these often ignited lingering resentments.

Kent did not want to ruin the "big city" occasion for Marion, but he found it hard to shake his mood. On Wallace Street he thrust back his shoulders and attended to new signs among venerable ones above the boardwalk—saloons, barbershop, general store, blacksmith and boot shops, and the telegraph office where Marion kept in touch with her father. On an impulse, he stepped inside the dimly lit barbershop with its small kerosene sconces beside a mirror on the wall. The only other light came through glass-paned windows on the narrow front of the building.

The genial old barber Kent had met before "was taken by pneumonia last winter and had to go south for his health," according to a younger man with a small, perfectly trimmed moustache. After relieving Kent of his bushy beard, he performed miracles with his equally dense moustache, allowing its ends to droop fashionably long. He trimmed Kent's sideburns along the jaw line, and eyed the mop of black hair flopping to one side. With a stroke or two he deftly combed the hair straight back and waited for Kent's reaction in the mirror.

"Oh, ho, I don't know who that is all of a sudden," Kent said of his reflection, but he knew he'd never accept the hairstyle of the clerk in the Recorder's office.

In a moment the barber styled it symmetrically with a deep part down the middle. "Say, I'd feel like a schoolboy with that look. How about taking a lot off the top and leaving the length in the back?"

Twenty minutes later he left his mood and a lot of hair behind. He stepped lightly up the street past Wells Fargo Overland Mail and Express Office, but not without stopping for cigars in the tobacco shop. He found Marion at Rank's Drug visiting with a young man in thick glasses whose hair was parted down the middle. Kent figured he knew where that haircut came from—and merrily swooped in to reclaim Marion.

"Where have you been? You go out a grubstaker and come back a complete gentleman! Won't you dare say?" she asked the young man who solemnly nodded. Marion patted Kent's sideburns and tweaked the ends of the moustache as if she couldn't believe the transformation. "Kent, you devil, whatever has got into you?"

He laughed and noted Marion had refreshed in their room at a nearby hotel and now wore the green silk gown from New York City. She had captured her fly-away hair with the abalone shell combs into the matronly bun of a married woman. He swept her out the door and up the street to one of his favorite places, the Varina Inn, that served a Southern-style supper in a refurbished dining hall. Dark maroon wallpaper touched with tiny gold lines gave a rather elegant appearance to the room. Low chandeliers with small kerosene lamps hung over the tables. Kent chose a corner for two where heavy velvet drapes tied back with gold cords created an intimate setting. Marion's eyes shone with pleasure, her excitement a mixture of youthful exuberance and the maturity she had revealed on the riverboat. Kent felt more grateful than he could say for her enduring spirit on what her sister called the "frontier." He pulled a small box from his inside pocket and placed a second ring on her finger.

"Kent—"

"You really must wear Norwegian Creek gold, darling. I had it made of gold we mined from *The Marion*. Did I tell you how much I adore you?"

Marion's stared wide-eyed at the man she barely recognized with sideburns and a stylish moustache. His twinkling eyes and heartwarming smile meant he chose to marry her again. Marion's voice became low, muffled. An uncharacteristic silence betrayed the depth of her emotion.

"Are you really the Kent I know?" she wondered aloud. "Or some amazing gentleman who keeps surprising me? Kent of the tender touch and daily thoughtfulness. You probably don't think I notice, but I do." She glanced around to see if anyone could overhear. "And surprising me in our pool in the creek!"

They laughed, the intimacy living again in memory, circulating within the narrow scope of their lives, invisibly binding them together.

Kent flushed. "We need to do that again."

Marion looked at the ceiling, her plate, her hands in her lap—and chewed her lip as if nothing in her previous life prepared her for dissolving into someone else's arms, life, dreams. Misty-eyed, she fingered the ring, lapsed into a quiet moment, then murmured, "I adore you, too."

Weeks went by and Kent focused on his claims with renewed energy. Summer days registered hotter in the dry climate at high altitude. He stripped off his shirt and bent more determinedly over the stout hickory-handled pick. His hands, rough and calloused already, became red and splotchy with sunburn. He had heard no more from Crocker Mining Company of New York and hoped the threat would go away. More pleasant thoughts replaced the worry since his honeymoon in Virginia City with the always sparkling Marion Patton. At unexpected times they recaptured moments in the Varina Inn, and talked of the perfect day at a forum in the grove of aspens on the upper reaches of Daylight Creek. Bearded souls had foot-stomped to tunes from a jaw harp. Literati had emerged to recite lengthy, heart-rending poetry, others expounded in German to the delight of knowing immigrants, and some read tattered classics offering bits of philosophy that were doubtlessly lost on many.

Women had opened great picnic baskets on blankets spread on the grass while children climbed trees or tried to catch minnows in the stream. Men gathered in small groups energetically discussing politics of the day or yields of their mining operations. From occasional boisterous laughter, it was suspected they surreptitiously passed around a flask or two—likely white lightning from a Southerner's hidden still, the recipe adapted to local ingredients.

Marion filled the weeks following their honeymoon with new enthusiasm, exploring the Tobacco Roots area where she had made her home. One day she ventured an idea she'd been considering for a few weeks.

"Kent, what would you think if I did not buy Rusty after all, but purchased a brood mare instead? I am in the mind to raise a few good foals that might form the basis for a horse breeding enterprise. I recall you once pursued that interest yourself."

"Of course, of course. We could certainly do better for horseflesh than Rusty, though he has been a reliable saddle horse in the meantime. Yes, do look into the matter at your own discretion. It may be a very rewarding enterprise for you, for us."

Knowing Marion's active nature and inquisitiveness, Kent was pleased to hear of her trips to town and neighboring farms to inquire where a suitable brood mare might be found. Unfortunately, horses in the Territories were generally brought in as trail or work horses, not for improving a breed. In fact, the reverse was true. Many were crossed with the free-roaming wild horses Kent loved, but whose attributes often included knobby knees, splayed hooves or Roman noses. Her quest so far had been futile.

"I need to find a mare bred for giving birth early next year. The difficulty of getting started in any meaningful way in this part of the country is tiresome."

"We can have a suitable mare sent from good Southern stock as soon as we can afford it. We may have built a home and proper horse facilities by that time." Kent felt stirred by the notion of incorporating past pleasures he'd known into their present lives.

"I'm not sure how I will occupy myself in the meantime," Marion said, making a mental note to whitewash the smoke-blackened wall behind the cookstove with calcimine.

Summer progressed and the shack, with its weather-stained vertical board exterior, remained the same as when the couple came from the East, except for a covered porch over the front door. They added a lean-to on the back to shelter a huge wood-pile of logs Ben had pulled from the timber for them. A larger corral had been constructed for the two horses, but that did not make the place high-class by any means.

"What do you want, Kent? I mean what do you want for yourself? Is it just go along with the diggings and homestead?" Marion's voice was careful but upset. "To be sure, progress has been made on the claims. I do not want to hurt you, Kent, but there is little evidence of anything else."

Marion sat with one leg crossed over the other, her riding boot tapping a restless beat on the wood floor. A fresh sunburn brought out freckles on her nose and cheeks, and lent color to strong forearms resting in her lap. A pout played over her lips, quickly replaced with the resolute voice she used with her father.

"The world moves on elsewhere and it seems no one notices on Norwegian Creek. Or perhaps no one cares. It is a strange world for me, you understand. Even though I was raised in the camps, the industriousness meant they were alive and indeed booming at times. Men had their visions of greatness or wealth or holdings, all of which contributed to a vigor among the workers and families."

The air in the shack felt close, sapped of its life-giving energy.

"I need to be a part of something much greater than I have ever dreamed, yet I am practically lost in the Territories."

Kent felt himself gulping down alarm, unable to address her dream—or his own.

"What do you really want?" she queried again in a strident tone that Kent was totally unaccustomed to hearing. "I do not know you sometimes. I see you with your shoulder to the plow when you once had others do such work. I fail to understand where your heart really lies." Her eyes dared, yet pleaded with him.

"You're right," he laughed uncomfortably. "I'm as much a misfit here as my former horses, Donegal and Bonnie, would have been. I never expected to settle in Montana Territory, but since I arrived two years ago I find this country gripping—it draws me back—the air, the stillness. I need that kind of peace." His brow knitted in an effort to deal with Marion's immediate confrontation.

"And I know I need you, Marion. I want you to be content. We will find a direction that will satisfy both of us. Your ambition is enough for two!"

Coffee cups clanked on the table while bacon congealed in the pan. Marion paced back and forth in the tiny room then sat down, the tension forcing Shag outdoors.

"Father had ambition—to be sure it drove my mother away, but I can understand his need to try things, to make multiple, if risky investments. All investors gamble in one way or another." Marion's voice became defensive. Her glance surveyed the dark interior of the shack and came back to Kent's sad expression.

"Perhaps it isn't in me to gamble," Kent said, "but my life has been unfolding in ways I never expected. I want to purchase land where potential for good hay and crops is greater than it is up this high. We could select a nice piece of property by a stream and build a house, Marion. With the increasing number of settlers, it would be prudent to obtain more land while we can."

Surveys undertaken by the government would soon elevate the profile of the vicinity. Until then claims, farms, and ranches featured creative if not chaotic boundaries. Residents were technically squatters for lack of exact ownership.

Kent's plans went right over Marion's flushed face and frizzy head of hair. Her round eyes sparked. "You seem to have a dream. Sometimes I don't know what I want. I do see great potential for businesses in the Rocky Mountains, but I'm not sure where I fit in, whether your dream would be mine. We are very different individuals. What is it about us? What do we have in common?"

The uncertainty Kent so often experienced rose in his gut with a familiar rush of panic. He couldn't reply, not that he knew the answer. Long days and nights of gradually finding his bearings now felt threatened by a logic he couldn't contest.

Marion rose, shifting her slight frame as if to move from one station in life to another, to put a strong face toward the world and a defense against the anxiety in her foot. She picked up her hat. "I'm going for a ride."

"Take Ben. He's in the corral."

After she galloped away heading east, Kent saw the interior of the shack through her eyes. Cast iron frying pans hung from nails behind the barrel stove. She had whitewashed a section of wall and hung a bit of muslin over shelves to protect dishes from dust and flies. The pail of water for inside use sat on a counter below the front window, while a dishpan and enamel wash basin remained outside during the summer. Kent realized he had let himself become equally shabby. Untrimmed, his beard had grown well down on his neck and his moustache trailed over his lips.

"Hell, I'm twenty-eight and probably look like an old man." His hair felt greasy with dirt and sweat since they hadn't bathed in the creek for awhile. "High time for a bath," he muttered, setting the galvanized wash tub in front of the stove for lack of a better response to Marion's demands.

Deeply disturbed, Kent recognized his ingrained childhood fear that a marriage could be irreparably broken, that one could disappear as his father had. He'd proven he was also capable of fleeing. Now this underlying sense of impermanence amplified his current fears. But Marion? She was so straightforward. Surely they could make better choices together.

He had to leave the bath and puzzling question of life's choices for later. The Colter brothers showed up, men he'd hired to relieve himself and Marion of heavy work. The fraternal twins, Patrick and Jackson, had agreed to provide day labor to augment diminishing returns from their own claims past Jake's old place on Norwegian Creek. Since many miners had recently joined a hastily organized militia, Kent felt lucky to get two good men. Indian troubles on the Bozeman Trail east of the Yellowstone River had unsettled the population. A massacre of eighty-one soldiers at Fort Kearney, Wyoming, in December the previous year alerted settlers and miners alike of the need for a strong military presence to guard against the Sioux, fierce Plains warriors defending their hunting grounds. General Thomas Meagher, Montana Territory's acting governor, called up six hundred men through late spring and summer of 1867. As a consequence, men from Virginia City and Sterling, many with military experience during the war, had been pressed into service.

Today, the trio met at Kent's place where Kent outlined the task at hand. "I'll have my neighbor blast my hard rock claims one more time this fall, then hold off until spring. I'm not an expert at handling that quantity of black powder, believe me. We may run into snow before we get the ore to the mill."

Kent started the men processing dirt and gravel from the last blast in a sluice box near the creek. They knew their jobs and worked without a break until lunch. Kent joined them beneath the shade of willow saplings hugging the water's edge. Western bluebirds flitted along edges of ravines and the sharp scent of yarrow crushed by their boots filled the air. They chewed hard tack and drank from the stream. Shag chased low flying killdeer whose melon-colored back feathers and ringing trill led the dog away from their nests.

"I expect to be moving on after this job," Jackson said. "I might go back to Boston and see the folks." He was young, maybe twenty, with an abundance of freckles and good manners that stood out in a crowd. Kent enjoyed the men who were more refined and educated than many of the miners.

"I'll be sorry to lose you, Jackson. You know, we could do a lot of hunting if you stayed!"

"Aye, that almost makes me want to stay, sir, but I think both of us better move on. They say the Indian uprising is coming this way, and I don't want to be called up to fight. How about you, Patrick?"

"I'm going to stay here. I'm thinking of applying for the schoolmaster position."

"You're kidding, Patrick. I can't see you teaching lads and lassies, or being locked up in a schoolhouse all day. What about dealing with their parents? Parents are worse than the students, I hear. Besides, we've never split up."

"Oh yeah?" Patrick arched his dark brows. "Maybe we ought to. A regular paycheck will keep me warmer than another claim. Anyway, they need a teacher for the new Sterling school. I hear the students plan to put a rattlesnake in the teacher's desk. I can deal with them if it's no worse than that." That triggered confessions of mean tricks dealt to teachers. Not one could claim innocence.

By supper time Kent trudged back to the shack to find that Marion had not returned home. Riding after her seemed futile this late in the day, but worry drove Kent to saddle Rusty and head out. What if there had been an accident—or an encounter with less than savory miners or outlaws? Kent kicked Rusty into a lope downhill, his gaze scouting the lower benches for Ben, visibility still a couple miles. Not a thing was moving. Dusk arrived all at once after the sun dropped behind the Tobacco Roots; a chill chased the last of the day's warmth.

Finally Ben whinnied from the next draw. Kent abruptly turned Rusty and followed the sound, soon catching up with

Marion. They rode home in silence except for the rasp of tall grass and sagebrush against the horses' legs and the clatter of hooves picking their way around badger holes and rocks. The moon cresting over the mountains gradually lit the darkness by the time they reached the shack. Kent sensed that Marion still bristled with defiance. Not wanting to rekindle the argument, he poked up the ashes in the stove and heated water for tea while she removed her riding boots and adjusted the kerosene lamp. Delicate patterns of grey and silver smoke inside the lamp chimney partially obscured the flame.

In the dimness she repeated her father's words, "'You will do what you will do, my strong-willed daughter.' You likely feel that way about me, too, Kent."

"I feel relieved you are safely home." They sat down to a late supper of cold ham and beans.

"I rode well past Lower Hot Spring camp and miles north along the river. A good many canoes, twelve or fifteen heavily loaded with Shoshoni, traveled downstream. They carried great handmade baskets of red and yellow currants as well as their tipi hides and supplies. They kept to the middle of the river and their own business," she added. "I picked some currants and gooseberries on the way back before I stopped at the Boaz mine and mill. It's about two miles south of the Bozeman Trail.

"There is more action around the Boaz than in Sterling right now. Tents and cabins clutter the hillsides. A two-story, stone house is under construction above Hot Spring Creek. Women were washing clothes in the warm waters of the creek, scrubbing overalls on the rocks. They washed their hair, too, all wet and shining in the sun, and they were all laughing. I wanted to join them. Children ran in and out of the water splashing, throwing water on the dogs, and playing their games. I later found a place to soak alone in the creek on the way back."

Kent noted that her hair was still wet and shining, her eyes shining, too, reflecting deeper feelings related to the story. She is lonely here, he realized, vowing to do something about that.

"The Boaz is working ore provided by multiple owners who bought out local claims for such an opportunity. I understand from talking with a few miners that their stamp mill is more efficient than some. The camp seems to be thriving." Such observations came naturally to Marion. Once again, she didn't notice how disconnected they were to her relationship with Kent.

He finished eating and sat back tamping his pipe, a luxury he seldom allowed himself. He hoped it would help him relax.

"I had to get away today, Kent. It's just my way." Her smile asked for forgiveness and at the same time chided him with its reserve. She struggled to explain her feelings, mostly of being pulled two ways—"I want the excitement of my father's world, but I do not want to live in his shadow. I want to plunge into enterprises and challenge my mind; yet I treasure the exquisitely simple manner in which you live—I feel safe and cared for with you, Kent—your gentle ways are so precious to me."

But Marion's lips trembled when she admitted feeling angry with herself and Kent both. "I felt badly all day about hurting you."

Across the table, Kent laid aside his pipe and took her two hands in his so he could see her face. "I was worried about you, Marion. Afraid something might have happened, though I know Ben would do his best for you."

The tears she fought all day with the furious riding fell unstopped, bouncing off her cheeks onto the plate in front of her. Toughness she could handle. Tenderness stole all her defenses.

"Oh, Kent, you are so kind to me. How could I have said those things to you? You do not think less of me? Or that I have acted like a child? My father would say so. I do not want to upset you, Kent."

Unaccustomed to Marion in this state, or any woman crying, Kent wanted to comfort her, to allay her fears, but he held back, sensing Marion had more to say, even if he didn't want to hear it.

"Tell me, Marion, why are you upset? Sometimes I fail to understand others—or myself—a great failing I want to correct."

"No, no, my fault entirely. I am so impetuous, or is it impatient or restless? You know, like my trip to New York. My father was solidly opposed to my taking such a trip alone. He wanted us to go together in the spring. But I had to go and get a sense of the City and the East! I gave little heed to his resistance, almost forcing him to accede."

She grinned mischievously, teasing him with her unpredictability. The tension eased and Kent poured two cups of chamomile tea.

"I have claimed you much too selfishly for my own. I am not sorry to have had you to myself these past months, but I understand you are isolated here. The farm is remote from any amenities or social life." This was the first time he had referred to the homestead property as a farm. The sound of it surprised him.

"Marry me, Marion, and we'll have a big reception worthy of East and West coasts!" Kent exhaled as if the words had long been held prisoner in his heart, as if the proposal exploded of its own course, as if the moment had come for clarity of their relationship, for commitment.

The outburst momentarily silenced them both. Kent suppressed the urge to promise a house and horse breeding operation—their lives felt entirely too fluid right now.

"A reception? Oh, my. I am already married to you, am I not? My life changed course because of you. Do you not feel married, Kent? It would be terribly awkward at this time. I couldn't possibly face anyone. I am fortunate to have you—how could I want for more?"

"Marion, you do want more. You deserve far more than I've realistically been able to provide—"

"It's not that—"

"I apologize, my dear, for having so little to offer you, for making assumptions without recognizing the limitations."

"I'm not clear what I do want."

"I didn't know either, when I came west, but I've found myself here, the person I didn't know I was. Somehow the Territory brought that out in me. And finding you brought such joy, I'm afraid I've been quite blind to anything else."

Fingers intertwined as each interrupted, words overflowing.

Marion's eyes dropped to her hands, tightly clutched in Kent's; her voice, hinting at resignation, sidestepped the issues of marriage and a reception and deserving and the surrender those words conjured, intimacies she'd hadn't yet discussed with her "husband" in their informal alliance.

"I could do something to entertain myself and I have been. I am not without resourcefulness. I shall go visit Mrs. Callahan and Mrs. Williams and the children."

Kent felt the slice of her withdrawal. He saw her deliberately seek to avoid revealing her deeper feelings, cutting him off as surely as if she again rode Big Ben down the mountain.

It was nearly two o'clock in the morning when they fell into bed. A shaft of moonlight through the small back window illuminated the bright colors of Dora's quilt. Marion's hair spread over Kent's shoulder and her arm rested on his chest. He lay awake a long time, emotionally drained from the previous day's events, waves of anxiety snatching any thoughts of rest.

11

Marion was still sleeping, her small body curled under the quilt, when Kent rose at dawn. He went out to check on Ben and give him extra feed. Kent figured Marion had ridden a good thirty miles, much of it at top speed.

"You'll maybe get a few days off," Kent said when Ben came for his oats. The wind had whipped Ben's thick black mane into matted witches' braids. Sweat brought dirt from under his hair to the surface where it formed greyish blotches over his powerful shoulders and barrel-like sides.

"You're a sight, fella. Marion will take care of you, just you wait."

Kent carried an armload of wood inside for the cookstove, made coffee in the battered pot, and heated a dishpan of water for cleanup. Marion threw her legs off the bed and motioned him to the bench, tucking her toes into the hem of her nightgown against the cold floor. Her arm worked around his waist as her fresh, out-of bed warmth brought a sense of calm he thought had been lost the day before. Her touch healed the distance that had stricken him last night, yet preserved her naturally reserved character. He left things the way they were only too gladly without voicing his fears.

"Would you like to meet the young couple who settled two or three miles down the valley? Or go to Virginia City for a few days of city life?" He was acutely aware he had begun to take her for granted, yet neither again spoke of marriage.

"Now you will worry about me, Kent. I am not like you. I don't worry but sometimes I have to sort things out. It seems the ride has calmed my mind. I am sorry I let my temper sway me. Truly, I am sorry. You are the way you are and I accept that. I want you to think well of me, Kent."

———————

Summer days wore on and the heavy work on the homestead broadened Marion's shoulders and strengthened her muscles, giving her a look of maturity. Her breasts and hips filled out and rounded to accentuate her naturally small waist. As her body changed, Marion became less boyish about nudity and more self-conscious. One mid-day after their bath in the creek, Kent dried her and wrapped her in a towel, then teased her by trying to take it away—or better yet—get inside it with her. Marion threatened to scream but said instead, "You are terribly handsome unclothed."

They captured these moments beneath the junipers with their greatest intimacies, freed by nature to share an uninhibited union, though neither reopened deeper feelings regarding their lives together. Later they sauntered back for the usual hard biscuits with honey, cheese and jerky, and black coffee. Marion had taken charge of Kent as she had with her father, a refreshing change for Kent from the subtle dependence that made his mother seem demanding. Kent headed downhill to work where he met his neighbor hiking toward him, breathing hard, a slouch hat pulled over his brow. His standard Army issue work boots were cumbersome, and his thick shirt and trousers appeared hot in this weather.

"Mr. Williams, what brings you here in such a hurry?"

Hyram Williams halted and wiped away sweat with the back of a huge sun-baked fist. "Did ye find the missus all right? We'se wonderin' aboot her last night."

"Sure, sure, Mr. Williams, she is home and just fine. She took an overly long ride yesterday, that's all."

"That horse was runnin' like a ghost was after it."

"We all have our ghosts, Mr. Williams, but I don't know that horses do," Kent laughed.

"Well, I come over to ask ye aboot that young feller, Benson, who lives down side a' my land. He's been acting mighty strange these days. Nice enough young man when ye talk to him, but sometimes he gits to talkin' to hisself and wanderin.'

"My missus, she sez to me, 'I seen him wanderin' down the valley, shakin' his head, and talking aloud to nobody, and he's half-naked with no hat or shirt. I be afeered of him. Be he mad, Hyram? she sez.'"

Mr. Williams ended his recitation to draw a breath or two. "I think he's gittin' worse. Not seein' him goin' home, I think I best let you know. I can't have him wanderin' round frightenin' the missus and the wee ones. But I sez to the missus, it's the war. Sometimes it does somethin' to the mind, Mama."

The news set off an alarm for Kent who had heard other reports that Benson had been acting strangely. "Thank you, Mr. Williams. About what time did she see him pass by?"

"It was dis mornin' sometime after breakfast. I's gone up to my diggin's and didn't git home till mid-afternoon. So it's been a spell and 'tis awful hot today."

"I'll get my horse and ride down the valley. He could be some distance. I will talk to the other neighbors, too. You keep a lookout, and it would be best if the family stays inside."

The two went their separate ways, something cemented in their relationship on the land, the way neighbors come together in times of trouble.

Late afternoon was hot and sultry, turning the bunch grass brown and dry. Ben was spirited, uncomplaining of another day's work. Marion insisted upon coming. Kent grabbed an extra shirt and hat from the shack, and they rode past the Williams' place several miles down the valley. Settlers were out caring for animals and farming; children ran about, excited to see riders passing by. No one else had seen a man wandering without his hat and shirt, so Kent and Marion spent precious, fruitless time riding up each draw and creek bed they passed without finding any sign of Benson.

Several hours later Kent said, "We've come almost to South Willow Creek. I'm glad to see the land here. It's rich with good grass and it's more livable than upper Norwegian Creek. I wish we had time to look around. I doubt Benson could have gone any further given the time lapse since Mr. Williams' wife saw him."

They looped back, taking a path parallel to the road toward Norwegian Creek. There Rusty spooked and jumped sideways as Marion struggled to stay mounted. Benson lay shirtless on an open patch of hot, sandy dirt ringed by rabbitbrush. He had fallen face down, legs spraddled, shoes untied and loose.

"Benson! Benson! Hey, man, let me see you."

Kent threw himself off Ben and kneeled beside the prone, stocky body. Benson's back was blackened by the sun that had scorched him on the dry ground. Kent felt for a pulse and listened for a breath, then grabbed the canteen off his saddle and poured water over Benson's head and powerful shoulders.

Benson roused a bit but could not lift his head. Marion dismounted to help Kent gently turn him over on the extra shirt and elevate his head for a sip of water. The water washed out of his slack mouth and ran down his chest where ants scurried among bits of debris stuck in sweat. Chunks of hair pulled from his head left strands under his discolored fingernails that looked grotesque on swollen fingers.

"We need a wagon fast," Kent said to Marion. She mounted Rusty and whirled for the next farm without hesitation. Kent moved Ben so the big horse's shadow fell over Benson. He continued mopping a damp kerchief over Benson's swollen eyes and cheeks, and talked encouragingly to him, one of the few miners he'd known for some time, but he couldn't say if Benson was his first or last name. Each man's past and privacy in the West was generally respected.

What had happened to Benson was apparent enough, heat exhaustion due to a delusional mind they called madness, if Mr. and Mrs. Williams were correct. He was still trapped in the war when Mrs. Callahan swept the Yanks out of the boarding house with a broom. Lately he had worked less on his claims and spent his time agitating in the saloons of Hot Spring District.

Left alone with the unresponsive figure, Kent checked Benson's irregular pulse until the neighbor's wagon pulled up with a couple buckets of water slopping over the edges. The three of them laid Benson on a pile of horse blankets in the back while Marion climbed in and continued efforts to cool him down.

"Besides water, I don't know what else we can do for him. They might be able to help him in Sterling." Kent hadn't met the driver before, a Mr. Blackburn, who shook his head at the sight.

"I'se had cows go down quicker'n this 'un."

"The rebellion was still going on in his head. He was fighting his own demons as well. The story of those might never be told," Kent said. They made haste toward Sterling, hoping to find a constable to take over.

"Pitiful fellow caught up in things he couldn't change," Kent shuddered, thinking it's the same mental battle for all of us to some degree, North or South. This could well be me. Leading Rusty, he rode behind and marveled at the physical stamina of the man fighting for his life.

"He was tortured by his father's death in the war, a burden that likely robbed him of his sanity," Kent said to Marion. "I wish I'd known him better."

Late afternoon mountain breezes fanned the procession while it traveled down the road. Benson roused enough to moan several times before he lapsed into unconsciousness.

"He's not breathing much," Marion said. "Shall I shake him or what?"

"Can you hurry the team, Mr. Blackburn?" Kent said. "He might be fading on us."

Marion continued to wipe his brow and face with cold water, and wrap his body in wet blankets. By the time they reached Sterling, Benson's breath was increasingly shallow and irregular. He died before further assistance could be obtained.

"God, to die like this—" Kent shook his head and looked away. Death in the camps happened frequently, but this was the first case of madness he'd heard of. Rattlesnake bite, horse accidents, bar fights, you name it, the Territory of Montana was known for it. Now the fearful prospect of self-destruction due to the war hung over their heads. Kent's feet felt too heavy to move.

Marion pulled him away and brought up the horses. "Leave this business for the constable. You did all you could. I recall you'd taken care of your friend Jake before my first trip to Sterling."

It was nearly midnight when they finally rode home and warmed a pan of chili. They ate supper in silence until Marion said, almost whispering, "Kent, you must tell me about your experience in the war."

Kent lifted tired eyes to scan her face. His lips failed to move.

"You needn't keep it all locked up to spare me even though I am reluctant to pry into your affairs. I know you came West after the war, but you like so many others have the Army boots and duffle bag, so I know you served. I am afraid of what it did to Benson. I must know more—." The words hung unattended in the still cool night like lost fawns, alert, listening, for a sign from the doe.

"Benson is not the only one," she continued. "Surely you have seen how men have changed after the battlefield. They came to California with all kinds of wounds, most that one could not see. I am afraid, like Mrs. Williams, of the madness."

Marion reached across the table to shake his wrist, her voice urgent, before Kent could grasp that this was it—the time he had dreaded—to tell Marion, anyone, what had happened to him behind the lines. Pale and choking, his voice unsteady, he began at last.

"Mother refused to let me leave her at first. Finally, eighteen months before the war ended, I joined the Army. It was going badly and the Confederacy was desperate for men. I put in for an administrative position where I could contribute my business and management skills. After we trained in those boots you saw, I was sent to Richmond for a post at headquarters. Mother was pleased to hear of it.

"I was assigned to a Dispatch and Supply department. It wasn't long before I was promoted to supervisor of distribution, issuing food, shelter and weapons to our troops. Orders came in round the clock for materials to be rushed to battlefields on land and sea, but what could we do?" Here Kent halted, his voice low, gravelly and shaky. He saw again the horses, mules and men that became skeletons—if they lived. Faces of those on the staff swept Kent's vision; he fell into noting those who died, those who did not. Marion squeezed his hand but refused to stop the painful flow of recollections.

"There was little food yet constant demands upon the men." He glanced at Marion, her face tense and white.

"It was the artillery that broke me. No, I was safe where I was, but I saw all the weapons we dispatched. My fear, my terror, was that every crate, every ship, train, and wagon load of artillery and rifles might be destined for use against my brother Rand. Or perhaps against my father—who knew where he was during the war." Kent's face contorted with grief as he relived the pain.

"Like Benson's tie to his father," Marion breathed.

"This beautiful person—my older brother, so handsome and confident—in my mind I saw him falling in battle—and I still do at times," he confessed. "Because I felt it would have been my fault. I became almost paralyzed in fear and guilt." He paused and shoved the now cold chili aside. "The blockade cut us off from the sea. Sieges from the west shut down supply routes. We had less and less of what was required to support our troops. I had no power to feed or clothe the men properly. On humanitarian grounds alone we--I--failed. This went on for months that dragged to eternity." He reflected back on his own sense of powerlessness, his breath shallow, forced.

"Besides the futility of what we were doing, it was not in me to fight. We couldn't achieve what we set out to do, to preserve the South. Believe me, Marion, I just wanted to go on living as we always had."

"As you always had?"

"Work the land in peace, Rand, Mother and myself."

Marion shook her head at the words, foreign to her ears. "'Just live as we always had.' That is a concept unknown in my life with my father." Her lips parted to probe what he meant, to understand this man, yet the halting story continued.

"One day I found myself down on the floor, half-conscious, crawling on hands and knees like a baby, unable to draw a breath—fainting like a coward when others were dying. I could not commit myself to the effort—it was like a curse, a hell of my own making. I--I--couldn't handle it, Marion, then or now—the thought of myself destroying Rand directly or indirectly. How any human being could be capable of that, I do not know. Rand was wounded, changed by the war, his fine spirit cut as if by a knife. I saw it when I was home. The greater injuries were inside. Even his wife respects the darkness there."

"It wasn't your fault," Marion interrupted. "I shouldn't have asked you to tell me—forgive me for opening these wounds." She stirred, shook the chill of his words and reached for her coat. The fire had died down to glowing embers that lit the room through the open firebox.

"Many others served admirably though they had similar fears." Kent gulped for air to regain his composure and finally went on. "They sent me to sick ward where I was treated with several days bed rest, then reassigned to accounting in another department. My brother served with distinction at the front. He has always risen above the ordinary. I loved him--love him--for it. Rand was brother and father, after father left us."

"It's over, my precious Kent. Leave it." Blank eyes returned her stricken look, raising currents of alarm and questions as if strangers occupied the room.

"I--I didn't want to burden you with this. Marion—"

Her lips parted, closed. She snugged the coat firmly around her body drawing her head within its folds."No, please don't go on. I can't bear to hear more."

But the thunder of hoof beats of wild horses again pulsed in Kent's ears and in his heart, shutting her out. His voice dropped to a mumble, the story unraveling of its own accord. "How could I go home and tell Rand I dispatched artillery? Or confront him for annihilating the South? Or resume our partnership on the estate? Truly, I became mad with the dilemma." He tightly covered his ears with both hands, uncertain whether the horses were outside on the hill or inside his head? Kent stared blindly at the far corner of the shack, desperately trying to find clarity, to sort it all out. "I had lost everything, and my mind, like Benson's, might have dealt the final blow if I hadn't escaped."

"Benson," Marion cried. "This all started with Benson." The vision of Benson succumbing to stresses all alone permeated the room. The shack creaked with a rising wind, and bullets of rain hit the roof, chasing the usual mountain breezes, overpowering the shrieks of the hawks. Marion smoothed Kent's cold, bloodless arms as if he were a small boy until he bolted to his feet and stepped out to piss over the edge of the porch.

Marion averted her eyes, stunned.

"That's not you, Kent. Come back to me—;" the charged air of the shack crackled, the tension ran hot and cold when he came back inside.

"I live in two different worlds—"

Marion's fear peaked, her anger flashed, "But I do, too. Maybe we all do. You needn't obsess over what's past. Your confession is like blowing up a mine. You've exposed the veins beneath. You are raw, Kent. I don't know if you are the same man. Or will be."

Her bitter assessment of what just happened stung. But lost in the familiar disturbing flashbacks, Kent failed to recognize how her understanding of him had shifted, how the discharge of his near-madness unleashed a blast that doomed any innocent views she may have harbored about him. The enormity of war that led to Benson's death and Kent's self-incriminations now loomed darkly over their lives together—exposing Kent's vulnerability and she a creature destined to creep around the edges of his pain.

Eventually her sharp rebuke forced him to breathe deeply, to drag remnants of his thoughts into some kind of order, to reorient himself to the one human being to whom he had entrusted his inner lode.

"The rebellion continues here, as you know. We keep it alive—with all its resentments. Will it ever end?" He rose from the table to sit on the front steps, his shirt open to embrace the bite of rain delivered by the summer storm, to hurt as badly on the outside as he felt inside, opening to the wind that raised the hair on his arms and reddish splotches on his chest; inviting nature's healing to rid the memories, trusting the land called Montana Territory would absolve him again as it had in the past year.

At last, wet, spent and trembling with cold, he reentered the shack, slumped onto the bunk and pulled the quilt over his head, his snores raking the silence.

———————

Marion sat at the table, numb from his outburst as well as her own. It was not the brutality of the war on her sensibilities as much as the chilling proximity to it she'd felt as he spoke. When she was young and living in California half a continent away, the War Between the States seemed remote, yet it was just a few years ago.

He lives with the horrors and remorse every day. How did I not know? Or realize that he had so many sides or contained such emotion? I wonder about myself—perhaps I miss a great deal, not knowing. Maybe I take things as they are; that might not be a fault. I'll leave the deeper involvement to others if it causes so much pain.

She knew her father was a veteran of border skirmishes, but he had never talked openly of his experience or what it had been like for him. Constant warfare to the south in Mexican Territory had occupied early residents of the land of *Alto California* before she was born, and the bloody Mexican-American War occurred twenty years ago. The U. S. military had since been compelled to defend the new state of California against occupation from the south, the ongoing conflicts a backdrop in her youth.

With the passing of Kent's own storm and the rain, night eased over the shack casting a kindly spell over its inhabitants, touching a tenderness in Marion's heart, releasing quiet sobs with gushes of tears. Marion dropped her head on her arms on the table and dozed fitfully. When she finally slipped into bed, the faintest light of dawn cast long eerie shadows over the land. Kent rose to prowl outdoors, grappling with the scourge of memories and their aftermath. Ever after, Marion could see the depth of sorrow behind his serious grey eyes.

Marion stayed close to Kent for weeks after her solitary escapade and Kent's confession. They did not talk about Benson's traumatic death or its subsequent exposure of Kent's intense personal pain. She tended to be unusually quiet and her features revealed a sobering reflection. When life again settled into a predictable routine of late summer chores and often excruciatingly hot "dog days" of August, she visited the Williams' to help hang the wash on the clothesline and look after the children. Mrs. Williams would stoke up the fire to boil jars of home-canned tomatoes, peas and carrots. Her root cellar, deep in the ground and covered with a mound of soil, was a treasure of stored foodstuff "put by" for winter. However, Marion had not yet found anyone of her age or inclination to spend time with, not unlike her childhood years growing up in Coloma, California.

When the long-awaited shipment of two stamp mills that Henry Ward, superintendent of Midas Mining Company, had ordered the past winter finally arrived in Sterling, Marion was one of the first drawn to the scene. Ward had ordered engines and boilers from New York to be shipped up the Missouri to Fort Benton, and quartz mills from San Francisco's Union Iron Works that would come overland. The silvery plume of a dust storm told Marion from afar that Sterling was the epicenter of an astonishing event. Never had so many horse and mule teams filled the roads into Sterling, an overflow of worn out beasts that shuffled impatiently for feed and rest, snorting in thick air raised by their own hooves. Freight wagons, many in tandem, jostled to unload over twenty tons of machinery plus tons of quicksilver in crates near the Midas mill. Quicksilver would be combined with ore to create an amalgam which was then treated with mercury and heated to distill the gold. Onlookers crowded in the way of miners hoisting massive gears and piston-like stamps with blocks and tackles. Marion joined women and children who poured out of doorways to be part of the excitement, despite the acrid scent of mule dung and sweat. Teamsters' shouts and curses competing with the mules' hee-hawing at ear-splitting decibels sounded like trains blowing through tunnels.

"Put 'er over there." A Midas manager indicated a cavernous stone building with a yawning mouth left open to receive the oversize mill components.

"Masons and builders are first to get jobs," scowled a slouched fellow whose wolf-like eyes hid behind a furry beard.

"Skilled labor like mechanics git the work puttin' this here thing together," drawled another.

"Look at them stamps. They'll crush ore you ain't even dreamed of yet."

"They'll need a hydraulic system like they had in Alder Gulch to feed this mill," disparaged a businessman in a clean, double-breasted suit and top hat.

"Nah, ain't 'nuff water in the crik to water them mules, let alone run a hydraulic pump." The old miner spit tobacco to the side. "I seen them washin' in California. Them pumps would wash the dirt clear down to the river."

On the steps of the boarding house Mrs. Callahan yelled, "How ye gonna feed 'em all, Pa?"

"Ain't likely they'd all want to sit down and eat with each other," Harland grinned, knowing the Missus took on challenges like a mess sergeant.

An official stood in a wagon box calling out items on shipping tickets, while another gentleman recruited miners to assemble the mill. A scuffle broke out about siphoning labor from one mining company to another.

"We're not falling for it. They're paying more in Alder Gulch." The jam-packed crowd wavered back and forth. Quiet stern faces of the bulk of the labor force, the Southerners, watched and waited. This could spiral in a way some yearned to see, some didn't. Liquor liberated old animosities, taunts and threats. With the festive atmosphere dampened, Marion slipped away to help Mrs. Callahan who'd been cooking since before daylight and gratefully accepted an extra hand. Marion shelled peas while they gossiped about affairs in Sterling and beyond.

Tentatively, Marion ventured to ask, "What kind of man is Kent, do you know Mrs. Callahan?"

"Ye'd not be asking that question if ye was properly married, now would ye?" was the quick response. Mrs. Callahan shook water from her hands and put new potatoes on to boil for dinner.

Marion's head came up in surprise with a little smile on her face. "Why, how did you know, Mrs. Callahan?"

"Cause if ye was properly married ye would have had a doin's," she said.

"A doin's?"

"Yes, a doin's. A shivaree they call 'em. A big to-do where everyone comes and somebody plays the squeezebox and everybody dances. Then there's a big supper at midnight. The women cook all day to bring something special to that. But, oh no, ye two come slippin' in without so much as a fair-ye-well and no doin's."

Marion laughed. "I'm sorry, Mrs. Callahan. Kent said you love to give a party. I seem to have everything backward and upside down these days! But please tell me, what kind of man is Kent? At times, I think I do not know him well at all."

"He's a good man, Mrs. Berrigan, a good man. He took care of his neighbor, Jake, who was shot one night for no reason nobody could find out. Buried him right on his own property, Mr. Berrigan did. He said a few words and an "Our Father" over the grave, a good and righteous old Catholic Bible it was—*forgive us our debts as we forgive our debtors.* Maybe he was asking that for us who're alive more than for poor Jake who was dead and gone."

The convivial chat had become too serious and dinner hour was near. The women worked silently preparing dishes and spooning them onto platters to serve family style. Marion donned an apron and began washing stacks of gigantic pans, ladles and knives. Mrs. Callahan's lye soap was deadly on her hands, but it was good for cleaning.

"Hey, hey, ye best be serving the dinner, Mrs. Berrigan, instead of washing them dishes. Ye go out and chat. Ye might hear some good bit of gossip!"

Marion gaily flung the dowdy apron on its peg and sailed into the dining room with a tray of ginger cookies in one hand

and a pan of bread pudding in the other. The men simultaneously turned to stare, a hush halting their conversations. This Marion found familiar and flattering, but the notion that she was married left her flustered. She forced a distant look on her face; at any rate, none of these men appealed to her whatsoever, not even the mill owners in fine long coats and top hats who assumed airs with the patrons of the establishment and with her.

"Dessert, gentlemen?" Marion asked politely, and deposited the desserts within their reach. They resumed discussing recent acquisitions of claims in the Lower Hot Spring area, a subject about which Marion was well informed. She lingered, offering small talk with some of the women, while she overheard portions of the men's conversation. Owners of the Boaz stamp mill had found quality ore in their claims, enabling them to operate their mill quite profitably, while others were failing. This was not news to Marion.

She moved to another table and sat with one of the settlers from Norwegian Creek who had come to town for supplies. After mentioning the sad fate of Benson, they both listened to animated remarks down the table about gold mining in Silver Bow.

"The newspaper headlines tout it as the next boom town. Believe it or not, the ore is loaded with gold, zinc, and silver, too, attracting miners from here. Surely investors should be looking into possibilities there."

"The newspapers, dey's behind the rushes. Rush here, rush der to sell papers, then dey write about something differnt to sell more papers. I say we should be in da newspaper business, ja."

The banter so amused Marion that she tossed her head to keep from giggling and ran back to the kitchen. "They are so funny, Mrs. Callahan, just like in California—men thinking they can find gold and riches right under their noses!" Her laughter peeled out over the rattle of dishes in the dishpan.

"Not one could long survive without women's cooking!" the women agreed.

Marion rode briskly home on Rusty with a huge sense of satisfaction from the day. It was nice to mingle in Sterling's transient society, yet return home to a steady if confounding husband.

"Dear Kent. I hope he's not too lonely when I'm gone so long," she breathed, galloping the horse into the corral. She stepped inside to find wide-open, welcoming arms and two huge rugs rolled in layers of brown paper. Even wrapped, the ends of the rugs already brightened the shack. Kent was pleased with her astonishment and the hail of kisses on his cheek.

Marion peered deep into his eyes. "I'm thankful I have such a man, not any other I've ever known. Truly, you're a good man—now whatever have you done here?"

"Mr. Williams dropped these off on his way back from Sterling. Tell me what you think."

"They are too lovely, much too elegant for me, for us. I shall hang them on the wall like the tapestries we saw in Virginia City when we first met, when I passed you in the doorway. These rugs are like Oriental tapestries, so rich in golds, reds, and blues. They must be kept up from the floor."

Shag was the loser in this proposition since she had only a stack of burlap bags for a bed, but the shack was soon transformed with the radiant, imported rugs which would serve as insulation in the winter as well as beautify the interior. Kent held Marion close until she asked about Mr. Williams being in town.

"I was there with Mrs. Callahan, but I didn't see Mr. Williams."

"He mentioned seeing you in the dining room, though he did not stay. He merely looked in for someone. You were very busy with customers, he said."

"Oh yes, I had such fun! They are such an ordinary lot, miners mostly, a few investors from the North. Nothing I hadn't seen or heard all the time growing up. Of course, I had to overhear gossip about the potential for the stamp mills. Quite interesting, Kent! I feel as though I have connected to my past!"

Her past may have seemed long ago to her, Kent thought, but it seemed recent to him—her business interests, her pent-up energy needing an outlet. The news Williams dropped that she was "entertainin" the men shook Kent. He was not certain from his story or hers what transpired at the boarding house, but clearly Marion was very happy—and happy to be home with him. He drew her into his arms, folding that bottled vibrancy to his lean body until their breaths came as one, the enchantment transforming the dull surroundings as certainly as the rugs. He allowed the concern to fade.

12

Only at night did silence reign over sage and prairie grass benches and juniper-filled gulches of the vast swath of land underlain by the Boulder batholith. Sixty million years ago, streams of magma forty-five miles long produced granite and igneous that rose to Earth's surface to cool. Eons passed as ridges of upturned, protruding granite carried veins of gold along fractures. Over time, erosion by wind and water created formations bearing heavy metals now probed by prospectors. A miracle of sorts, Kent marveled, these unimaginable bouquets of precious minerals like gifts at our feet.

"Now I am part of the process, turning over the soil and rocks in my minute way."

Scars and chips lent character to his double-sided pick. Any ego he had as master of a small estate in Woodland Hills had shrunk to a well-grounded humility. He, Marion, and Patrick Colter worked Kent's claims; the clamor of picks, hammers and stamp mills up and down the gulch indicated that other miners worked all daylight hours, too.

Norwegian Creek endured infinite depredations during mining days that would make it one of the richest placer discovery sites in Hot Spring District. Besides excavations by prospectors, the Denton stamp mill operated on the upper end of the creek, augmented by water from the Meadow Creek ditch.

Downstream, Kent diverted Norwegian Creek water into his sluice box. He shoveled heavy, rock-filled dirt into the upper end of the box, and Marion spread it with a long-handled hoe. When the bulk washed overboard, Patrick scooped remaining sand, gravel and heavy metals for panning into buckets beside the sluice box.

Kent hauled remaining quartz rocks to the Denton for crushing and amalgamation, a process of separating gold with mercury. His last batch of ore had a surprisingly rich yield and indicated no readiness to "flare out." The returns brought him that much closer to acquiring land and building a home on South Willow Creek, property he'd admired the day they found Benson.

A neighbor blasted Kent's quartz mines for him. The blasts threw prickly pear cacti, bunch grass, small junipers, and white quartz over a wide area around each claim. He and Patrick put in a good day's work moving rubble while Marion took a break. A sizeable empty hole of hard rock remained, a symbol characteristic of exploitation of the land that Kent found difficult to rationalize.

Later, Kent and Marion rode to Sterling to mail a box containing ore samples to the assay office in Virginia City. In exchange, the stagecoach brought a packet of mail for Kent which he stuffed into his saddle bag before they went to Callahans' for supper.

At home that evening Kent dumped the mail on the table. Beneath outdated *Montana Post* newspapers a letter addressed in a woman's hand lay in plain sight. He slowly picked it up and immediately recognized the handwriting of Miss Olivia Spencer. He glanced at Marion who intently witnessed everything from the other side of the table. Kent casually slit the durable envelope with a butcher knife and opened the letter.

Dear Kent, it said, followed by news of Olivia's promotion as a teacher of advanced contemporary literature, the sorry state of

Reconstruction, and a bit about his mother and Aunt Margaret. She continued,

"My mother, like yours, has decided to move to Savannah, and of course, poor Father can do nothing but leave the land where he was born and raised to be with her. My mother has been quite ill for some time from the strain of the war. I believe the memories constantly disturb her thoughts and dreams. Father is leaving the plantation in the very capable hands of the manager who has been a loyal employee for over twenty years. As you know, I am the sole family heir to the property since my sister died from the pox as a child. I am writing this to tell you that in the event the gold rush comes to naught, you would have a home and established plantation to come back to, should you choose to do so. It would be most heart-warming to have you back, Kent, and I wait impatiently for your reply."

Kent idly thumbed the two sheets of vellum and handed them to Marion. The notion of returning was so distant from his immediate experience that it was laughable, and he had forfeited any participation related to his own family's estate. Kent was astounded, not at Olivia's proposal, as it was, but at the finality of his own leave-taking.

"My supper is quite ruined," Marion said, shoving back her chair. "I wonder that you have been corresponding with a woman and dared to open her letter in front of me, Kent." She rose, flipping her skirt as she stepped outside. Kent sprang to his feet, instantly drawn to his present situation in life, one that seemed imperiled by this intrusion from the past.

"There has been no correspondence, Marion, and truly this comes as a surprise, one I have no interest whatsoever in pursuing. Had I suspected something so distasteful to you, would I have dared to share it?"

Her back toward him radiated indignation, not an invitation for an overture.

"Sure'n all, I'm sorry," Kent said, unconsciously using an expression of his father's. He blinked, thinking how unpredictable Marion could be. There were bound to be times when they would have disagreements, but this apparent jealousy was unexpected and bittersweet. Sweet, he thought, that she cares that intensely, but unfortunate if she feels threatened. Or worse, that she feels she could be displaced.

"I expected more of you than to encourage this woman when you went home."

Kent paused. Clearly she was not to be dissuaded from her view. "What can I tell you?" he said at last. "When I described my life here, she declared even her father's swine would not be required to live in such deplorable conditions, and that if I ever wanted to rejoin civilized society I was welcome, but I would need to be retrained like a horse."

Marion turned with a sly, forgiving look. He met her in his arms with a huge sense of relief. The images generated laughter at a sorely needed time. Olivia's reputation as a prude was firmly established.

The rest of the packet contained legal notices related to homesteading in Montana Territory, jurisdictions of various governing authorities, and advertisements. The matter of the proposal was soon dropped.

The newspaper advertisements offered a mixture of refinement and opportunities in Virginia City, yet the quality of life Kent had envisioned for Marion remained questionable, if not remote.

Ladies high button shoes and bonnets
Fresh Gallatin Valley farm produce
Dancing every night except Sundays

Urgent Notices:
Unload oxen trains in backstreets
to eliminate jamming main street.

Toll road contracts open for bidding.
Road improvement needed

Public Health Notice:
Citizens of Virginia City, clean up garbage
in front of your businesses and homes.

Triggered by the stated civic needs, Kent gave Marion an overview of Territorial affairs. The biennial Legislature designated by the Organic Act met under Governor Sidney Edgerton, who allotted seven Council members and thirteen representatives to each county. Southern Democrats dominated politics except for federal appointees to territorial positions of Governor, Attorney General and Supreme Court Justice. Hezekiah Hosmer, Chief Justice, held part ownership of claims on Norwegian and Rattlesnake creeks. In contrast to vested interests, the citizens, largely Rebels, muscled their influence more or less by mob rule. This power of the people precluded voting for welfare funds to care for the ill, poor, and elderly, or raising taxes for roads, bridges, or civic enhancement such as garbage cleanup.

The weeks of Montana Territory's short summer slid past while residents of Norwegian Creek hastened to wrap up their mining. Marion's outlook tended to slip, comparing her life in this remote place with that of the city, until she mentioned a woman she'd like to spend time with.

"By all means, Marion. Please do. I hope you'll enjoy her."

"Mrs. Nathaniel Thompson has requested a woman who might drive with her to Helena. I would like to accompany her." Marion spoke without preamble.

Kent's heart did a momentary skip. At his blank look, Marion hastened on. "Mrs. Thompson travels there regularly to visit her sister. Yes, she drives the buggy herself with quite a fast pacer, if I understand correctly. I am sure the trip would be expeditious with appropriate accommodations along the way. You would not have to worry, Kent."

The worrier in question let out a long breath and asked if she had talked to Mrs. Thompson herself.

"No, not directly. The request was conveyed by Mrs. Callahan, who spoke with Mr. Thompson when he picked up a shipment for his mill in Alder Gulch. To be sure, there is considerable respect for Mr. Thompson and therefore his wife. I understand they are doing well from their acquisitions in Summit District, and they can afford these little adventures."

To Marion, it was an adventure. To Kent, it was a possible encounter with robbers or at the very least, the vagaries of weather, road conditions and wild animals. He stalled for time, reiterating her father's belief that she was a strong-willed woman who would do what she would do.

"I need to notify Mrs. Callahan right away that I am available, and that it would be most agreeable for me to accompany Mrs. Thompson." Marion preemptively made her own decisions, a habit honed with her often inattentive father. A spark already lit her features.

"I certainly understand your desire to go—." He found he could say no more, either encouraging or discouraging the enterprise.

The next day Marion galloped Rusty into town on a shopping spree at the Mercantile. She bought suitable shoes to replace her usual riding boots. Otherwise, a long dust coat would cover her identity except for a small face beneath a snugly tied cotton bonnet. She purchased a sturdy purse for coins that could be hidden about her person. She planned to stash the balance of her funds discreetly in her baggage.

Despite his undeclared misgivings, Kent was caught up in the flurry of preparation. Marion's endless excitement became infectious. He baked a tin of molasses cookies and wrapped venison jerky in brown paper for the ladies in case of an emergency or delay in arriving in Helena, over ninety miles to the north through the rugged Elkhorn Mountains. Far braver men would think twice about the journey and few would do it alone, but Kent kept his own council, acutely aware of Marion's recent flight.

"You women have a whole different outlook about the West than I do," Kent muttered, finding he once again addressed the back of her head.

The women settled as comfortably on the high, firm seat as the top buggy would allow, sheltered from sun and rain by a tight but minimal canvas. A springboard type, it had a black leather upholstered seat anchored above slim wheels, those in back larger than those in front. Dandy, a sleek black pacing horse of a breed sought after by the well-to-do, clicked off the miles, his head arched high on a thin, curved neck.

"He wouldn't even fill Ben's shadow," Kent groused, when he saw the women off from Sterling early in the morning.

Mrs. Thompson and Marion immediately recognized something of themselves in the other—a spirit of independence that set them apart from traditional homemakers. Mrs. Thompson and her husband lived in Virginia City, but they had mining interests throughout the Gravelly Mountains as well as Last Chance Gulch. She might have been in her mid-thirties, a trim, dark-haired, confident woman with a pleasant countenance. Her hands were strong and capable of holding the reins of the energetic Dandy. Mrs. Berrigan was, well, not really Mrs. Berrigan, but her traveling partner was either unaware of the fact or did not care.

Temperatures in the mid-range for late summer made the trip swift and enjoyable. By following the South Boulder River north up "Peace Valley" as it was known by Natives, the independent Thompson party reached Boulder Hot Springs stage stop at dusk. The hot springs, another of Montana Territory's thermal wonders, was located in the Elkhorn Mountains. Three dozen or more springs brought forth 102 degree Fahrenheit water from deep within the earth. The women planned to stay over a day to enjoy the beautiful setting and the healthful effects of "taking the waters."

Travelers were accommodated by a tavern and an unpretentious hotel with a dining room. Mrs. Thompson and Marion dressed smartly for supper, glad to be relieved of their cumbersome, dusty travel garments. Each helped the other pin up their hair in loose buns—Marion's secured by the abalone combs. Trailing curls representing a bit of naughtiness in married women encircled their faces and necklines.

The clientele at the hotel included some "dandies" in black top coats and tails, who were on their way to Butte on business. Others were local folks celebrating a wedding, arthritic individuals who came for the waters, and passengers from stagecoaches on the Helena to Bannack road. Several gentlemen found reasons to stop and talk with Mrs. Berrigan and Mrs. Thompson, and the women had no lack of company before or after supper. With remarkable acuity, both discussed mining interests with the best of them, but declined offers to stroll on the grounds after dark despite the security offered by kerosene lanterns along the driveway.

The full day and two nights at the hotel went by too fast. The women walked up tributaries that filtered into the South Boulder River, which cut a winding path down the valley.

"This is quite a resort for the frontier," Marion exclaimed. "I'll be spoiled by the bathhouse!" They lazed in soaking pools for women only and completed the evening reading in rocking chairs, their room lit by a blazing orange and yellow sunset until it melted behind the mountains.

Before dawn next day Mrs. Thompson had Dandy and the buggy brought around to the carriage entrance. Mr. Bower, the hotel owner and manager, scurried out to meet the women.

"I see you are prepared to depart ahead of the other travelers. It is not yet light. I advise you to wait a few hours until they will be on the road with you." He grasped the buggy handrail as if to secure it by force, signaling he had the best interests of his patrons at heart.

"Mr. Bower, I do thank you for your kind solicitousness for our welfare, but I have traveled this way several times without incident. My horse is extraordinarily fast, and we will make short work of it, I assure you."

"No doubt, no doubt, madam," he muttered, pulling his short beard. "Same and all, the passes have been dangerous. It's best to go with an armed escort. You never know what perils may be lurking in those places."

Mrs. Thompson glanced at Marion to see if she was agreeable to go despite the warning. Marion shrugged and Mrs. Thompson turned firmly to Mr. Bower.

"My husband is fully confident of my ability to arrive safely in Helena. I intend to do so as swiftly as possible if you will kindly permit us to leave. The Boulder route is the shortest from Virginia City. Thank you for your hospitality, Mr. Bower. It has been most refreshing."

Dandy pranced and tugged on the reins held by the livery boy. The women climbed onto the seat, Mrs. Thompson careful to avoid exposing her ankles to any ogling Mr. Bower might engage in. Dandy sped off, his shoes striking the stone driveway loudly enough to awaken all the occupants of the hotel. Mrs. Thompson and Marion laughed and cheered him on.

The narrow Boulder valley lay serenely sheltered on the east and west by chains of beautiful mountains, thereby providing optimal growing conditions for sparsely located farms and ranches. Marion noted that forage was dense and plentiful far up from the valley bottom, and the land was generally unspoiled by mining.

"I shall have to tell Kent about the richness of this valley. He could prosper here without struggling against the winds and mining conditions on the east side of the Tobacco Roots." She pictured lovely pastures with fine horses that Kent would enjoy, and fences around a substantial house with at least rudimentary indoor plumbing.

"I could live here—like this—," she mused, entertaining the thought of establishing herself in Montana Territory and making a proper marriage of their common law arrangement. Yet these notions became an uneasy distraction that Marion hastily dismissed. A hesitancy, a nameless restlessness, claimed her inner being; unnamed yearnings bid for her attention while the present persistently occupied her time.

Besides day-dreaming, the hours of traversing the remaining twenty-eight miles to Helena afforded her the opportunity to tell Mrs. Thompson about the gold camps of California. Mrs. Thompson's keen interest prompted Marion to describe her father's business. Left out of the story were his frequent risk-taking forays, an admission of which might deter her from her as yet unclear ambitions.

"All of this is terribly exciting and impressive, especially from a woman as young as you."

With such a rapt listener, Marion felt encouraged to relate her travels to New York City.

"Not so!" Mrs. Thompson exclaimed. New York seemed as remote as Paris to many living in the Territories.

"Oh, it was not nearly as adventurous as this very trip," Marion said, excusing her boasting. "Transportation is quite advanced from St. Louis northward. Rails and canals make connections to the coast easily accessible, and little hardship or danger remains for one's travels over land or water there. The country has developed beyond imagination. Surely, much has been spoiled in the process, however," she added, echoing Kent's reservations about exploiting the land.

Mrs. Thompson wasn't to be dissuaded. "I must accompany Nathaniel when he visits investors in the East next spring. We cannot be bound by the hardships of travel, not to insult poor Dandy, nor by these wretched roads in the Territory when it is possible to travel to New York, as you so readily recount."

"The telegraph is almost commonplace there, while our line to Virginia City is a rarity in the Northwest." Marion's voice became wistful, bereft of involvement in the outside world.

Mrs. Thompson personally knew the enterprising Creighton brothers who had installed the western portion of the telegraph line and instruments. "We are fortunate to have it, but it can be unreliable since storms, vandals and wild animals cause frequent disruptions."

Each woman envisioned the telegraph in her own way, both foreseeing impending connections from coast to coast and north to south reaping limitless benefits for business and industry, a fact of vital interest to the women.

At noon they stopped near a stream that welcomed them with its dense, shady willows and tall cottonwoods, but hoards of horse and deer flies, mosquitoes, and gnats descended upon them when they set out the lunch basket. They wolfed down the petite ham sandwiches and applesauce cake Mrs. Thompson had ordered from the hotel kitchen and hurried on.

The road followed a steady incline from the valley floor past the rough cow town of Boulder City, gradually gaining altitude to Helena. Dandy slowed to a walk when they neared the first pass where the road narrowed and wound around a promontory of jutting rocks. Tension mounted as they recalled Mr. Bower's admonition that they travel with armed escort. They listened intently to birds and other sounds that might alert them to any presence or movement beside the thoroughfare.

As they neared a blind corner, Mrs. Thompson raised her voice, chatting nonchalantly about the sewing she was doing for her nieces. Catching on, Marion responded with an anecdote of her own until they both ran out of stories and began to sing. Dandy picked up the energy, and with a burst of speed, took the buggy sailing over the bumps through the pass to the open barren hillside beyond.

"I do believe we have passed through safely," Mrs. Thompson said. "Let's hope the following outfits do the same."

The journey continued uneventfully for some time, though the women noticed a scraping noise coming from the buggy's back wheels. Soon a distinct wobble alerted Mrs. Thompson that she needed to stop and determine the problem. Marion jumped down from the high seat and immediately saw that the slim metal rim had jarred loose from one of the tall, skinny wooden wheels. It no longer aligned properly as the wheel revolved, and it was in danger of coming off with further use. Repair would not entail considerable difficulty; however, Marion could think of nothing they had aboard to fix it. Mrs. Thompson slowly pulled Dandy off the road and seated herself on a large boulder.

"Doubtless the stones in the road over the pass and Dandy's haste caused the damage," Mrs. Thompson said. "We shall have to wait for assistance." Mr. Bower's prediction that other outfits would be two hours behind them meant they would lose all the fast time they had made, but it was not to be helped.

Eventually a cloud of dust and racket signaled the arrival of outriders associated with the first wagon train. Two men galloped up to the stranded travelers and doffed their hats at seeing the women. The smaller fellow was missing all his front teeth and the remainder formed uneven lines toward the back. His face and clothing were very dirty--obviously he did not partake of the waters at the resort—but he offered a jaunty smile and whatever assistance they might require. The problem was readily apparent. He dismounted to help.

"C'mon, Ned, git off yer horse and quit gawkin'. The ladies need to have the wheel fixed, cain't you see?"

Ned was a heavyset young man with braided black hair, maybe Salish, Marion guessed, though she was unfamiliar with northern tribes. The men jiggled the wheel and tried to shove the rim back on, but it wouldn't budge. The smaller man puffed and blew hard attempting to elevate the wheel on his shoulder, then gave the task over to Ned.

"Heft that there wheel up so's I kin fix this rim on with stout wire, will ye?" He retrieved a small roll of wire and a pair of pliers from his saddlepack.

Ned turned his powerful back and shoulders to lift the rear end of the buggy and free up the wheel. "Heaviest damn thing I ever heard tell of," he growled. They both glanced in the rear luggage compartment that extended under the seat, but saw nothing except the ladies' trunks.

"This 'll hold ye till ye git to Helena." The men left with their outfit.

True enough, with Mrs. Thompson carefully pacing Dandy so slowly that a stream of travelers passed them, the buggy and occupants arrived two or three hours after the others. They rattled down the hill toward Last Chance Gulch hoping the wire wouldn't wear through. Marion began to search for the livery.

"Oh, I must first attend to business," Mrs. Thompson said. "I shall immediately look up my husband's associate, Mr. Turnage, who will make all the arrangements for Dandy and the buggy. You will be pleased to make the banker's acquaintance."

The bank, built with locally made red bricks, was distinguished by tall east-facing windows, a symbol of Helena's rapid accumulation of wealth from a number of extraordinary strikes—Last Chance, Confederate Gulch, and the Holter Lake discoveries. Mrs. Thompson stopped at the curb in front of the bank. She and Marion stiffly alighted when Mr. Turnage hurried towards them.

"Mrs. Thompson, madam, you have once again arrived safely, bless you. Please introduce me to your companion."

Mr. Turnage took a hand of each woman in his smooth palms and smiled broadly into Marion's eyes. Several gold teeth made Marion wince; it seemed like ill-gotten gain compared to their Good Samaritan who had few teeth at all. She curtsied briefly without replying. Mr. Turnage led the horse and buggy away himself, and Mrs. Thompson proceeded inside for a private meeting. The office was located on the mezzanine overlooking the lobby and, indeed, the entire Helena valley to the northeast.

A few moments to herself gave Marion the opportunity to refresh in the powder room upstairs. From a back window Marion overlooked the carriage port at the rear of the bank. She glanced down to unexpectedly see Mr. Turnage unlocking what appeared to be a hidden drawer under the luggage compartment of the buggy. Two swarthy gentlemen wearing no-nonsense holsters stepped forward to lift the heavy drawer onto a waiting hand cart. They wheeled it without delay into the vault section on the first floor.

"What in heaven's name?" Marion breathed, her hand flying over her mouth to curtail a string of profanity. "Whew! We were sitting on a shipment of gold!"

She grasped the window sill, her legs trembling, the tales of hijacking and robbery at gunpoint raced through her mind— the haste, the heavy buggy, Mrs. Thompson's chatter now made sense. Marion sank onto a velveteen settee in the powder room, pausing to absorb this information and its potential ramifications.

"Was I duped into this reckless scheme? We could have been robbed or killed—oh my, Kent would be horrified." She glanced around to be sure no one else witnessed the scene below. Rushing back to the window she found the carriage port empty, Dandy had been led away, all evidence of a delivery of gold erased as easily as one wave washes over another.

She caught her bearings; she was safe; they had made the delivery—yet she felt as though the wind was knocked out of her.

Taking a few moments to arrange her composure in an elegantly framed mirror, her hand nervously knocked over a French porcelain soap decanter that shattered on the marble-topped washstand.

"Whew," she breathed again before she walked downstairs. "I wished for excitement, but this is more than I asked for."

Mr. Turnage had ushered Mrs. Thompson out of his office when Marion returned.

"My assistant will telegraph your husband in Virginia City of your safe arrival," he said. "Now you ladies be sure to enjoy a lovely supper at the Last Chance Hotel."

Mrs. Thompson motioned for a public carriage to convey them and their trunks to her sister's home. She talked eagerly of giving the children items she had embroidered for them since her last visit. "Dear children, they do go through pinafores in a hurry."

No mention was made then or later of the delivery of gold from the Alder Gulch mines. On the uneventful return trip Marion was notably quiet with plenty of time to contemplate what had occurred. She could only shake her head again and again with "Whew!" If this is how business is conducted in Montana Territory, I'm not sure I'm cut out for it. What would father think if I became involved in the mining business in the Rocky Mountains? If I resorted to such a subterfuge? Oh, my, this woman surpasses me for adventure—I wonder—is that what I want?

13

While Patrick worked the claims alongside Kent and occasionally helped prepare the new plot of farm land, Marion had a great deal of time to visit a young couple who recently settled on the lower bench towards the Jefferson River. Samuel and Genevieve Sayles had come from Missouri in the spring to homestead in Montana Territory. They built their small hand-hewn log cabin, leaving time to put in a garden and build a cow shed. Samuel troweled chinking between the cabin's logs as insulation against the coming winter's fierce temperatures. Their red Jersey milk cow had a three-month-old calf that bounded after its mother on the open plains.

"How do you get them to come home so you can milk?" Marion laughed.

"I rattle the pan of oats and Helen comes running up with Daisy after her." Genevieve hardly missed a beat rotating paddles of the churn while she talked. She was a tall, slim woman with high cheekbones and large brown eyes. She bunched her dark hair loosely with ends falling in all directions. A plaid gingham dress proved to be her one everyday work dress, except washday, when she put on a frayed, white muslin covered by the usual long white apron.

"Please sit down and let me bring you some cold mint tea," she offered. "Our first task was to dig a well since we are not located on a creek. It produces fine, cold water. We met many of the neighbors when we had a well-digging day."

Genevieve related their efforts to become established on the land before a notorious Montana winter. "It is so open here that any wind, let alone blizzard, is sure to whip mercilessly across the place."

The two women soon exchanged stories of their backgrounds and experiences. "My family was desperately poor after the war and it seemed best that Samuel and I seek our fortunes elsewhere," Genevieve said. "My older sister, Danielle, will join us in a few months since I am with child. I will find her presence comforting."

The couple already sold eggs and milk products to the miners for a small income, and they had planted a garden to see them through the winter. In the meantime, Samuel labored much as Kent did, his shoulder to the plow.

"If things don't work out here in a year or two, we might proceed to Oregon's Willamette Valley," Genevieve said, "but we love this beautiful country."

"I often wonder about my destination, too—which direction my life is taking me. Sometimes I'm uncertain whether I fit in here, or what I will do."

If Genevieve noticed Marion's apprehension about her future she did not reveal it, continuing their get-acquainted conversation.

"I will admit the grasshoppers are terrible. People who've lived here awhile say it's a bad year for them. Here, this butter is churned." Genevieve let Marion have the pleasure of bringing it to a finish, a huge yellow lump oozing whey in the one gallon churn. Genevieve salted the butter and set some aside for Marion to take home. This began many days of women-talk that Marion had scarcely found time or inclination before in her life. She taught Genevieve how to make sourdough bread, while Genevieve shared her family's yeast recipes from the South.

In late September when Genevieve's pregnancy was about five months along, Danielle came to stay. She was a strikingly tall woman, a little older than Genevieve, with dark, searching eyes and thick black hair combed severely under a white cap. Marion instantly found her distant and unsmiling, hardly evidence she was a sister to Genevieve. She was entirely lacking in the openness of other women in the West.

Danielle, whom Marion addressed formally as Miss Hartman, kept to herself though her beauty gave Marion pause. Kent couldn't fail to find her attractive, in fact, he would find her quite lovely. Marion let the thought pass—until she might need to deal with it another day. Danielle tried to be unobtrusive in this home that was not hers, but when she entered a room the air became charged; a whisper of heavy skirts announced her presence, her gait almost servile until she strode outside among Sayles' cows and chickens.

At home with the butter, cream, and a bowl of homemade sauerkraut, Marion asked, "What do you think of me now, Kent? Genevieve will make a good wife of me yet! How could I have grown up without any domestic skills whatsoever? My sister Dora would laugh at me for donning an apron after all these years. Mother never corralled me long enough to teach me how to make a respectable pie, much less become ladylike. She would love you, Kent, for your good influence on me!"

She sang the praises of Genevieve and Samuel who were preserving meats and garden produce in jars for the winter.

"My head fairly swims with this chatter about 'putting by.' I'll have to do something about a cellar," Kent murmured one night after supper when he flopped on the bunk. Marion unbuttoned his heavy work shirt to rub down his tired biceps and chest.

"The cellar can wait," he grinned.

She pulled out his shirttail, removed his shirt and hung it on a peg outside to air. Her strong hands deftly massaged his sore muscles while she rambled about filling in her time sewing an apron for herself. Kent was well relaxed when she asked him to roll over so she could work on his shoulders and back. Marion massaged a handful of thick Jersey cream soothingly from his hairy neck to the waist of his trousers.

"Genevieve said the cream was good for dry, sunburned skin."

Kent soon fell asleep, reminding Marion of a small boy, a boy who kept baby birds in his room and grew up to love wild horses—as contented as big ol' Ben after a rubdown at the end of a day's work. Marion sat up by the kerosene lamp struggling to sew a perfect cross stitch and capture the balance of wayward French knots with a needle to adorn a dishtowel. The thread became tangled like her uncertain sense of her destination—she opened the firebox in the stove and thrust the dishtowel inside.

Pleasant weeks of the golden Indian summer of 1867 were full for the settlers and miners. They made last minute efforts to gear up for a change of season, heralded daily by crisp mountain air. The mercantile's stock of canning jars and hundred-pound sacks of sugar for home canning still kept the women occupied. Kent discussed preserving some venison in the fashion of the settlers. Even an old buck would be tender if it was canned, but the cellar did not get dug. He planned to give most of any sizeable kill to the Williams family, keeping enough for jerky and current use until cold weather provided a natural deep freeze.

On the fifteenth day of October snow accumulated on the east side of the mountain above the shack. Kent rose before dawn and dressed for the cold, then quietly headed out to hunt elk. He and Marion had been out of wild meat for some time, not counting sage grouse, pheasants, and an occasional wild turkey that were plentiful and easy to shoot on the benchland. He had counted on the herd grazing lower slopes, but he tracked them up the mountain. Ahead of him, magpies shrieked warning calls announcing his presence, and the wind carried his scent into stands of timber. Bagging big game wasn't to be without nature on his side.

Kent returned empty-handed from the tough, fruitless climb up the ridge. He stamped snow off his boots on the porch and stepped inside. The room was cold. His first glance took in the fact the stove had not been lit that morning. Marion was not in the bunk. The heavy handmade quilt from Dora was gone.

Kent stood in the doorway. Melting snow ran off his beard, a drip suspended in time, falling, falling—the floor rising up to meet it; drip and floor wavering before his eyes, engulfing his senses until the drip spattered in tiny colored rivulets. Kent's heart tumbled in slow motion, a deadweight crashing at his feet. A chill claimed his legs, iced his toes wet from the hunt, and set his teeth ajar. He'd sensed she might leave sometime, but it couldn't, shouldn't happen like this—not now when they were so content, at least he thought so. But the quilt was gone.

Hardly breathing, Kent forced his legs to move outside and found Rusty was missing from the corral. And the quilt was gone—one of the few things in the shack that was truly Marion's. His thoughts collided: An emergency? A trip to town or to Genevieve's? Possibly but not likely without leaving a note. He was sure she had left him. Hopelessness besieged him, akin to that he'd felt on the promontory above Sterling with the depths dropping away, his anguish bare, inconsolable.

He stumbled back inside, his mind thick, sluggish. Maybe she couldn't face winter in Montana—she was born and raised in California. What ever happened? Not the disagreements they'd had. Not the hardship and deprivation. Marion could handle all that and was indeed thriving upon it. But she was gone.

Kent felt his life spark drain away, like dampering down the stove to curtail licks of flames. Bird calls and winds rustling the junipers ceased, the music of the mountains silenced. His breath became short and rapid, but air didn't seem to reach his brain. He held his head, feeling dizzy and helpless. "Why? Why now?" Red and yellow flashes shot behind his eyes. He sank heavily into a chair.

Did I anger her last night? What did I say? I didn't notice anything was amiss? Did she want freedom—the freedom she had before we met?' An unnerving hour passed while he moved in a trance, hurt, haunted, renouncing any emotional attachment he had to her, or would ever have with anyone. Later, a rising anger roused him from his confusion. He spun around to dig under a pile of coats in the corner. Marion's small trunk was there with the key dangling on a little chain, but he did not touch it.

Shag crouched underfoot, her quizzical eyebrows signaling questions. She clung to him, needing to touch his hand, sniff his clothing, lick his boots. Her fat, long-haired body paced to her empty bowl and back to his side. Kent heard his own hollow footsteps cross the wooden floor as if a distant echo. He blindly walked to the corral and rested his forehead on a frosty top pole. Shag brooded over him, made small whimpering sounds, and trailed his every step.

Kent brought in a fresh bucket of water for the day, fed Shag, and lit the fire in the stove. A smoldering anger kept him going. Anger at the sense of betrayal, that Marion had been less than honest to resort to this—that she may have wanted someone else. But he didn't want to look at that right now. His tightly clenched jaw gave him a throbbing headache. He went out to feed Ben and shovel out manure. Back in the shack he found the interior as dark as his life felt. The bright handmade rugs hanging on the walls like tapestries now appeared tasteless in the rough surroundings. Two coffee cups on the table told unbearable, jarring stories. The joy had taken flight. To California? To Mexico Territory? Images of Ray, laughing, playful, suddenly roused his temper. The only tangible rival that inexplicably came to mind. The thought was entirely irrational, but he fumed, "I should have left him in jail."

The day stretched unmercifully long, over agonizing hours in which he found little to do but pace. He chopped and stacked wood until his arms ached, glancing down the valley expecting a red sorrel horse to come flying up the hill—he knew that was irrational, too. He knew deep down she had purposefully left him for her own reasons.

The next day and the next he couldn't help peering in the distance for approach of horse and rider, though he found she had returned Rusty to the Sterling livery stable. He gritted his teeth at the constant, bruising disappointment, the sense of desertion and rejection. The casual, disinterested brush-off was worse than outright fighting—left him fighting cobwebs, entangled in a familiar cycle—his father had left, he left Mother, now Marion abandoned him.

"Maybe it's the madness that drove her away—I must have appeared as out of my mind as Benson that night," he muttered, unraveling more sympathy than a defense. She begged me, and I revealed too much. The effects of the war she experienced here must have been too much for her to bear, for any woman to bear—Benson's death, my mental anguish, the lives of men that women should not be privy to.

But he'd expected they would both put his story aside, and that would have been the end of it. Now it flooded back in waves of unresolved loyalties, self-blame and flashbacks. "The flashbacks and night sweats are a part of me neither I nor she can forget. How dare I pursue her? I doubt I'll change, though my circumstances may improve."

His inner voice became a relentless tryant: I can't go back to those days—haunted before she came. I moved on before. I can do the same with this, choose to forget the whole damn affair. Yet I need something, someone to hold on to. My very existence depends on—depends on—what? She isn't coming back, I know. Maybe I leaned on her too much. He argued until his shaggy head sank into his hands, supported by elbows on his knees. He pictured Ray in jail. He and Ray both essentially asking, "Where do I go from here?" "Does it matter?"

Shag stayed close at his heels, quiet, worried, squirming in Kent's discomfort, foregoing her food when he failed to eat his. He rose to stare down the valley where Norwegian Creek wound its silvery course between unsightly diggings, acutely aware of the wrenching times, avenging and exposing the depths of souls in this land ruled by nature's fierce temperament—but the onslaught of grief refused to obey his demands to cease. Aching and gaunt, he stumbled up the creek, scrambled over boulders and snagged his wool coat on branches. At last wounded sounds emerged from deep inside, muffled in the still air. Shag brooded and crossed her front legs, her head resting upon her paws, her sorrow-filled eyes reflecting Kent's pain.

Three days later Genevieve stopped by on her way back from Sterling. She had a new crochet needle and pink and blue skeins of thread for Marion. Kent straightened from putting new shoes on Ben. His skin was haggard and grey.

"Marion isn't here," he said, his throat hoarse, barely able to utter the words. "She left a few days ago."

The neighbors spoke silently into each other's eyes. The skeins of rainbow hues with their magical potential lay limp in Genevieve's hand.

"This is very unexpected," she said gently.

"I should have known, I suppose, but I did not see it coming. She must have let me know, some sign—some indication—that I was too obtuse to recognize. She had always been so direct in many regards, though often reluctant to state her feelings." Kent put down his hammer and nails and sat on a barrel, motioning Genevieve to rest on a bench. He was grateful to have someone to talk to. For too many years he had habitually kept it all to himself.

"Perhaps I did not want to see that life here was unfulfilling for her, Mrs. Sayles, nor openly discuss any thoughts she might have about me—about living with me—or about her reluctance to reveal how she felt." His voice cracked. The casual arrangement had given him concern at times, but it seemed Marion continued to make it her choice. Certainly he had no hold over her.

"I'm sure she experienced more than enough of my personal family problems. And I know she harbored unfulfilled dreams—"

Genevieve waited for Kent to regain his composure.

"Do you know of any plans that might have taken her away? I do not want to intrude upon any confidences she may have shared with you, so do not feel obliged to reply. I just wonder what she chose to do and why."

Genevieve slowly shook her head. "I did not know Marion other than as a delightful companion. She did express wonder about her destination, possibly questioning it, but nothing more. Believe me, I will miss her greatly." Genevieve had the grace and empathy of his mother, Kent noticed.

She rose to go. "I am sorry, Mr. Berrigan. I can understand your deep loss. I wish you well."

Was this the way it had ended for Mother when Father left—and again when I left after the war? The circle of choices and abandonment swirled like an unhinged universe around Kent's head, an enveloping system he couldn't escape. In disgust he picked up Ben's hoof to finish shoeing.

It was late when he went inside and opened the small trunk. There lay Marion's pointy, high button shoes on top of the green silk gown from New York. She had taken the inlaid combs he gave her on the riverboat. He paused a moment, then rummaged in the corner of the room under his hunting outfits. From beneath, he pulled a pair of new shearling boots he had secretly hand stitched for Marion for the winter. He tossed the boots into the trunk and closed the lid.

———————

Marion returned to her hometown in Coloma, California as Miss Patton, not Mrs. Berrigan. The freightline driver, Mr. Cobb, had alerted townspeople she would arrive by stagecoach from Salt Lake City. The news aroused no great attention from anyone except her former riding partner, Ray, who had ridden to the stage stop leading his finest horse, saddled and ready to go.

"Ray, are you a mind-reader?" Marion said when she saw him waiting. "Of course, I want to ride, why not?" She shook his hand and took the reins in the other.

"I call 'im Bruno but you call 'im what you like. He's three years old." Ray's audacity in meeting her caught up with him. He suddenly became awkward and schoolboyish. Bruno, a bronze chestnut, danced impatiently.

"Do--do--you ride side saddle now you been to New York and all?" He grinned and Marion had to laugh at his fear that she had become sophisticated and ladylike. She noticed his missing tooth on the left side. He picked up her two bags, asking if he could give directions for transfer of her trunk.

"My worldly belongings are in these bags. The large one contains Dora's quilt," she said, patting it with a weary hand. "You will be pleased to know I left New York culture and style quite intact after my brief visit." They walked their horses down the street, discussing whether she would be staying in Coloma and where she might stable Bruno. This gave Marion an opportunity to sneak a good look at Ray. She sensed he was practically a grown man. Women they passed gave him sidelong glances and bobbed their skirts in brief curtsies.

"Who are you these days, Ray? Mayor or something?"

Ray cleared his throat and looked down at his boots, pulling his flat-brimmed hat lower over his brow. He couldn't seem to find words to reply. He had grown a couple inches taller in the past year. A black silk shirt showed off his wide shoulders, and leather riding pants fit tightly over his long muscular legs. Ray stuffed his hands in his pockets, reins and all.

Marion stared at him as if he were a stranger. In turn, he glanced sideways at his formerly free-spirited friend in the split skirt and high-heeled riding boots. Her womanliness now unnerved him, though the worn skirt and boots were the same.

He is dashing, Marion breathed. No wonder women practically faint on the street when they meet him. It was becoming clear to her that Ray's solicitousness in greeting her at the stagecoach may have had a deeper meaning. With a sinking feeling, she realized he was no longer the young lad she had taken for granted the last few years. She realized, too, that she was far from ready for this kind of involvement.

"Please, Ray, I must stop in the office and see my father. No doubt he has been wondering when I'd arrive. You understand, I'm sure." She handed the reins back to him.

"The horse is yers. I stable him for you 'til you be ready." Ray's voice sounded disappointed and a little concerned. He had a hard time meeting her surprised gaze. Marion read his guilt for acting rashly—his feelings overwhelming his judgment when he wanted to make a good impression—in reality to claim her for his own. It was there all over his downturned face; the man is hopelessly in love with me, Marion thought. Why hadn't I noticed before? She wondered how long this had been going on. Indeed, it took the admiring glances from other women to make her do a double-take at Ray, and see his reserved maturity in contrast to the youth who had hung around town and sometimes got into trouble.

"Thank you," she said simply.

Ray walked away with the horses while Marion tried to subdue a wave of emotion she'd successfully kept at bay during the trip from Montana Territory. She entered the office of the International Consolidated Mining and Shipping Company with a tight smile, waved to a new person behind the desk and strode quickly to the open door of her father's office. The pale green wallpaper with a tiny floral pattern was the same, also the brass chandelier with hanging crystal baubles. The mahogany file cabinet and substantial safe were familiar, but she felt changed.

Her father instantly bounded to his feet, holding wide his great arms that always felt so comforting. Marion slipped into them just as quickly, dismayed when her tears stained his starched shirt front.

"Marion, let me see you! You've become a lovely woman and so strong and healthy! Is that what New York has done for you? Or was it the Territories?" He laughed, wiping her face with his handkerchief. "But, come, you are weary and travel is arduous.

"Mr. Cobb happily notified us that you were en route. How that man knows everything. He is like a one-man telegraph system!" Father jubilantly steered Marion out the door and down the street to the nearest dining room for coffee and whatever else Marion desired.

This exceptionally warm homecoming felt almost too heated for Marion to comprehend. Father had all but forbidden her to leave last spring when she'd headed East. She only knew that she needed rest and time to think—and a long while to adjust. With attempted gaiety she related as much of her story as she could, leaving out anything that would bring another flood of tears— and that was most of it. Instead, she deferred to her father's willingness to discuss current company enterprises with her.

"As you know, the Company made investments in minerals in Brazil. Thanks to my personal assessment there, these have been remarkably timely expansions of our business abroad. It remains to be determined how we can further our interests in the United States now that the perpetual wars have finally abated. We're considering new discoveries of gold in Northern California. It has always been that way in your life, Marion, so much afoot. I wonder how you could bear it otherwise!"

Marion looked at him blankly, failing to grasp an insinuation that her stay in Montana Territory surely must have been tedious, given news of the failure of many mining companies. Her father enthusiastically described the potential for investment in railroad and communication contracts that appeared daily in financial circles, reiterating Marion's earlier prediction.

"Please, Father, I shall be interested in hearing more of this later, but now I need to go directly home and get refreshed." She rose and moved towards the door, hot tears behind her lashes. The full realization of what she had left behind assailed her.

Marion slept for three days, intermittently wandering about in her night gown when no one was around. She only sampled a few delicacies the cook left for her in the kitchen, great slabs of prime rib, German potato salad with generous chunks of bacon, and fresh hot doughnuts that at another time would have been mouthwatering. Her father threatened to call Dr. Hatch for a house visit, but Marion refused to see him or anyone.

Her mind played tricks on her—she saw Kent in the Coloma coffee shop looking like a travel-worn mountain man with his black hair, beard and hands furrowed with grime. She envisioned the tall poised gentleman with calm grey eyes, his stride beside her on the ferryboat, and heard his low drawl in her ear, his warm concern—no—love that now drove her to regrets.

I wonder if I am pregnant, Marion thought. If so, I don't want Father to know—or to know myself. It can't be, but it's possible after six months with Kent. I never thought it would— could happen to me. Fears slammed her already fragile being.

"Not now, for heaven's sake," she cried. She paced behind pulled curtains and fretted for days. Just when she convinced herself she was carrying Kent's son her natural cycle occurred. This became a major letdown amid lost dreams, but admittedly not the tragedy it would have been to be with child.

"How could I have faced him? Or father? What would my life have been then? I must have been childish to have risked such a possibility. But his son? Now that might have filled my restless heart. And his."

After a particularly dark day, Marion could no longer tolerate the walls around her or another moment of painful reflection.

"Father, I have been quite remiss in sharing my recent experiences with you, and if you will promise to forgive and let me suffer from my own errors, I am willing to open my heart." Marion's once oval face was now a study in prominent cheekbones and long sad lines. "I am at a loss to explain, otherwise, how this melancholy has overtaken me, when I came home with such optimism."

Henry Patton sat down on the nearest chair and gave his daughter his full attention. Marion shifted uncomfortably on a stool opposite and placed her hand on his knee. "I fell in love, Father, with the man, Mr. Kent Berrigan, who visited Coloma last fall. No, it did not happen then nor even later when we both traveled with the wagon train to St. Louis. He returned to the South to visit his family at the same time I traveled to New York. It was largely coincidence, for me at least, to have been in his company at that time.

"On my return trip, we encountered each other again. I was persuaded, with my full compliance to be sure, to continue on to Montana Territory with him. Since then, Father, I lived with Kent as his wife—to anyone who cared to know—and we were gloriously well-suited to each other. He was so thoughtful and kind, and I was terribly content. A contentment I have never known. Now I have thrown it all away."

"And you loved this man, my daughter?" Mr. Patton cut to the essence of the difficulty as surely as if he himself had tread this path before.

"Yes, Father, and I still do. I do not understand how I left him as I did. We were perfectly happy with our lives. Oh, I was restless at times, and he suffered from the war, but my abrupt departure is most bewildering. I must have a character flaw that is extraordinarily damaging to those around me. I am afraid for myself—and afraid for Kent, for how I may have hurt him." The tears were long past but Marion felt herself falling again into depths where she confused half-formed yearnings with loving and losing.

"Your bereavement is a natural thing, darling. I felt that way when your mother left for San Francisco, though she did not close me out of her life. It will heal in time. You may find that hard to believe at this moment. I wonder that you should care so much for this gentleman, Kent, and not bring him into the family and the business."

"That was not possible, Father. He is quite wed to the land— he says he's found something in Montana that he needs to hang onto."

"The gold mines?"

"The beauty, the peace of mind he's found there, the hope of acquiring more land. I believe his withdrawal is due to his experiences in the war. He was from a once proud family. He could have married into a plantation in the South with position, wealth and recognition, but he did not aspire to any of those. I could not understand it." Privately she added, he could have married Miss Olivia Spencer but he only wanted me. Tears brimmed over once again, and she hid her face in the lace ruffles of her gown.

"I--I failed to recognize the finer attributes of a man like Mr. Berrigan. You may go now, Father. Thank you for hearing my sad story. I promise I will commence working on your behalf and that of the Company as soon as possible."

Marion's health improved quickly after she cleared her conscience, accepting responsibility for the disaster she made of her first love. The sharp click of her heels on the boardwalks was heard early and late when she resumed socializing about town, greeting old friends and making acquaintances with newcomers, but she avoided the office and board members of her father's company, knowing any commitment would overwhelm her.

"Ray, I am thinking of your generous gesture with the horse. I believe I am ready to try him, at your convenience, of course," she announced one day when she met Ray on his way to work at the freight loading dock.

Ray threw back his head and laughed. "And he's ready to make yer acquaintance, Miss Patton. He be rarin' to go after these days in the stable. You may have yer hands full! I think I best ride with you this evening after work."

But by afternoon her restlessness drove her to attend a board meeting with her father at the Company office. She notified Ray of her change of plans, much to his disappointment. Marion carefully selected suitable clothing from the free-standing wardrobe in her bedroom, a collection of apparel accumulated from her youth to the present. Earlier favorites had no chance of fitting her mature figure. Finally, she settled upon a Gibson-sleeved linen blouse in pale ochre and a straight floor-length brown skirt, a proper matronly style. With a wide brown homespun shawl and sensible walking shoes, Marion surveyed her image in a wavy glass mirror that had been her mother's. Dowdy and dated, oh my! These would be working class in New York City. What have I come home to? She straightened and left the house purposefully to pick up the pieces of her life and, hopefully, leave behind her tumultuous personal affairs.

Adam Feingold, operations manager, stood first when Marion swept in the door and moved toward her seat, a generously-sized red maple captain's chair. She felt his slightly bulging eyes take in everything at once; her attire, her sun-bronzed complexion, her uncustomary diffidence. His smile lacked the least bit of warmth, which did not bode well for any role she might entertain of herself as an associate in the Company.

The other gentlemen removed their hats and bowed graciously in her direction, offering pleasant remarks about their pleasure in seeing her again. In return Marion curtsied the least bit and sat down. On her right sat Adam's son, Harold, mid-twenties, with a clean shaven face and smartly trimmed goatee. To the left she was happy to find "Uncle" Jeddiah, a longtime teamster and friend of the family, likely retained on the Board as acknowledgement of his past services rather than for present realities.

The meeting proceeded solemnly with the usual formalities, many of the reports expensively typeset or in elegant longhand script. Mr. Patton rifled through frayed, parchment-like leaves of a shipping order file organized on several rings. Columns of entries filled hundreds of pages documenting the history and survival of the Company over sixteen years. Marion, along with the others, felt genuine respect for the files.

Eventually, he mentioned that since Marion had traveled extensively across the continent, "she might be able to enlighten us as to the conditions, and more importantly, the attitudes in the aftermath of the war."

Marion suddenly felt small and insignificant in the enormous captain's chair. The scope of the subject was daunting, and Marion feared she'd reveal her yet unhealed, highly personal experiences to this group of gentlemen; however, it seemed to be forced upon her. Father was inordinately proud of her acumen about most things.

She found her voice to begin. "To be sure, so soon after cessation of hostilities, I found emotions to be raw in many parts of the country. These are times of most trying adjustments for individuals and companies in both the North and South. Losses in deaths alone claimed over a generation of young and middle-aged men from both sides. The South was especially devastated proportionately, as you know." Here her voice wavered. "In many cases those involved are still fighting the war with each other or within themselves."

She thought of Benson's losing battle and Kent's confession—maybe the raw emotion he revealed at her insistence had driven her away—a fleeting insight she stifled before continuing.

"On the other hand, the country is vigorous and shows signs of prospering at an astounding rate. Completion of the trans-continental railroad will soon make all parts of the Union easily accessible, even the remote Northwest Territories, not to mention the contribution of the telegraph system." She winked at her father. "I was obliged to report my whereabouts and well-being when I visited New York City and the Territories. With these assets, in my opinion, we will see a migration such as we've never dreamed to the farthest corners of the United States."

She paused a moment to take in the weight of this concept, the States now united in one forceful mass of expansion. Beneath the table her hands twisted a small handkerchief into a limp ball. The board members either waited for more or paused to evaluate her comments. More likely they were checking the winds to see which way they blew, to determine if their positions were threatened.

"Thank you," Marion whispered to Jeddiah, who kindly acknowledged her contribution with a reassuring smile. A nod of his head sent his badly cut grey hair tumbling over his brow.

Over the next few days, Marion suffered a relapse into the rawness. The open wounds of her love for Kent, the wounds Kent carried from the war, the horrors of Benson's death—all rose up as ghostly images accosting her at every turn. Marion became desperately ill with a fever, and Dr. Hatch ordered bed rest for the following week. He prescribed passion flower and valerian root, and stayed at the house most of the next few days. Despite the sedation, Marion threw herself over and over in bed, winding the sheets into knots, chilling her skin and raising her temperature. Fits of memories and nightmares dragged down her invincible constitution. Mr. Patton engaged a night nurse to attend to her every need.

"This appears to be more than an ordinary influenza," Dr. Hatch said. "Has she been exposed to something we might not know about? Or has she been under recent strain?"

"Appears so, Dr. Hatch, appears so. I am not clear on this myself. She cries about the war spoiling her life along with the lives of others who suffered, all this brought up by her trip North.

I must admit my experiences in the border skirmishes years ago left deep inner wounds.

"I was swept up in the tide of defending our borders, though it is now debatable whether it was defense or aggression—many think the latter. The conflict still haunts me." Mr. Patton's voice trailed off when he reflected on the barbarism of man against man over the U.S. and Mexican Territorial border.

"Ironically, these are the same men we want to do business with now."

"Excuse me, Mr. Patton, but I wonder if you can talk with your daughter about her experience and yours. Perhaps it would relieve her mind and yours as well." Dr. Hatch gathered his few belongings in a trademark black bag and left Mr. Patton sunken in his chair with his memories. Marion was sleeping evenly when the night nurse arrived.

Word quickly spread that Miss Marion was ill. Ray paced the streets looking for her, and he rode Bruno twice that week before turning him out to pasture, uncertain when they might ride together. When he next saw Marion, he whistled under his breath. *"Ella es como una cáscara vacía de sí misma."* She is like an empty shell of herself. Her spirit and gaiety were all gone; Marion was a matchstick figure with gaunt cheeks and hollows around her eyes, evidence of what she had gone through. She greeted Ray eagerly, yet her voice was weak and halting. Stricken, he was without words to express his shock and dismay. Embarrassed by the impasse, they went their separate ways.

Marion knew without a doubt that the overpowering forces of war that had crushed Kent in so many ways had at last caught up with her, and that she brought the ordeal to California. One morning while silently breakfasting with her father, Mr. Patton brought it up. He rattled his china coffee cup in its delicate saucer and cleared his throat.

"I am sorry, my daughter, for your great pain from recent experiences." He hesitated a moment, then went on, "Would it help if I told you I carry much of the ongoing border war with me?"

Marion's eyes flicked to his earnest face, willing at last to let her into his inner being. This from the father she did not know as a person—or had ever expected to—as if that person had disappeared long ago into roles of parent and breadwinner, even investment gambler. She said nothing, allowing her father to speak, knowing that, like Kent, if he did not do so now he likely never would.

14

Blizzards of the historic winter of 1867-68 in Montana Territory nailed tenderfoots and hardened settlers alike with icy blasts. Cattle suffered frostbit limbs or perished in fifty degree below zero temperatures. Storms whipped through cracks in homes, freezing water in teakettles and wash basins. Only smoke rising in the frigid air from scattered cabins, and a few wagon tracks across snowy benches denoted human existence in the Arctic weather. Kent relied heavily on his neighbors for solace and warmth. He valued Genevieve's friendship, indeed that of both women, more than he could say. He had plenty of opportunities to meet Genevieve's sister, Danielle Hartman; Genevieve made sure of that. On whose behalf she worked so assiduously Kent was uncertain.

Over supper one night at the Sayles,' Kent saw the hunger in Danielle's eyes though she tried to hide it in every way imaginable. In reality, she was unavailable for any overtures except the most polite, mundane conversation. Give it up, Genevieve, Kent stormed inside. I'm not a commodity on the market, and she is the driest of dry goods left on the shelf. Oh, Danielle is a beauty all right, but she is as tightly wrapped as Marion was loose—then he stopped himself. Oh hell, I can't compare these women this way—but I would like to shake this one. Maybe the other one, too, damn it.

After supper the family usually read aloud by light of candles and a boisterous fire under an open mantle. Samuel offered a Scripture reading with a brief commentary, applying it to their daily lives. One could not but be helped by the guidance and inspiration, Kent thought. The women selected poems or short stories for entertainment. They were all often laughing when Kent headed out to ride Ben home in the dark.

Several winter months were mercifully behind them when the Callahans prepared a holiday Open House for surrounding neighbors, the only remaining inhabitants in Hot Spring District. Weather had shut down the mills, and workers had scurried home or elsewhere to a better climate. True to her love of a celebration, Mrs. Callahan arranged for one of the settlers to play the squeezebox, giving a raucous effect over already noisy chatter due to generous libations before and after her sumptuous holiday meal.

Huge casseroles and platters were still mounded with her best dishes after everyone was more than adequately served. Kent sat back from a scoop of mashed potato and carrot mixture that Mr. Callahan topped with smooth brown gravy.

"I'm stuffed like the wild goose. I have to let this meal settle a bit before I even consider homemade ice cream and mince meat pie."

"You'll like the mince pie," Harland grinned. "It's made of apples, raisins, and the venison you gave us."

On impulse, Kent invited Danielle out for a short turn up and down the street "to settle our suppers." Lanterns dangled from shops, though most of the businesses had "Closed for the Winter" signs in the windows. She hesitated an instant before Kent took her arm and steered her outdoors into a blast of cold air that felt welcome after the overly-heated room in the crowded boarding house.

They turned off Hill Street to walk near a livery stable where Kent halted. "I would like to know you better, Miss Hartman," he said, touching her throat above the prim lace neckline that framed Danielle's face, a gesture he at once felt was at odds with his formality.

Danielle did not reciprocate with a gesture of her own, nor did she shrink. Hot Spring Creek gurgled beneath crusted ice marred only by rabbit tracks. Wind rattled saloon shutters in concert with distant voices and music at Callahans'.

A sudden bizarre, inappropriate image of Kent's standoff with Rand behind this same stable struck Kent—he saw himself striking Rand, an act unthinkable in his normal life. He dropped his hand as if had been burned and shook his head to clear the image, to clear effects of the spiked cider.

"I'm sorry, Miss Hartman, forgive me—my mind--ah--I do truly mean it about knowing you better. Can we be friends if not more?" He stood helplessly lost for words as the strength drained from his body.

Something about his vulnerability allowed Danielle to acquiesce. Her eyes softened and she put out her hand which Kent gratefully accepted. "Please do come see me when you have time," Danielle whispered as they rejoined the others celebrating inside.

The Sayles acquired goats in March. Four young black and white nannies and a ram scampered up on the sod roof of the chicken coop playing king of the mountain, then over the fence to mingle with the sheep. Daisy, the calf, cavorted with the goats in the pasture, kicking up her heels and butting heads with the best of them except the ram. The goats' bleats added chaos to the cackling of chickens making the homestead a proper working farm.

Care of the small animals fell to Danielle, especially after the birth of little Peter Sands Sayles. Genevieve needed her rest to meet round-the-clock nursing demands of the hearty child. Danielle hastened to do early chores when the rooster crowed and dim light crested the Gallatin Range to the east. Samuel rose to light the woodstove for breakfast.

Kent rode over one day to visit during a warm spell that Montanans called a Chinook. His loneliness had soared and mood plummeted as winter threatened to hang on. Shag had her virtues, but carrying on a conversation was not one of them. Unusually at ease, Danielle spoke to Kent of her special time of day.

"Mornings are frosty if not gales of horizontal snow, but always clean, crisp, sharp to the senses."

She stood in her long wool coat on the cabin steps, breathing in astoundingly pure mountain air that swept from the highest reaches of old Hollowtop. "The scooped out top of the peak is such a landmark. It is like a best friend to me, bent kindly in my direction from its lofty altitude."

Clouds circled or hung low at the peak's command, its climate ranging from sultry to stormy mistress around its bald façade in summer or stern, glacier-like snowcap in winter.

"Stunning," she breathed, before picking up a pail of cow's milk saved last night for the chickens. "The goats will soon have their first offspring and produce surplus milk. Samuel will sell goats' milk as well as the thick yellow cream we spoon off the Jersey milk."

Kent saw that the activity and invigorating cold of the short winter days brightened the time for Danielle. Her skin glowed, her high red cheeks set off a new light in her eyes.

"We substitute extra cream or applesauce for eggs in cakes, cookies and pancakes if hens are not laying." Danielle laughingly escorted him about while the goats tried to suck her fingers or butt human backsides. Chickens came running for table scraps she scattered for them. Shag's nature prompted her to herd these unruly beasts and fowl, but Kent signaled her to stay beside him.

"You are finding homesteading agreeable, I presume," he said, amazed at Danielle's radiant face.

"Oh, yes, I am so happy to be of assistance to Samuel and Genevieve. The opportunity to help with the animals has given me responsibilities thoroughly suitable to my present situation in life. See how amusing they are!" She pointed to two agile goats standing on their hind legs chewing an old towel hanging from the clothesline.

Kent laughed, too, not at the goats which he found distasteful, but at Danielle's sudden ease and charm. The couple walked over the benchland, leaving jagged snow trails behind as they casually talked of daily happenings, foremost of which was about her nephew, Peter Sands, "Sands" being in honor of their Scotch grandparent on his father's side. Shag sprinted aside in pursuit of an enormous jackrabbit in its white winter coat whose long legs easily put it out of range.

"And tell me of your situation in life," Kent asked gently. Since she'd referred to her "present situation," he took the opportunity to be more personal than either had previously allowed. Nevertheless, Danielle was caught off guard, but she braved her nerves for the disclosure.

"I am married," she said. The open land spread before them like empty pages of a journal to be filled at last with her long hidden story. Boots crunched through the crust of unbroken snow in an otherwise silent world that stood waiting for the entries. Looking straight ahead, Danielle gathered her thoughts. Kent saw only the tip of her nose past the heavy wool shawl covering her head.

"I married young and we lived with his parents in Boonville, Missouri, not far from my childhood home. Genevieve was still a child. I spent as much time as possible with her when she wasn't in school, and she helped us with extensive gardens that provided a livelihood for both families. Melons, peppers, corn, the usual gardens they have there."

She was not telling him about her husband or the marriage, Kent noted, but he had all winter, all year, or the rest of his life if necessary to hear more. He did not hurry her.

"Fort Sumter fell and changed our lives. The state was in a flurry of for or against. Everyone was talking about it and neighbor went against neighbor. It all became very hurtful. The newspapers roused people even more with their fiery headlines. Politicians railed from their soap boxes, gathering great crowds that often came away more unenlightened than before. Even the churches joined in.

"My husband became obsessed with the currents of secession whipped up by the news and these spokespeople. He joined the Army and went on a campaign in the North. It was not long after that I last heard from him."

She ended with a sense of finality.

"You last heard from him?"

"He has been missing since, either dead or deserted. There has been no news of him these past seven years."

"I am so terribly sorry." The crushing weight of her situation became painfully obvious to Kent. He understood at once her former distance from him, indeed from life itself.

Danielle turned to face him. "There is more. My husband had exceedingly strong views about the destiny of the country, and of the church and its teachings. He left on something of a crusade, if I may say so, that alienated my family and myself. I cannot say that I am so sorry any longer—after these past years." Her usual soft voice hit strident notes revealing another side of her character.

"So you see, I find myself bound by what may be mythical ties at this time. His family and mine are Southern Baptists of a more conservative order. I have not failed to notice that you enjoy Scripture readings here, but I am afraid since you are Catholic that we have no common ground. I could not bear further condemnation such as I frequently experienced as a young wife. I fear getting into another impossible—situation." The words "relationship" or "marriage" seemed far too threatening to utter.

Kent felt the "impossible situation" was flung like a challenge which he chose to ignore, while he tried to absorb the fears held so close to her heart, the tears having been shed long ago.

"You fear condemnation from me? Surely you know of my recent companion, Miss Marion. I'm hardly in a position to be critical and I wouldn't intend to be. I'm not sure that being a Catholic, in name only, has any bearing on this. I wonder if you have unfairly separated yourself, Miss Hartman, by harboring these fears."

"You are kind, Mr. Berrigan, thank you. Perhaps I have waited too long for the axe to fall—fearing my husband's sudden return or claims on me if I remarried. Not knowing has cost me dearly."

Kent rode home murmuring, "If I had to endure seven years of this present pain, I could not tolerate it. Here we are, Danielle and I, each hardened by our losses in different ways. It is a cruel world at times." Her fears concerned him most, her fear of condemnation by the church and fear that her husband may one day return. An unfair situation indeed, though her fears regarding him were unfounded. It seemed she might distrust her own choices with men having had such a bad experience. It all struck too close to his own minimal defenses and wounds from loss, and he wrenched his thoughts away.

Other bad news quickly put their problems into an immediate perspective. Four men had been killed in a mining accident in Alder Gulch a few days prior, including Nathaniel Thompson, owner of Summit Mine and Mill and husband of Annette Thompson, who had delivered gold to Helena. The news swept the county and beyond due to the sudden and unlikely nature of the disaster. The shock made more than one miner rethink his occupation. By the time Kent and Ben reached his shack, he had made up his mind to get out of mining. He decided to speed up his acquisition of the South Willow Creek property he had admired last summer.

———————

Settlers had found fertile, open valleys on the east and west sides of the Tobacco Roots before the gold discoveries. They were well rewarded for their early arrival by the Preemption Act of 1841 that granted one hundred sixty acres free to those willing to file for the land and settle there. Their farms, allotted in quarter section parcels, soon turned undeveloped federal land into privately held properties. The Homestead Act of 1862, signed by Abraham Lincoln, further represented expansionist policies of the United States government, albeit at the expense of native inhabitants. Originally opposed by the South, residents of both North and South now exploited the opportunity to seize homesteads. Increasing numbers of immigrants raised beef for the miners.

"Some folks came out, put down roots, and planned to stay awhile," Kent marveled, the thought striking a chord in his need to buy land. He researched remaining government parcels in the county offices. The wedge of prime grazing land between the northeast flowing Jefferson and Madison rivers was already occupied by the Williams, Blackburns, Sayles and others. He found a half section of 320 acres for sale near South Willow Creek. The region was favored by bountiful water flowing from the Tobacco Roots—Norwegian Creek, Canadian Creek, Rattlesnake Creek, colorful names that Kent enjoyed.

In spring 1868, he hastened to acquire desirable acreage he'd only dreamed of, and began to build at the earliest opportunity. He bought lumber from dismantled stamp mills before timbers and boards were snapped up for Territorial bridge building. He had little difficulty buying quantities of steel rods, pipes and wiring auctioned off by managers trying to recoup funds for irate investors, many of whom had been sold "a bill of goods" on their initial investments. One of the mills, Midas Mining Company, had barely begun operations before gold became scarce. Others had been closed for the winter ahead of Montana's bone-chilling blizzards, this year setting record low temperatures. By spring owners found that gold, laborers, and enthusiasm had largely disappeared. Many men had joined the campaign against the Sioux to keep the eastern portion of the Bozeman Trail open. However, Kent hired eminently qualified craftsmen from the old countries who remained among the settlers.

Moving from the shack entailed various hard decisions. Kent gave Mrs. Callahan the tapestry-like rugs he had bought for Marion, and Angel was delighted with a gift of the small trunk, though Mrs. Callahan looked knowingly at Kent. He had also cut down the shearling boots to fit Angel, and made a small warm pair of shearling mittens for Finn. The New York tailored dresses and contents of the trunk had been distributed to other miners for their women.

Harder to separate were the immense losses associated with the shack, namely his beloved "wife" Marion, but he had learned that fighting shadowy memories and regrets only engaged them further. Embracing the worst of them gave him relief and a measure of peace he desperately sought. With a sense he had released ties one by one, he closed the door of the shack behind him. Patrick Colter, the new teacher in Sterling, would occupy it for the school term. Kent maintained title to the homestead and his claims, which he would have to work each year as required by law. A greater demand on his time was running for election as justice of the peace. He had agreed to serve one term on behalf of his fellow citizens if elected, but with the house building under-way he let the moral imperatives lie at the moment. Instead, he dropped by the Sayles' place on his way to South Willow Creek.

"Going for the election, are ye?" Samuel asked.

"News travels fast by pigeon or something around here," Kent laughed.

"We'd like to see ye get it. Frontier justice isn't what it should be. It isn't Christian, the hangings and all. And ye know as well as I do the officials been skimming fees from the poor miners sure as we skim cream from Jersey milk. They say beware of wolves in sheep's clothing. Anyway, ye best look out for yourself. It might not be safe to nose about."

Samuel shoveled out stalls while he talked. Genevieve, with little Peter Sands in a sling on her back, scrubbed clothes on a washboard in a tub outdoors. Danielle heard Kent's voice and came from the cabin, dripping soap suds from her elbows.

"How are the goats?" Kent asked.

"We have some little ones." She excitedly motioned him to follow her, unlike her formerly distant personality. Happiness sparked her dark eyes and turned up the corners of her mouth, a sight at once appealing and threatening to Kent. He trailed her to the pasture where the goats ran pell mell to meet them. Danielle soon had her hands full petting each one and pushing their hard heads with nubs of horns away from Kent.

"What is that smell?" Kent passed his sleeve over his nose.

"Smell? Oh, the ram! It's the ram in rut!" Danielle laughed at Kent holding his nose.

"God, the odor—I can't stand it." Kent edged away coughing and rubbing his eyes.

"Forgive me, Miss Hartman, but I find that scent intolerable. If you will excuse me, I shall be on my way."

"Oh, you must be upset with me as well as the ram—"

He tried not to breathe as he stumbled back to Ben.

"T'would be an ill wind that blew that smell to my new home," he muttered. Shaking his head at the perplexed Danielle, he waved that he had to go, thankful the South Willow Creek property was a good distance further from the Sayles than his last place.

15

Winters ended early in California with a curious mix of bracing pine-scented air from the Sierras and sweet smell of buds bursting on cherry and plum trees throughout settlements in the foothills. The eighteen-year-old town of Coloma, meaning "beautiful" in Native language, began to fade after the initial gold rush boom of '49. Remaining establishments and businesses including the International Consolidated Mining and Shipping Company faced similar changes.

Its owner, Henry Patton, had bared his soul to Marion, wringing the story of his experience in the border wars from deep in his past. He could now expect a warm kiss on the cheek from her at breakfast, a mellow, amiable time together each accepted with gratitude. Their cook's scones, served with fresh apple jelly Marion prepared, soon put weight on Marion's bones. No mention was made of her attending board meetings. Father briefly summarized proceedings when they were deemed of interest. In turn, Marion declared she'd heard nothing from Kent, nor did she write.

"He followed me here once, Father. He isn't likely to do it twice."

In the meantime, Mr. Patton knew she often disappeared for hours. He related some of this to Dora's upcoming wedding in San Francisco. Elizabeth Patton had been instrumental in making an arrangement for Dora with a respectable family, and wedding festivities were to occur around the holidays. Mr. Patton expected the marriage might be both a happy and sad occasion for Marion who so recently suffered the loss of her own so-called union, and he did not pry into her whereabouts.

One morning Marion breezed in with a quick hug around her father's shoulders. "You're feeling right pert today, Marion," he said, pleased that she seemed like her former self.

"The inactivity is becoming unbearable for me, except that I am training Bruno. You know that Ray—or Ramos—gave him to me? The training is coming along well. He is a splendid horse."

Henry Patton winced. The mere mention of a man in Marion's life set off his acid indigestion, and the mention of Ramos in particular gave him heartburn. He stared balefully at Marion, utterly at odds with her cheery disposition. He was not unaware of Ramos' exploits in the small town of Coloma, but he'd previously tolerated his association with Marion. Admitting that he'd never become a horseman himself, he felt his daughter was safer riding with someone. However, it was more difficult to turn a blind eye to Ray's gift of a horse. He hoped most people did not know how it had come about. At least no one, particularly his rather rigid board members, had raised the issue. Mr. Patton had always been touchy about how he had raised his daughter.

Marion poured herself a cup of coffee. "I've been seriously thinking of the Company expanding within the borders of the United States. As I alluded to at the board meeting, I believe we could prosper with early assertive moves, particularly in the Southwest. That section of the country is ripe, I think. Construction of a railway to Santa Fe, delayed by the war, will doubtlessly be completed before long. The telegraph will accompany it, if not before.

"I have a particular fondness for the telegraph because of my use of it in New York. How fast and convenient it was to connect us all the way across the country. Did you not find it enjoyable as well as utilitarian, Father?"

Mr. Patton had long ago learned that when Marion had been "thinking," trouble was sure to follow. Her idea would likely shake up the stolid investors on the Coloma board of his International Consolidated Company. How it might go over with its San Francisco managers he dared not speculate.

"Your observations appear to be sound and the implication we put our money in the Southwest has merit. Do you have recent evidence to support your claims?"

"It is based more on intuition, Father. I am cut off here from information to be had in larger financial centers. I asked as many questions as appeared decent when I visited New York City. In Manhattan I studied available news and literature of the investment firms, financial offices, and mining company headquarters."

Mr. Patton knew full well when he left the breakfast table he'd be challenged to stay ahead of his daughter—and that he'd be a better man for it. Opening a company branch in Santa Fe would be an opportune time to merge the provincial Coloma office with headquarters in San Francisco. However, he was deeply suspicious of Marion's motives. She might break away from the Company and make an independent foray into the bruising world of commerce. It was apparent that Marion aimed to mingle in the midst of greater financial circles. He immediately grasped a sense of her ambition, not unlike his own. Henry Patton understood a calling and the challenge that entailed as well as anyone. Clearly, her sojourn in Montana Territory with a man she professed to love had not been enough for her, for whatever reason.

"You realize, of course, that every able-bodied man from sixteen to forty would like to stake a claim to your affections. I fear for your future—and your safety—on these ventures you undertake so casually. Truly, Marion, I am at a loss for what to do with you. The loneliness and deprivation in the camps is rampant. The prospects are not at all promising for you. Outside San

Francisco or Los Angeles, there seems little that would be suitable or of interest to you."

"Father, I fear you underestimate your daughter and only foresee the worst for me, though I did not mean to upset you—"

"Take Dora now," Mr. Patton interrupted. "She's engaged to an exemplary fellow, excuse me, gentleman, who is faultless in good manners and has a secure position for the future. Would that I be so fortunate as to see such a match for you."

Marion edged away from the dissertation on acceptable prospects, but Henry Patton observed a flush in her cheeks. He had no inkling Marion's upbringing and innate good manners had not prevented her from capering about nude in nature with Kent Berrigan.

"I probably will not conform to your expectations, Father." She slipped away to meet Ray for a horseback ride. Their undeniable mutual attraction would have made her father apoplectic.

At the next board meeting, Adam Feingold, operations manager, disdained the notion of concentrating their efforts elsewhere when they were so heavily invested in gold and iron ore enterprises in South America.

"We have committed considerable resources to the operations in Brazil, which means sizeable demands upon the finances of the Company."

"I think we are indebted to El Dorado County and those locally who gave the Company its start and continue to make it prosper," added Feingold's son, Harold.

The contentious meeting ended with Henry Patton pushing through his plan to close the Coloma office. Adam Feingold chose the security of working in the San Francisco office along with Mr. Patton, while several other members resigned to remain with their homes and families in the foothills. Jeddiah, bless his soul, whose years of freighting had acquainted him with the Southwest, was more encouraging. He stoutly defended the expansion and agreed to accompany the small group that would establish temporary headquarters in Santa Fe. Marion was to occupy a position in the new branch office.

After the decision had been made, Mr. Patton spoke to Marion with an assurance he did not feel. "This exercise on your behalf leaves me concerned but confident that you'll keep your feet on the ground, my Marion. Santa Fe is the oldest capital city in the country, surely a center of traditional culture and religion of very conservative people. There should be amenities you would enjoy and find more than adequate."

He arranged for the date of Dora's wedding to be advanced so Marion could attend the festivities before leaving on the long, difficult journey to the Southwest. Dora's betrothed, Martin Brisbane, was a handsome, well-dressed gentleman some years older than Dora. The usual wedding preparations were compounded by selling the Coloma home and packing for the move to San Francisco.

"You might discuss the living situation with Mother," Marion cautioned. "She has been quite independent for a good many years and may be set in her ways. She may want to continue the existing arrangement."

Henry Patton recognized this to be in keeping with his own need for independence. As a consequence of the intuitive nature and foresight of his daughter, he rented a flat uptown in San Francisco suitable for his comfort and need for entertaining business associates.

Marion's childhood mahogany wardrobe was sent by barge to San Francisco and unceremoniously hauled to Dora's new husband's spacious Nob Hill home where the couple would reside. Marion's meager belongings would be dispatched in the opposite direction to Santa Fe.

At the wedding, Marion wore the abalone combs Kent had given her, a touching sentiment of her short term "marriage." The gift now represented the entirety of their relationship from first love on the riverboat to end, when she left the shack taking few belongings—one of them being the combs. The mementos no longer made her cry. Instead, they kept her union with Kent Berrigan foremost in her mind when her sister made her vows.

Marion found the overland trip skirting the southern end of Death Valley even more tedious than she expected. The scent of long-dead dust stirred with pungent rabbit brush and the scraping of shale against shale were in harmony with her inner world. A visceral tug across the vast Southwest Territories of the United States to Montana made her stomach queasy, her temper short. Her lips firmly forbid a return to often idyllic summer days with Kent Berrigan, though her gold "wedding" rings were packed in her jewelry box. She hadn't mentioned their existence to her sister—that she, too, had been married, at least symbolically. Even Ray's charisma failed to dissuade the reflections, the farewells to a lost love, rather an abandoned love. That she did the abandoning set off a wave of introspection, unusual for Marion, but perhaps in response to the gravity of her loss. *What is it about me that I would seek this gentle soul? The very oasis of quiet when I have yet to live so much of my life? I wonder what fate aligned our paths.* But her youthful energy tried to lift the mood and strain while she and Jeddiah rode the bumpy wagon.

"Are you all right, Uncle? I hope this is not too much for you."

"I'm farin' well enough, and you?"

"Well enough. The trail is trying and I'm afraid it is tiring you."

The hardships of rough travel were in stark contrast to the speed, comfort and excitement of the riverboat, railroads, and trams she had been privileged to experience on recent journeys. She envisioned the transformation that steam-powered railways would bring all the way from El Paso to Los Angeles. The significance of the route to the newly unified United States could not be overstated.

In the meantime, they found themselves among hundreds of freighters, many loaded with hand-made Indian blankets and goods, traveling the Old Spanish Trail from Santa Fe to Los Angeles.

"It's the oldest, longest damn trail in the whole United States if you ask me," Jeddiah said. "I done it more than once with caravans of pack horses and mule trains. The trail goes back two hundred years or more. You know all about that, Ray."

"Santa Fe belong to Mexico then. It was the capital of Province of New Mexico. Mexico had very rich trade in old days."

Only Uncle Jeddiah and Ray, whom Jeddiah had picked up for a guide, made the trip tolerable. They could not know of Marion's misgivings after Dora's grand wedding. Marion tried to hide the uncertainty of her own future. Ray's presence was comforting while he served as outrider, repairman or baggage handler, as need arose. He proudly rode Bruno, the young chestnut he'd given Marion that she relinquished when they left Coloma. One night as the last embers flickered in the campfire, Marion quietly asked him if he knew Kent Berrigan.

"We rode with Kepling, wagonmaster from Montana Territory, to Salt Lake City las' year. Why you ask?"

His curious face neared Marion's when she replied in a low voice, "I, too, traveled with Mr. Berrigan when I went East."

"*Debería haberlo combatido antes de que eso suceda.* I shudda fight him back then 'fore that happen," Ray chuckled aloud, surprising Marion. She had no idea what he meant.

"Tell me about him, please."

"He's a good man, save a lot of wagons from goin' over in the rivers. That big horse of his pulled 'em out. Never say bad word about nobody no matter rich or poor or color of their skin. He be a gentleman to the ladies, too," he added with a twinkle, trying to annoy her.

"Oh, pshaw, you can't be serious. There are few ladies in the West, believe me. I've been there." She flicked his leg with her hand. Ray retreated to his bedroll, failing to disclose that Kent had bailed him out of jail; more importantly, he never disclosed another closely held secret—that he, Ray, had followed Marion on her first trip to Montana Territory, and he'd looked for her in Sterling. Their wagon trains had missed each other in the interminable miles, weather, and mishaps.

The branch office of International Consolidated Mining and Shipping Company determinedly threaded its way southeast. Days later, with fatigue penetrating every joint and muscle of their bodies they crossed southern Utah above the Arizona border. Ray asked Marion if she would like to visit the sacred tribal land of monuments known as Valley of the Rocks. Delighted with the diversion, Marion traded her place on a wagon for a horse from one of the outriders and headed south with Uncle Jeddiah chaperoning.

To any traveler, the spires rising into a cloudless, pale blue Arizona sky would be awesome. For Marion, who had lived intimately with vast snow-topped ranges of the Northwest, high, timbered peaks of the Sierras, and rambling hills characteristic of both East and West coasts, these delicately carved sienna landmarks were in a class by themselves—a whole new concept of Spirit and the Holy made itself known.

"Sacred land of ancient people, now Navajoland," Ray explained, adding that Hopis occupied land to the east. All tribes revered the valley with its labyrinth of eroded columns. In breathless silence, the riders passed over coarse sand and mounds of slick rock, craning their necks to peer overhead through great holes in cavernous formations created by drops of water and the timeless grating by wind. Rainbow-like arches framed views to the south, Three Sisters towers marched to the east, and a stone Chief Thunderbird held a solitary vigil on a promontory facing west. Marion could easily have become lost in the monuments but for Ray's sense of direction. They followed a circuitous route through narrow, secret passages between enormous red walls where it was always cool. Scrub willows grew in damp hollows hidden from the ravages of the desert. Pictographs on high smooth walls told stories in symbols of people, animals, and weapons as if they'd been painted recently.

"We follow trail of caches, storehouses for food," Ray said. "Navajo hide crops from harvest in holes in mountains." He pointed to a three-foot-square hole higher up in the wall than could be reached by horseback. "Corn, grain, dried food they hide from the soldiers, then cover holes to look like the wall—'cept these caches open, they been raided."

"By the soldiers?" Marion asked.

"First by Spanish soldiers then *Californios* and then United States soldiers come steal food. United States soldiers come few years ago to starve tribes and drive them out of homeland. I tell you story sometime."

"Border conflicts," Jeddiah said. "They went on a long time, each side gaining and losing this territory. The United States did not own this land until the Mexican-American War. The bloody wars, one after another, caught desert tribes in between. No wonder they cleverly hid what food they could."

The full impact of the story Father had told Marion of his war experience hit her for the first time. He had barely survived the skirmishes leading up to the Mexican-American War, a war fought with bayonets and machetes amid foot or cavalry marches to the Rio Grande and beyond. He'd been about Dora's age and felt foolhardy and indestructible in those early conflicts. A good thing, Marion thought, because the barren land sweeping hundreds of miles in every direction would be enemy enough with its scarcity of water.

Evening light disguised sparse vegetation in a strange turquoise glow and the monuments in hushed lavenders and purples. Surrounded by enchantment, Marion felt how diminished humans were in this landscape. Eroded layer upon layer of rough red sand strained their horses' legs when hooves sank to their fetlocks. A few wild flocks of Navajo sheep nibbled tufts of grass among scattered empty hogans. Tattered window coverings and sagging door frames suggested long abandonment.

The next day they came upon a vast bank of sand dunes deposited by tireless desert winds. Ray goaded his horse to plunge upon a dune and hurdle several hundred yards over it in great lunges. Bruno's powerful legs rose and fell, his nostrils flared and his thick mane flew like a sail. His wide hooves sought tenuous footholds to support horse and rider. Ray yelled and laughed with youthful exhilaration and waved his hat for Marion and Jeddiah to follow.

Marion's horse tenderly moved ahead, snorting and fearful of the unstable ground beneath his feet. His nose went to the sand time and again, his depth perception thrown askew and senses uncertain. Only Marion's firm hand conveyed trust in his ability to make the crossing. Jeddiah followed close behind until he spotted a drop to the left that appeared to be a shortcut, and veered his mount around the higher, central portion of the dune. Shortly, Marion heard the thrashing of Jeddiah's horse in a frantic struggle to remain upright.

"Uncle, where are you? Please, what has happened?" She saw his hat crushed by his horse's hooves into the dune.

Ray had seen the bad choice from afar. Away from hardening winds the dunes gave way like butter on the leeward side. He and Marion were there in moments to find Jeddiah tumbling head over teakettle down the dune, raising a dust storm far below while the gelding's flaying legs sought footholds above. Marion knew she couldn't get off and find footing herself, but Ray dropped his reins and plunged down to give Jeddiah a hand. The old man struggled upright to find his suspenders broken and his trousers full of sand and stickers. Ray whooped and laughed at the sight, relieved that Jeddiah appeared to be all right.

"The devil be hanged," Jeddiah cursed all the way back up the dune. "What's goin' on, me takin' a spill at my age?" Ray pulled him uphill and retrieved his horse, suppressing any more untoward laughter. Marion squeezed her lips. Jeddiah's hat would never be the same after his horse danced on it.

Leaving the dunes, they followed Ray's unerring recall of the topography toward what looked like a sheer, blank red wall behind wispy greenery. He rode ahead with Marion into a low rounded alcove. Both removed their hats to clear the stone overhang. Water! The damp earthen scent drew the horses inward to a turquoise pool. Jeddiah rested and waited beyond the scraggly bushes that camouflaged the opening.

The pool of clean cool water filled a natural bowl in the slick rock. As their horses drank thirstily Ray leaned far over from his saddle, and gave Marion a long slow kiss, only their lips touching, as if at last melding two worlds, that of the Anglos and *mestizos*, the Spanish Indians. Marion's eyes flew open at last and she gasped, "Whew!" They both fanned themselves with their hats.

"*Por todos los santos!* By all the saints!" Ray's boyish laughter rang out past Jeddiah, suddenly excluded from the inner circle of young folks' goings-on.

Is that what women are sensing about him? Marion mused, as she and Ray retreated to let Jeddiah water his horse.

Their trysts came after the plodding wagon train crossed New Mexico and arrived in Santa Fe. In the meantime, Ray made no more overtures. The trio settled into a routine with Ray showing off the country where he'd grown up. He's at ease, Marion thought, more outgoing and confident with a maturity she had not seen before. Now twenty-one, his body appeared as strong and graceful as an athlete, and the goatee had given way to a handsome mustache. She kept more of an eye on him than she dared to admit.

When they left the monuments behind, Ray turned his horse to look back. Marion and Jeddiah stopped, too. "Remember the mountains," Ray said, his arm sweeping the length of the range that melted into the distance in shades of hazy blue and purple.

The desert presented endless miles of deepening color that brushed against steep shale-covered foothills. Cholla forests topped high rugged mountains, their exquisite fuchsia-colored blooms defying cacti thorns on the chollas' many arms. Blooms likely seen only by our eyes, Marion thought. Mounds of funnel-shaped claret cup clung to crevices amid fat barrel cacti, a mosaic of the distinctive colors of the Southwest with scarlet red, yellow, and orange blossoms. A dry, rasping sound of empty yucca pods, excited by wind and passage of horses, called attention to the yuccas new growth of razor sharp blades that served as leaves. The hardy plants promised pale ivory flowers drooping like tulip bells on long stems later in the season. Now, their rhythmic rattle and the constant clicking of horses' shod hooves on stone produced a meditative song in the otherwise enormous silence of the desert backcountry. Slim pasterns of the horses rotated with each tentative step, searching for secure footing in the heavily eroded volcanic sediment.

"The dark jagged skyline isolates this strange land from civilization," Marion said. "Early Spanish settlers must have named them the Black Mountains for the same reason. These are some of the most remote ranges I could ever imagine."

Here even the stars represented excess; millions of stars, many times brighter than elsewhere, pin-pricked the blackness of the desert nights. Late that evening Ray told the story of why the Diné, "the people," were absent from their hogans in the monuments and throughout much of northern Arizona. Four years earlier the U.S. military forced them on the three-hundred-mile "Long Walk" to the reservation at Fort Sumner, where the Bosque Redondo Indian Reservation spanned the borders of New Mexico and Oklahoma. The Navajo were currently interned there, along with their enemies the Apaches.

"Empty hogans mean Navajo people still not come home."

"Where are they?" Marion asked.

Pausing as if he needed prodding, Ray finally began the story of where they were and what happened to them.

"United States soldiers come in night to Canyon de Chelly and Chaco Canyon and then here. Capture all peoples—men, women, children and take their food. Some tortured to tell where caches were hidden. All made to ride or walk in the dark, hands tied behind. Many barefoot, go east with soldiers' guns pointed at them.

"Little girl, eleven years old, keep lookin' back, seeing mountains in moonlight. Then they push her on. Only nex' day she keep lookin' back and git mountains in her head. She remember them and they cannot take memory away from her.

"Some captives try to escape in night but soldiers find and shoot them. All walk for weeks, not much food to eat, very hot days, cold nights. People suffer terrible much, many old people die. Long, long way from Navajo homeland.

"One night little girl crawl out under tent where women sleep—ran like deer in dark past soldiers, going home toward west. They come after, shoot, yell 'halt', shoot more. But she run faster than the wind. She fall down and still hear soldiers come."

His voice dropped, a breath of bitterness tracing the suffering. "She lie still and they cannot find her. She git up and run again. When so tired, can run no more, and afraid of soldiers, she climb a tall tree and hide in eagle's nest. Eagle spread its wings and covers her. Soldiers no can see little girl. They go back.

"Girl remember mountains and keep walking long time until finally see same mountains she remember. She come to homeland of monuments. To Spirit place. She like a mother. She save land for her people to come back to."

Quiet settled over the campfire. The three figures huddled in the dark as if they were listening for soldiers in pursuit. Marion shuddered. Maybe on this road, among these hills as witnesses, residents of the land were torn from all they had ever known.

Surely, their weary footsteps echo at this moment, their cries, heard as eagle cries, still lingering in the air. Ray bowed his head, a sense of kinship with those oppressed evident in his reverence.

Jeddiah cleared his throat, "Thems' people, too. We don' think about that when we round 'em up like cattle and drive 'em off their land. Happens all the time with one group or another we have some fight with."

Ray caught Jeddiah's eye, a signal they both thought of the Mexican-American War and the ongoing prejudices and displacement of people. They were crossing what had once been the vast reaches of Mexican Territory that originally extended north all the way to Wyoming.

"This right here Spanish *ranchos grande* all way north," Ray said, "then war come and brown-skin people be run off like it's not their homeland."

"That was yet another North-South rebellion before you were born," Jeddiah explained to Marion. "The wars took the land back and forth and stirred up hate on both sides."

"Yeh, that why I lost my tooth," Ray said, pointing to the gaping hole near the front. "Anglos still have bad feelings for *mestizos.*"

How can one claim the land and dispossess residents, Marion wondered. The vast ranges of unoccupied, almost undiscovered mountains of New Mexico extended into the distance in every direction. Determinedly their own, they defied the advance of civilization with its conquering, naming and recreating. Attempts to own these lands were harshly rebuffed by climate and geography, but not immune to human invasion, invasions using this very trail of Geronimo.

By day, their horses held to precarious side hills above rock-strewn arroyos that offered a deadly demise if one slipped. Enveloped in a sense of history and a pervasive sadness about human failings, the riders plodded rough trails of unyielding desert highlands in a generally eastern direction toward Santa Fe. At last Ray could stand the low spirits of his charges no longer.

"We go to fine ranch, I take you. Meet good people and see how Spanish people live."

"Fine ranch where?" Jeddiah demanded. "My britches are already on fire from this damn saddle."

"Here, put this sheepskin top 'a yer saddle." Ray yanked one of the two skins from under his saddle.

"Wal, I guess, but no more detours after this, you young'uns," Jeddiah grumbled. "If we're this close already it might be a good idéer if we go."

Setting off at a good pace again, the riders plunged south across land where rusty implements and skeletons of miners' homes bore evidence of earlier residents. The land and people have been exploited and robbed, Marion observed, a belief Kent often expressed from his experience in a mining community.

Kent. His profound gratitude for the riches of the earth and the natural world had worked its way deep into her psyche. A wave of sadness swept over her. She asked Ray for a rest stop. Sweat-drenched hair fell over her brow and became smudged with grime from the trail. She slapped a dust-caked leather canteen on her thigh before taking a small swallow, well aware the scarcity of water begged cautious use. Here nature held power over travelers such as they, while horned toads wisely scuttled under dry bushes and timber rattlers sought shady crevices.

From Jeddiah's acquaintance with the territory he drew upon its history. "Mogollon Indians lived here maybe four hundred years ago. They built pit homes around a courtyard." He pointed out remnants of a village above a sheltered stream.

The next day they followed a winding dry wash named after Cuchillo Negro, leader of the Tchihenne tribes. Overhanging fendlerbushes bobbed with sweet white blossoms, a delicate contrast to the rough dirt-sided canyon. Underfoot, a watercress-like plant flourished in small pools that reflected the startling blue New Mexico sky. Around a bend they came upon three curious wild donkeys staring steadily at them, their great ears upright like sails. Marion was able to ride closely enough to see long eyelashes on outsized eyes and heads compared to their tiny hooves. She noticed their greyish-black hair was patchy and shaggy, a sign of worm parasites in the desert creatures.

"We visit my friends Domingos." Ray said. "They good people, don' bother nobody. They jist want to live where they always live."

Hidden far back in the mountains, a Spanish community of half a dozen adobe homes survived among ragged pole and stick corrals. The riders first glimpsed the spire of a tiny white Catholic Church on a knoll above the town. Ample green grass for livestock ranged up and down the draws along the creek bottom. A large beehive adobe oven dominated the town square.

Ray introduced Marion and Jeddiah to Señora Domingo, dressed in a full length, black skirt gathered at the waist and a wide-sleeved, loose blouse tucked under a long red and blue sash. Her dark eyes appeared tired beneath wisps of black hair that escaped artfully decorated combs.

"Many generations Domingo family live on this land. Our son will carry on when we are gone." She invited the visitors to pull up chairs in the shade of huge, old cottonwoods while she used a long-handled shovel to bring steaming hot loaves of flat bread out of the oven. Señora Domingo urged the visitors to break off chunks and dip them in fresh salsa she placed on the table.

"Heavenly." Marion relished the aroma of fresh baked bread after their dreary camp fare. Another woman set out a huge pitcher of lemonade. The notion of communal bread was not lost on anyone. "This seems fitting with the place and times, here with a family that goes back hundreds of years," Marion said. "A tradition that touches the heart."

Señor Domingo rode up fast on a gaited Spanish mustang that fairly pranced, prompting Ray to explain, "*Sí, el caballo de paso fino*, a fine walking horse." These extraordinary horses were brought to the New World by Spanish explorers and bred at the missions for their endurance and ability to carry heavy loads, Ray explained to Marion. "Horses the Apaches stole and took north and west."

"Hola, Señor Ramos! Buenos dias. Estoy feliz de verte. I am happy to see you!" He waved and dismounted. He wore a floral-stitched western shirt and hat similar to Ray's. Silver conchos decorated the headstall on his horse and saddle and his belt buckle displayed fine silver craftsmanship. His saddle, topped by a thick sheepskin, rested on several layers of colorful handwoven, wool blankets. At sight of the soft seat, Jeddiah caught Ray's eye and winked.

Señor Domingo unsaddled and turned his horse loose in the corral with mustangs, judging by their sturdy legs, thick manes and tails, and large wide hooves. He joined the visitors at the table along with several extended family members who spoke little English. Ray excitedly carried the conversation in Spanish with occasional translations for Jeddiah and Marion. Jeddiah was alert, interested in the discussion, and intervened with a few words of Spanish.

"How have you managed to stay on the land for many generations?" he inquired.

Señor Domingo chose his words carefully. "No one can find us in the lost canyon," he grinned. "It has been through our good relations with other folks that land grants have been respected. We sell beef. We maintain the Church, always. It is the Church that protects us, we believe."

Marion and Ray fell silent, absorbing the wisdom that had surely come with time for this family. They and their ancestors had been caught in the middle of many political and military forces that swept their nation back and forth due to the expanding country to the north. Ninety percent of all Spanish-Mexican landholders lost their *estancias* within ten years after signing a peace treaty with the United States, according to Marion's father. He said much of the United State's aggression seemed arbitrary and unjust as he came to understand it in later years.

"*Sí*, the governments come and go, but the Church, she remain the same for hundreds of years."

Jeddiah nodded, deep in his own recollections. "I been wagonmaster for over forty years," he said. "I drove freight for anyone who could pay. This war and that war. I freighted supplies for Cherokee-white conflicts in South and drove Missouri mules to Confederates in war. Then I brought iron, silver, and gold from Mexican Territories to North for its war treasury. I hauled rifles to Texas for border wars. Then I hauled for your father," he nodded to Marion, "when California gold was needed to pay for more fighting. I don't see the sense of it. We jist go on to the next war." He shook his shaggy mop of hair and looked wearily at those silently nodding in agreement. Jeddiah's bronzed face with its heavy creases, drooping lids, and jowls behind the rough grey beard bore a map of all those years on the wagons.

"*Sí*, exactly what I mean." Señor Domingo jumped at the chance to express his privately held opinions to someone who might understand. "Same God, same hope for families, same pain. We want respect same as everybody. This family know that. We get along no matter what troubles come next."

Marion sensed this sharing was of a higher order than she was accustomed to, an exchange that would alter her own thinking—if only she carried the charged emotions from this humble table to other arenas.

She, Ray and Jeddiah followed the Domingos to the small frame church that stood serenely over this hidden place, hallowed by the individuals who resided here if not by the Church itself. Inside, they all removed their hats. Señor Domingo knelt, a deeply reverent genuflection that, to Marion, represented centuries of deep connection with the church in the Southwest. The altar was draped in layers of fine embroidered cloth with handstitched white lace scallops. A profusion of gaily painted figures and a clay vase with dried flowers filled the space around several unlit candles.

"Such bright and colorful folk art," Marion whispered to Jeddiah. She had little knowledge of the significance of any of the figures except the Holy Family. On the wall, the Virgin Mary was represented in an icon of early Italian-style with a halo and rays of the sun encircling her head, art both Christian and pagan, Marion supposed.

Señora Domingo talked softly about how the few families of their small community had preserved the church. Priests were often shared by many villages and sometimes came only in times of crises or death. It is the long view, certainly, Marion gathered, an extremely long view of past generations and those to come.

Outside, they all shook hands, and the visitors gathered their horses. They left with the sense of interdependence that *rancheros* and their families had for one another, transcending land ownership be it Spanish, Mexican or Anglo. Indeed, they had encountered a remarkable family that engendered good relations with others.

16

In Montana Territory, mining activity in Hot Spring District continued into the summer of 1868, although a number of mills failed and their assets were auctioned off. Kent Berrigan benefited by using cast-off materials from defunct stamp mills to build his dwelling on South Willow Creek. The "barn raising" spirit of laid-off miners and the remarkable craftsmanship of guildsmen quickly laid down tree-size mill timbers on solid rock, and built thick walls of rough-cut six by eights. The goal was to finish the roof as soon as possible against coming inclement weather.

Kent hammered ladders and sawbucks together from poles and scrap lumber to facilitate the progress of the carpenters. Privately, he liked to wander through the comparatively spacious interior which included one bedroom, pleased to have a home many times the size of his shack. He often despaired that Marion was not at his side, that they were not planning their home together. Scrolled woodwork on the Queen Anne style gables begged a woman to occupy the residence. But he found the antidote to despair was plunging into work, and he generally felt buoyed by a sense of achievement. He and the workmen finally hoisted heavy rafters up over the center beam and secured them in place with V-notches, as the carpenters had done at the corner joints.

One day Genevieve and Danielle drove over in their wagon with little Peter Sands Sayles. "We haven't seen you for awhile.

We had to come satisfy our curiosity about what is keeping you away." Genevieve, always warm and good natured, glowed from new motherhood and summer outdoors.

"You have a handsome son, Genevieve. He will soon be gathering eggs and milking the Jersey."

"Not that soon, I hope," Genevieve laughed. "I already have a time keeping him clean."

Kent remembered how Gracie used to drag him and Rand off for baths. "Nice to see you, Miss Hartman–er, Danielle. How are all your charges?"

"All thriving and keeping me busy. We are building additional shelters for the winter. We have quite an impressive stack of hay put by, too."

Kent kept an eye on the men laying roofing over the rafters and watched Danielle at the same time. She seemed shy in his presence today and reluctant to get out of the wagon. He felt a twinge of regret for his less than gracious leave-taking over the odor of the ram. He extended his hand for her to step down; her closely tied bonnet concealing her features.

"Come see my future water system," he motioned to the women. At the rear of the house a series of long metal pipes were laid out along a slight slope. Kent had more than enough materials and parts from the auctions to indulge in innovations. "These will be buried sufficiently to prevent freezing at subzero temperatures. With luck I should have water on tap in the house year round."

"True, you are way ahead of most of us. You will be enjoying freedom from toil that this provides." Genevieve shifted Peter Sands to the other hip and walked about admiring the homesite with Danielle. Not wishing to interfere with the construction they soon left, reminding him that he could drop by for supper anytime.

These good people would boost anyone's spirit, Kent thought, their visit a blessing and a good omen, a friendly Montana welcome to me in my new home.

The impromptu crew of miners and farmers bantered and cheered, but proved they were skilled and efficient. The stone mason directed building the wide hearth in a floor-to-ceiling fireplace, while a blacksmith forged oversized iron hinges to hang the heavy front door, and the carpenters installed windows and finished off the gables and eaves. The house was soon enclosed, warm and dry.

With Patrick occupying the shack while he taught at the Sterling school, Kent and Shag settled into their new place. Kent found himself alone at last with echoes and the fresh smell of sawdust inside and out. Wearily, he pulled his single chair near the fireplace and lit a well-earned cigar. He was soon lost in a long, pleasant smoke where dreams merged with reality, the reality that this home was his own creation, the beginning of a new identity—or at least an extension of the person he had become in Montana Territory.

A few days later Shag ran to the door, barking at the clattering of a horse outside. Kent stepped out to find Dandy, the black pacer, panting through flared nostrils. Mrs. Thompson unwound her black headscarf, sign of her widowhood, and gingerly stepped down from the buggy. Kent rushed out in his sock feet to give her a hand, while a young lad climbed down from the other side.

"Mrs. Thompson, may I help you? You are far from home."

"Yes, and I have come on urgent business as you can see from poor Dandy's heaving sides. This is my son, Bradley." She moved ahead toward the house without waiting for a reply, her black crepe mourning dress rustling with every step. Bradley tied Dandy to a tree and followed. Inside, Kent offered to take her coat and adjusted the one chair for her in front of the flame. If she noticed the sweet scent of cigar smoke, she gave no indication.

"I am terribly sorry about the accident, Mrs. Thompson," Kent ventured, "my deepest sympathy to you and your son." He looked at Bradley who was probably fourteen or fifteen and extremely uncomfortable at the moment. Everyone had been shocked about the horrifying mining accident in Alder Gulch a few months earlier in which Mr. Thompson had been killed, along with three of his men.

"Thank you. That is why we have come—about my husband. About his long overdue financial affairs. As you may be aware, he owned the Comet, the largest mill in Summit. Few people knew he was also invested in operations in Brown's Gulch and up Williams Gulch in the Ruby valley. He had also made recent acquisitions in Last Chance Gulch. To make the story short, the financial situation he left us," she indicated herself and Bradley, "is exceedingly complex. I have come to you for assistance."

Kent waited, unclear of her expectations. It appeared that she required an attorney to settle the estate.

"It has come to me from several sources that you have accounting expertise and, more importantly, that you are a trustworthy individual from whom a poor widow might seek assistance."

Kent was at once alert and alarmed. This trust she reportedly felt in him was not something he was ready to receive. On the contrary, he earnestly desired—no—required, a personal distance and privacy right now.

"Madam, I do truly express my sympathy for the loss of your husband as well as the three other men. I can imagine such a shock has yet to fade from both your life and Bradley's. However, what time and experience I have would surely be limited for such a task as you propose."

"Frankly, Mr. Berrigan, my husband, bless his soul, handled all the finances. The ledgers, dozens of them, have been stored in his vault since his demise. His—our own superintendent, Mr. Rhodes, is pressuring me to make decisions, foremost of which is to pay workers, families of the deceased, and creditors. I am able to handle many affairs of the Company, but the estate with its entanglement of legal and financial obligations requires the work of independent persons skilled in those areas." In the long silence following these prepared remarks, Mrs. Thompson stared steadily into Kent's rather bewildered eyes, assessing perhaps more about his character than his "skill in those areas."

Bradley squirmed, distressed by hearing these disclosures that made his now uncertain world even more insecure. A flat wool cap pulled far down over his brow left his ears prominently showing through tufts of dark hair. His mother remained ramrod straight in the chair, her feet in sensible but expensive boots set primly on the floor. Kent couldn't help but recall Marion's unbelievable tale of Mrs. Thompson's delivery of a huge quantity of gold to Helena. Here was a remarkable woman who was persuasive as well.

"The Territories offer little in the way of assistance to the poor," she went on. "I understand the county and good people of Virginia City have taken care of the families thus far, but this matter needs to be resolved as quickly as possible. A settlement from the Comet will come later."

"Yes, yes, to be sure," Kent mumbled his agreement.

"It is I who am sorry to disrupt your exciting home building with so unpleasant a mission. If you will consent, however, I will have the ledgers brought to your house." Her glance surveyed the interior where two sawbucks with boards across served as a temporary table holding Kent's kitchenware and an Army duffle bag. Dropping the business tone, she said, "The room feels comforting. I do feel as though I can trust you, Mr. Berrigan."

Kent guessed the feeling came from yellow-orange flames flickering from red embers and the lingering tobacco smoke since all else was construction related. He pulled his beard and stared into the fire—listening to his mind say no and his intuition say yes. At last he raised his glance to meet dark, somber eyes set in the deep hollows of Mrs. Thompson's pale face.

"I may be able to help you settle immediate accounts," Kent said, plainly not over-committing, but not willing to refuse the widow and her son, either.

"Thank you, Mr. Berrigan," Mrs. Thompson said quietly. "I am grateful for your assistance. Mr. Rhodes will bring the ledgers and you may stipulate your terms to him." She rose and extended her gloved hand. Kent took it in both his large palms, then went out to get the buggy. Bradley swung up and pulled his mother to the seat beside him. Without formalities the pair drove off at a brisk trot with Dandy again in Mrs. Thompson's capable hands.

In New Mexico, the crushing fatigue from desert travel failed to extinguish Marion Patton's dream to establish a branch office of her father's company in the Southwest. The wagons from Coloma bearing home furnishings, office files and equipment wound their way toward Santa Fe. Marion, Ray, and Jeddiah, still complaining of his saddle sores, came from a southerly direction and met the wagons not far from their destination.

"I'm turnin' this horse in for a permanent seat on the wagon," Jeddiah declared at sight of the outfits. Gratefully, he hauled himself onto the highest wagon, his kindly, weathered face beaming with satisfaction.

"I couldn't have done this without you, Uncle, you know that," Marion said.

"You young 'uns keep a feller goin', I'll say." Jeddiah gave no indication he was relinquishing any of his chaperone responsibilities.

Within weeks, Marion succeeded in renting a building in Santa Fe in a prime downtown location on a square surrounded by immense old cottonwoods. She supervised setting up the office to suit her, enjoying her first taste of independent business decisions. She moved into an apartment upstairs, and Jeddiah occupied quarters behind her suite. When her feet trod worn adobe walkways on the square, she had a recurring sense of stepping into another time, an age she'd experienced on the trail of Geronimo.

"I am here," she breathed, inhaling the dry desert air and scent of profuse, purplish clematis blooms on tangled vines. Foothills of the Sangre de Cristo Mountains to the east framed the sprawling hot, tired city. Marion felt she'd been lifted from all she'd ever known, yet she felt entirely at home. Pieces of her dreams had fallen naturally into place. She admired the handsome, hand-carved wooden door to her building, seeing it not as it was but with a discrete bronze plaque bearing her name. For some odd reason, an image of cream turning into butter skipped through her mind—it felt that natural and inevitable that she would establish a business.

Neighboring merchants and members of firms soon paid their respects, formally at first with much bowing and doffing of hats. When news spread that the newcomer was a young woman, a round of invitations followed. Marion found the gatherings hugely exciting. Parties occurred in the cool shade of parks with ever present mariachi bands or in the courtyards of extravagant *haciendas*. Giant bougainvilleas covered adobe walls, adding an interesting contrast to the potted barrel or claret cup cacti.

To complete her connections, her side door was always open for frequent visits by Ramos, as he was known here.

Candle lanterns burned down late one night while she studied a stack of proposed contracts. At Ray's tap on the door, she stuffed the business papers into a drawer, hiding her world of risky financial affairs that represented her longing for "something far greater than I ever imagined," and switched to another passion.

"I'm always amazed you come back," she managed to breathe, unwrapping herself from his embrace. "I feel as though we're bounding over sand dunes in the Monuments, heedless of consequences!"

Ray threw back his head and laughed, the low rolling chuckle she loved.

"Shhh, Uncle will hear you," and they both laughed, remembering their first kiss in the hidden alcove. Ray's charm and passion met rarely tapped desires in her own nature, a zest for living, a thrill of adventure—their combined youthful energy sustained their relationship behind closed doors, heightened the clandestine affair, and challenged cultural prohibitions across ethnic lines.

The trysts with *su amante*, her lover, went unobserved by Marion's attentive chaperone and the business community as far as she knew. Marion banked on not getting pregnant since she had not conceived with Kent. It doesn't seem to be in my make-up, she concluded, releasing the worry to a beneficent Spirit and the caprices of a woman's body.

17

Summer ended abruptly in Montana Territory when September night temperatures hit freezing. The men working on the Berrigan home laid down their tools for hunting season. Kent had hoped to get a trench dug for the water pipes, but with the cold he, too, struck out for the mountains. Snow in higher elevations would drive elk down from summer grazing grounds. He rode out early on Ben for the next few days but was unable to get within range of the plentiful herds that bolted at the slightest disturbance. Mule deer and pronghorn antelope were the opposite, often curious to a fault, so he never came home empty-handed.

But he felt the quiet times he spent riding alone were highly satisfying. His mind pulsed with random thoughts, even a snippet from the poet Tennyson who penned *"the sweet music here that softer falls."*

Miss Olivia Spencer was indeed right about me—I am deeply touched by nature, Kent smiled.

He rode for hours over land so crisp and beautiful it seared one's soul. *"Be still and know that I am God,"* came to mind from Samuel's Scripture readings. Truly, the heavens touched mountain crests all the way around, Spirit sang in cleansing winds, and the rattle of dry aspen leaves inspired awe. He had no doubt the abundance of antelope, wild turkeys and geese, trout in the streams, and birds in the air surely came from the Providence of God.

Relishing the nose-tingling air spiced with juniper and pine, he mused, I wouldn't exchange a minute of it right now. Nature is kind yet fierce, magnificent beyond comprehension. "That is why I choose to live here," he said, patting Ben's sweating neck and shoulders.

The depth and breadth of the country drew him to forfeit other avenues of his life; it exercised its power, yet lent serenity, and teased any would-be complaisance with unpredictability. The land offered healing qualities that, like the wild horses, he couldn't fathom yet couldn't leave alone. But he was always glad to hurry Ben back down the mountain to find the comfort of a hot fire and Shag's eager welcome.

One evening as he cleaned his rifle, Kent felt a rare sense of orderliness to his life on South Willow Creek, and he concluded he'd done the right thing in accepting the admittedly unpleasant job that Mrs. Thompson had entrusted to him. Later in the week the superintendent of Summit Mining Company arrived with the ledgers in a buckboard.

"Ezra Rhodes," he said, extending his hand. He was a stocky man of medium build with a sun-reddened neck set on wide shoulders. He removed several armloads of bound, grey ledgers and placed them on the sawbuck table. He opened a volume revealing pages of computations, some in an elegant pen and ink script, but most scrawled with pencil. He was direct and forthcoming about all the designated entries. "This is as far as I could go with the last few columns that Nathaniel—Mr. Thompson— had entered concerning operations that I manage. I am uncertain whether all the necessary entries have been made since he was wholly in charge of the bookkeeping. In addition, the Company had other connections of which I am not fully informed."

"I would need all current outstanding bills and a list of creditors with their accounts if we want to bring this to date," Kent said.

Mr. Rhodes reached into his inside coat pocket and pulled out a wad of outstanding bills, most from the Overland Express for freight, and a list with a handwritten tally of the miners' names, hours and wages. "As Mrs. Thompson may have indicated, we must settle with the hired men in a most expedient manner, and settle with the families of miners who were killed." He looked up hopefully from page after page of figures and notations.

"Yes," Kent said. "I think I can get started with this. But I wonder—can you tell me what caused the accident? I have heard only rumors."

Mr. Rhodes scuffed the floor with the toe of his boot. "Landslide," he said after a long hesitation.

"My god, how could that happen?"

Mr. Rhodes sized Kent up before he related the story. "We'd been blasting for a week, following a lead on the west side of Alder Gulch near the Comet mine up at Summit. I left to work up Brown's Gulch for a few days. The men—my men—continued to set more charges, bringing down tons of soil and rock that evidently cut under an unstable overhang. The landslide didn't happen then. I was notified of the blasting and rushed back to Summit to find they'd ripped off half the mountain, more than I'd given orders for. So, you see—I should have been there to supervise."

He stopped to collect himself. "Those young men, they don't have a sense of the danger of unbalancing a steep slope." He pinched off a wad of snuff as Kent nodded agreement. "Nathaniel and three men went over there to determine the direction of the vein, and the whole damn mountainside let go over all of them. Now I've got to live with that." His voice trailed off, weary, older than his forty-some years. "We shut down all our mining so we could dig down to recover the bodies."

Kent felt that there was nothing he could say.

Mr. Rhodes went on. "Naturally, the rest of the men want to get paid and move on. Get away from the memory. The county's funds for destitute families are pitifully inadequate. Two of the three men were married with children. Folks generously chipped in at first. Now we need to settle with them so they can move on, too. Me? I'll work for Mrs. Thompson until this is cleared up. The Comet is shut down. Maybe it'll never open again, I don't know."

He turned to leave, then coughed. "I saw it happen." He spit a long stream of tobacco juice into the fire and shuffled away.

Shock waves kept coming from the Alder Gulch tragedy, pulling Kent into the aftermath despite his resistance. He dreaded further involvement that brought up his own losses and Benson's death, both barely eased by current diversions, yet the need to address immediate problems compelled him to be of assistance. His life had gradually reoriented, and he felt like a pillar of strength compared to the shattered states of Ezra and Mrs. Thompson. However, he realized after Mrs. Thompson's visit that he needed rudimentary home furnishings more quickly than he'd planned. Since he would be well compensated for the unexpected work, he sent a mail order by stagecoach without delay. The order included a modest four-poster bed, a bureau, a buffet with framed mirror, and a marble-topped washstand. In a burst of extravagance, he chose selections from the catalog of Gillison's Fine Furnishings in Salt Lake City.

Four days later he'd completed a packet of reports for Mr. Rhodes, indicating what funds from the Wages and Compensations account were available for payroll. Kent rode Ben over to the shack to have Patrick mail the packet in Sterling on his way to school the next day.

"How is the teaching going?" though Kent hardly needed to inquire. The dark-haired new schoolmaster sat with chin in hand, a baleful look framing his strong features.

"I don't think I am cut out for this, sir. What am I going to do with all these books? Fifteen lads and lasses from six years old to fourteen. Only half can read these." He shoved aside an armload of readers and Webster's Spelling books that tumbled off the table.

Kent stifled a laugh. Clearly Patrick was not in a humorous mood. Transitioning from a self-employed placer miner to public service was more than he'd bargained for.

"There's a preponderance of boys, but one of the girls is more trouble than all of them, the lass from the boarding house—"

"Careful there, man, that is Angel—rightly or wrongly named, she's my goddaughter, or I like to think so, it not being official."

"She's been bringing in pockets full of marbles and 'losing' them on the floor. We've had more than one kid's feet fly out from under them." Kent tried to hide his smile and poured himself a cup of Patrick's black coffee.

"Somebody reached under the desks and sliced another lad's pair of new rawhide shoelaces right down the middle. The culprit won't be found, but I will get in trouble with the parents." His always serious demeanor now slid to the grim side.

"I wish I could help you, Patrick. I only hope they are paying you well."

"Not as well as you did, sir. Believe me, using a pick ax on quartz rocks is a lot easier than teaching eight different grades."

Evening wrapped around the shack as they sat without speaking. Kent tried not to peer at the room Patrick now occupied, but he noted Patrick's saddle, blanket and packs were on the wide bunk, dry and handy for early morning rides to school. He had built a single upper bunk for his own use, maybe a hint of delicacy knowing Kent had slept with Marion in the other.

"Maybe I should have joined Sterling Company on a campaign against the Sioux. The militia would have been a whole lot simpler, don't you think?"

Kent had to chuckle. "And short-lived. I understand major confrontations were over when our men reached the battlefield east of the Yellowstone. I hear we'll see men return with shiny new rifles, uniforms, and some of the Army's horses. Evidently they feel entitled to the outfits despite lack of action."

"I'm glad my brother Jackson is safely on the East Coast. These uprisings throughout the West seem to be happening more often. I'm afraid they will get worse."

Kent had not seen or heard from Mrs. Thompson since her initial visit with Bradley six weeks ago, when they came to engage him as their accountant. He began to wonder if the position would pay for the houseful of furnishings he had rashly purchased, though he enjoyed the relative ease and comfort of the furniture. Socks and underwear went in a drawer in the bureau rather than in his duffle bag. Dishes and small foodstuffs such as butter, jam and honey that might attract mice and flies were safely stored in the buffet. The cherry dining table with matching chairs, their upholstered seats cross-stitched in a floral pattern, could have competed admirably in any elegant setting. His concerns were alleviated when Mrs. Thompson drove over alone.

"I have matters requiring immediate attention." She paused momentarily when she entered the room, now so beautifully equipped, but she quickly glided to a chair at the table and sat down without commenting. Soon she and Kent had their heads together over the ledgers, deep in study to determine the assets of Summit Mining Company. The often foreign language of accounts was quite readable to Kent, but Mrs. Thompson needed to have everything explained to her. Hours passed while Shag drifted in and out the door to check on Dandy dozing in his harness.

"I would say from the looks of the accounts after payment of debts that there are substantial provisions for you and Bradley for some time, Mrs. Thompson," ventured Kent. He was unsure what motivated her or contributed to her anxiety.

"I would like to say so, truly, but I fear extenuating circumstances may adversely impact our future livelihood—the mining business is so uncertain, you know."

"I imagine you have worried a great deal since your husband's passing. I would like to complete the accounting so you could rest assured about your future. To date, I have only ledgers from the operation of the Comet mine and mill. These have apparently been well kept and fail to present the entanglements you are alluding to. Is there something more I need to know?"

"Yes. My husband had an associate who had an interest in the Company. He was not a partner. Rather he provided loans to my husband for startup of some operations in exchange for a certain percentage of returns—Ezra—Mr. Rhodes, tells me."

"I see." Kent absently calculated how adverse this revelation might be for Mrs. Thompson, but he tried to allay some of her fears. "In due time, this problem will resolve itself."

"You are most kind. When my year of mourning is over, Kent, you shall have to marry me. It is not good for man or woman to be alone."

The statement hit Kent like a dash of water. And not cold water—even his ears felt hot. He blinked at this daring woman some years older than himself who looked expectantly at him like Shag or Ben often did. Her face crinkled into a smile at his obvious confusion.

"My name is Annette. May we call each other by first names?"

The walls closed in with a mix of fear and unrealized passion neither chose to discuss, though their location far from other homes lent intimacy to the moment. Kent murmured assent, embarrassed that Annette's lingering smile had as much to do with his flushed face as her designs upon him. Her usually somber dark eyes turned very feminine under long dark lashes, her breath sweet and warm, both startling Kent. He'd seen her in command of herself, her horse and her situation—failing to have seen her as the vibrant, intelligent woman who sat comfortably next to him—and undeniably excited him. Unable to sort through a rush of thoughts or emotions, he shifted his gaze.

They breached the awkward moments with small courtesies and Annette soon left. Kent found himself feeling acutely alone; being single suddenly felt lonely as hell, but the need to have someone in his life quickly clashed with another familiar feeling, that of getting in too deep for comfort.

Danielle's goats had strayed some distance down the road since there were few fences around any of the properties. Wearing her washday dress of faded print gingham under a torn apron, she was driving the goats home, shaking a long stick at the stragglers, when Mrs. Thompson drove her buggy along the road from Kent's place.

"Oh, I imagine you are Miss Hartman," Annette said, stopping beside Danielle.

"Yes indeed, and not in my finest, I'm sorry to say." Danielle retied her bonnet. "We have not met."

"Mrs. Thompson, widowed as you can see by my dress and shawl. My husband was Nathaniel Thompson, bless his soul. Now Mr. Berrigan, Kent, is taking care of me—of my affairs."

"Kent is what?"

"Taking care of my affairs."

Danielle stared hard at the other woman, seeing a striking, rather sophisticated older woman in black with perfect pale skin.

Mrs. Thompson broke the silence. "I have only now come from his home. We have many hours of work to do together on the estate of my late husband."

Danielle dropped a brief curtsy when she realized who she was talking to. "So dreadful an accident, Mrs. Thompson. I offer my deepest sympathy."

"Thank you. I am Annette—to Kent."

Danielle saw her goats escape in every direction to consume stalks of yellow clover and weeds along the road, but she held her ground, her hands on her hips. "It appears, Mrs. Thompson, that your affairs with Kent may be of a personal nature."

"Inevitably, yes. I doubt you would be aware that he is my accountant. As I said, we have many hours—"

"Together you said, of which you are now boasting." Danielle's voice became low, icy. "I wonder, Mrs. Thompson, if you are boldly telling me you have Kent's affections while you are still in widows weeds."

"A pity, Miss Hartman, that you may lay claim to his affections as well, it is rumored," Annette retorted.

"I would think the gossip would be about you coming to his home alone—"

"On business to be sure, all quite proper and necessary for conducting the Company business, but being a goatherd, you—"

"I am a widow, too, Mrs. Thompson, my husband killed or missing in the war seven years ago. Do you care to insult one who has suffered and now shares a similar unchosen fate as a widow?"

Annette paused and saw the tall, beautiful woman with high cheek bones and flashing black eyes as a formidable rival. She snapped the seldom-used buggy whip over Dandy who leapt ahead with his mistress and pounded the hard earth on his way back to town.

A batch of burned-down candles and several kerosene lamps with smoky chimneys framed the papers on Kent's long cherrywood table. He worked late into the night on the ledgers which were laid out chronologically, pages marked with scraps of paper according to relevant entries. He found years of investment transactions for new and modern equipment for the

Comet mine. Costs of overland transport were included as well. The purchase of a hydraulic system was well documented, as well as sale of the system when its use was discontinued. Kent was struck when he read entries showing orders for quantities of gunpowder, and more recently, for dynamite that replaced gunpowder for blasting. The pages of the grey ledgers told the story of the tragedy.

Kent also gained a sense of how Territorial offices came by inside information. Registration of claims and their locations clearly mapped a course of mining exploration, explaining why officials were often sought after by investors, including bankers, to become partners or affiliates with the larger, more successful operations. He suspected he'd have a docket full of complaints if and when he was elected justice of the peace.

A new, partially filled ledger described the investment in Last Chance Gulch near Helena in terms of payments, loans, and contractual agreements. The numbers read like a book to Kent. Missing were the accounts on activities in Brown's Gulch and up on the Ruby, both of which Mrs. Thompson had referred to. However, he was able to generally complete the accounting of ledgers in hand and provide Mrs. Thompson with information to help the fatherless families of the deceased.

Finally, he turned to an unmarked ledger containing daguerreotypes stuffed into the front pages. Kent held up a portrait of the family when Bradley was about five years old, the age of Finn now. Nathaniel Thompson, a square-faced, stocky gentleman a bit on the heavy side, looked stiff in a ruffled shirt, high collar, and black day coat exposing a gold chain looped across his wide chest. Annette appeared considerably younger in a wide-brimmed white hat, its low crown bedecked in flowers and tied with a swath of silk under her chin.

The ledgers contained bank statements from Helena, blurred ink entries made with quill pens, and more pencil notes. Kent groaned, guessing that Mr. Thompson had made the pencil entries himself when he was busy. At any rate, there was enough work and income to pay for all of his home furnishings. When Ezra Rhodes returned before Thanksgiving, Kent gave an accounting of income and expenses which was beginning to look perilously unfortunate for Mrs. Thompson's future and that of her son. The deliveries of gold, the knowledge of which Kent had kept quiet, represented far more than was suggested by the income of the Comet.

"Did I get this straight?" he asked Mr. Rhodes. "The investment in Last Chance Gulch was financed based on profits coming from the Summit mines."

"Yes, I 'spect that is true."

"It appears that despite the tremendous assets of the Comet, the expenditures are in excess of the income. That is mostly due," Kent hastened to say, "to the heavy investment in equipment as well as satisfying loans for operations. Am I correct in these findings?"

"No doubt, no doubt. I am not an expert at such things as bookkeeping. But I do know all of us, Nathaniel, myself, and Mrs. Thompson used the loans to work all three of the properties."

Aware there was more to the story, Kent again mentioned missing ledgers that might pertain to holdings Mrs. Thompson had referred to earlier.

Mr. Rhode's head shot up. "I have two of them. Brown's Gulch and *The Dolly* up William's Gulch on the Ruby." He looked directly at Kent, again assessing whether he should continue. "Nathaniel did not want these to fall into the hands of anyone else."

"*The Dolly?*"

"Yes, Nathaniel called Mrs. Thompson 'Dolly.' 'Dolly and Dandy' he often said with a great deal of pride. He named the mine for her." Ezra paused with a deep sense of sadness recalling the fondness between Nathaniel and his wife. "The holdings in William's Gulch are in her name only, but we worked both mines with funds from the Comet, therefore the discrepancy you see in the amount of income and outgo attributed to the Comet."

Kent must have looked puzzled because Mr. Rhodes continued. "The gold that was delivered to the bank came from all of our holdings."

"Uh, my wife, who has since returned to her family in California, accompanied Mrs. Thompson to Helena," Kent revealed at last. "She related to me that they delivered a sizeable shipment of gold to Mr. Turnage at the bank. Could Mr. Turnage be the 'associate' Mrs. Thompson mentioned to her? I wonder if the bank has more of an interest in the Company."

The superintendent shut down at the suggestion, clearly wary of any more disclosures. In fact, Kent felt he shouldn't have tipped his hand so soon. There were already too many hands in the till.

In San Francisco's financial district, Henry Patton felt the loss of his daughter, Marion, who had been a constant in his adventurous life. Communication with the branch office in Santa Fe proved to be painfully slow and cumbersome. Her letters became worn from transport over the Old Spanish Trail through Las Vegas and on to Los Angeles, where they were shipped up the coast. Employees at the headquarters of the international company heard plenty about Mr. Patton's uncertainty regarding the remote office as months went by. He fussed and fumed over delayed business reports and outdated information about Marion. With increased uneasiness about allowing her to risk such an undertaking, Mr. Patton wondered about his judgment in backing such an enterprise. At last the strain of not knowing about her well-being and the status of his investment was alleviated when a report arrived from Marion.

"*Barnstone and Company Contract Secured*" read the telegraph he found on his desk. The company, which he had never heard of, would provide telegraph service to Santa Fe, an investment Marion deemed worthy of his money, his Company.

"What is this? I cannot believe my daughter has accomplished this in so short a time! I really must see for myself," Mr. Patton said to anyone and everyone who came into the San Francisco office that day. "Remarkable! I believe she has inherited a good bit of my business acumen, if I do say so!"

The astounding news inspired him to travel to Santa Fe. Impulsively, he offered to pay the fares for the newlyweds, Dora and Martin Brisbane, should they care to join him on what would be a six week trip.

"We could comfortably sail on one of the better Pacific Mail steamships to Los Angeles. I sailed from Panama City to San Francisco on that line when I returned from Brazil. From Los Angeles, the trip would entail overland travel by stagecoach for a good many miles, but we could take the Armijo Route branching off the Old Spanish Trail for a shortcut." He mentally calculated the cost of the tickets, comparing them to his laborious and expensive crossing of the Isthmus by rail, mule, and finally by ferry to the boat on his return from South America.

Dora's response to the invitation had nothing to do with the business. She was sure the trip would be a second honeymoon, their first having been spent in a small chateau at a vineyard in northern California. The Patton family arrived in Santa Fe late in the fall by way of San Bernadino, Las Vegas, otherwise known as "the meadows," and Abiquiu north of Santa Fe, six months after the Company had been precipitously uprooted from its founding location in Coloma. In that time Marion had launched her fortunes in the Southwest.

"Really, Father, Barnstone and Company is ideal for this time and place. I saw their offices in New York City on Nassau Street off Broadway. I found upon inquiry that they specialized in making telegraph connections to lesser known cities such as Santa Fe. They supplement Western Union lines between New York and the West Coast by extending services to hard to reach places. This service is badly needed. To notify you of the contract I had to send my message by mule to a telegraph station in

California." Marion's former youthful exuberance had become a settled self-assurance, placating Henry's fears about her ability to conduct business affairs.

Juanita's Hacienda on the Square served a sumptuous supper of grilled *arracheras*, strips of steak, with handmade tortillas. Dora glowed in the new desert finery she'd shipped inside a trunk for protection against the elements. She wore a full-sleeved silk blouse of light cactus flower yellow above a sandstone cotton pleated skirt, accented by a flowing gold and rust silk scarf.

"Oh, what a stunning scarf, Dora. How fine it looks on you! Aren't you the picture of a happily married woman!"

"The scarf is yours, Marion. How could I keep it, knowing it suits your hair so perfectly? You may have it this minute. Let me drape it properly around your shoulders. And, yes, Martin and I are very content, thank you." Up close, Dora could see the strain and weariness around Marion's eyes.

"Are you all right, my sister? You appear quite fatigued. I'm wondering if this business is too much for you." Dora whispered in her ear.

"I'm quite all right, Dora," Marion said. Ray had run away with a young Spanish girl after a beastly bar fight over her. A raven-haired beauty, they said. The couple would be safely across the border by now.

Marion bit her lip—she had hidden her life in men's world of business, while he also led a separate life of which she'd heard only rumors.

She mentioned nothing of her affair to her father or Dora.

Thanksgiving dinner, 1868, in Sterling, Montana Territory, had all the markings of surpassing last year's feasts. Holiday banquets always stirred Mrs. Callahan to produce her finest dishes. In addition, local fiddlers and accordion players supplied lively crowd-pleasing tunes from early Christmas carols to foot-stomping polkas and square dances. The population of Sterling and its vicinity had dwindled considerably since last year and dozens of businesses were closed; however, saloons remained open in winter. Citizens were only too happy to come to town to celebrate with food, drink, music and billiards.

But the celebration Kent Berrigan most enjoyed took place earlier at the little Sterling school one frosty afternoon. Most of the students were settlers' children from far and wide in Hot Spring District. When Kent rode up on Ben for the program, the school yard was already full of parents and relatives stamping their feet in the snow to keep warm. School would be dismissed over mid-winter months due to severe weather, but now silver bells jangled from horses' bridles and clouds of the horses' hot breath circled the jumble of wagons. The schoolmaster, Mr. Patrick Colter, almost unrecognizable in a full-length wool coat and a hat with ear muffs, stood on the steps of the one-room school that rocked with the noisy bunch of students inside.

"The students will give their presentations outdoors class by class," Patrick announced, since there was little space inside. Once the first graders were assembled a hush fell over the crowd; even students waiting their turn quieted in anticipation, their usually bare feet snug in woolen socks and heavy leather shoes.

In remarkable performances, the students singly or as a group, sang traditional carols or recited poems they had memorized. Older students read short pieces they had written or found in their readers. Snatches of Longfellow's recently fashionable poems, "Song of Hiawatha" and "The Wreck of the Hesperus," were heartily applauded. The display of accomplishments was followed by a quick dash to Callahans' boarding house for hot spiced apple cider. Parents congratulated the schoolmaster. Neighbors visited with neighbors.

A few days after the school closed, Patrick rode over to South Willow Creek with little Finn Callahan riding behind his saddle, tightly clutching the schoolmaster's wide belt. Kent came in from the meadow with a fat wild goose he'd shot.

"Hallo, I've brought someone to read to you," Patrick said.

"No! To read to me?"

"Yes, Finn would like to read to you."

"Naw, I don't believe it! You don't go to school, do you?" Kent grinned, hanging the goose on a peg outside the door.

Finn shook his head and slid down from the tall horse, shy as usual. His sister, Angel, always spoke for both of them, so Finn had grown like her shadow, but today he apparently wanted to shine on his own. The child clutched a slim volume that Kent had given to him.

"Angel taught him to read at home," Patrick assured Kent. "By the way, I brought over a parcel left for you at Callahans." He handed Kent a well padded rectangular box that had come from Rand. Kent could almost taste and smell the fresh cigars before he unwrapped the surprise gift on the dining table.

"Holy smokes!" Patrick exclaimed. Kent joined him in laughter. Kent felt even better after reading the enclosed heavily embossed card of congratulations on "building your fine home in the wilds." This came as a warm and thoughtful outreach by Rand that touched Kent deeply. In addition, Rand requested that Kent consider becoming a regular cigar taster of the new and exciting varieties Rand was developing under a new label, Brogan Premium Cigars.

To Kent, the deal sounded like a winner all the way around. The "Brogan" designation honored their father, who decades earlier had encouraged a crop yielding light ochre leaves for their mild taste and sweet aroma. These leaves were fermented and charcoal cured, then rolled relatively intact into manufactured cigars in their own tobacco leaf wrappers.

"He promises to send more samples," Kent winked at Patrick. "This could be a good winter for us, my friend! Keeping Rand's mind and hands busy will do far more than anything else to restore his spirits after the war."

Finn wandered about the new house, his hands holding the book behind his back. The children had evidently been taught to keep their hands to themselves when visiting the Mercantile or anyone's home.

"Now let's hear you read." Kent indicated a chair at the table for Finn, the cigar box and wrappings pushed to one side. Kent sat next to him, towering over the five-year-old whose feet did not reach the floor. Finn's light blue eyes were large and round as he opened the book to the first story. A small, dirty forefinger moved slowly under each word while he read in a perfect Southern drawl. He struggled over a few words so Kent knew he had not memorized the text.

Kent looked up questioningly at Patrick regarding the drawl which was foreign to the Callahans' Northeastern clipped accent. Patrick shrugged. Page after page, Finn read intently without looking up until the end of the story.

"Say, lad, how did you learn to read like that?" Kent patted Finn on the back.

"That's how ye read," Finn said, confidently reverting to his normal accent.

Kent reared his head back with a huge belly laugh. "Glory be, you're a fine young lad!" He'd occasionally read the children stories, and hearing his adopted "godson" Finn sound like him was more than gratifying.

"We came to talk to you about getting more books," Patrick said. "I need a classical education before I dare venture into any profession—possibly attending Harvard at some point. Would you kindly assist me this winter, sir?" As an afterthought, he added, "I believe it would be invaluable, too, in helping me teach the older students beyond the basic requirements of literacy. For the most part they have good minds that might be stimulated by an enriched curriculum." Patrick's serious demeanor always impressed Kent, but this time he revealed a deeper motivation, an ambition that surprised him.

"Enough, enough, I am with you already on your proposal." Kent leaned back on his chair. "I can't think of anything more welcome than renewing my acquaintance with the classics, as well as the opportunity to catch up with new American and British writers. My school friend, Miss Olivia Spencer, would be delighted to know I am salvaged from the dire influences of the hinterlands."

"But ye do not have any bookshelves," Finn said quietly. "We have libeery shelves at school."

"Right you are, son. I am not salvaged until I have bookshelves so the mice can't chew the books. Let's go out and get some boards. The three of us can fix that little problem right now."

Finn was off his chair before Kent finished speaking. Patrick picked up a hammer and nail pouch from the corner of the room. Outside, they dusted snow off the sawbucks and set to sawing, hammering and nailing in high spirits until a serviceable cabinet with doors was complete and ready to hang inside on the wall. Not long after, Miss Spencer received a telegram to the effect *"Have Shelves, Need Books."* She readily wired back, offering to supply classics currently used at the Women's Academy.

By return mail, Randolph Berrigan in Woodland Hills, Georgia, received a long, expert analysis of the merits of Brogan Premium brand of tobacco, a treatise he could use for marketing. It also signified that Kent was firmly and happily in partnership with him on the quality control end of the business. In a postscript, Kent requested a shipment of his own childhood readers for a mentoring project he had undertaken. *"That is, of course, if my nephew and niece are not using them."*

18

Ezra Rhodes soon made his last trip to South Willow Creek, and settled with Kent according to the terms of their agreement. They loaded the Summit Mining Company ledgers into his buckboard, but he hesitated before departing. The accounting work was complete with the exception of the two missing ledgers. Those pertaining to the Brown's Gulch holdings and *The Dolly* mine detailed how financial assets of the company were systematically reapportioned—if anything was written down. Remaining were documents that presumably would go to Mr. Turnage, the assumed associate, after Kent's "independent" appraisal and balancing of the books. The banker's involvement appeared to be forthright and trusting. Any implications that the scheme was other than a loss to the immediate family appeared highly unlikely.

"As you know, there is little value left in the Comet. We want to get away from it. I haven't been able to work for months." Ezra shook his head, his hair now showing more grey. "I've been haunted by the accident—by the thought that I should have prevented it. Or worse, that I may have directly contributed to it."

"My god, what do you mean?" Kent's startled grey eyes searched Ezra's face. To Kent's surprise it appeared Ezra was taking him into his confidence, a trust more personal than he'd yet experienced with him.

"We were blasting in Brown's Gulch the day before, as I mentioned earlier. Four men set explosives at six different mines—I own most of them, but several belonged to another man. They weren't extensive mines but deep enough to have shafts sunk into the hillsides. All the mines were linked, I think, on the same strata of granite that contained quartz outcroppings, which is the reason I staked as many of these claims as I could in the first place."

"Did the charges all go off at once? That would be a sizeable blast!"

"No, in a series—spaced—but I've been worrying the blasts might have set off vibrations deep down that may have disturbed the other side of the mountain in Alder Gulch. It's not a great distance as a crow flies between the two watersheds up that high."

"I'm not a miner these days but it seems unlikely—aren't those mountains in the Gravellys similar to the Tobacco Roots, mostly solid granite beneath weathered exteriors?"

Ezra leaned heavily on the buckboard. "Could be a coincidence—I'd like to think so, but then there's my crew undercutting the damn ledge, making it unsafe. I've said it a thousand times, if only we could go back and do it differently." He pushed thick, sweaty hair back from his brow.

"That I understand. The regrets—they're tough to live with and they don't go away."

"Not when I feel that I killed my brother, Nathan."

"Your brother, 'Thompson'?" Kent's knees felt weak.

"Yes, same mother, different fathers. Not many people knew—better for business if they didn't."

"Come in and sit down, Ezra." Kent motioned that Ezra enter the house and take a chair by the fireplace. He pulled up his own chair, feeling as though he'd had the wind knocked out of him. The reason for his reluctance to take on the Rhodes-Thompson affairs became obvious—the regrets flooded back even though years has passed. He'd been relieved of flashbacks at times, but residual pain persisted, surfacing when he least expected it.

"I–I understand," Kent said again. "Not long ago, I felt the same, almost, about my brother."

"War?" Ezra asked looking up.

"Yes."

"Union here. Antietam, '62."

"Richmond, Dispatch, towards the end."

Ezra at last heaved a deep sigh. The men sat in silence, each alone in their own epic struggle but with a sense of being together, communing, in the room.

"Yes, Dispatch," Kent continued. "The where-with-all to defeat the "enemy" who happened to be my brother with Union troops. How could I? Even now I shudder—I fail to comprehend—oh, yes, he survived the war, thankfully, but we both carry scars. Mine are more in my mind." Images surfaced of Benson harboring the war, fighting real and imaginary enemies, holding on to it until his death.

"You're damn right," Ezra said, "Scars that don't scab over—at least not yet—not mine with Nathan."

Breaths came hard for both men, chests swelled, rose and fell as vivid images revived dramas that danced and whirled in a frenzied burst of recollections, arousing sharp stabs of regrets, fear, and anger. Their lips firmly forbid the cries, the outbursts their hearts desired; this time the men appeared to cave in under thick flannel shirts as if they had both sprinted a last lap. Finally, Kent reached for the fine, hardwood box of Brogan Premium Cigars and extended it towards this former stranger who seemed closer to him than he would ever have imagined.

Ezra gratefully accepted the proffered box and carefully fingered a smooth, tight yellow cigar that obviously was of a higher quality than he had seen in the West. Kent chose his, bringing up a wooden match to light Ezra's, then his own. After a few long-savored puffs, Ezra sat back, unburdening himself of some of his worries.

Kent crossed his long legs and stared out the window. Ravens flew by, carefree, intent upon adventures in their own lives.

The sweet Premium smoke caught a swell of air and lifted to encircle the room, stirring the recent outbursts and sorrows with a calming presence. One of Ezra's horses whinnied and Ben answered, rousing the two men from their thoughts.

"Annette and I will be moving back East. I--uh--will care for her. Her health is not good since losing Nathan and most of her fortune. She is frail and melancholy these days." He paused. "It is not good for man or woman to--uh—to—"

"—to be alone," finished Kent.

Ezra nodded, thankful for Kent's understanding. "I sold my holdings up Brown's Gulch, of course. The Comet went to pay debts owed Mr. Turnage, the associate. *The Dolly* will remain in Mrs. Thompson's possession for Bradley someday."

At last he dropped the stub of his cigar into the fireplace and stood up, taller it seemed, again in charge of himself. His hand shot out with a firm grip which Kent returned. The two gentlemen stepped outside.

Ezra's visit brought up much of Kent's own anguished past—and showed by comparison how far he had come in healing those old wounds. At some level the conflict related to the war had become distant, more settled in his mind. Indeed the moments with Ezra built a bond, a bridge uniting their humanity despite geography of North or South.

The emotional residue edged in, overshadowing his current outlook. Food lost its taste, even the great pots of stew that Genevieve sent over. His enthusiasm waned for the collection of classics Olivia had promised to send, and his dreams were disturbed with pointless forays into mishaps, reigniting old losses. True to her nature, Shag worried and fretted over him like a mother hen. Her morose stare furthered his discomfort. She burdened herself with his cares, moped in his moods, and denied her own pleasures to remain in his company.

In addition, the coming holidays of December 1868 portended a reawakening of troubled times until Kent's restlessness drove him outdoors. He cleaned the Henry again in preparation for one last big game hunt, a task that reminded him Marion left when he had gone elk hunting over a year ago, the awareness deepening his mood. A mood alleviated only by the occasional realization he had crossed what was once a "no man's land" of the enemy in the North and found instead a friend in Ezra.

But nagging thoughts of Marion surfaced with startling reality. He recalled the sweet, fresh scent of her skin and felt her soft, warm breath on his neck when she stood in her high-heeled boots, her head barely reaching his shoulder. The sense of her body yielding to his touch maddened him; memories of holding her submerged in the chill water of the pond evoked a sad smile. "You must have been terribly hurt to feel so deeply," she had said.

"Marion," he breathed. The utterance came from an immense backlog of feelings held in check so long he had forgotten their weight upon his soul. Adrenalin flushed his cheeks, wrenched his gut, followed by his body twisting in response to no one, only the thought, only a fantasy. A living dream or nightmare. "My god, I'm not done with it—with her," he managed to say, sinking into a chair, head in hands, long avoided grief heaving his sides. The rifle stood forgotten by the door.

Images of other women filtered unbidden through his mind—the striking Danielle Hartman, braced by her new life in the Territory; Annette Thompson, persuasive and capable, yet fearful of being alone; even Olivia Spencer, a fading link to his past of culture and refinement. Their collective portraits represented milestones he couldn't disavow, nor did he want to, but only another woman, Miss Marion Patton, held his heart.

Sometime later he stomped about the room searching for pen and paper. He began to write rapidly, uncensoring, knowing undue contemplation would shutter the words once again in a prison of his own making.

Berrigan's Ride

My Dearest Marion,

I have put my conscience to rest as well as I might regarding the ordeals and divisions of the War. By chance and the Lord's blessing, I have found some measure of reconciliation with my own guilt and shortcomings, and that of the once implacable foe, the North. You, my one and only love, are again the first to hear this baring of my soul, the depths of which it was your misfortune to endure when you were at my side. This report is hopefully welcome and improves your opinion of yours truly, the ever soul-searching Southerner in Montana Territory.

Remaining to unsettle the tenuous peace I am experiencing is my overwhelming sense of loss—loss of you, your love and the comfort you brought me at a critical time of rootlessness, alienation from family, and burdens of self-condemnation. Now I profess, from an established home and regained sense of self-respect, my gratitude for your radiance that brought laughter, joy and beauty to my humble shack, for your sensuous side so in tune with Nature that delighted and surpassed my own reserve—truly, you taught me how to live, my Marion! Please accept my deepest appreciation for this, and for every treasured moment of our being together.

I will telegraph the San Francisco office for your address. I had to, at this late date, declare my devotion and express my apologies for whatever happened to divide us. Possibly there is no resolution—or rather, not always the desired outcome of relationships such as ours since we have chosen different paths. I only wish for you, if you require it, and for myself, the sense of peace that comes from arranging broken fragments into some kind of order within ourselves.

Your always devoted,

Kent Berrigan

Without pausing to reread or pass judgment on this outpouring of closely held pain, suffering he had vowed never to revisit, Kent wrapped the letter for mailing. He yanked on his hunting coat, picked up a warm, flat tweed cap with ear flaps, and set out for the stagecoach to Virginia City to telegraph for her address.

Weeks lapsed after he mailed the letter. He did not count them. His empty stare over the open benchland replayed dramas backwards: finding Benson dying in the dirt and sagebrush, he and Marion moving into his shack with the smell of mice, feeling her gloved hand on his arm on the riverboat, their first embrace in the stable—his heart still tied to this determined woman who was so certain of her ambitions, yet uncertain, until the last, about him.

I should have known, Kent accused himself. I didn't want to see it—then or ever—the emancipation she felt riding to Helena with Mrs. Thompson. Her zeal for the industriousness of New York. Perhaps even her fear of losing herself in our union. And of course the madness—Kent refused to think of it.

Then a slim packet of hand-lettered mail arrived from Santa Fe at the new Sterling post office.

My Dearest Kent,

Your letter was most gratefully received. I found my heart stirred once again by the depth of sentiment you express. I often wonder about the strange turns one encounters in life; impulsive, possibly, or predetermined. One does harbor misgivings at times and surely my abrupt departure was one of those. A love like yours, ours, was more than any woman could wish for. My restless heart has yet to find a home or to return to you.

On a wider stage, I have witnessed the healing that you refer to, from the mestizos in the Southwest where I now reside, to my father in the West, and elsewhere across the country. There seems to be a coming together despite earlier wounds, mortal for too many and too terrible to comprehend for Benson and others such as yourself.

I am thankful you have found some measure of peace in your beautiful Montana Territory.

I am your ever willful but affectionate,

Marion Patton

———————

Ben's wooly winter coat made him a caricature of himself, fluffing his belly inches further out on each side. His long chin whiskers collected a frosty beard. This time Kent placed the Henry in the scabbard and mounted. Ben was eager to go and Kent let him set a fine pace, not toward the mountain peaks where elk might come down on high benches for winter feed, but east towards the river, a course Marion had once taken, running from tensions between them. Kent felt the wild horse surging beneath him, the gelding's powerful legs driving into frozen sod, his mane a banner of wild herds that continued to thrill Kent on South Willow Creek. Their drumming flight echoed now in Ben's hooves pounding the earth, the legacy of mustangs living on in Ben, and in a sense, in Kent's immersion in the land.

Kent rode past Lower Hot Spring where the Boaz mill sputtered with minimal energy this late in the season. Harsh unsightly diggings of the mining district gave way to small meadows of dense dry grass flanked by rambling foothills, entrees to heavily eroded cliffs composed of granite thrust up hundreds of millennia ago. Overcast skies hung low over these steep walls of the Madison canyon. Small dark juniper spears clung to improbable places here and there among the rocks. Kent noticed the absence of winter wind that often whipped through the narrow passage of Fifteen Mile Canyon and chastised the Bozeman Trail. Ben slowed, his ears flicking forward, then back towards Kent as if aware of his master's deepening mood and their solitary presence in the canyon.

At this time of year the river ran wide, cold and black between stark icy borders forming jagged lines far out from the edges. Flocks of white pelicans that frequented the river during summer were gone. Instead, beaver, muskrats and mink found winter forage along the sheltered banks. Only deer tracks blemished the light snow.

Kent dismounted near a tangle of leafless currant and gooseberry bushes; an empty bird nest dangled from the barren branches. His mind drifted back to the day that seemed ages ago when Marion joyfully described seeing the flotilla of Shoshonis glide downriver with their colorful baskets of berries. He imagined their paddles lifting silently from side to side of the handmade canoes, gently creating waves that closed behind them leaving only a memory of their passing, as silent and sure as the memory he held of the woman he loved.

Lost in his reflections, the grey day faded before him and became the warm, bright afternoon Marion had described. She had exclaimed about the women of the mining camp washing clothes in nearby Hot Spring Creek, and laughing as they washed their hair while children ran around playing. He smiled at the scene under a clear blue sky, embraced by a rush of pure rippling waters and the pageantry of women. One of the women became Marion, laughing, her rusty-gold sunburst hair wet and shining in the sun.

Historical Novels Set in Montana Territory
by Jan Elpel

Berrigan's Ride

Kent Berrigan never expected to settle in remote, raw Montana Territory, 1866 when he fled the South after the Civil War to avoid facing his brother—and his own conscience. He identifies with the wild horses in the mountains in Madison County, unsure of who he is and his future until he encounters Marion Patton, a woman from California gold country. When his friend is murdered, he pursues Miss Patton, who has a vision of the future of the country if not her own destiny.

Healers of Big Butte

Carrie Tarynton saves the life of a prized Irish horse, but she and her intuitive women friends are confronted by the use of modern medical practices in the silver camp of Big Butte, Montana Territory, 1875 – 1877. Carrie faces her greatest challenge trying to save her husband, cattleman Mac Tarynton, and their marriage. The women have visions and intuitions that portend tragic events so frightening that Carrie seeks her mentor, a Shoshoni Wise Woman, and brings the ethnic women of Big Butte together in solidarity before the Nez Perce war.

Heirloom China

Patrick Colter marries Shelley Norton in a double wedding in Big Butte, Montana Territory, 1877, and finds his dream job as a law clerk, until his investigation of a murder brings threats against his life. He whisks his family to safety in the East where he attends Harvard, and Shelley becomes a rising star in the women's movement, along with an unlikely friend, Irmgarde Meyer, a prostitute. Shelley and Irmgarde unexpectedly overcome challenges that would keep them in their place, forcing Patrick to make adjustments of his own.

Healers of Big Butte

Carrie Tarynton and Jackson Colter tied their horses away from the corrals to avoid startling the sick horse—if he was still alive. They edged towards the new stable around barking dogs, setting off howls from hunting hounds kenneled to the rear of the barn. Carrie wanted a chance to see the stallion prior to Mr. Huckins coming from the house. The large dapple grey stood in a side pen, alive but swaying unsteadily, unaware of the presence of visitors.

"Blind," Carrie whispered, "or almost blind with all that blood and damage."

******

"What about that horse? Is it going to be like this, you with the stud and me having coffee by myself?"

Carrie leapt to his side almost toppling both of them. Mac stood and she rushed into his arms, choking sobs amid a mischievous grin that he didn't see. He crushed her in his long, powerful arms, his face pressed against her hair.

"I thought I was your love," he muttered, nudging her cheek much like King did.

"You are my love, my one and only. I care only for you, Mac, you know that, darling."

Wrapped in each other's embrace, memories cascaded through her mind—their marriage, their loss of two-year-old daughter Christina, the ranch work that sapped energy from their love making. A good many years had passed them by, or had they lived them to the hilt?

"Sometimes with your healing obligations I wonder if I have a wife at all. If you start healing sick horses, I'll be a lonely man."

******

"Kent Berrigan from Madison County is a longtime representative of people in Hot Spring District. He has experience in both mining and business. Please welcome our next candidate for Commissioner."

In a diplomatic effort, Kent praised … "the vigorous nature of the growing city of Big Butte, much respected for its citizens of diverse cultures and for its industries essential for the entire nation"….at that moment Kent looked up to see a woman moving confidently through the crowd of miners, ranch hands, and a few women. A pert green bonnet trimmed in cream satin with ties under her chin did not disguise the person he knew so well. Nor did the rusty-gold, frizzy hair that trailed from beneath her hat. Miss Marion Patton. His train of thought derailed, Kent attempted to conclude his remarks.

—Available from www.HOPSPress.com—

Acknowledgments

I am indebted to Jeffrey J. Safford for permission to "mine" the wealth of original research in his book, *The Mechanics of Optimism: Mining Companies, Technology, and the Hot Spring Gold Rush, Montana Territory, 1864-1868*. Professor Safford's research, published in 2004, thoroughly reconstructs the life and times of the gold camp of Sterling in Hot Spring District, among other mining communities with which my family and myself are so well acquainted.

This story was initially inspired by the late Tom Sargent of Virginia City, Montana, who wore his Union blues to Victorian balls, igniting passions long after the Civil War.

My gratitude to Ingeborg Hayes and the Gypsy Rhythm Writers of Bozeman and the Pony Writers who encouraged and nourished this debut novel.

My heartfelt appreciation to my family, Thomas Elpel, publisher, and Jeanne Elpel for relentlessly editing; also to insightful editors: Cynthia Logan, Margie Peterson, Diane Elliott, Marjorie Smith, and Florence Ore. A big thank you to Linda Griffith for cover design, and to my artist friends for their encouragement and mentoring. A special note of gratitude to Tim and Roberta Jackson whose family lived what is now the history of Sterling.

And to the following:

A.J. Noyes, eyewitness to early day Bannack, Silver Bow, and Madison County, who narrated his experiences in *The Story of Ajax: Life in the Big Hole Basin*.

Larry Barsness for vivid descriptions of the mining camp of Virginia City in *Gold Camp: Alder Gulch and Virginia City* that gave the pulse and flavor of the mining district.

Those whose tales I was privileged to hear firsthand, Bruce Flesch, late of Pony, and the Navajos of Monument Valley who so earnestly hosted our horse ride there.

Others included Dr. Michael Malone's numerous works, Phyllis Smith's *Montana's Madison County, a History*, Dorothy Johnson's, *The Bloody Bozeman*, Tom Leeson for his lyrical *Inventing Montana*, and Bruce Levine's 2013 *The Fall of the House of Dixie* which explores the deep wounds on both sides in the War Between the States, and Professor John Kohl's *Fascinating Facts and Figures of Civil War* (Railroads).

Also Ken Robison's many works portraying Montana Territory and its people during and after the Civil War, and Virginia Cole Trenholm and Maurine Carley for *Shoshonis: Sentinels of the Rockies*, William Least Heat-Moon for his experiences on the Missouri River in *River Horse*, and Craig Childs for his personal exploration of the Southwest in *House of Rain*, as well as Terry Tempest Williams' Navajo stories in *Pieces of White Shell*. *Sing Down the Moon*, a truly precious children's book by Scott O'Dell, relates the story of the Long Walk in cultural context.

For the line of poetry "There is sweet music here that softer falls," I credit Alfred Lord Tennyson's *Song from the Lotus Eaters*.

To the dedicated collectors at the Butte Archives, Fort Benton Archives, Montana Historical Society, and Montana Heritage Preservation of Virginia City, my appreciation for preserving a sense of the short period that was Montana Territory.

Not least, my humble gratitude for the riches of the Earth that have yielded so many hopes and promises and given many of us reflective moments over a gold pan. Gold in Alder Gulch, Hot Spring District (now Norris), and the American River in California—of these yarns are spun.

About the Author

Jan Elpel, Psy.D, grew up near the Headwaters of the Missouri River. That sense of history frames the stories she creates set in the mid-nineteenth century. Her family's (Jewett's) lifestyle among descendants of early immigrants in the 1940s was little different than that of the settlers in *Berrigan's Ride* eighty years earlier. She wrote the 1958 John Colter pageant for the original Colter's Run in Three Forks, Montana. Her family later moved to historic gold camps of Virginia City and Pony. Elpel's series of

Photo by Kathy Allard

historical novels celebrate the wild horses of Madison and Jefferson Counties, and the Jewett's herd of horses that thundered off the dry hills to water at the handpump in front of the Parker Homestead.

Wild horses of Madison County